Opposites Attract

National
Bestselling Authors

Lynn Kurland
Elizabeth Bevarly
Emily Carmichael
Elda Minger

It's
what
they
have in
common
that counts...

JOVE

$6.99 U.S.
$9.99 CAN

EAN

Lynn Kurland's
The Icing on the Cake

He's a writer working on his new novel, and baking wedding cakes on the side. She's an Alaskan wilderness buff more experienced at fending off grizzlies than men. But she's about to discover the joy of coming in from the cold . . .

Elizabeth Bevarly's
The Short, Hot Summer

He was as out of place in Alabama as she would be in Manhattan. But the temperature spikes whenever an executive stuck in town for a big-time deal and his small-town landlady are together—creating enough heat to rival the sultry summer nights . . .

Emily Carmichael's
Pride and Prejudice

A double-booked hotel room during a prestigious dog show pits a cartoonist and her pet papillon with an award-winning Border collie. What ensues is a sexy contest of wills. And it's winner take all . . .

Elda Minger's
The Princess and the Adventurer

She stuck out like a debutante at a monster truck rally. What was a lady doing in a cantina on the border of the Mexican jungle? Little did Matthew Kincaid realize, he was just the man she was looking for . . .

Opposites Attract

Lynn Kurland

Elizabeth Bevarly

Emily Carmichael

Elda Minger

JOVE BOOKS, NEW YORK

This is a work of fiction. Names, characters, places, and incidents are either the product of the author's imagination or are used fictitiously, and any resemblance to actual persons, living or dead, business establishments, events, or locales is entirely coincidental.

OPPOSITES ATTRACT

A Jove Book / published by arrangement with the authors

PRINTING HISTORY
Jove edition / July 2000

The Penguin Putnam Inc. World Wide Web site address is
http://www.penguinputnam.com

ISBN: 0-515-12865-1

A JOVE BOOK®
Jove Books are published by The Berkley Publishing Group,
a division of Penguin Putnam Inc.,
375 Hudson Street, New York, New York 10014.
JOVE and the ''J'' design
are trademarks belonging to Penguin Putnam Inc.

PRINTED IN THE UNITED STATES OF AMERICA

10 9 8 7 6 5 4 3

contents

The Icing on the Cake

Lynn Kurland

one

It had been the morning from hell.

Samuel MacLeod carefully avoided the last chuckhole, turned the engine off, and unclenched his teeth. He carefully leaned his throbbing head against the steering wheel of his once clean and shiny Range Rover and let out a long, slow breath.

"I am," he said to no one in particular and with a distinct edge to his voice, "too old for this."

He should have known from the start that it would have been a day better spent in bed. He'd had a lousy night's sleep and was suffering from an incredible case of writer's block. He could have made a soufflé, put his feet up on the coffee table, and wallowed in eggs and spectator sports. Or he could have propped his feet up on the fat leather ottoman in front of the picture window, settled back into the matching leather chair, and stared out into the wilderness surrounding his rented cabin. The deep green forest could have held his attention, as could any number of critters that might have used the front yard as a hiking trail. Fall was his favorite time of year, and fall in Alaska was like nothing he'd ever before experienced.

Yes, he could have been comfortable. He could have been warm. He could have been entertained by wild things.

But instead of following his better instincts, he'd risen

at five, determined to work out the kinks in his plotline. He'd planned to finish chapter twenty by ten o'clock, leaving him plenty of time to get to town and back.

The way the lights had been flickering should have told him it wasn't a day to be tempting the Fates.

First had come the power spike at eight, wiping out three hours of irreplaceable prose. He'd gone outside to check the generator and heard the distinct, unwelcome sound of a locked door closing behind him. Breaking in through the window had left him with cuts on his hands and his sweats. He'd headed back outside, determined not to let his rented house get the best of him this time.

Fixing the generator had gone rather well, though he didn't have a clue as to what he'd done. Banging it a couple of times with a wrench and threatening it had seemed to do the trick.

Unfortunately, that had been the only success of the morning.

He'd tried to ignore the lack of hot water midway through his shower. He'd laughed off the small kitchen fire that had resulted from a misbehaving toaster. He'd even kept a smile on his face, insincere though it might have been, when he discovered he'd forgotten to turn on the dryer the night before and all his clothes were soaking wet. He'd simply put on dirty jeans and headed out to the garage to warm up the car—

Only to encounter a creature of indeterminate origin who glared evilly at him before hiking its leg and relieving itself on Sam's tire. Sam had made it into his four-wheel-drive sustaining no damage to himself. Of course, that had been rectified nicely after he'd had a flat on the way into town and been forced to change said tire.

And, heaven help him, it was only noon.

He clambered out of the Range Rover, casting an eye heavenward to check for falling satellite parts, and stepped knee-deep into one of the chuckholes he had so carefully tried to avoid. He saw stars. He indulged in a few choice swearwords before he uttered what summed up his feelings about the past three months of his life.

"I hate Alaska."

Of course, the blame for that—though he was loath to admit it—was something he could lay only at his own feet. He could have been back in New York, hobnobbing with the well-heeled and dabbling in his artistic pursuits. He could have been worrying about a date for the opera, struggling to decide who to take to a gallery opening, wracking his brains for a suitable miss to gaze adoringly at him while he listened to an obscure poet read even more obscure poetry.

He also could have been listening to his family ridicule his two passions: writing and food. They couldn't fathom why a man with a perfectly good eight-figure trust fund seemed to find it necessary to ruin his manicure with manual labor.

He'd pointed out to them that somewhere back in their family tree there had been a MacLeod or two doing plenty of manual labor on Scottish soil—likely in the form of cattle raiding and sword wielding. His father had hastened to inform him that they were kin to a long, illustrious line of Scottish lairds, and that stealing beef and waving swords around didn't count as manual labor.

Sam had tried to explain his driving need to put words on paper by reminding his kin that the first American transplant from their ancestral clan had made his living as a newspaperman. His older sister had ruined that excuse by pointing out that said newspaperman had actually been an "editor in chief and very wealthy newspaper owner."

Sam had given up trying to probe any further back into his well-documented genealogy for examples to back up his arguments. He'd settled for informing his family that not only had he been writing, he'd also been studying with one of New York's most famous chefs. His mother's week-long attack of the vapors upon hearing that news was what had finally driven him to seek sanctuary as far away from New York as he could get and still remain on the same landmass.

Sans his trust fund—and that by his own choice, no less.

"Alaska," he grunted.

He was an idiot.

He sighed and reminded himself why he was there. Alaska was the last vestige of untamed wilderness and he was a MacLeod. Sword wielding wasn't all that legal anymore, but he could do mighty things with a pen and the occasional spatula. He could do those things on his own terms and by the sweat of his own brow.

But there were times when he wondered if Southern California wouldn't have been wilderness enough. He suspected a ramshackle house on the beach would have been a great deal easier to manage than his rented cabin with its accompaniment of deer, bears, and other sundry and perilous wildlife.

He sighed deeply, then tromped across the mud and up the worn steps to the general store. Smith's Dry Goods and Sundries seemed to be the precise center of whatever hubbub was going on in Flaherty, Alaska, population three hundred. The store was the gathering place for anyone who was anyone to discuss everyone else. Sam suspected he'd had his share of space on the gossip docket. He opened the door and stepped inside, avoiding the rotting floorboard near the door. No, sir, he wasn't going to put his foot through that twice in a lifetime. He wasn't a greenhorn anymore.

He ambled over to the counter and nodded to the usual locals holding court next to the woodstove, chewing the fat and their tobacco. Sam pulled out his neatly made supply list and handed it to Mr. Smith, the proprietor. It was a lean list, of course, because he was still living on the proceeds from a couple of articles he'd sold to a cooking magazine. He was beginning to wonder now if he would have been better off to have traded out for six months of groceries.

A throat near the stove cleared itself, coughed, then hacked into the brass spittoon. "Yer the writer fella?"

Sam identified the speaker as an old-timer he'd never met before, a grizzled man who probably hadn't had a haircut since World War II.

Sam nodded, smiling slightly. "That's right."

There was a bit of low grumbling. There was always low grumbling after he admitted to his vocation. Since he didn't like to hunt, fish, or chew, he had left the Clan very un-impressed. Sam would have liked to point out to them that his great-great-great-grandfather had come across the sea and cut a swath through Colonial America that even the Clan would have been impressed by, but then he might have been questioned about his own deeds and he didn't dare admit the kind of soft life he'd left behind in New York. He suspected that in Alaska lynching was still an acceptable means of population control.

"Heard yer up at the Kincaid place," another bearded octogenarian demanded. "That right?"

"That's right," Sam agreed.

The grumbling rose in volume until it reached outraged proportions. The spokesman rose and stomped to the door.

"Just ain't right," he growled. "It just ain't right."

The rest of the group departed after giving Sam disapproving looks. Sam looked at Mr. Smith, an older man with a merely rudimentary sense of humor.

"What did I say?"

Mr. Smith shrugged. "Reckon you'll find out soon enough."

Sam wondered if that could possibly be anything he would want to investigate further. Then again, forewarned was forearmed. He took a deep breath.

"Care to translate?" he asked.

Mr. Smith shook his head. "Better to let you find out for yourself."

Sam leaned against the counter and tried not to let the ambiguity of that statement unnerve him. With the way things were going, finding out for himself could be downright dangerous.

The door behind him opened and shut with a bang.

"Joe, when are you going to get this damned floorboard fixed?"

Well, now the sound of *that* voice was almost enough to make all the misery of the past three months worth it. Sam leaned heavily on the counter while his knees recovered. It was a voice straight from his most favorite lazy Saturday-morning dreams, the voice that belonged to his warm and cuddly football-watching partner. He was tempted to whip around immediately and make sure, but he resisted. Surely the sight that awaited him was even more luscious than the sound of her voice. Better to let the anticipation build for a bit. Sam closed his eyes and gave free rein to his imagination.

Maybe she would be a Nordic type, with legs up to her ears and pale hair streaming down her back. Or perhaps she was a brunette, petite and lovely with a mouth just made for kissing. A redhead? Sam considered that for a moment or two, wondering just what kind of fire a redhead could really produce when put to the test. One thing was for sure: Whatever awaited him had to be a ball of sultry femininity, no doubt bundled up in a nicely done fake-fur coat and boots. He straightened, unable to wait any longer. He would look. Then he would investigate. Then he would likely invite her out to dinner. He put his shoulders back, then turned around, afire with anticipation.

He looked.

Then he felt his jaw slide down on its own.

The creature before him was covered with something, but it wasn't a fake fur. It looked more like mud. The dirt was flaking off her coat in layers while clinging to her hat and scarf with admirable tenacity. And not only was she filthy, she smelled. The fact that he could ascertain that from twenty paces was truly frightening. It wasn't anything a gallon of Chanel No. 5 couldn't cure. Sam stared at the apparition, unable to believe it was a woman.

"Good to see ya, kid," Mr. Smith said with an indulgent chuckle. "Roll in this mornin'?"

"And not a moment too soon," the swamp monster grumbled. "You should see what's been done to my—"

"Boy, here's your things," Mr. Smith interrupted, shoving Sam's box of supplies at him. "You'd best be headin' home. I have the feeling there's going to be a storm brewing right quick."

Sam didn't need to hear that twice. The last storm that had brewed had left him stranded in twelve inches of mud in the middle of the road to his rented cabin. If the Tenderfoot Patrol hadn't come to rescue him, he would have starved to death. He grabbed his box and made a beeline for the door, slipping twice on the mud the creature had dragged in with her, but skillfully avoiding the rotting floorboard by the front door.

" 'Bye, Mr. Smith."

"See ya around, boy. Better batten down those hatches."

Sam didn't bother to say anything to the woman as he passed her. He was far too busy holding his breath so he didn't have to inhale her fragrant Pig Pen–like aura.

He pulled the door shut behind him and let out the breath he'd been holding. He paused to clear his head, giving it a shake for good measure. Nothing like a little fresh air to bring a man back to his senses. He carefully negotiated a path to his car, threw the supplies in the back, and mucked his way around to the driver's side. Twenty minutes and he'd be home. Maybe he'd go back to the old standby of writing on a legal pad with a smooth, round number two pencil instead of playing power-surge roulette with his computer. That would certainly save him some aggravation. Then he'd make a filet for supper. He'd hole up in his nice warm cabin and weather whatever storm Alaska saw fit to throw at him.

two

Sydney Kincaid stood in Smith's Dry Goods and Sundries and praised the wonders of civilization. She pulled off her filthy knit hat and dragged her fingers through her hair. She'd never felt so dirty in all her life, and it had been her boarder's fault. Damn the woman if she hadn't left the garage door open. The remains of a critter invasion were readily obvious to even the most plugged of noses. A broken window and no hot water had been the last straw. Well, that and the fact that the place was clean. It had taken her almost a half an hour to make it feel like home again.

But now home was comfortably strewn with clutter, and her stomach was about to be filled with something besides trail mix. Life was improving all the time.

"So, Syd," Joe said, pulling out another box and beginning to fill it with Sydney's standing order of just-add-water suppers. "How'd it go?"

"How does it ever go?" Sydney grumbled as she crossed the store to toss her hat on Joe's counter. "I've spent the last four months pulling one city boy after another out of places they never should have been looking at in magazines. Don't people realize this is *wilderness* up here?"

"Reckon they don't," Joe said, rearranging a few cans of stew.

"If that wasn't bad enough," Sydney continued, irritated,

"I go home to find my house clean. Just what kind of neat freak did you rent my extra room to, anyway? I thought you said she was a writer. I expected lots of crumpled-up balls of typing paper hiding under the coffee table."

"You could have done worse," Joe offered. "Tidy isn't bad."

"I don't like it," Sydney groused, reaching into Joe's candy jar and helping herself to a piece of licorice. "I didn't see any curlers in the bathroom, but I'll bet she's just as lily white and frilly as they come. She's a baker, too, can you believe it?"

Joe pushed Sydney's box at her. "Hurry on home, girl. There's a storm brewing, and I wouldn't want you to miss out on it."

"You mean be out in it, don't you, Joe?"

"Reckon so."

Sydney pulled out another piece of licorice. "Who was that man?" she asked casually. He might have been a potential tour-guiding customer, and she wasn't one to miss out on a business opportunity.

"What man?" Joe asked, blinking innocently.

Sydney chewed even more casually. "You know, that city guy. Old man Anderson was grumbling about him being a writer or something."

Joe reached under the counter and pulled out a magazine. "There's a piece in here of his. Read it myself. It wasn't bad, if you like that sort of thing."

Sydney looked at the cooking magazine and dismissed it as something she'd be interested in only if hell froze over. She turned her attentions back to the matter at hand. "Is he planning on staying?" Of course, she wasn't *truly* interested, but she could appreciate a fine-looking man as well as the next girl.

"I wouldn't know what his plans are. I suppose you could ask him the next time you see him."

Sydney shook her head. "We're attracting these writer types like flies up here. The next thing you know, we're going to need a stoplight or two."

"We just might," Joe agreed.

Sydney shoved the magazine in her box and made her way out to her mud-encrusted Jeep, trying to put the man out of her mind. She'd probably never see him again, so there wasn't much use in worrying about it. Especially since she wasn't a girl on the lookout for romance. She had her father's trail-guide business to keep running, and her own reputation to maintain. City boys with eyes as green as spring leaves and hair the color of sable just didn't fit into her plans. The man probably couldn't put a match to a handful of dry kindling and get anything but smoke.

She drove home slowly, tired to the bone. Four months of being out in the wild, going into Anchorage only to wash her clothes and pick up another group of greenhorns, had left her aching for home and hot showers. Of course, her shower today might not be hot, thanks to whatever damage Samantha had done, but that could be fixed in time. First a shower, then maybe she'd come out and find a hot meal waiting for her. The cake sitting on the counter had been delicious. Sydney hadn't meant to eat all but one slice, but she hadn't had a decent meal in weeks. Sam was good for something, even if just for cooking. Joe had been annoyingly closemouthed in his letters, not dropping a single hint about what Sam wrote.

Sydney braked suddenly, sending the Jeep into a skid. It settled to a stop, and she looked off into the distance, feeling dread settle into the pit of her stomach. Sam was a Samantha, wasn't she? It really was possible that two writers had moved into Flaherty over the summer, wasn't it?

She knew all she had to do was pull out the magazine Joe had given her and check.

She shook her head. Joe wouldn't have rented out her house to a man. He was a terrible matchmaker, but even he had to draw the line somewhere. Besides, it was a food magazine. What kind of guy would write for a food magazine?

Sydney put the car back into gear and eased the clutch out until the tires caught. Sam was no doubt pleasingly plump and terribly maternal—just the kind of roommate

Sydney had been looking for. If she could be convinced not to try to fix anything else electrical, that was.

The door to the garage was closed, and Sydney took it for granted that Sam had parked her car inside. A lecture about keeping the door closed could wait until after dinner. No sense in upsetting the cook. Sydney'd had enough trail rations over the past few months that she was willing to keep her mouth shut in exchange for some real food.

She left her Jeep in the gravel pit that served as a driveway, then walked into the house, dropping her muddy coat on the floor and discarding her hat, gloves, and scarf along the way to the basement. She went down and made a few minor adjustments to the water heater. Someone had been trying to turn it up and turned it down instead. Sydney shook her head in disbelief. She'd have to put her foot down about Sam loitering anywhere but the kitchen. It could be hazardous to their health.

She discarded the rest of her clothes on the way to the bathroom. Sponge baths in the privacy of her tent just hadn't cut it for her. Already she could feel the hard spray washing away the layers of grime, taking the tension with it. Baby-sitting helpless executives was hard on a woman. Maybe Sam would hear her washing up, take the hint, and start dinner. Maybe she would even warm up the last piece of that chocolate cake and top it off with some ice cream.

The guest room door opened, and Sydney hastily reached for a towel to cover her otherwise naked self. She'd say a quick hello, then duck into the bathroom for her well-deserved shower. After all, she wasn't exactly dressed for a long conversation.

Sydney looked at her housemate.

Then she blinked again, just to make sure she wasn't imagining things.

Yes, she recognized that hair the color of sable, those spring green eyes, and the rugged, handsome face. Worn jeans hugged slim hips and long, muscular legs. A long-sleeved rugby shirt revealed muscular arms and a broad chest—and probably hid a nice, flat belly. It was a hard body, one she had only glimpsed in the general store, one she had actually thought might serve as tasty dream fodder later in front of the fire.

And then full realization hit.

Sam was anything but a Samantha.

"You!" she squeaked.

"*You!*"

Sydney fled into the bathroom. "What in the hell are you doing here?" she shouted.

"Me?" the man yelled back. "What in the hell are *you* doing here?"

Sydney locked the door. Then she put the clothes hamper in front of it for good measure.

"This is *my* house!"

"Your house?" her unwelcome greenhorn responded, sounding more annoyed than he should have, given the circumstances. "Lady, you're losing it. You might be Sydney's girlfriend, but you can still haul your butt right out of that bathroom and get moving because he's not here right now to clean you up."

Sydney couldn't believe her ears. "You idiot, *I'm* Sydney Kincaid and this is *my* house."

"You're Sydney Kincaid? But Joe told me—"

Sydney wanted to scream in frustration. It was pure frustration, not fear. No, she wasn't afraid. She was never afraid. She'd faced down three grizzly bears, four groups of chauvinistic city boys, and an army of wilderness inconveniences and come out on top. A tenderfoot writer from New York was nothing compared to what she'd been up against. She pulled the rifle down from its hook over the commode, loaded it with the shells hiding in the empty can of Noxzema, and pointed it at the door.

"Joe's an old fool and I'll give him a piece of my mind just as soon as you get out of my house so I can get dressed," she said, putting her no-nonsense-now-boys edge in her voice. "Beat it."

"Look, lady, I've got rent paid up through December—"

"I'll give it back." She didn't want to say it, because she certainly couldn't afford to be without a boarder over the winter. And damn Joe if he hadn't given Sam a cut rate that guaranteed Sydney would have to keep him on or starve. Her guide services were pricey, but not pricey enough to feed her much past February. She took a deep breath. "Just get your stuff and go."

"I'm not going anywhere," came the annoyed growl. "And since I'm going to be staying, I suggest you start wearing a few more clothes on your way to the bathroom."

Sydney clamped her teeth together and swore silently. She cursed some more as she propped the rifle against the side of the tub and started the shower. She cursed her father for having put only one bathroom in the cabin. She cursed whatever quirk of fate had brought Samuel, not Samantha, MacLeod to Alaska to move his annoying self into her house. She cursed her situation, because she would most definitely have to make Sam go and that would leave her wallowing in very dire straits indeed.

And she finally, and most thoroughly, cursed Joe for allowing Sam into her house.

Because, despite his convenient cover as owner and operator of Smith's Dry Goods and Sundries, Joe was first and foremost a matchmaker.

And she knew she was number one on his hit list.

three

"Damn woman," Sam grumbled as he flipped a chunk of butter into the pot of drained potatoes. "First she tracks mud in this morning"—he dumped in a splash of milk—"then she leaves all her gear stinking up the front room"—he jammed the beaters into the mixer—"then she does a strip-tease with clothes that ought to be burned, not washed." He turned the mixer on and savagely beat the potatoes to a pulp. "As if I had time to baby-sit a barbarian!"

"What are you still doing here?"

The voice was as smooth and husky as whiskey and immediately brought to mind the vision of a cozy evening spent cuddling in front of the fire on a fur rug. Sam turned off the mixer and shook his head, amazed that such an appealing voice could belong to such an unappealing woman. He wanted to get to know Sydney Kincaid about as much as he wanted to get to know the porcupine that ambled across the front yard every now and then. He turned, prepared for battle.

And forgot every word of the speech he'd thrown together over the past half hour.

It was no wonder she hid under all that mud. Her hair was as dark as midnight, her skin flawless and not needing a speck of makeup to enhance its beauty. Sam put down the mixer and walked over to her, mesmerized. He couldn't remember the last time he'd been so affected by the sight of a woman in a ratty bathrobe. Without thinking about it further, he put his hand under her chin, lifted her face up, and bent his head to kiss her.

And then he froze at the feel of something hard against his belly. He really wanted to believe it was the belt of her robe. Really.

"Get your hands off me," she said in a low, rather unnervingly calm voice.

"Sure thing," he said, lifting his hands and backing away slowly. "Don't shoot. That thing isn't loaded, is it?"

"Want to find out?"

He smiled weakly. "I'm right in the middle of cooking dinner. Filet mignon. Know what that is?"

The sound of the gun being cocked echoed in the stillness of the kitchen.

"I guess you do," he conceded. "Are you hungry?"

"Starved. And I get kind of cranky when I'm starved."

"Yes, I can imagine that's true," he said, wondering how in the world such a good-looking woman could have such a bad temper. He backed up until the counter stopped him. "Think you could put that gun away?"

She gave him an assessing glance. "Why would I want to? It isn't as if you've been very gentlemanly."

"Well, how does 'I can't cook under stress' sound?"

Her eyes narrowed. "Did you make that chocolate cake I saw today, or did you buy it?"

"I made it."

She considered, then lowered the gun. "You won't try anything?"

The barrel was on level with his groin. He looked quickly at her face and knew she realized just where she was pointing her weapon. He shook his head vigorously.

"Wouldn't think of it."

The gun was uncocked, then lowered. "Well, then. I'm going back to change. You finish cooking."

"Yes, ma'am."

With a toss of her shoulder-length, unbelievably silky looking hair, she walked out of the room. Sam leaned back against the counter and blew out his breath. Sydney Kincaid was definitely not what he'd been expecting.

He finished the mashed potatoes, pulled the steaks out from under the broiler, tossed a salad, and hastily set the table. He was just pouring water into glasses when Sydney came back into the room. She sat down at the table and started to eat. Sam couldn't believe what he was seeing. He walked around the counter and plunked down a glass of water in front of her.

"Haven't you ever heard of waiting until everyone is sitting at the table before you start eating?"

"Got to get it while it's hot," she said, her mouth full. "And before anyone else gets to it. It's the only way to survive in the wild."

"Well, this is civilization. We can reheat things in the microwave here."

She ignored him. Which was just as well, to Sam's mind, because he was still trying to figure out just what in the hell he was going to do for the next three months, living with a woman whose face said "touch me" and whose actions said "do it and I'll geld you." Oh, why had he ever decided Alaska would be a nice place to hide and write?

He really should have headed for California. Nice, warm beaches overflowing with women whose come-hither looks probably meant come hither. Trying to second-guess Miss Wilderness was too complicated for his poor overworked brain. All he wanted was to go back to his room, turn on his computer, and deal with characters he had control over. The character sitting across from him was way out of his league.

"This is all there was?"

Sam blinked at the sight of her empty plate. He looked at his housemate and blinked again.

"Where did you put it all?"

"I haven't eaten a decent meal in almost four months. Are you going to finish yours? No? Well, I'll do it for you."

Sam watched as his plate was removed from under his nose. She finished his supper, then sat back with a sigh.

"I'm going to sleep now," she said, putting her hand over her mouth and yawning. "Don't be here when I get up."

"Look," he began, "I signed a contract . . ."

"You also let a who knows what into my garage, screwed up my water heater, and cleaned my house. If that wasn't breach of contract, I don't know what is."

"You've got to be kidding."

"I never kid." She rose. "I sleep with a gun, so don't think about trying anything funny."

"I'd rather waltz with an angry polar bear."

Her mouth tightened into a thin line. "I'm sure you would. Which is just fine with me, mister. You can stay the night, but you sure as hell better be gone when I wake up."

And without a single compliment about dinner, or even a thank-you, she left the room. Sam gritted his teeth at her rudeness. No wonder Mr. Smith had laughed so gleefully when Sam had signed his name on the dotted line. Sam had never thought to wonder why no one had wanted to board at the Kincaid house. It had been a cabin straight from one of his Sunday-morning, lots-of-snow-on-the-ground snuggling fantasies. How was he to know the snugglee would rather be snuggling with a rifle than him?

Sam sighed and rose, cleaned off the table, then made himself a peanut-butter-and-jelly sandwich. Though he was tempted to stay just to irritate Sydney, he knew he was probably better off cutting his losses and leaving. But not until after Friday. He needed Sydney's kitchen for his day job. She could put up with him for a while longer.

He cleaned up the kitchen, then headed back to his room. He sat down and turned on his computer, ready to dive into chapter twenty-one.

And then he found himself staring blankly at the computer screen, distracted by the image of a beautiful woman with dark hair and pale eyes. He sighed and turned off the machine. Creation would have to wait until morning. He needed to go to bed before the day could hand him any more surprises.

Though he doubted the Fates or Mr. Smith could top what he'd been handed already.

• • •

Sydney woke, disoriented. Then she realized she was in her own bed, under a toasty-warm comforter, and she smiled. There was nothing quite like coming home. It was one of the reasons she enjoyed her work so much. She never appreciated home more than she did after three or four months out in the wild.

She fumbled for her watch, wanting to know the time and the date. She flopped back on her bed and groaned. Twenty-four hours gone without a trace. She vaguely remembered a trip or two to the bathroom, trips made without encountering her housemate.

She sighed deeply and burrowed back down under the covers. Much as she wanted to kick Sam's arrogant, overbearing self right out the door, she knew she couldn't afford it. Though she was just as good a guide as any man out there, city boys were reluctant to use her. She'd had to cut her fees drastically just to get business. It was the reason she'd decided to rent her spare bedroom. Joe had assured her he would find a suitable renter. Damn him, anyway.

Well, it was either keep Sam or starve. She couldn't give him back the rent money he'd paid all up front because she'd already spent it. She hated the thought, but it looked like she was stuck with him until December.

She rolled out of bed and pulled her robe around her. She rubbed her arms vigorously as she left her bedroom and made her way to the kitchen. She was used to traveling in the dark, when necessary, and had no trouble finding her way. Or spotting the creation that sat cooling on the counter.

Cake. Sydney's mouth began to water at the sight. She wanted it to be warm, but no, that might be too much to hope for. She got a knife, for the sake of propriety, and cut herself a generous slice right out of the bottom tier. Whatever else his flaws, Sam certainly could bake rings around Sara Lee. Sydney closed her eyes and brought the slice up, then opened her mouth to bite.

"Stop!"

Her eyes flew open. She squinted into the beam of a flashlight.

"Don't move."

Sydney stood, frozen to the spot, as the flashlight approached. The cake was very carefully and gingerly removed from her hand.

"Hey—" she protested.

"Quiet," Sam growled. "You just ruined six hours worth of work, lady, so right now it would be a very good idea for you to just wash your hands and go back to bed."

"It's just cake—"

"It's a wedding cake!" Sam exploded.

"You're getting married?" This guy was certifiable.

"It's not for me! It's for Eunice and Jeremy. Tomorrow afternoon at one o'clock."

His face was illuminated by the flashlight he held between his forearm and chest as he carefully set the slice of cake onto a plate. And she wanted to laugh.

"You make wedding cakes?"

"It pays the bills. Turn on the light. I've got major surgery to perform here."

Sydney obediently turned on the kitchen light, then she caught an unobstructed view of Sam's face—and his furious expression. She backed up a pace in spite of herself.

"Uh, I'm sorry . . ."

Sam reached behind her and jerked a cake knife out of the pottery utensil holder sitting on the counter. He didn't spare her a glance.

"I didn't realize . . ." she began.

Sam was pulling ingredients out of her cupboards, strange things she didn't usually keep, like flour and sugar. He didn't respond as he got out a bowl and started mixing these foreign substances together.

"Look," she began, his silence starting to make her uncomfortable, "can't you just fix it? Patch it together? It would probably take a lot of time to rebake it."

Sam stopped and turned his head slowly to look at her. "Too bad you couldn't have thought about that before you ruined it."

"I didn't mean to!"

"That hardly matters now, does it?"

"I didn't ask you to come live here," she said, sticking out her chin stubbornly, struggling to find some way to defend herself.

"That really isn't the point, is it, Sydney?"

Sydney felt lower than the lowest grubworm. So she bristled even harder.

"You should have told me not to touch it."

"You've been asleep for twenty-four hours. I didn't want to wake you and find myself without my family jewels." He turned and reached into the refrigerator for a plate encased in Saran Wrap. He handed it to her. "Roast beef sandwich. Here's a can of pop. Go eat it somewhere I don't have to look at you."

"This is *my* house," Sydney said in a last bid to save her pride.

"Yeah, well, this is *my* kitchen at the moment and I don't want you in it."

Sydney clutched the cold can in her hand and walked out of the kitchen with her head held high. No, she wasn't upset. Sam's kindness in making her dinner didn't hurt her. His anger didn't bother her. His assurance earlier that he'd rather dance with an angry bear than touch her didn't trouble her either. After all, she was Sydney Kincaid, wilderness woman. She was every inch her father's daughter, bless his crusty old soul. She'd survived on her own since her seventeenth birthday, since Sydney the elder had died on his way back in from the woodpile. She didn't need anyone. She'd made it all by herself, and damn anyone who tried to imply differently. The very last thing she needed in her life was a man, especially a man who would probably starve to death five yards from the house unless someone showed him the direction back to the kitchen.

She shut and locked her door, put the supper Sam had fixed for her on her nightstand, then threw herself onto her bed and tried to burst into tears.

It didn't work. So she rolled over on her back and looked up at the ceiling. She hadn't cried in thirteen years, not since before her father's funeral. If she hadn't cried then, a simple snubbing by her housemate certainly wasn't going to bring tears to her eyes now.

She ignored her supper and crawled back under the covers. Tomorrow was Eunice and Jeremy's wedding. If she didn't go, the town would think her a chicken and the Clan down at the store would grumble about her cowardice. If she went, the women would shake their heads sadly and pity her that she couldn't find a husband.

Not that she wanted one; no, sir.

No, she reminded herself again as she drifted off to sleep. The very last thing she needed was a man.

Especially one as handsome and useless as Sam.

four

The next afternoon Sam stood in Flaherty's dilapidated Grange hall and felt as if he'd been transported to another planet. His mother would have succumbed to another fainting fit if she could have seen his current surroundings. He found, however, that the place was growing on him. There was something good and solid about the beat-up wood under his feet. He looked around at the reception guests and felt the warmth increase. These were good, honest people. At least he never doubted where he stood with them.

"Oh, Sam," Eunice gushed, "you're *so* talented!"

"It's just a hobby," he said modestly. But if the bride was happy, then so was he.

"Well, I've never seen anything so fancy," she said, looking adoringly at the three-tiered wedding cake adorned with icing flowers. "And look, Jeremy, there's already an indentation where you should cut the first piece. Sam, how in the world did you bake it that way?"

"That's my secret," Sam said pleasantly. He looked over Eunice's head for the culprit. He and Sydney hadn't come to the wedding together, which was no doubt safer where she was concerned. He had the feeling he would have been tempted to strangle her if he'd had her alone in a car in the middle of nowhere.

"You know," Eunice continued, "Mother has already recommended you to all her friends. I'm afraid you'll soon have more business than you can handle."

Sam grimaced. He would spend his mornings baking and his evenings repairing whatever damage Sydney did to his creations. He could hardly wait.

Besides, he already had more business than he could handle. Though the Clan at the general store seemed to find him somewhat lacking, the mothers of Flaherty did not. He was certain it was that author mystique. It would pass. But hopefully not before December. Baking cakes for the local Ladies Aid Society provided him with spare cash and free lunches every Wednesday. A guy couldn't ask for much more than that.

His mother was, however, apoplectic over the news that he was making a living elbow-deep in flour.

His older sister periodically sent him papers to sign that would transfer his assets to her account, on the off chance that his dementia extended to his signature.

Sam turned his thoughts away from his family and back to the wedding guests. It was shaping up to be an afternoon for the annals.

First he was accosted by Estelle Dalton and her eighteen-year-old ingénue daughter, Sylvia. Sam took one look at Sylvia and decided against it. No matter that he was thirty-five and almost old enough to be her father; the girl looked like she couldn't fix a broken fingernail, much less a leaky sink. They would drown within a month.

Then there was Ruth Newark and her daughter, Melanie. No, definitely not. Both of them looked like they'd just stepped out of the pages of *Vogue*. Sam had visions of watching his royalty checks be spent faster than he could haul them in. Then Ruth announced that she fully intended to live with her daughter and future son-in-law. Sam wondered why. Then Ruth pinched him on the behind when Melanie's back was turned, and he understood. He fled to a safer corner of the reception hall.

Next there was Bernice Hammond and her daughters Alvinia, Myra, and Wilhelmina. Sam immediately had visions of the women dressed in breastplates, brandishing swords and making him listen to Wagnerian opera for hours at a time. Not that having a handywoman around the house wasn't an appealing thought. But a quartet of Amazons just wasn't for him. These were mountain women. They needed mountain men. He didn't want to grow a beard, and he wasn't all that fond of plaid flannel shirts—his ancestry aside. No, these gals were not for him.

Sydney walked through his line of vision, and he felt a scowl settle over his features. Now, there was definitely *not* the right woman for him. She was irritating. She was selfish. She had no manners at the dinner table. It was no wonder she was still single.

"Well," a smooth voice purred from beside him, "would you look at that?"

Sam looked down and gulped when he saw Ruth Newark sidling up to him. He suppressed the urge to cover his backside.

"What?" he asked, not really wanting to know the answer.

"Sydney Kincaid. Have you ever seen such a pitiful creature?"

Sam looked at Sydney. She was wearing jeans and a dark blue sweater. Not exactly wedding-reception attire, but it certainly suited her. She must have felt him looking at her because she turned around. She looked at him and smiled weakly. He started to smile back, then remembered how annoyed he was with her. He scowled at her. She turned away.

"Joe's been trying to set her up for years," Ruth continued. One of her hands disappeared behind her back. Sam took a step to his left, moving his buns away from certain trouble.

"Oh?" he managed.

"No one will take the bait. Why would they? She can't cook, she can't keep house. Perfectly worthless as wife material." Ruth turned to him and put her hand on his chest. "Poor Sam, stuck out at the Kincaid place with that creature. Why don't you move in with us, honey?" She dragged her fingers down his chest. "You can have my bed. I'd be more than willing to sleep on the couch just to get you out of that wild woman's house. Or maybe we could share the bed. If you want."

Sam watched Ruth's hand slide down his belly, over his belt. He hastily backed away with a muffled yelp.

"Now, Sam," Ruth coaxed, "don't be shy."

Sam had never considered himself a coward; rather, he was a man who knew when to cut his losses and run. So he ran, straight for the men's room.

He hid out there until the men who came in started to look at him strangely. He knew better than to hang around any longer. His reputation was tattered enough as it was. So he crept back into the reception hall, keeping his eyes peeled for Ruth the Bun Molester.

The Clan from the general store stood huddled near one end of the buffet table. They looked terribly uncomfortable in their Sunday best, but Sam noticed they didn't let that stop them from noting everything that went on around them. The reception would no doubt provide fat for them to chew on for quite some time.

The Ladies Aid Society stood at the other end of the buffet table, probably discussing the Clan. Then again, maybe they were discussing the Jell-O salad Mrs. Fisher had brought. Sam had overheard someone say she'd used regular marshmallows instead of the mini variety. The ensuing uproar had been enormous.

The rest of the population stood around in groups, dividing themselves up by age. Sam felt comfortable with none of them, so he remained against the wall, hoping he could blend in with the woodwork.

The bride and groom stepped up to the table, and the cake ceremony began. As Eunice made a comment about Sam's cake-cutting-guide indentations, Sam searched the room for his misbehaving housemate, determined to give her a few more glares before the afternoon was over.

He found her without much trouble. She was at the far side of the reception hall, leaning back against the wall in the same way he was. She was alone and watching Eunice and Jeremy with an expression he didn't understand right off. When he finally figured out what it was, he felt like someone had slugged him in the gut.

It was hunger. It wasn't envy, it wasn't disdain; it was hunger, plain and simple.

He watched people drift past her. Men her age ignored her. Women her age gave her looks that would have made most women break down and weep. Sydney did nothing, but her spine stiffened with each look. Even from across the room, Sam could see that. The Ladies Aid Society snubbed her with a thoroughness that made Sam's blood pressure rise. Not even the Clan came to her rescue.

Sam's scowl faded into a thoughtful frown. This was something he hadn't expected. If there was one thing he wouldn't have figured on, it was that Sydney Kincaid would be vulnerable. But there she was, looking so lost and forlorn that he could hardly stop himself from striding out into the middle of the room and blasting the general population for ignoring her. Sydney might be irritating and pig-headed, but she didn't deserve this. The men should have been fighting among themselves to get at her. Instead, they avoided her like three-day-old fish.

Then Sydney met his eyes. She pulled herself up to her full height and threw him a scowl that would have only infuriated him ten minutes earlier. Now he understood exactly why she was glaring at him.

But there was no use in letting her in on his realization. So he glared back while his mind worked furiously, trying to assimilate what he'd just learned and understand what he wanted to do with that knowledge. Was it pity he felt? No, he didn't think so. It was something that went far deeper than that. Seeing Sydney vulnerable, watching her draw her dignity around her like a cloak, had touched something deep inside him, something he'd never felt before.

When he realized what it was, he had to lean back against the wall for support.

She had awakened his chivalry.

It was frightening.

It was obviously a latent character flaw that had been lurking in a forgotten corner of his Scottish soul. He wondered if there was some ancestor he ought to be cursing for it.

But as he turned the notion over in his mind, he found that the waves of noble sentiment that coursed through him were irresistible. He wanted to stand straighter. He wanted to find a sword and wave it around his head in an Errol Flynn–like manner, scattering enemies like leaves. The thought of rescuing Sydney Kincaid from injustice was tantalizing beyond belief.

Assuming she wanted to be rescued.

He shook aside that niggling doubt and put his shoulders back. He would rescue her. In fact, he was going to make the best damn knight in shining armor she'd ever seen.

Carefully, of course. He had fond hopes of fathering a few children in the future. No sense in getting Sydney's trigger finger itching too badly at first.

He took a deep breath. Then he fixed his most formidable frown on his face and crossed the reception hall to her, threading his way through the dancers, skirting the Ladies Aid Society and the Clan, and rounding the buffet table to where Sydney stood against the wall, looking as if she were going to run at any moment. But she stood her ground. He smiled to himself. Yes, sir, Sydney Kincaid would never back away from a fight.

He slapped his hand against the wall next to her head. "I suppose you heard about my cake-cutting guide."

Her pale eyes flashed. "What of it?"

"You just about ruined my reputation. I'd say that means you owe me."

"I don't owe you anything—"

"The Clan tells me your father always paid his debts. A pity his daughter doesn't have the same sense of honor."

Ouch, that had to have stung. He waited for her to slap his face, and he knew he would have deserved it. Instead, she started to wilt right there in front of him. And that he couldn't bear. He had to do something drastic.

"Giving up already?" he demanded.

Well, that took care of the withering. The fire immediately came back to her eyes. "All right. What do you want?"

"I've already paid up through December. I'm moved in and I don't want to move out. The way I see it, you owe me a place to stay." She started to balk, and he quickly continued. "You wouldn't want word to get around that you're a chicken, would you?"

"That's blackmail," she snarled.

He nodded.

She gritted her teeth and looked away. Sam watched the wheels turn, wondering what she wrestled with.

"I won't bother you," he said, in a low voice. "I'll be a perfect gentleman. You won't even know I'm there," he lied. He fully intended to give her no choice but to notice him. And he had the feeling he knew just how to do it.

"You'll cook?" she asked.

Bingo. "You bet."

"Cakes?"

"Whatever you want."

She looked back up at him and frowned. "Don't break any more windows. And don't mess with the water heater."

"Done." He held out his hand. "Truce?"

She ignored his hand. "Get out of my way. I've had enough of this wedding garbage. And come home soon. I'm ready for dinner."

Come home soon. Sam rubbed his fingers over his mouth to hide his smile. Maybe there would come a day when Sydney Kincaid would say those words and mean them in an entirely different way.

Now all he had to do was figure out how to convince her that she wanted to mean them in an entirely different way.

Because, whether he wanted it or not, he had just fallen head over heels in like with the orneriest woman west of the Hudson.

five

Sydney brought in an armload of wood and shivered as she dumped it in the bin next to the fireplace. It had taken her an entire week to chop enough to last until the new year. On Monday she'd been a bit irritated that Sam wasn't coming out to help her. On Tuesday she'd been completely annoyed with him. Either she wasn't very good at hiding her emotions, Sam was very bright, or he had begun to feel guilty, because he'd come out Wednesday morning, dressed in sweats and sneakers, ready to help.

He'd succeeded only in almost chopping off all the toes on his right foot.

Sydney had decided right then that chopping the wood herself was far less aggravating than watching over Sam while he helped. So she'd sent him back inside to play on his computer while she worked like a dog.

Well, at least they'd be warm for the next couple of months. The cabin was actually centrally heated and had two backup generators in case the main power supply went out. The wood served as merely a last resort, as well as something of a luxury. There wasn't anything Sydney liked better than to turn off all the lights, sit in front of the fire and dream she was sitting there with an attentive man. He didn't have to be gorgeous, or built like a football player;

he just had to be nice. Of course, if he was gorgeous and built she wouldn't argue.

And just such a man was living with her.

She brushed her hands on her jeans and walked into the house. She had to get out. Fast—before she started to let her imagination run away with her. She backed her Jeep out of the double garage, then got out to close the door. Sam bounded out onto the porch.

"Where're you going?"

"Town," she said shortly. *Please don't say you want to come along.*

"I want to come along. Wait for me, Syd."

She closed her eyes briefly and prayed for strength. It wasn't that he was handsome. It wasn't that he was built like a linebacker without the excess pudge around the middle. It wasn't that he could cook up a meal like a trained chef.

It was the way he said her name.

She got into the Jeep and slammed the door shut. She closed her eyes and rested her head against the steering wheel. Letting Sam stay had been a very bad idea. Guilt was a very bad thing. She would have kicked him out if he hadn't held that stupid cake over her head.

The passenger door opened, the car dipped slightly and the door closed.

"Hey, what's the matter?" His low, husky voice washed over her like a soothing, warm wave. "Want me to drive?"

"No, I'm fine." She lifted her head and rubbed her eyes. "I'm fine."

"You've been working too hard." Strong fingers were suddenly working their way under the collar of her coat to massage her neck. "I should have helped you with the wood. I'm sorry, Sydney."

"You would have lost a limb by the end of the week," she said, pulling away. "I just haven't been sleeping well."

Sam retreated back to his side of the Jeep. "You'll have to come home and take a nap before dinner. Let's get going."

Sydney eyed the package on Sam's lap as they drove toward town. "What's that?"

"First draft. My agent thinks I've been doing nothing but napping all summer." He flashed her a smile that made her knees weak. "She has a rather inaccurate impression of my manliness, I'm afraid."

Sydney doubted that. No woman with eyes could have formed an inaccurate impression of Sam's manliness. Sydney concentrated on the road.

"Do you ever read espionage novels?"

"Never," Sydney fibbed firmly. "I haven't got the patience for them."

"Romances?"

"Not those, either," she lied. Wow, two lies in the space of ten seconds. With any luck, Sam would never look in her room and see what filled her bookshelves. "I've only got time to read up on work stuff. You know, trail information and things. Wilderness studies. Hunting techniques."

"You're such a stud," he said with a laugh.

Normally, that kind of comment would have stung deeply. But the way Sam grinned at her took all the sting away. She smiled weakly.

"I have a reputation to maintain."

"I hear you're the best."

"Oh?" Now, this was news. "Who from?"

"Mr. Smith. The Clan. Even Mrs. Fisher, who doesn't know when it's polite to use regular marshmallows and when it isn't. She was complaining Wednesday at the Ladies Aid meeting that someone needs to marry you and saddle you with a dozen kids before you run her sons out of business. A backhanded compliment, of course, but it was still a compliment."

"She's an old biddy," Sydney grumbled. Secretly, she was pleased. Maybe things were starting to look up.

Then why did the thought of half a dozen sable-haired, green-eyed children running around her house seem more appealing than showing dozens of spoiled executives the beauty of her land?

The general store saved her from speculating about that disturbing thought. She pulled to a stop and turned off the engine.

"Anything you want inside?" she asked.

"I have a list. I'm just going to run to the post office, then I'll come meet you." He tapped the end of her nose with his finger. "Don't leave without me. I'm making apricot chicken tonight."

"I'm convinced."

He looked at her with a strange little smile before he got out of the car and made his way across the street to the post office in his high-top sneakers. Sydney shook her head as she walked up to the porch of the store. She needed to think about something more practical than Samuel MacLeod's smiles.

His feet. Yes, that was the ticket. Sam needed boots. Maybe Joe had an extra pair lying around. If not, he could order a pair. Sam wouldn't survive the winter without them.

She walked into the store, nodded to Joe, and approached the Clan. They grunted a greeting. Sydney jammed her hands in the pockets of her jeans and bestowed a rare smile on them.

"What's new, fellas?"

"Kilpatrick's heading south," Zeke grumbled. "I said he'd never make it up here. Born and bred in California. No spine at all."

"*I* said he'd fold," Amos said, leaning over to deposit a hefty bit of spit into the spittoon. "Guiding's a man's job. Ain't that so, Sydney?"

"You bet, Amos," Sydney said, rocking back on her heels. It was no easy feat in her boots, but she'd had plenty of practice. "Not for cowards."

Zeke looked up at her with a disapproving frown. "Still got that writer fella out at your place, Sydney?"

"He's paid through December," Sydney said defensively.

"I heard Ruth Newark offered him a place. He shoulda taken it. Ain't right to have him out at your house, Sydney. Your pa wouldn't have liked it."

Sydney frowned right back at him. "He's paid through

December," she repeated. "Money's money, Zeke."

"And he's a single boy, Sydney."

Sydney felt her good humor evaporate. "It isn't as if he wants anything to do with me," she said sharply, then spun around and walked over to the counter. She shoved her list at Joe and pretended a mighty interest in the contents of Joe's glass case. She could name all the flies there and could tell which ones were best for what kind of fishing. Yessiree, that was certainly the kind of knowledge she needed to attract a man.

She looked up as the door opened, expecting to see Sam. Instead, she saw Melanie Newark and Frank Slater. Frank was the only male in Flaherty who had ever given her the time of day. He thought it was great that she had her own business, and he had even asked her out on a date. Once. Her one and only date.

"Hey, Sydney," Frank smiled, coming over to her. "How's it going?"

"Great, Frank. How are you?"

"Frank, stop," Melanie hissed.

Frank threw Melanie a faintly annoyed look. "What?"

"What are you doing, you idiot?" Melanie spluttered.

"Well . . ."

"Frank, you come away from her."

"Now, Melanie . . ."

"You know she's desperate for a husband. Or maybe she isn't. Either way, you don't want to stand too close. And I certainly don't want you talking to her. It will ruin your reputation. Mother says no self-respecting man would get within ten feet of Sydney Kincaid."

"Sure, Melanie," Frank mumbled, moving away. "I guess you're right." He didn't spare Sydney another glance.

Sydney looked back down at the case, blinking furiously. She didn't care what Melanie thought, or Frank for that matter. They were just stupid. Stupid, idiotic, ignorant jerks who didn't have a kind bone in their bodies.

"Here's my list, Joe," a deep voice said directly behind her. "Alphabetically, just how you like it. Sydney, did you give Joe your list?"

She nodded, keeping her head down, mortified that Sam had probably heard all of Melanie's diatribe.

"Why, Sam," Melanie purred, "how nice to see you again."

Sydney peeked to her right in time to see Melanie shove Frank out of her way so she could get closer to Sam.

"Mother wanted me to invite you out for supper tonight."

"Hey," Frank complained, "I was coming out for supper—"

Melanie glared briefly at Frank, then smiled at Sam. "What do you say, Sam?"

It was the last straw. Sydney knew when to concede the battle. Not that she wanted Sam. No, sir. But he was her housemate, after all. She couldn't help but feel a little proprietary where he and his chocolate cakes were concerned. She backed up, intending to make a clean getaway before Sam started discussing his dinner plans.

She backed up straight into Sam's hard body. He grabbed a fistful of her jacket and held her immobile.

"Can't," he said cheerfully. "Sydney's going to teach me how to fish this afternoon, then we're going to fry up our catches tonight."

Sydney turned around, as best she could with him still clutching her coat, and gaped at him.

"Isn't that so, Syd?"

She could have sworn he winked at her. She couldn't even manage a reply. He pulled the hood of her coat up over her hair.

"Why don't you go out and warm up the Jeep? I'll get Frank to help me out with the goods. And, Syd, do you think I need boots for the winter? Joe, have you got any boots? Get moving, Sydney. We haven't got all day. The fish will be asleep by the time we get out to the river."

Sydney got help to the door. Sam kept up a steady stream of nonsense conversation as he steered her past the booby-trapped floorboard and pushed her out the door.

"Go start the car," he said in a low voice. "I want a quick getaway before Melanie's mother gets here. Move it."

Sydney moved it. She walked out to her car, crawled in

under the wheel, and started the motor. Then she put her head down on the steering wheel and tried to cry. It didn't happen. She steeped herself in the humiliation she'd just been through, repeating Melanie's words over and over again in her head. No tears were forthcoming. Not even the knowledge that Sam had wanted to leave quickly not because of her but because of Melanie's mother brought any tears to her eyes. As if he would actually want to stick up for her!

Though he had. Rather nicely, too. She shook her head. He hadn't meant it. He was just a nice person. He wanted nothing to do with her. He probably felt the same way all the other men in Flaherty felt. Sydney Kincaid wasn't good wife material. A woman who couldn't cook or keep house was a bad bet for marriage. Best stay away from her. Wouldn't want to ruin your reputation or anything.

The driver's side door opened. "Keys."

Sydney didn't move, so Sam reached in for the keys. She listened to him load their supplies into the back. By the sound of it, the supplies were numerous enough to last them through the winter. It was just as well. It would start snowing soon enough, and then they'd be trapped together. Alone in her house.

Too bad nothing would happen.

"Move over, sugar."

Sydney looked up at Sam—handsome, kind Sam who stood inside the open door.

"What?"

"I'm driving home. Move over."

"But—"

He picked her up in his arms, carried her around to the other side of the car, unlocked the door, and put her in. He buckled the seat belt, returned to the driver's seat, and started up the motor. And he said nothing, all the way home. Sydney grew more miserable with each mile that passed. Maybe he was having second thoughts. Maybe Melanie had talked him into coming out to dinner. Maybe he was going to stay once he got there. She wasn't sure why it bothered her as much as it did, but there was no denying it.

She unloaded the groceries with Sam, then helped him put them away. And when they were done, he plunked her down on the counter as if she'd been a rump roast and slapped his hands down on either side of her.

"We've got a problem," he said, looking her square in the eye.

She could hardly swallow. "You're going to dinner at Melanie's?"

"Hell, no. Her mother fondled me at Eunice and Jeremy's reception. At the reception, mind you. No, I am definitely not going to dinner at Melanie's house."

Sydney couldn't stop a small smile. "That's really a compliment, you know. She doesn't grope just anyone."

"I'd rather be snubbed. Which brings me to what I want to discuss."

Sydney's smile faded. He was leaving. He was leaving and she was stupid enough to want him to stay.

"The way I see it," Sam continued with his hands still resting on either side of her, "we both have what others would consider a problem."

"We do?"

"We do. I can't find a wife because I can't tell one end of a hammer from the other. You can't find a husband because you can't cook. That about sums it up, doesn't it?"

She nodded slowly. "That's about the size of it."

"So," he said, clearing his throat and looking at something behind her, over her right shoulder, "I figure we can help each other. You can help me become mechanical, and I'll help you learn how to cook. Of course, this means I'll have to stay here with you longer than I'd planned. Probably three or four months more." He sighed. "I'm really hopeless when it comes to fixing things. It might take you that long to rectify my lack of studliness."

He was staying. Sydney blinked back the tears that should have been there at his announcement.

"You think a man wants a woman who can cook?"

"Absolutely. And not just cook. She has to be a fabulous

cook. It'll take me at least six months to teach you what you'll have to know. Maybe more if you really want to become marketable. Especially since I'll have to keep working on my revisions."

"So you won't be able to help me every day?" *He was staying.*

"We'll see. What sorts of things do you do during the winter? Will you be busy a lot?"

"I just read. And watch television." She paused and looked at something behind his left shoulder. "I could fix you lunch and things while you work. Just to practice," she added hastily.

"Of course," he nodded, just as hastily. "All right, let's have a plan. We'll get up in the mornings and make breakfast together. Can you scramble eggs?"

"If it doesn't come prewrapped and precooked, I can't deal with it."

Sam smiled. "Eggs first, then. Once we've finished breakfast, you can teach me something to increase my machismo. I bought boots today, so I don't have to worry about losing any toes."

"Good point."

"Then we'll make lunch. Then I'll either work on my book in the afternoon while you read up on your trail-guiding studies or I'll teach you how to bake. How does that sound?"

"Fair enough," she said. In reality, it sounded like bliss. Maybe if she were exceptionally inept, Sam would stay until spring.

Or summer.

Or fall.

Or forever.

He tapped the end of her nose. "Go take a nap, sweetheart. Your eyelids are already at half-mast. I'll wake you up in time for dinner."

"Apricot chicken?"

"What else?"

She hopped off the counter and pushed him out of the way. "I suppose this is a good thing," she said, trying to sound businesslike. "I guess it's about time I got married, and I'm sure not attracting any prospects the way I am."

He smiled. "We're doing each other a favor. All I'm getting is my butt pinched the way I am now. I'd like to be respected for my prowess in the tool shed."

Sydney nodded and left the kitchen. She was happy. For the first time in years, she was happy. And that happiness lasted until she closed her bedroom door and flopped down onto her bed. Then her happiness was replaced by hollowness. How many nights had she lain in that very bed and dreamed of a man who would want her? Too many to count. She'd pretended it hadn't hurt her feelings. Men were stupid, and she hadn't wanted any part of them.

Until Sam. He was handsome and funny and kind. And he couldn't stand Melanie Newark's mother. That said a great deal about his character. He wasn't afraid to bake mouthwatering cakes. He couldn't start a fire on his own, and she half wondered how he managed to work the oven without help.

But she wanted him to want her. She wanted him to look at her with those leaf-green eyes, smile that secret little smile of his, and say, "Yes, Syd, I think you're perfect and I want you." And if he thought the perfect woman was a woman who could cook like a French chef, then that's what she would become.

She closed her eyes and fell asleep, dreaming about flour and sugar.

six

Sam came out of the bathroom a week later to the sound of pots clanking and a certain wilderness woman cursing. He walked through the living room and stopped just shy of the kitchen, curious as to what Sydney was up to. The smell of burnt eggs immediately assaulted his nose.

"Damn it, anyway, I'm going to burn all the winter supplies before November if somebody doesn't start cooperating right now! Go down the disposal, you ungrateful little sonsa—"

Sam indulged in a grin. It was no wonder Sydney had such a tough reputation as a trail guide if she talked to her city boys the way she talked to her breakfast ingredients. The woman was adorable. Sam could hardly stop himself from striding into the kitchen and kissing her senseless.

No, that wouldn't do. In the first place, he'd promised to be a gentleman. In the second, he had the sinking feeling that she had her heart set on Frank Slater. Why, Sam didn't know. The guy was a wuss. All right, so he wasn't exactly a wuss. He could hunt and fish and do all those Alaska things, but he couldn't tell the infinitive form from the subjunctive, and Sam had his doubts he knew what a pronoun was. And he was dating Melanie. If that didn't say something about his character, and his intelligence, Sam didn't know what did. No, Frank Slater wasn't for Sydney.

Now to convince her of that.

Carefully.

Sam cleared his throat and entered the kitchen.

"Hey, Syd, what's for breakfast?"

"Oh," she said, blinking innocently, "eggs. Just like you taught me, Sam. I'm just getting ready to cook them," she added, waving the pan around, probably to make the smell of burned eggs dissipate.

"It sounds great. Want me to make the toast?"

"No. You just go on in and sit down in the living room. I'll call you when it's ready."

Sam let her off the hook and went to hide in the living room. After a week of lessons, Sydney still couldn't scramble eggs to save her life. They were either too runny or too dry. Sam didn't care either way. One day she'd be making runny eggs just for him, and he'd eat them with just as much gusto then as he did now.

Half an hour later, he sat facing a plate of quivering eggs. It was a lucky thing he usually liked his over very easy or he might have been slightly sick at the prospect facing him. Sydney looked like she wanted to cry, so he ate not only his breakfast but hers, then he made her some unburned toast. And he started to gird up his loins for his humiliating part of the bargain: his wilderness-man studies.

He didn't care about hammers. He didn't care about wrenches or screwdrivers or power tools. He didn't care about what made the generator tick. It provided light and heat, and power for his computer. He didn't want to know where that power came from or what to do when the power was off. Sydney would be around for that.

But today was different. He was going to learn how to fish. Sydney promised him she would teach him what kind of lures lured what kind of fish. Sam could thread a needle about as easily as he could jump over the moon, so he anticipated a great deal of difficulty in hooking the lures to the string. Fishing line. Whatever they called it, he knew it was going to give his fingers fits and Sydney would have to give him a great deal of help.

And if that wasn't enough to make a man grin, he didn't know what was.

He buzzed through four chapters of the revisions his agent had requested, then cheerfully waited in the living room for Sydney to go get their fishing gear. She came in with a tackle box and two rods. Sam opened the box the moment she set it down and peeked inside. He held up a little silver fish with three hooks hanging from his underbelly.

"Cute," he noted.

"No, not cute," Sydney corrected. "Clever. Efficient. Practical. Lures are never cute, Sam."

"I'll keep that in mind. Whatever happened to salmon eggs? Or worms?"

"Minor-league stuff," Sydney said, reaching for a rod. "You're fishing with the big boys now, Sam."

"Do your city boys know all about this when they come up?"

She shrugged. "Some do. Some would like to think they do."

"Why do I have the feeling they don't like hearing what they're doing wrong from a woman?"

"Because you're very bright, Sam. Now, pay attention. I'm going to explain the parts of the reel to you."

He leaned back against the couch and moved just the slightest bit closer to her. "I'm listening."

"This up front is the drag knob. It adjusts the tension. Then we have the spool. See how the fishing line is wound around it, then fed through the guide?"

Sam nodded obediently.

"Now, when you're casting, you release the line here, by pressing this button. Then you drag the lure back toward you by cranking the handle . . ."

Sam stopped listening after that. It wasn't that he wasn't interested in fishing. He didn't mind salmon, barbecued with lots of lemon on it. He found he just couldn't concentrate. Sydney was just so doggone beautiful. He wondered why in the world every male in Flaherty over the age of ten wasn't beating a path to her door. Frank Slater probably was. Sam didn't care for that thought.

"Sam?"

He blinked and realized she was looking at him. Her pale blue eyes were wide and her lips parted just slightly. Sam had the overwhelming urge to bend his head and capture her mouth with his.

"Sam, you look flushed. Did my eggs do you in?"

"I'm fine," he said. But his voice sounded suspiciously hoarse, even to his ears.

"Do you want me to go back over the parts of the rod?"

"No. Keep going."

She launched into a discussion of lures, and Sam did his best to follow. But her perfume kept getting in his way. He couldn't decide if it was something she'd put on, her shampoo, or the dryer sheets he'd used in the last load of wash. He leaned closer for a better whiff and bumped his chin on her shoulder when she suddenly leaned back.

"Sam!"

"Sorry," he said, rubbing his jaw. "I was just moving in for a closer look."

"Here, let's put the tackle box on your lap. It'll be safer that way."

Sam let her put the heavy box on his lap, then he sniffed unobtrusively when she leaned over to pull out a lure. Could have been shampoo. Could have been the dryer sheet. Whatever it was, it was sexy as hell and it was making him lightheaded.

"Sam?"

"I'm just a little dizzy," he said, drawing his hand over his eyes. "It'll pass. I must have stayed up too late."

"Oh, no," she said, lifting her arm and sniffing her wrist. "It's that insect repellent I put on. I'll try not to get it under your nose again." She met his eyes. "Then again, maybe I should go wash it off."

He felt himself falling. And then he felt himself falling. Literally. Sydney caught the tackle box.

"Sam!"

"Oh, this is bad," he moaned as he lunged to his feet and

ran for the bathroom, where he summarily lost both breakfast and lunch.

"Sam, open up!" Sydney shouted, pounding on the door.

Sam flushed the toilet, then rinsed out his mouth in the sink. He looked at himself in the mirror and smiled weakly at the pale shadow that stared back at him.

"Sam, good grief, what happened?" Sydney had pushed open the door and caught sight of his face. She blanched to about the same color. "I did this to you," she whispered.

"Bad eggs. Not your fault. Just help me get to bed."

She put her arm around him and helped him into his room. Well, now, this had been one way to get her there. Not exactly how his chivalrous self would have planned it, but drastic times called for drastic measures.

"Oh, Sam, I'm so sorry."

"Honey, it wasn't you," Sam said, sitting down gingerly and willing his stomach to stop churning. "It might not have been the eggs. It could have been the chicken from last night."

She looked like she just might cry for real this time. Sam took her hand and squeezed it.

"Syd, this is going to give you a great chance to hone your pampering skills. Every man loves to be pampered. I'll show you just what to do."

"You're right," she said, sounding relieved. "Let's get you comfortable, and then I'll wait on you hand and foot until you're better."

And whoever said food poisoning couldn't be fun?

seven

Thirty-six hours later Sydney sat at Sam's bedside and prayed she hadn't killed him.

First had come twelve hours of staying out of Sam's path to the bathroom. She had decided he looked mighty fine in a pair of red-and-blue-plaid boxers.

Then had come half a day's worth of shivers, when she'd piled every blanket she owned on top of him and he still begged her to turn up the heat.

Then his fever had raged and he'd wanted nothing on him at all. She'd had to fight to make him leave his underwear on.

Now he was sleeping peacefully. He looked like hell and she felt like hell. She had done this to him, laid this beautiful man low with one turn of her spatula. It was no wonder she couldn't find a man to marry.

She leaned forward and brushed an unruly lock of hair back from his face. He opened his eyes and smiled at her.

"Hi," he croaked.

She couldn't return his smile. "Sam, I'm so sorry."

"Hey, you're doing a great job of pampering me."

"Oh, Sam . . ."

He took her hand and pressed her palm against his cheek. "It wasn't your fault, sugar. It was Joe's fault for selling us rotten eggs. We'll bake him some brownies with laxative frosting in a few days as repayment."

She pulled her hand away. "I'm never setting another foot in that kitchen."

He pulled himself up against the headboard, wincing as he did so. "Oh, yes, you are. When you fall off a horse, you get right back on. Go take a nap, Sydney, while I clean up. Then we'll make soup for supper and find a good movie on television. Tomorrow we'll start over. You promised to teach me how to change the oil. I don't want to miss out on that."

"The Ladies Aid Society thinks I killed you," she said in a small voice.

Sam laughed softly as he swung his legs to the floor. "I'll set them straight next week. Now git."

Sydney rose, then stopped at the door. "I can make soup." She met his eyes. "It comes in a can, you know."

"Then you go make soup. I'll be out to eat it in half an hour."

She nodded and closed his door behind her. At least soup wouldn't kill him. Saltine crackers would be a nice addition, especially since someone else had cooked them. And ice cream for dessert. Yes, Sam would certainly be safe through dinner.

Half an hour later, she heard the TV go on in the living room. She brought out a tray with two bowls of soup and a package of crackers. She set the tray down and watched Sam try to start the fire. When he started to swear, she knew the time for aid had come. She knelt down next to him and smiled.

"You're pitiful, you know?"

"Yeah, that's what I hear."

"Try kindling under the log, Sam. Newspaper and twigs. Works every time."

He used too much paper and wasted half a dozen matches getting the blaze going, but she didn't complain. He sat back on his heels with a smug smile.

"Piece of cake."

She nodded solemnly. "Of course. Now come eat your dinner before it congeals."

He followed her over to the couch and sat down, looking at the tray on the coffee table. "It's a feast!"

"Well, at least it won't kill you."

Once dinner was consumed, she cleaned up, then went back into the living room. Sam was relaxing on the couch with his feet propped up on the coffee table and a blanket over his legs. He smiled when she came in.

"There are so many channels, I don't know where to start."

She sat down on the opposite end of the couch. "Pick whatever you want. It doesn't matter to me."

Sam started to flick through the channels, then he slid a glance her way.

"You know," he said, "we're missing out on a perfect opportunity."

"How's that?"

He shrugged nonchalantly. "For snuggling practice. It's my understanding that the skill can never be too refined."

"Really." Was that her voice sounding so breathless?

"From what I understand."

"I'm sure Melanie already knows how to snuggle."

"I'm not interested in Melanie."

Sydney didn't want to know who he was interested in. But her mouth had a different idea.

"Are you interested in someone else?"

Sam looked away. "Yes."

"Oh," Sydney said. Funny how there was that little cracking sound when your heart broke. She'd never expected to have it hurt so badly.

"What about you? Planning on making Frank Slater a wonderful wife?"

She looked up and met blazing green eyes. She blinked. "Frank?"

"Yes, Frank, damn it."

"I'm not interested in Frank."

"Oh." He looked taken aback. "Then, are you interested in anyone?"

"Yes."

He looked like she'd slapped him. Then he started to scowl.

"Whoever he is, he isn't good enough for you. I want to meet him. What's his name?"

"That's none of your business."

"It sure as hell is my business. Who is he?"

"What do you care?" she retorted.

He growled. And he scowled some more. Then he thrust out his hand.

"Come here. We might as well get on with this snuggling business. I'm sure the fool will appreciate it eventually."

"I think he might." If Sam only knew!

He took her hand and hauled her over to him. Sydney found herself pinned between his heavy arm and his hard chest. He dragged her arm across his waist and pushed her head down against his shoulder.

"This is snuggling," he grumbled. "And that's *Singing in the Rain* on TV. I hope you like both because I'm not giving you a choice about either."

Sydney didn't care what was on television. They could have been watching a televised correspondence course in advanced calculus and she would have been perfectly content. After a few minutes, Sam relaxed, and she relaxed against him. She closed her eyes and sighed as he began to trail his fingers over her back. She snuggled closer to him and pressed her face against his neck.

"That feels good."

He cleared his throat. "Compliments are, of course, always appreciated. As are comments about the snuggling partner's warmth."

"You're very warm, Sam."

"Yes, like that," he said gruffly. "You're getting the hang of it."

"No, not quite yet. I think it might take another couple of hours."

She could hardly believe the words had come out of her mouth, but it was too late to take them back now.

"Yes, well, it might." Sam sounded positively hoarse.

"We'll see how it goes tonight. We might have to do this often. Just so you perfect your technique."

"Of course."

"And so you can please Sasquatch. Or whatever the hell his name is."

"Right," she agreed.

"I don't want to know who he is."

"I wouldn't think of telling you."

She felt the weight of Sam's head come to rest against hers. "Are you comfortable, Syd?" he murmured, the annoyance gone from his voice.

"Very," she whispered. "This is nice. Thank you, Sam."

He sighed deeply. "It's the least I can do for the woman who's going to take her life in her hands and teach me how to change the oil in my Range Rover."

"You'll do a great job."

He said nothing, but tightened his arms around her.

Sydney closed her eyes and smiled. She didn't think about whoever it was that Sam was interested in. *She* was the one in his arms at present, and if his embrace was any indication, he didn't want to let her go.

There was a nagging doubt at the back of her mind about the identity of Sam's woman, but she pushed it away. There would be time enough tomorrow to be irritated and miffed.

For the moment, Sam was hers.

eight

Sam swung the axe down, and it split the wood with a satisfying crack. Yes, there was something therapeutic about chopping wood. Especially when you could do it and not worry about losing toes in the process. He didn't need to chop any wood, but it was keeping him busy. And it was certainly the only positive thing in his life at present. His revisions were worse than the first draft, and his plan to woo Sydney was turning out worse than his revisions.

And it had everything to do with her mystery man.

He finished his stack, put the axe back in the shed, and walked into the house. Sydney was lying on the couch, her nose stuck in a book on trail guiding. He wished for once she would read something else. Something he'd written maybe. The woman claimed she wanted to learn how to cook. A little foray into a cooking magazine wasn't too much to ask, was it?

She looked up as he clomped by. He glared at her. She returned his look coolly.

"Ready for our lesson?" she asked, her tone as icy as her look.

"I can hardly wait. Let me shower first."

"Please do."

He slammed all the doors he could on his way to the shower. It had been a week since their snuggling lesson on the couch. Sydney had awakened the next morning in a sour mood, one that matched his perfectly. He'd lain awake all night wondering just who the hell this man of hers was. Sydney didn't know any men. Was he some New York investment jockey with plans to take Sydney to the Big Apple? The thought of Sydney Kincaid being yanked out of her native environment rankled. The thought of someone else besides him doing the yanking just plain infuriated him. If anyone was going to be doing anything with Sydney, it was going to be him.

He had no idea why she was so angry. Maybe she was reacting to him being such a jerk. He didn't know. He almost didn't care. Damn her, she was the one making him miserable, not the other way around. She knew he didn't have any ties. He never received mail or phone calls except from his agent. She sure as hell couldn't imagine that he was after Marjorie.

He took a shower that used up every bit of hot water in the tank. Then he went into his room and scowled for half an hour.

Love sucked.

He finally walked out into the living room. Sydney was asleep. He hauled her up without warning. She threw her arms around him in self-defense, so he picked her up and carried her into the kitchen.

"Cookbook," he barked.

She rubbed her eyes as she reached for it and handed it to him.

"Pay attention," he growled.

"Stop being such a jerk," she growled back, the sleep fading from her eyes, to be replaced by anger.

"Me?" He threw up his hands. "Women! Go figure."

He grabbed his keys off the rack and slammed out the front door. Might as well go check the post office box while he was out acting like an adolescent. He drove to town and found nothing in his box. Frustrated, he made his way to Smith's Dry Goods for a cold root beer. He thought about taking up smoking, then discarded that idea. No sense in taking more years off his life than Sydney had already taken.

He leaned against the counter and sipped his root beer. "Joe, does Sydney date much?"

"Reckon she doesn't," Joe said, polishing a shiny lure.

"Has she dated much in the past?"

"Once," Joe said. "Frank Slater."

Sam gritted his teeth. Frank Slater. It figured.

"Only one time, though," Joe said conversationally. "Her pa wasn't much on seeing her married."

"Just one time? You gotta be joking."

"I never joke."

Sam didn't have any trouble believing that. "But she says she's in love with someone. Some Sasquatchy mountain man."

"I reckon she's lying," Joe said, unperturbed.

"Then who could she possibly be in love with? Some city boy?"

Joe looked at him. "Now that's a thought."

Sam frowned. "Do you know who she's been taking around this summer? Names? Phone numbers?"

Joe held the lure up to the light and buffed it a bit more. "I'd look a little closer to home if I were you, Sam."

"Then I'll need a map of Flaherty and names of who lives where. And ages of the men, if you have them."

Joe gave an exasperated snort. "You don't need a map, boy. Just go back home and see if you can't figure it out from there."

Back home? Well, Sam supposed it wouldn't take all that long to plow through Sydney's copy of the phone book.

Then the proverbial light bulb went on his head.

Home?

"You're joking, right?" he said in disbelief.

Joe looked at him and pursed his lips.

Sam held up his hands. "I know, I know. You don't joke."

Joe took away Sam's root beer bottle. "Go home, Sam. And don't you dare hurt her. You are planning on staying in Flaherty, aren't you? Permanently?"

Sam thought about it for the space of ten seconds, then he realized there was nothing to think about. He didn't have to live in New York to write. He could take Sydney down to Seattle or San Francisco for a few weeks every now and then so he could do his research. There was absolutely no reason to leave. His mother, his sisters, and his trust fund would survive quite nicely without him.

"Yep," Sam nodded. "I am."

"Then get on home, boy. And see what you come up with if you look hard enough."

Sam took Joe's advice and headed home. He wasn't quite ready to accept the fact that he was the one Sydney was interested in, but there certainly wasn't anyone else in her neck of the woods. He'd go home and keep an open mind about things. Who knew what he would find out?

He entered the house quietly and immediately sensed that Sydney was in the kitchen. He followed the sound of her curses and walked in to find her in the middle of the biggest mess he had ever seen. Every bowl in the house was dirty. There was flour all over the floor, the counters, and the cook. And the cook was furious.

"What," he asked in a strangled voice, "are you doing?"

"I'm cooking," she snapped. "What does it look like I'm doing?"

It looked like she was making a mess, but he wisely chose not to point that out to her. He crossed the room and put his hand under her chin, tipping her face up. He gently wiped the flour from her cheeks.

"What are you making?"

"A cake. But it isn't going well."

"Want some help?"

"Yes."

"Let's clean up first. It'll be less stressful if you start with a clean kitchen."

Sydney wasn't much better at cleaning than she was at cooking, but he had to admire her enthusiasm. He kept back the necessary bowls and put the rest in the dishwasher.

Then he opened the cookbook, laid out all the ingredients, and proceeded to show her what to do.

"It says 'fold in the dry ingredients.' What does that mean?" she demanded.

"Here, turn the mixer back on," he said, standing behind her. "Take the spatula in your right hand and the bowl of flour in your left. Just dump in a little at a time and let the mixer do the work."

"But that's mixing, not folding."

"Same thing."

"Then why doesn't it say the same thing?"

"I don't know." He didn't. All he knew was that Sydney Kincaid was standing in the circle of his arms, concentrating on something else, leaving him free to concentrate on her. The fragrance of her hair wafted up and forced his eyes closed. He breathed deeply, savoring the smell.

"Now what do I do? Sam, are you falling asleep?"

"No."

"The cake's folded. What do I do now?"

"Preheat the oven, then pour the batter into the cake pans."

He leaned back against the counter and listened to her hum as she poured the batter into two pans, then slid them both into the oven. She set the timer, then turned and smiled.

"Now what?"

"Now you come over here and listen to me apologize for being such a jerk these past few days."

Her smile faltered. "You weren't, Sam. I'm not the easiest person to live with."

He reached out, took her hand and pulled her across the floor. "We're going to practice making up now, Syd. An important part of any relationship. I'm going to say I'm sorry. You're going to listen, forgive me, then hug me. Got it?"

She nodded.

"I'm sorry."

"I forgive you."

"Now, hug me."

"But . . ."

"Hey, I need the practice too. For Miss Sasquatchette. It's as easy as snuggling, only you can do making-up anywhere."

She moved closer to him, slowly. When she was close enough, Sam put his arms around her and drew her close. And he closed his eyes and sighed. Yes, he'd come home.

"Where did you go, Sam?" she asked softly.

"To have a root beer down at Joe's."

"I was worried about you."

Sam smiled into her hair. "I'm sorry, Sydney. I won't go like that again." He stroked her back. "I'll stay right here for as long as you want me to be."

"Miss Sasquatchette won't be angry?" Sydney asked, her voice muffled against his shirt.

"Somehow, I just don't think so."

"Then you'll hold me for a few more minutes?"

"I sure will."

He held her for forty-five more minutes, to be exact. And he cursed the timer when it went off and pulled Sydney away from him. Her toothpick came out clean, and she grinned as two perfectly baked rounds were pulled from the oven. Sam showed her how to put the cake on a cooling rack, then she made frosting. They waited for the cake to cool, then Sam leaned against the counter and watched her frost her chocolate cake. He had to smile at the concentration on her face.

Then she stood back and admired her handiwork.

"It's beautiful," she said reverently.

"No," he said, taking her hand and pulling her closer, "*you* are beautiful."

"Sam . . ."

He put his finger to her lips. "You're going to practice taking compliments. It's a skill I'm sure will come in handy in the future."

"You think so?"

He nodded. "I do." He put one arm around her shoulder and pulled her closer, then smoothed his hand over her hair. And he tried to find the words to say to tell her just how beautiful she truly was and what fools the men of Flaherty were never to have seen that. How could they have overlooked those haunting eyes, or that exquisite face? Her hair was soft and luxurious, hair that a man could bury his face and drown in without too much trouble. He met her eyes and saw the hesitancy there.

Or was it desire? He honestly couldn't tell, but there was one surefire way to find out. He lowered his head until his mouth was a mere inch from hers.

"May I kiss you?" he whispered.

"More lessons?"

"Definitely."

"If you think it will come in handy in the future."

His only answer was to cover her mouth with his own. He pulled her closer to him as he explored her lips. By the time he was finished, Sydney was shaking like a leaf. And it occurred to him, accompanied by the most Neanderthal rush of pleasure he had ever felt, that she had probably never been kissed before.

"Are we finished?"

Sam opened his eyes. Sydney's teeth were chattering.

"Do you want to be finished?"

She shook her head.

"Are you afraid?"

"Me?" she squeaked. She cleared her throat. "I've faced down grizzlies bigger than you and not broken a sweat."

"Well," he said with a smile, "that says it all, doesn't it?"

She rubbed her arms. "I think I'm cold."

"I'll build you a fire. I'm getting pretty good at it, you know." He took her hand and led her out into the living room. He built the fire quickly, then took off his shoes and pulled a blanket down in front of the fireplace. He looked up at Sydney.

"Join me?"

"Shouldn't I start dinner?"

"We'll have sandwiches later. We'll practice our cuddling tonight."

"Cuddling?"

"A completely different technique than snuggling," he said with a nod. "So get comfortable. We could be here a very long time."

The thought was singularly appealing.

nine

Sydney picked up the nail, then straightened, certain that Sam's eyes were raking her from the heel of her cowboy boots to the waistband of her jeans. She doubted he got much further than that, but she didn't care. She turned slowly, savoring the feeling of power she had somehow acquired over him in the past couple of days.

"This," she said, holding the item out for inspection, "is a nail. We don't leave these lying around on the floor. Someone might step on them, and that would hurt. Oh, look. There's another one." She bent right in front of him and brushed his chest with her forearm on her way up. "We have to be careful out here in the workshop, Sam. Safety is no laughing matter."

Sam grunted in answer. Sydney smiled sweetly and turned back to the pegboard. She set about explaining all the various tools and giving him possible uses for each. In reality, she had no idea what she was saying. All she knew was Sam was standing only inches behind her and he was paying as little attention to what she was saying as she was.

Three days had passed since he'd kissed her in the kitchen, and she was fast learning that he was determined that she practice kissing as often as possible. If he could be persuaded to work at all, he was never in his room for more than ten minutes without coming out to check on her.

And Sydney loved it.

She didn't want to speculate on his reasons. He didn't want to discuss Miss Sasquatchette, whoever she was. Sam never got personal calls, and Sydney was desperately hoping that he didn't have anyone waiting for him in New York.

"Oh, Sam," she said, pointing at a crescent wrench to her right, "would you get that for me? I can't seem to reach it."

He muttered something under his breath and reached out to take it down. Sydney slid her hand up his forearm and over his hand to take the wrench from him. She could have sworn she felt him shiver. She definitely heard him curse.

"Oh, not this one," she purred. "The one higher up." She leaned back against him as he reached, thoroughly enjoying teasing him. Never in her life had a man looked at her with anything besides impatience or disdain. Sam looked at her with lust, plain and simple. Oh, there were those other looks, those looks that a less sensible girl might have mistaken for love. But Sydney was nothing if not sensible.

"Maybe the one higher up," she said, pointing. "Yes, I think that's the one . . ."

She jumped as Sam grabbed a rag, swiped it over the bench surface, spun her around, and plunked her down on the wood with enough force to make her teeth rattle.

"All right, enough is enough. You can only tease me for so long before I snap. And I'm snapping."

"Tease?" she said, putting her hand over her chest and blinking in surprise. "Me?"

"Your jeans are so tight I doubt you can breathe, your shirt is unbuttoned far enough to give you pneumonia, and you're wearing makeup. Which you don't need, by the way."

"I don't—"

He covered her mouth with his and cut off her words. Well, he certainly was effective when it came to making a bid for a little silence. He kissed her until she forgot what she'd been about to say, then she forgot her name, and she came close to forgetting to breathe. She had only enough presence of mind to notice the last because the lack of air was starting to make her ears ring.

She froze. That wasn't her ears ringing. It was the doorbell!

"Sam," she gasped frantically. "Let me go."

"No," he murmured, holding her more tightly.

"Someone's at the door!"

Sam stiffened, then lifted his head. His eyes were wide. "Oh, no."

"Oh, no, what?"

"I invited the Ladies Aid Society over for lunch."

"Sam!" she wailed.

"I forgot," he said, releasing her and stumbling back. "You go answer the door. I'll be right there."

"Me?" she screeched. "I look kissed!"

"And I look aroused. Give me five minutes to let things, ahem, settle down." He smiled at her hopefully. "Please?"

She jumped down off the bench and tried to resurrect her hair. It was useless, so she dragged her fingers through it and straightened her clothes. Putting her shoulders back, she tried to recapture some of her dignity.

"Syd?"

She turned at the door. Sam was staring at her with a gentle smile.

"I love you."

She froze. Then she gestured to the bench. "Because of—"

He shook his head sharply. "No."

"Oh, Sam."

"Go answer the door, honey. This is going to be the shortest Ladies Aid meeting in history."

Four hours later, Sydney was ready to throw the Ladies Aid Society out of her house without any regard to where they landed. Sam ushered them out with his usual charm, and Sydney went in to start the dishes. One thing she could say for Sam—he'd taught her how to keep a clean kitchen.

She jumped when she felt arms go around her.

"Only me."

She leaned back against him. "Did you mean what you said before?"

"Yes." He took the last dish out of her hand, stuck it in the dishwasher, then turned her around. He smiled down at her. "Let's go snuggle on the couch. I'm beat, how about you?"

"The Society is exhausting."

"But very impressed with your brownies."

"I couldn't care less."

Sam laughed. "I know. And that tickles me." He kissed the end of her nose. "Let's go."

She grabbed a magazine off the counter as they went into the living room.

"What's that future Pulitzer prize–winning article you have there?" Sam asked.

Sydney smiled. "Yours, of course."

"I thought you didn't read cooking magazines."

"I lied. Joe gave me a copy."

"And do you like it?"

She smiled at the way he wouldn't meet her eyes. "I loved it. You're great, Sam."

He stretched out on the couch, then smiled up at her. "Those were the magic words. Come down here, gentle reader, and let me kiss you in gratitude for preserving my delicate author's ego."

Sydney let him draw her down next to him on the couch and then sighed as he kissed her.

He lifted his head and smiled at her. "Come with me to the Ladies Aid Society dance Friday. I want to rub this in Frank Slater's nose. And Sasquatch's. Whoever he is."

"He's you, silly. Who did you think he was?"

"I had no idea. Joe told me to look close to home. I figured he was some mountain man, hiding in your woods."

"No, he's a writer, hiding in my kitchen."

"Speaking of kitchens, do you want dinner?"

"Only if I don't have to cook it."

He sighed and rose. "A man's work is never done. If I have to go, you have to come. The least you can do is praise me while I work."

It seemed a fair trade to her.

ten

When Friday night arrived, Sam found himself pacing in the living room, waiting for Sydney to come out of the bathroom. He paced for other reasons as well. He'd spent Wednesday night snuggling with her on the couch while she'd slept contentedly in his arms. Yesterday they hadn't spent a moment apart. Sam had the feeling he was going to have to move to a hotel until the wedding.

Assuming, that is, that Sydney wanted to get married.

He stopped his pacing once he caught sight of her standing near the fireplace. His jaw went slack.

"Oh, no," he said, shaking his head. "You aren't going anywhere dressed like that."

Her face fell immediately and she turned away. Sam strode across the room and caught her. He turned her around in his arms and tipped her face up.

"You're stunning. Breathtaking. Exquisite. And by the time the evening is over, I'm going to be bruised, bloodied, and broken from fighting off all those wilderness men who'll want you. Where is that gunnysack I found for you?"

She smiled hesitantly. "You like this?"

"Sydney, you look sexy in jeans, but this?" He stepped back and looked her over from head to toe. She was wearing a long navy blue dress and no-nonsense work boots.

He was quite certain he'd never seen anything like it in New York. He was even more certain he'd never seen anything sexier. He sighed deeply. "You knock my socks off."

She didn't look all that convinced. "I don't know how long I can take this whole dance thing. We don't have to stay long, do we?"

"We'll only stay as long as you want to. You say the word and we're out of there."

The town hall was filled with Flaherty folk of all ages, and the band was already warming up with a few golden oldies. Sam greeted the Clan and his Ladies Aid Society. Sydney greeted the Clan and Joe. And then she and Sam went out to dance and they didn't pay attention to anyone else.

Sydney was asked to dance by plenty of men. She refused each one. Sam avoided being pinched by Ruth Newark and made it plain to hopeful mothers that he was off the market. As if they couldn't have told that by the way he was holding Sydney as they danced. Even the Clan seemed to accept it. Grudgingly, of course. Joe was simply beaming.

Sam couldn't take his eyes off the woman in his arms, and he found that he couldn't let go of her either. But he'd already made up his mind that she deserved a wedding before anything else, so dancing with her in public seemed the safest way to hold her and not get carried away.

He geared himself up on the way home to pop the question. His palms were sweaty. His heart was racing. In fact, his chest hurt so badly he feared he might be having a heart attack. A man didn't make it to the ripe old age of thirty-five without having had a healthy aversion to that "Will you marry me?" question.

He took a deep breath. His chest pains were from something he'd eaten at the dance. His palms were sweating because he didn't want Sydney to say no.

"All right," he said, with another deep breath. "Sydney, will you marry me?"

There was no answer.

Did she have something stuck in her throat? Had her

powers of speech been swiped by aliens? Sam scowled as he looked to his right to find out why in the world she hadn't answered him.

Her mouth was open. Her eyes were closed. Her head was lolling back on the headrest.

Great. He let out the breath he'd been holding and turned his attention back to the road. This probably hadn't been the most romantic way to do it, anyway. He would gird up his loins yet again the next day and see if he couldn't pop the question while the lady in question wasn't drooling.

And he hoped this wasn't a sign.

The next morning Sam stumbled out into the kitchen to find Sydney standing over the stove, making pancakes. She looked incredibly well rested. Sam felt his eyes narrow, which wasn't all that difficult since he hadn't slept a wink.

Sydney turned and smiled at him. "Sleep well?"

"No."

"Okay," she said slowly. "Would breakfast help?"

"I doubt it."

"What's your problem?"

Sam dug his fists into his eyes and rubbed vigorously. "Lots on my mind. It's nothing that concerns you."

Sydney's spatula dipped, and she looked as if he'd slapped her. Sam found, to his faint dismay, that he couldn't seem to find anything to say to fix that. He'd spent the night going back and forth, wondering if he'd lost his mind or his heart.

He wanted to marry her.

But would she want him? Or would she just chalk up his devotion to too much cabin fever beginning to prey on his overworked imagination?

The phone rang. Sam had never been more grateful in his life.

"I'll get it," Sydney said, but he reached it first.

"Hello?" he said.

"Sam, I'm at the airport," a crisp voice announced with all the diction that six generations of finishing-school attendees could instill in their posterity's genes.

Sam blinked in surprise. "Marjorie?"

The sigh from the other end of the phone almost blew his hair off his scalp. "Who else? I've come to see about the condition of your revisions."

Revisions? Sam frowned. Marjorie would hardly make a trip all the way to Alaska to check on his revisions. She was obviously on a mission to see what he was up to. But there was no sense in going into that over the phone. "All right," he said, resigned. "I'll come get you."

"Hurry," came the demand. "I'm appalled by the dander floating in the air—inside the building, mind you."

Sam hung up the phone before he said something he would regret. Marjorie was his agent, after all, and she was reported to be a very good one. She was also his sister, which meant it would be very embarrassing to be dumped as a client.

He looked at Sydney and wondered what she would say when she learned about the life he'd left behind. And then he looked at her and really saw her. And he knew all over again why he loved her.

Because she loved him. Samuel MacLeod, struggling writer, respectable cook, and pitiful handyman.

He took her by the shoulders, hauled her to him, and kissed her smartly on the mouth.

"I've got to go get my agent. But I'll be back as soon as I can. I have something to ask you."

She blinked. "Okay."

"I'll find her a hotel, then come home."

"Oh, she can stay here," Sydney offered. "If you want."

Sam paused. He wasn't sure he wanted them in the same enclosed space before he had a chance to explain a few things to Sydney, but maybe it was best to get all his cards on the table before he asked her to marry him. He smiled weakly.

"She won't stay long. I promise."

"It's fine. Really."

"I'll kick her out in thirty-six hours, forty-eight max. Can you put up with her that long?"

"Of course."

"I'll be back late," he said.

"It's supposed to snow. Maybe you should stay overnight."

An evening alone with his sister? The thought was terrifying, but even more terrifying was the thought of getting stuck in a snowdrift with her.

"All right, tomorrow," he agreed. "I'll miss you."

She nodded and held him tightly. "Can Marjorie cook?"

"She studied cooking with some of France's finest chefs." Why that was okay for Marjorie but not him was something he'd never understood, but getting all riled over the sexism of it wouldn't do him any good at the moment. "She can make a soufflé that'll just knock your socks off."

He hurried and packed an overnight bag, gave Sydney one last kiss, and headed off toward Anchorage. This was a good thing. He'd get some input from his agent, get his life out on the table with his future wife, then get on with things.

Sydney watched Sam drive away, and her heart sank. She had no idea who Marjorie truly was. Sam said she was his agent. Was she also an old girlfriend? Sydney couldn't bear to think about it. All she knew was that Marjorie used to be a chef. She was probably beautiful and she was from New York.

Sydney began to pace. Marjorie and Sam had probably been lovers. He probably had plans to go back to New York and sleep with her some more.

Sydney almost cried.

Then she stiffened her spine and marched herself into the kitchen. A soufflé, was it? She pulled out a cookbook and looked up the recipe. And she frowned.

Eggs. Her old nemeses.

Well, they wouldn't get the best of her this time. She'd make a damn soufflé if it took her the next twenty-four hours to do so. Then Sam would see Marjorie had nothing on her.

And then he would stay.

eleven

Sam drove back to Flaherty, skillfully avoiding the potholes. He'd managed to do the same with the verbal land mines that his sister had scattered in front of him—up till now. But he sensed his luck was about to run out.

"Just what are you so mysterious about?" Marjorie asked tersely.

There was no sense in postponing the inevitable any longer. Sam took a deep breath. "I'm in love."

"Oh, please, Sam," Marjorie said, rolling her eyes with enough force to stick them up in her head permanently. "Please be serious."

"I am serious, Marj. She's the best thing that ever happened to me—"

"She runs a trail guide service, Sam. She's out alone in the wilderness with horny executives for months at a time."

Sam fixed his blond companion with a steely look. "Watch it, Marjorie. I have no qualms about letting you out right here and watching you hoof it back to Anchorage. Now, if you can't exert yourself to be civil, let me know so I can pull over."

"Now, Sam, don't get testy. All this country living has certainly put you in a foul humor." Marjorie looked at her long, manicured nails. "You really should come back to the city."

"I'm moving here. Get used to it."

"Mother will have a fit."

"I couldn't care less."

"She'll cut off your trust fund."

"Marj, the trust fund is under my control. I never use it, anyway. Keep up with the times."

"Of course not. You bake those ridiculous cakes."

"I'm very good."

Marjorie gave a very unladylike snort. "I don't understand this compulsion you have about working. You've got gobs of perfectly good money sitting in accounts all over the world. Why dirty your hands?"

"You work," Sam said pointedly.

"I represent the current century's literary geniuses," Marjorie said haughtily. "It's a service to mankind."

Sam snorted. He knew Marjorie's true reasoning. If publishing had been good enough for Jackie O. and John Jr., then it was good enough for her. Unfortunately, her attention span was short, and she couldn't spell to save her life, so editing was out of the question. Fortunately for Marjorie, the rest of her mind—the part not in charge of putting letters in the right order—was like a steel trap, and the survival instinct flowing through generations of Scottish Highlanders had been honed to a fine killing point in her. In short, she was a barracuda in half-a-year's-salary skirts who could dissect a contract faster than an eighth-grade boy could dispatch a frog. Her clients loved her, editors feared her, and other agents envied her.

Sam was, of course, her pity case.

But he was realist enough to know that it wasn't easy to get published and that maybe being a good writer might not be sufficient. If his sister could get him a read or two that he might not get on his own, she would be worth her fee.

"She's probably not a virgin, you know."

Then again, maybe throttling her would be more rewarding than being the recipient of any of her called-in markers.

Sam slammed on the brakes and the Range Rover skidded to a halt.

"That's it," he snarled. "Get out."

"Now, Sam . . ."

"Don't you now-Sam me, you cynical socialite. You're dead wrong about Sydney—"

Marjorie gasped. "You slept with her?"

Sam gritted his teeth. "No. But I know her."

"Thank heavens," Marjorie said, sounding vastly relieved. "To propagate the species this way . . ."

"Have you ever considered the fact that I might want to have children?"

"And pass on your father's gene pool? Definitely not."

"He's your father too. And just because he considered selling his seat on the Exchange—"

"Oh, Sam," Marjorie gasped, "please don't bring up that painful memory!"

"That doesn't make him a bad person," Sam finished. "You're a snob."

"And you're an incurable romantic." She turned the full force of her pale blue eyes on him. Sam was almost certain his head had begun to smoke from the laser-beam intensity of her stare.

"Come home to New York," Marjorie said with a compelling tone of voice that any vampire would have been proud to call his own.

"No."

"You can stay at my place until you find something suitable."

"I'm happy here."

"I cannot imagine why."

"Exactly," Sam said, deciding that there wasn't any point in discussing things further. Besides, Marjorie hated the silent treatment, and he was enough of a younger brother to relish giving her a little of it.

Sam put his 4X4 back in gear and eased back out onto the road. He ignored Marjorie all the way home, then left her to bring in her own luggage while he ran up to the house and banged on the door. He owed it to Sydney to prepare her for what she would soon face. He should have done it sooner.

Sydney opened the door, then walked away before he could hug her. He followed her into the kitchen and pulled up short. There were at least a dozen egg cartons on the counter, as well as what could have been mistaken for a soufflé.

Had it risen, that is.

"Sydney?"

"I was trying to make a damn soufflé, all right?" she snapped. "I couldn't do it. Satisfied?"

"Good heavens, what is this mess?"

Sam threw Marjorie a glare over his shoulder. "Shut up, Marj."

"And this must be your country girl," Marjorie said, extending her hand like she was a damned queen and holding a handkerchief to her nose delicately. "How quaint."

"Marjorie," Sam growled.

"Attempts at a soufflé, my dear? How charming. But don't you just eat grits and things up here? Or is it raw bear meat right off the bone?"

"Marjorie!"

Sydney fled from the kitchen. Sam threw up his hands in frustration.

"You *shrew*," he exclaimed. "I love her, damn it!"

"Now, Sam," Marjorie said, unperturbed. "Don't be so rude."

"You're fired," Sam bellowed.

"You can't fire me. I'm your sister."

"You're a pain! Get out of my house."

Marjorie peered out the kitchen window. "Oh, Sam, I do believe your little bumpkin is driving away. Does that mean I can stay for dinner? What time do we eat out here in the country, anyway?"

Sam ran out of the kitchen and back to Sydney's bedroom. On her bed was a note, along with an envelope. He grabbed the note.

Sam, I know I can't compete. Here's your rent money back. I'll stay away until Saturday. That should give you time to move out. I hope you have a happy life. Sydney.

"Marjorie!" Sam roared.

"Yes, darling," she called.

"How are your clerical skills?"

"Nonexistent, my love. Why?"

"Better brush up," he yelled. "You're going to have to get a real job when I get you blackballed in the city!"

Sam drove his sister/former agent into Flaherty and paid one of the Clan members a hundred dollars plus gas to take her back to Anchorage. He watched with narrow-eyed satisfaction as Marjorie bumped off in a truck that didn't look like it would get five miles without breaking down. Her luggage had been dumped in the truck bed and would probably be covered with dog hair and a nice thick layer of compost by the time it reached the airport. Sam couldn't have been happier about it.

After assuring himself that Joe had no idea where Sydney had gone, Sam retreated back to the house to plan.

And prayed that Marjorie hadn't ruined everything.

Sydney crept back to her house Saturday afternoon. Sam's car was gone. She knew she should have been relieved, but she wasn't. She was heartbroken. All it had taken was one look at Sam's "agent" to see that there was no hope of winning Sam away from her.

And so she'd run. She'd scampered off with her tail between her legs like the coward she was and spent three days licking her wounds. She had the feeling that no amount of licking would heal them.

The house was empty when she entered. She didn't bother to check Sam's room. She sat down on the couch and tried to cry. It was a futile effort. If she hadn't cried before, she certainly wasn't going to cry now.

She sat there until the darkness was complete. The days were growing shorter all the time. Soon there wouldn't be much light at all. Fitting. She would spend the winter in the gloom.

She flicked on the light in the kitchen and pulled up short.

There, on her very own counter, was the top of a wedding cake. It was the most beautiful thing she had ever seen. It must have taken Sam hours to finish. And there was a note beside it. She picked up the note with trembling hands.

My beautiful Sydney, you have two choices: you can either eat this cake or you can go to the refrigerator, pull out the rest of the frosting, and fill in the blank. And if you're brave enough to come down to the reception hall, you just might find someone waiting with the rest of the cake, someone who has a few things to explain to you and something to give you. Love, Sam.

Sydney pulled out the bowl of frosting, then closed her eyes briefly before she looked at the top tier of the cake. It said: Congratulations, Sam and . . .

Oh, what did he mean? Why had he left the cake blank? Did he want her to fight for him?

Wasn't that what she'd been trying to do with the soufflé before she'd chickened out?

Sydney reached for the cake-decorating kit laid out conveniently close to the cake and spooned some frosting into the pouch. She could hardly spell her own name but that didn't matter. Her courage returned with a rush. She loved Samuel MacLeod and damn Marjorie if she thought to steal him away. A man didn't take his life in his hands to learn to fly-fish if he didn't love you, did he?

She carefully lifted the cake top and ran out to her car. Sam was waiting for her. She couldn't get to the reception hall fast enough.

And so, like clockwork, she got a flat tire.

It took her over an hour to fix it because she was so upset. By the time she was on the road again, she was filthy. And she was weeping so hard she didn't notice she was drifting off the road until her Jeep went front-end-first into the ditch. Sydney got out of the car, cursed fluently, then grabbed her precious cake top and started to walk.

And, of course, it started to rain.

It couldn't have been snow, so she could have died a very pleasant death from exposure. It had to be rain, which soaked through her coat, plastered her hair to her head, and left her with no choice but to tuck the cake top inside her coat.

She started to sob.

She wasn't sure how long it took her to get to town, but she felt certain it was half an eternity. She stumbled into the reception hall just as things looked like they were about to be packed up. Sam was standing in the middle of the room, looking defeated. And then he turned and saw her.

And he smiled.

Sydney didn't know where all her tears were coming from, but there was a whole new batch handy for this round of weeping. She threw herself into Sam's arms, squishing the cake top between them.

"I got a flat t-tire," she hiccuped, "then the c-car slipped off the r-road."

Sam wrapped his arms around her tightly. "It's okay, sweetheart. I've got you now."

"I crushed the cake," she wept. "I even put my name on it."

"The rest of the cake is here, honey," Sam said soothingly. "We'll eat it without the top. Or I'll make you a new one after we get home. Will that make you happy?"

She lifted her face and choked on her tears. "Y-yes, it would." She clung to him. "Oh, Sam, I thought you loved Marjorie."

"She's my ex-sister," Sam said, wiping the tears and rain from her cheeks. "I have a lot to tell you."

"She can make soufflés," Sydney blubbered.

"I'll tell you a secret," Sam said, bending his head to press his lips against her ear. "I hate soufflés. I think I even hate eggs."

"Oh, Sam!"

He gave her a gentle squeeze. "I want a woman who can change the oil in my Jeep and can tell the difference between a flat screwdriver and a Phillips. Now, if you'll tell me you've been waiting for a man who could bake with the best of them, we'll go in and get married."

She lifted her head and smiled up at him. "I love you."

"I love you, too. Does that mean you'll marry me?"

"It does."

"Then let's go."

"But I have cake smashed on the front of my sweater."

Sam unzipped her parka, then hugged her tightly.

"Now, we're both wearing it." He grinned down at her. "You look wonderful. Let's go."

She couldn't argue with a man who ruined his tux with wedding cake just to make her feel more comfortable. So she took his hand and let him lead her into the chapel.

And she became Mrs. Samuel MacLeod, wearing not only her cake but a smile that she was certain would never fade.

It matched Sam's perfectly.

twelve

Sam sighed and stretched, then saved the last chapter of the second book in his espionage series. He turned off the computer and stood, wondering what Sydney was up to. He looked down at his calendar, just to assure himself that it really was the last week of August and all her little city boys and girls would be going home soon. He could hardly wait to have his wife to himself again.

He walked out on the porch and looked over the front yard. He couldn't see the new addition to the house on the opposite side of the garage, but he knew it was there. It was conveniently far enough away that he could work in peace, but close enough so the inhabitants could be rescued at night if the need arose. Which it did. Often.

Camp Alaska was Sydney's baby. Sam had encouraged her and funded her, discreetly at first, until the application checks had started to roll in. Joe had called in a handful of favors, and the addition on the house had been constructed in May and June, then filled with six city children who had come up for two months of the wilderness life.

Sam had also come clean about the life he'd left behind, but Sydney hadn't been all that impressed. As she said, all that money didn't mean much if it was just stuck in a bank. Sam suspected they would eventually do something with all his loot, but they were still discussing how best to use it. She promised to go to New York with him eventually, but neither of them was in any hurry to leave Alaska.

Sam leaned against a porch post and smiled as his very own wilderness woman shepherded her children across the lawn.

"Will Sam fry up the fish for us?" one of the boys asked. "We'll clean 'em for him."

"No, Sydney, you cook them," one of the girls said, holding Sydney's hand. "Then maybe Sam will make us brownies. Do you think he will?"

"If you ask him, he just might," Sydney said, looking up and catching sight of Sam.

A little blonde darted away and threw herself up the stairs and into Sam's arms. "Will you, huh, Sam? We let you write all day long, didn't we? We stayed out of your hair, didn't we?"

Sam laughed and gave Jennifer a hug. "Yes, you did, sweetheart. And I'll make you brownies if you run on in and get out all the ingredients. Doug, you're in charge. Don't let anyone mess up my kitchen."

"Sure thing, Sam," Doug said. He was fourteen and took his leadership responsibilities very seriously. "Come on, brats, let's get moving. No, Chrissy, you can't stay outside with Sydney and Sam. They probably want to do something gross, like kiss."

There was a chorus of gagging sounds and childlike laughter that disappeared into the house. Sam rolled his eyes as he gathered his wife into his arms.

"How did it go today?"

"Nobody drowned. I call that a success."

Sam laughed and kissed Sydney softly. "You're great with them. It's going to be very hard next year to choose from all the applicants. We may have to build on a few more rooms and bring some of these kids back as camp counselors or something."

Sydney trailed her finger down the front of his sweater. "Yes, we might have to do that." She looked up at him. "Build on another room or two."

Sam kissed her, his heart full of love for the passionate,

beautiful woman in his arms. He thanked his lucky stars that the men of Flaherty had been too stupid to see what was right under their collective noses.

"About the rooms, Sam," she said, looking in the vicinity of his chin. "I know we've got the loft, but we're going to have to build something else too. On the ground floor."

"Whatever you want, Sydney."

She met his eyes. "Sam," she said patiently, "don't you want to know why we need more rooms?"

"More campers?"

"No, Sam."

"You aren't letting Marjorie move in, are you?"

"Sam, sometimes you really aren't very bright."

He stiffened. "You aren't inviting any of the Clan in, are you?"

"Sam, I'm pregnant!"

"Oh," he said, with a smile.

Then he choked. "A baby!"

Sydney smiled serenely. "A baby. Maybe two."

"Oh, Sydney." He gathered her close and hugged her tightly. "Oh, Syd."

"Tell me you're happy about it."

"I'm thrilled."

"I didn't think you had enough headaches with just the kids during the summer," she whispered in his ear. "I thought a few distractions year-round might make you happier."

He lifted his head and looked down at her. "Did you say two?"

"The doctor in Anchorage says no, but Doc Bolen says he's sure it's twins. Sort of a variation on the spit-in-Drano test." She smiled up at him serenely. "He's never wrong."

"Oh, heaven help me. Twins."

"Maybe triplets. He wasn't quite sure."

Sam started to laugh. He leaned on his wife and laughed until tears were running down his face. Then he kissed her soundly.

"Oh, Sydney, you never do anything halfway, do you?"

"Never."

He pulled her inside, then made her sit while he gave his camp cooking and baking lesson for the day, then he pitched in with his six little helpers and cleaned up the dishes and the kitchen. Then he tucked them all in and tried not to get misty-eyed thinking about how he would be tucking in his own children in a few months.

And so he practiced once more by tucking his wife in. Then he untucked her and slid in beside her. He made love to her slowly and sweetly, then they shed a few tears of happiness together. Sam gathered Sydney close and counted his blessings. They included every chuckhole he'd ever bounced his Range Rover over, every minute on the Clan gossip docket, every Wednesday afternoon spent with the Ladies Aid Society to give his report of his and Sydney's activities and, last but not least, every bit of matchmaking Joe had done on their behalf.

Yes, it had been a match made in heaven.

And as he drifted off to sleep with his love in his arms, he promised himself he would check Joe for wings the very next time he went to town.

The Short, Hot Summer

Elizabeth Bevarly

one

"I don't want to go. You go."

"I don't want to go, either. You go."

Preston Atherton IV eyed Preston Atherton III with what he hoped was a steely, relentless gaze. Unfortunately, at thirty-two years of age, Preston IV was no less intimidated by Preston III than he'd been at three-point-two years of age. His father topped six feet, had shoulders the size of the Brooklyn Bridge and forearms the size of sanitation trucks, and his brown eyes were made all the more menacing by the dark forelock of hair that fell down above them.

Of course, Preston IV was virtually his father's mirror image in every respect, minus twenty-five years, but that was beside the point. Preston III was his father. And even though Preston IV had been brought up to follow in the old man's footsteps, the old man wasn't ready to move out of those footsteps just yet.

Besides, Preston IV couldn't help thinking, just because he'd been brought up to follow in the old man's footsteps didn't mean he wouldn't mind making a few tracks of his own off the beaten path. But that, of course, was beside the point too. Beside his *father's* point, at any rate.

Preston IV was still only an executive vice president, even if he was the COO of Atherton Industries. He was still the second-in-command—to his father. And his father was a long way from retiring. There were times when Preston was convinced that he himself would go to that big executive washroom in the sky before his father did.

At any rate, the business was much more his father's than it was his. If his father told him he would be the one to go, then Preston IV would be the one to go.

Unable to maintain the steely, relentless gaze he'd been practicing for months and had thought he'd perfected, Preston relented. Then he turned his attention to the massive windows behind his father—the ones that offered such a breathtaking vista of New York City from the twenty-seventh floor of the Atherton Building in the heart of a bustling Manhattan. The towering structure was a sight to behold from outside, all steel and glass and moxie rising high into the sky, a modern manifestation of the dreams and hopes and tears and sweat that six generations of Athertons had poured into what had ultimately become one of the nation's leading corporations.

But from inside, the building was even more breathtaking. All Art Deco styling at its very best, with elegant curves, sophisticated angles, and color schemes that changed from floor to floor, ranging from soothing pastels to exuberant primaries to arrogant darks. Preston's father had chosen that last for his own decor, as had Preston himself. Come to think of it, he mused, his own office was quite a lot like his father's. The same hunter-green walls and dark mahogany paneling, a massive Oriental rug spattered with rich jewel tones covering much of the dark wood flooring.

He really was far too much like his father for his own liking, Preston thought. Even though he assured himself there were significant differences between the two of them—he was sure of it, even if he couldn't come up with a single one at the moment . . . well, except for the cowardice with which he himself always backed down from an argument, but no others—there were times when he feared he might just wind up exactly like the old man. And even though he'd been groomed for precisely that since day one,

Then he opened the cookbook, laid out all the ingredients, and proceeded to show her what to do.

"It says 'fold in the dry ingredients.' What does that mean?" she demanded.

"Here, turn the mixer back on," he said, standing behind her. "Take the spatula in your right hand and the bowl of flour in your left. Just dump in a little at a time and let the mixer do the work."

"But that's mixing, not folding."

"Same thing."

"Then why doesn't it say the same thing?"

"I don't know." He didn't. All he knew was that Sydney Kincaid was standing in the circle of his arms, concentrating on something else, leaving him free to concentrate on her. The fragrance of her hair wafted up and forced his eyes closed. He breathed deeply, savoring the smell.

"Now what do I do? Sam, are you falling asleep?"

"No."

"The cake's folded. What do I do now?"

"Preheat the oven, then pour the batter into the cake pans."

He leaned back against the counter and listened to her hum as she poured the batter into two pans, then slid them both into the oven. She set the timer, then turned and smiled.

"Now what?"

"Now you come over here and listen to me apologize for being such a jerk these past few days."

Her smile faltered. "You weren't, Sam. I'm not the easiest person to live with."

He reached out, took her hand and pulled her across the floor. "We're going to practice making up now, Syd. An important part of any relationship. I'm going to say I'm sorry. You're going to listen, forgive me, then hug me. Got it?"

She nodded.

"I'm sorry."

"I forgive you."

"Now, hug me."

power that the old man held. Preston III had worked every bit as hard in his youth—for Preston II—as Preston IV was working now. And deep down, in spite of his upbringing, Preston wasn't sure that Atherton Industries was the right life partner for him. Yet it went without saying that, someday, eventually, Preston *would* take over the reins of Atherton Industries from his father.

Whether he liked it or not.

But that wouldn't be happening today. Obviously. Today he couldn't even win an argument with the old man, let alone wrest control of the company away from him. Not that he wanted to *wrest* control, anyway. Or even win it. Or have it given over.

Honestly, Preston wasn't sure what he wanted to do. Except work. He did like that part.

"All right, I'll go," he conceded. Somehow he refrained from stubbing the toe of his Gucci loafer into the plush rug. And he told himself he did *not* sound petulant when he added, "But I want full control over this merger when I do."

"Fine," his father agreed easily. "You'll get no argument from me there. In fact, I was going to suggest it myself. It's time you flew solo, Preston. You need to learn to handle these things by yourself."

Although Preston knew perfectly well how to handle these things by himself, he didn't argue with his father. There was no point to it. They were too much alike, and neither would ever concede a victory to the other. He was content, for now, to let it go.

After all, he had other things to worry about at the moment, things that were far more important than the balance of power in Atherton Industries. Preston was about to embark on a very dangerous mission, one that would require every last instinct and brain cell he possessed. He was about to visit a completely alien environment, a place unlike any he had ever visited before.

For this trip, he would need to keep his wits about him. His destination was one that was utterly foreign to him, completely removed from everything he held familiar and dear. It would be so strange, this odd and distant land. Socially, culturally, politically, ideologically. The local citizenry spoke in ways he did not understand, ate bizarre and exotic foods, listened to weird and unfamiliar music, and embraced a lifestyle he would never fathom. Preston would have to be on his guard the whole time he was visiting this far-off place.

This far-off place called . . . Alabama.

"Just be careful," his father told him, sounding genuinely concerned.

Preston nodded. "I will."

"And for God's sake, take some Evian with you, all right? There's no telling what's in the water down there."

Preston inhaled a deep, fortifying breath. "I bought a case yesterday," he said. "It's already been shipped to the hotel where I'll be staying."

His father's dark eyebrows shot up in surprise. "You found a hotel in Butternut, Alabama?"

"Well, in a manner of speaking," Preston qualified. "It's actually, I believe, more of a guest house. Or . . . something." He cleared his throat before pronouncing, "Miss Mamie's Bide-a-Wee Bed and Breakfast, to be precise."

"Do you have your schedule organized?"

Oh, please, Preston wanted to mutter. As if he wouldn't. The very idea. "Of course," he replied unnecessarily—and not a little snottily. Then, as if he wanted to hammer home the fact, he recited, purely from memory: "Flight five-seven-two leaves JFK tomorrow at ten-forty-seven a.m., arrives Birmingham at twelve-fourteen. My rental car will be waiting for me at twelve-thirty, and I'll be on the road by twelve thirty-five. I'll stop for lunch on the way at one p.m., resume travel at one-twenty, reach Butternut by one-fifty-five. Check into the Bide-a-Wee at precisely two, catch up on work until four-thirty, then prepare for dinner with Samuel Butternut. Dinner itself will be at exactly five-thirty. By seven-thirty, he and I can return to the Bide-a-Wee for after-dinner drinks and, it goes without saying, a good cigar."

His father grunted an indistinct response, but seemed to

be reassured. Then, looking more concerned than Preston had ever seen him look, he met his son's gaze levelly and repeated, "Just . . . be careful, son. I mean, Alabama. It's just so . . . so different there. The way of life those people embrace, well— Their ways are just foreign to us, you know?"

Preston nodded, clenching his jaw. "I know, Father."

"Don't be shocked by anything you see or hear, son. Or, at least, try to hide your shock as best you can. I know it will be difficult at times, but I have faith in you."

Preston steeled himself. "Thank you, Father," he said. "And don't worry," he hastened to add. "If anyone can handle Samuel Butternut—and Alabama—it's me."

Samuel Butternut was the quintessential self-made Southern millionaire, a man who had turned a small textile mill into a multimillion-dollar industry just because he had wanted to. His forebears had been the founders of the small community in Alabama, and Samuel himself was the owner of Butternut Industries, which he'd recently put up for sale so that he would have more time to fish. Yes, that was correct—to fish.

Because Samuel Butternut was also the quintessential Southern eccentric. As he had stated in his letter to Preston III upon accepting—with a few conditions—Atherton Industries' offer to buy him out, he never, ever, traveled north of the Mason-Dixon line. So anybody who wanted his company was going to have to come to Butternut to get it. The letter had gone on to explain that Samuel also did not, under any circumstances, trust anyone who didn't know what a "goober" was. If the Prestons Atherton—both III and IV— wanted Butternut Industries, then they were going to have to work for it. One of them—III or IV, Samuel wasn't particular—would have to come down to Butternut himself. And, as a gesture of good faith, and to show that he knew his goobers from his gumbo, he would have to bring a bag of goobers with him in offering.

At first Preston IV had resisted. There was *no way* he was going to take a bag of goobers *anywhere*. The thought of even collecting a bag of goobers had made his stomach heave. Why the very idea of what that would involve was simply too revolting to consider. However, his secretary, Martha—who had relocated to New York from Atlanta—had assured him that the endeavor wouldn't be nearly as distasteful as he was expecting it to be, and that in fact, goobers were quite yummy boiled.

Preston had been debating whether or not to dismiss her on grounds of mental instability—among other things—when she had told him what a goober actually was. Preston had felt a little silly, but his relief had far outshadowed any embarrassment. A peanut. Well, who knew? Fine. He would buy a bag of peanuts before flying down to Butternut to meet with the elusive, industrious Samuel Butternut. And he would win the old man's confidence and buy the business for a fair price. Then Samuel could fish to his heart's content, and Preston could prove to his father that he was perfectly capable of running Atherton Industries.

He just wished he could convince himself of such a thing as easily. Not just that he *could* run Atherton Industries. Of that he was already reasonably certain. He just wished he could convince himself that running Atherton Industries was what he *wanted* to do. For the rest of his life. Until a Preston V—in whatever strange, or even biblical, manner that might come about, seeing as how Preston IV had no intention of marrying or procreating, something he decided not to ponder at the moment—could take the reins from him.

He sighed and met his father's gaze. "I'll take care of everything," he vowed. "You can count on me."

"I know I can, son," his father assured him. "Just . . . you know. Be careful. And Preston?"

"Yes, Father?"

"Don't forget your goobers."

two

The words "Miss Mamie's Bide-a-Wee Bed and Breakfast" had conjured up a very immediate and very specific image for Preston when he had first heard them, and as he rolled his rental car to a stop in front of the establishment, he was amazed at how utterly accurate his assessment of the place had been. In fact, all of Butternut, Alabama, was looking to be *exactly* the kind of place he had visualized it would be.

More's the pity.

Just as his schedule had dictated, he'd driven precisely forty-two minutes beyond the Birmingham city limits before reaching Butternut's city limits—or at least what he supposed passed for city limits when the city in question was, well, limited. Then he had unwittingly driven through and past downtown Butternut before even realizing he was there.

The business district evidently covered roughly three blocks along Main Street—a moniker that Preston found to be a trifle redundant, since it seemed to be the *only* street in downtown Butternut. Said business district—and he knew it was the business district only because a sign stating BUTTERNUT BUSINESS DISTRICT had told him so—was pretty much completed by a bank, a bakery, a post office, a market, something called a five-and-dime (though he couldn't imagine what kind of merchandise such an establishment would boast at those prices), and an eatery of questionable origin called Fern and Moody's. The words "Home Cookin' " were stenciled on the window, and somehow, it told Preston all he needed—or wanted—to know.

As he thrust his car into park at the curb of Miss Mamie's Bide-a-Wee Bed and Breakfast—the only other business he could see as being part of Butternut's business district, and on the very edge of it, at that—he marveled at how easy it was to find a curbside parking spot here in Downtown Butternut. Well, maybe he didn't marvel *too* much. But he did notice.

The Bide-a-Wee itself was a massive Victorian house that looked to have been recently renovated. A fresh coat of creamy, pale yellow paint gave the place a warm appeal, which was enhanced by elaborate, and flawless, white gingerbread trim. Huge baskets of hanging plants spilled fat pink and purple blossoms at regular intervals all along the wide wraparound porch, and more flowers burst from boxes beneath the front windows. The walkway, too, was lined with an even broader palate of color, orange and yellow marigolds, red and white begonias, and petunias so purple they looked to be velvet.

Having grown up in Manhattan, Preston had never seen so many splashes of color growing in one place before. Even the Athertons' summer home in the Hamptons, so carefully tended by Bates, the gardener, had followed a strict seasonal color scheme. Bates would *never* have allowed purple and orange within a good quarter acre of each other. Whoever had landscaped the Bide-a-Wee, however, had been far more exuberant in his—or her—technique. And although Preston usually had no use whatsoever for exuberance—unless, of course, one applied it to one's work—he had to admit that here exuberance held a certain strange appeal.

Switching off the engine and exiting his car, he was immediately struck by two things. Thing number one: Butternut was a very quiet place, remarkably absent of sounds like blaring car horns, barking cabbies, howling sirens, and pounding jackhammers. And thing number two: it was hotter than the dickens.

He immediately reached for his necktie to loosen it, cursing himself for his sartorial lapse as he completed the gesture. Honestly, though, the temperature must surely be pushing one hundred degrees. In New York, that would make for a very uncomfortable day. Here in Alabama, however, it made for an unbearable one. Everything just felt so . . . wet. So . . . heavy. So . . . oppressive. Although, normally, he wouldn't even have *thought* of compromising his corporate uniform of suit and tie, by the time he had removed his briefcase and garment bag from the trunk of the car, he was so hot, he was ready to strip down to his underwear.

He made do with shedding his jacket instead.

But the small concession brought little relief. Reluctantly, he unfastened the top button of his white dress shirt, then went after the cuffs. By the time he reached the front door of the bed-and-breakfast, praying that the big building was air-conditioned, Preston felt like a limp rag.

And it was still very, *very* hot.

He fairly dragged his luggage behind him as he pushed through the screen door, and he was relieved to find that the inside of the house was, in fact, a bit cooler than the outside. Not because of a sophisticated climate control center, however, he realized quickly, to his dismay, but because of three wide, lazy ceiling fans that swoosh-swoosh-swooshed laconically overhead. He had stepped into what appeared to be a large dining room populated by naught but half a dozen empty tables. To his left was a sweeping staircase that led to the upper floors, and beyond the staircase was what appeared to be a small sitting area.

The furniture was old, elegant, beautiful, and the hardwood floors were buffed to a honey-colored sheen. The wallpaper was faded but pretty, fat cabbage roses of pink and lavender climbing a background trellis of white. Real roses, and other large blossoms, sprang up from vases and bowls and bright bits of majolica scattered around each of the rooms, their sweet fragrance nearly overwhelming him. The place, on the whole, looked like someone's Southern grandmother's house, and, oddly, he immediately felt welcome here.

Miss Mamie, he thought, knew how to make a place feel like home.

The proprietress herself did not seem to be about, however, something that didn't escape Preston's notice. Probably, he thought, she was napping. In this heat, an elderly woman would no doubt need to rest. He told himself he should probably go across the street to Fern and Moody's for a little while, maybe have something cool to drink while he waited for Miss Mamie to rouse herself and return to work. But those words "Home Cookin'" came back to haunt him, and he thought better of the idea.

Besides, he had a rigid schedule to keep. He glanced down at his watch and was shocked to discover that he was already running a full two minutes behind. He hadn't counted on the heat making him so sluggish. He was going to have to be careful not to let this happen again.

Therefore, it was with much purpose that he made his way over to what appeared to be a registration desk and reached for a small brass bell that sat on the counter. RING FOR SERVICE, a hand-lettered sign beside the bell instructed. Unsure why he did so, he hesitated before ringing.

Poor Miss Mamie, he thought. She was probably upstairs right now, lying in her bed, barely conscious from the effects of extreme heat, unusual fatigue, and advanced age. She'd no doubt have to totter down all those steps to greet him and check him in. In this heat, her heart would probably give out, or she'd become disoriented and fall and break a hip or something—those old bones were always so fragile.

Then again, if the old woman couldn't handle the workload, she never would have opened the place, would she? He revised his image of her some. She was doubtless one of those stalwart Southern women with magnolias of steel— a bingo-happy, blue-bouffanted, polka-dotted, bosomy Aunt Bee. Yes, surely she was made of stern stuff, and wouldn't let a little something such as overwhelming, hell-like heat slow her down. Picking up the bell, Preston shook it quickly several times, then returned it to the counter.

He had pretty much perfected his image of Miss Mamie and her magnolias when he heard a sound to his left and turned toward it. He was still envisioning that bosomy, polka-dotted Aunt Bee and her ilk, so it was with no small astonishment that he noted the woman who passed through a door on the other side of the room. The young woman. The red-haired woman. The woman who was utterly lacking in Bingo card, blue bouffant, and polka dot.

"Miss Mamie?" he asked dubiously.

"Yessir?" she replied slowly, leisurely, turning two short words into one very long one.

Oh, well, Preston thought. At least he'd gotten the bosomy part right.

The rest of her, however, came as quite a surprise. He would have sworn, quite adamantly, that no member of his generation could possibly claim the name Mamie. And even if he had been proved wrong in that regard, he would have sworn, quite vehemently, that a Mamie couldn't possibly look like this woman did.

Instead of polka dots, Miss Mamie was dressed in short—very short . . . good God, they were short—cut-off blue jeans and a brief—very brief . . . good God, it was brief—red halter top. Her hair was a riot of dark auburn curls spilling out of an unsuccessful attempt to bind them, made more riotous, no doubt, by the intense humidity. Her shoes—well, her shoes were, quite frankly, nonexistent. Her toenails, however, sported quite fetching, bright-red polish. On her hands were what appeared to be gloves, which she wore—just a shot in the dark here—for gardening and not because of the temperature outside.

All in all, she was in no way the kind of woman for whom Preston normally experienced an immediate—and very profound—sexual reaction. Oddly, however, Preston experienced an immediate—and very profound—sexual reaction to her.

It was odd not just because she was a complete

stranger—though, true, he didn't usually go around being immediately and very profoundly aroused by complete strangers on a regular basis. No, it was more because there wasn't a single quality present in—or on—her person that he normally liked to see present in—or on—a person. At least, a person of the opposite gender. He was drawn to women of a much more . . . sophisticated, elegant . . . and much less . . . voluptuous, earthy . . . nature. Women who dressed in streamlined, efficient suits, who wore their hair conservatively cut, who worked in positions of corporate power, who lived in sleek Manhattan abodes, and who enjoyed tasteful, expensive pastimes. Going out with such women was like going out with . . .

Well, it was like going out with himself, Preston thought happily. And what could possibly be better than that?

Miss Mamie, on the other hand, was . . . not. Not Preston. Not *like* Preston. Not by a long shot. And certainly not like any of the women to whom he had ever been attracted, either. Still, there was definitely something about her. He just couldn't . . . quite . . . say what.

Mamie Calhoun eyed the man standing in her lobby with much apprehension. Although she'd been expecting him—and only him, seeing as how she didn't have any other reservations for the night . . . or for the summer, for that matter—she had thought the big-shot corporate guy from New York City would look like, well . . . like old Sam Butternut. Sam was the only other businessman Mamie knew, and even though he wasn't a big shot—not by New York City standards, anyway, she figured—she just pretty much assumed they probably all looked like that.

This fella, however . . .

Well, he was actually kinda cute. In a rumpled, confused, sweaty sort of way.

"You must be Mr. Atherton," she assumed, taking a few steps toward the registration desk.

He smiled, seeming relieved to be identified. "Yes, I am, as a matter of fact."

"You got here a littler earlier than I thought you would,"

she told him. "I wasn't expecting you until late this afternoon."

He gaped incredulously at her offhand comment. "I *beg* your pardon," he bit off crisply. "I'm *exactly* on time." Then he mumbled something under his breath that sounded, oddly enough, like "Give or take two minutes."

Goodness, judging by his outraged reaction, she might as well have just accused him of wearing women's underwear—old, holey women's underwear, at that. She stopped dead in her tracks and stared at him. "I'm sorry, I didn't mean to imply that you were—"

"What?" he demanded.

"Uh . . . irregular."

He arched one eyebrow in what was obvious offense.

"I mean, um . . ." she tried again, "not punctual."

In response to that, he only jerked impatiently at his wilting necktie, and said, "I believe I have a reservation."

Mamie nodded as she strode forward again, tugging at a gardening glove. "You sure do. For two nights. Am I right?"

"Yes, that's right," he said. "At least, I'm hoping it won't be for any more than that. If it is, will that be a problem? Or are you booked up?"

She laughed as she pulled her other glove off and dropped both on the counter, then reached beneath for her registration cards. "No," she told him. "It won't be a problem at all. You're sorta my only guest."

Then again, she thought, he looked like he might provide her with more than enough business—and not just hotel business, either—to match two dozen guests. With that dark, unruly hair and those puppy-dog brown eyes, he could melt a woman quicker than butter on a hot knife. It didn't help that the shoulders and arms beneath his wilting shirt looked broad enough and strong enough to pull a barge.

Nope, he was nothing like Sam Butternut, that was for sure. But then, not too many people were.

"Summer must be your slow season," Mr. Atherton said as she began filling out a registration form for him.

"Yessir, it is," she said. "But then, so is fall, winter, and springtime."

She spun the card toward him and made a quick X for his signature. Automatically, he took the pen from her and began to scribble his name along the line.

"The place looks prosperous enough," he said as he signed.

Mamie nodded. "That's 'cause I've been working my fanny off for the past two years—ever since inheritin' it from my aunt Gert, who raised me up—to make sure it does. *Look* prosperous, anyway," she clarified. "The actual *bein'* prosperous part, well . . ." She shrugged. "That depends on whether or not the Butternut town plannin' commission—"

"You actually have a planning commission here?" he interjected. His expression, when he glanced up, midsignature, was lightly incredulous.

"Well, yeah," she told him. "Sam Butternut organized it himself. They're tryin' to build Butternut into a major tourist attraction."

Mr. Atherton eyed her curiously. "A major tourist attraction?" he echoed.

"Sure," she insisted. "You may not know this, but Danny Jim Robinson himself was born right here."

"No, I didn't know that," he told her. "Nor do I know this Danny . . . Jim . . . Robinson."

This time Mamie was the one to gape incredulously at him. "Danny Jim Robinson just so happened to be a very famous hero of the frontier."

"I've never heard of him."

"Well, that's 'cause you're not from Butternut," she said. "He's *very* famous around here. Shot himself a bear when he was only three."

Mr. Atherton eyed her suspiciously. "I thought that was Davy Crockett."

"Danny Jim did it first."

"Ah. I see. And you think that this being his birthplace will bring in tourists by the droves?" Mr. Atherton asked, clearly unimpressed, as he went back to complete his signature.

"I dunno," Mamie answered honestly. "But it wouldn't have to be that many droves of tourists. Just one good drove would fill the Bide-a-Wee right up."

He completed his signature with a flourish, then turned his attention to her face. For a moment, he said nothing, only focused on her eyes, looking at her as if . . . as if . . . well, as if she were something worth looking at. It was an expression that put Mamie on alert for some reason. His scrutiny was so lengthy, in fact, that she began to grow uncomfortable.

Okay, so she knew she didn't look as great as she probably should for greeting a customer, but she hadn't expected Mr. Atherton to arrive for another couple of hours, and the rosebushes out back had needed a trim real bad. Maybe she didn't look or smell as good as the roses out there, but that was no reason for him to stare at her like she was some kind of animal that just wandered out from underneath the porch.

Feeling self-conscious, Mamie lifted a hand to her hair and brushed a few errant curls off of her damp forehead. But still her guest only gazed at her face, focusing his attention on her eyes.

"Mr. Atherton?" she finally said. "Is there somethin' wrong?"

Instead of breaking his spell, her question only seemed to compound it. Because he shook his head very slowly, then parted his lips very slightly, as if to say something—but he said nothing at all. Mamie was about to speak again, when finally, finally, Mr. Atherton replied.

"You have the greenest eyes," he said softly.

Okay, so granted that wasn't exactly the reply she'd been expecting to hear. It was a nice thing for him to say. It was a very *confusing* thing for him to say, but nice, too. And funnily enough, it made her feel hotter than she had felt out in the yard, under the glare of the afternoon sun, and until now, she wouldn't have thought such a thing was possible.

"Um, thank you," she said, her voice as quiet as his own. "That's, uh . . . that's very nice of you to say so."

But still his gaze remained fixed on her eyes, and still he seemed overcome by some kind of hazy, vague trance. "No, really," he said, more insistently, but still very softly. "I don't think I've ever seen eyes that color before in my life. It's like the water off St. John in the Virgin Islands. Just . . . gorgeous."

Mamie swallowed hard. She wasn't the most knowledgeable woman in the world when it came to the opposite sex, but she was pretty sure that Mr. Atherton here was—what did they call it—coming on to her. Yeah, that was it. And to be perfectly honest, she had to admit that she wouldn't mind having him come on to her, either. And he could just stay on her for as long as he pleased, too.

For a minute neither of them said a word. Mr. Atherton just continued to gaze into her eyes, and Mamie just continued to do her best not to melt into a puddle of ruined womanhood at his feet. She'd just hate to mess up those nice shoes of his, after all.

Fortunately, that didn't wind up being a problem, though. Because as quickly as Mr. Atherton had fallen into his trance, he snapped right out of it again. And when he did, he turned back into that upright, forthright, do-right kind of businessman she had expected him to be from the beginning. Just, you know, a lot cuter. Because now, on top of looking so yummy, he was blushing. As if he were embarrassed by the things he'd just told her about her eyes. Which was just as well, 'cause she felt a little embarrassed, too.

Nice to know they had something in common, she thought. Still, it probably wouldn't be a good idea to start thinking along those lines. Even if he was cute, he would only be in Butternut for a couple of days. And it was pretty clear that, except for the embarrassing thing, there was absolutely nothing to bind the two of them together.

At his realization of what he had just said to her, his back went ramrod straight, and the dreamy little smile that had begun to curl his mouth went flat. The wistful, faraway look in his eyes turned focused and piercing, and he didn't look at all happy to be where he was.

Really, Mamie supposed she couldn't blame him for not wanting to be here. There wasn't a whole lot to Butternut. Heck, pretty much the only way to arrive here was by getting lost or getting born. Those who got lost in Butternut eventually found their way out again. Those who got born here, like Mamie, well . . . they tended to stay.

But that was okay with Mamie. She liked the slow, languid pace, the leisurely days and indolent nights, the simple ways and down-to-earth people. She wouldn't trade her existence here for anything. Not even a bright-lights-big-city slicker like Preston Atherton IV.

And now that she thought more about it, Preston Atherton IV was neither lost in Butternut, nor had he been born here. No, he'd come here *on purpose*. This might just be a first for the community. It oughta be real interesting to find out what Butternut had in store for him for the next couple of days.

Smiling for the first time since his arrival, Mamie took the registration card back, filed it neatly away under *A,* and said, "Mr. Atherton, if you'll follow me, I'll just show you right to your room."

three

Room, Preston realized, was a very deceptive term. In a connotative sense, it rather suggested large size, and in relation to a hotel, or other such establishment, it was generally meant to indicate more than one room. At least, it meant one room *and* a bathroom. At the Bide-a-Wee, however, a bathroom did not seem to come with his room. Nor, he realized, much to his dismay, did *room* seem to come with his room.

But first things first.

"No . . . facilities?" he asked Miss Mamie, striving to mask his dismay and voice his concern in the most polite way he could.

When he glanced over at her, it was to find that she was looking back at him in a manner that indicated quite clearly her absolute befuddlement. "Facilities?" she echoed curiously.

He nodded. "Yes, the, uh, the powder room?" he tried again.

"Oh, you're lookin' for the toilet," she said, clearly relieved.

Well, that made one of them, Preston thought. He was nowhere near feeling relieved himself, and wouldn't until he knew the actual location of the . . . facilities. "Actually, I was more concerned about a shower," he lied.

"No need to be concerned," she told him easily. "Shower and toilet both are down at the end of the hall."

And that wasn't supposed to concern him?

"I see," he said, even though logic would dictate that such a thing was impossible, because he saw neither understanding nor facilities. The latter, after all, were at the end of the hall, and the former was, to put it simply, not there.

In spite of that, he sighed his resignation and considered his alleged room again. It *was* somewhat cozy, he reluctantly conceded. The antebellum ambiance had carried from the first to the second floor, and the room to which Miss Mamie had led him was similar in style and furnishings to what he had seen below. More flowered wallpaper, though a bit less faded here, and more old furniture, though a bit more worn. One reason the room seemed small, he noted, might possibly have been a result of the fact that the bed was so enormous. Enormous enough to require stairs to get into it.

Truly. Stairs. To get into bed. Ah, well, he reminded himself, he'd known going in that this was going to be a foreign culture. He told himself he shouldn't be surprised by anything he encountered.

He was still surprised by Miss Mamie, though. He hadn't expected her at all.

Likewise unexpected was his reaction to her. Certainly she was a reasonably attractive woman—in her own, folksy, earthy, y'all-come-back-now-ya-hear kind of way. Oh, all right, she was an *extremely* attractive woman, he conceded, no matter which way he looked at it. Or her.

Whatever.

In fact, upon further inspection—which he completed in the most unobtrusive way he could manage—he realized she was rather, well, beautiful. Her complexion was as golden and flawless as raw honey, and her eyes were the color and clarity of an ocean view. And her mouth . . .

Well, best not to think too much about her mouth, he decided. It was, after all, a very hot day. No need to make matters worse.

In spite of her undeniable beauty, however, Preston could think of no reason why he would have such an immediate and profound reaction to her, yet that was precisely what was happening. There was just something about her, he realized. Something in her spoke to something in him that had never before been addressed. And the language that the two things were speaking was quite . . . extraordinary. Mamie was . . . unusual. Different. Exotic. She was utterly removed from the refined, well-groomed, perfectly attired women he normally met in his other life—his *real* life.

And that, he told himself, could be the only explanation for why hc was so captivated by her. It was not, he assured himself, because of anything else. Something like, oh, say, a soul-deep, life-altering emotion for another human being that must be present before one could even consider tying one's life to that person forever.

Nah.

"Will you be wantin' to eat your meals here, too?" Mamie asked, stirring him from his troubling, though not entirely unpleasant, musings.

Imperceptibly, Preston shook his head, hoping to clear it of the few clouds left lolling about. "Well, I was under the impression that it was bed *and* breakfast. It does say so on the sign out front, after all."

She grinned at him, and he was taken aback by how the skies opened up just then, and how the angels lifted their heavenly voices in chorus, and how all the planets aligned themselves into total and complete harmonic convergence.

How very, very interesting.

"Oh, heck, yeah, it's breakfast," she told him. "All the breakfast you can stand. Lunch and dinner, too, if you've a mind to sample those. 'Course, there'd be an additional charge for the two extra meals."

What Preston wanted to sample—with or without additional charge—Miss Mamie didn't want to know, he decided. Bad enough that he was entertaining such ideas himself. It was with no small shock that he realized just how wayward his thoughts had become in the last few minutes. And it was with no small effort that he pushed them away and cleared his head for more important matters.

"Yes," he said. "I've a mind to sample . . . those."

Damn. He really had been trying to keep his mind on track.

"Meals?" Mamie asked innocently.

Preston nodded vigorously. "Yes, those as well."

She narrowed her eyes at him. "As well as what?"

Quickly Preston spun around and made his way to the open window. "Just add the additional meals to my final bill. Is it always so hot here?" he asked, hoping to change the subject. Then again, introducing the topic of heat probably wasn't much changing the subject.

"It is in August," she told him. "But never in June like this. This summer seems to be worse than most. I'm sorry the Bide-a-Wee isn't air-conditioned," she added, reading his thoughts. "Most times it truly isn't necessary. The house is well shaded, and the ceiling fans blow off the worst of the heat. When it gets like this, though . . ."

She left the statement unfinished, as indeed, it needed no conclusion. Obviously, when it got this hot, there was nothing to be done but grin and bear it.

Or grin and bare it.

Damn, it had happened *again*. Preston really was going to have to have a little chat with his libido. So, before his thoughts could stray too far, he did what he always did when he felt a bit lost. He glanced down at his watch.

Good heavens. Was that really the time? He'd veered nearly twenty minutes off his schedule. If he didn't get his laptop up and running in thirty seconds, there would be no way to recoup his temporal loss.

"I really must get to work," he told Mamie. "I have a tentative arrangement to meet with Samuel Butternut at five-thirty for dinner." He paused for a moment, thinking. "I suppose it would be a good idea to touch base with him beforehand, to make sure the allotted time is still doable for him."

He glanced quickly around the room, looking for something he now realized it was probably foolish for him to be looking for. If there weren't facilities in his room, there most certainly wouldn't be a—

"Telephone?" he asked hopefully anyway.

"Downstairs," Mamie said, pointing her finger in that direction. "You can use the one at the registration desk, or, if you need privacy, there's one in the kitchen."

And that was supposed to be private?

Well, so much for checking his E-mail on his regular hourly schedule, he thought, mentally—and hastily—recalculating his daily agenda. Still, that might buy him twenty extra minutes a day for business matters. With a few more quick calculations, he realized that the added time might potentially be very profitable indeed.

So once again he sighed deeply his resignation—and hoped he didn't end up hyperventilating over the next two days with all the deep sighing of resignation he seemed to be doing since his arrival here in Butternut. "The telephone at the registration desk will be fine," he told her. "There's nothing private about my negotiations with Samuel Butternut."

"Okeydokey," Mamie said, and Preston found himself smiling. No self-respecting New Yorker would ever say . . . that. "Follow me," she added lightly.

She spun around and strode slowly out of the room, her lush lower body swaying to a tune Preston certainly couldn't hear himself. Still, it was a remarkable walk. And he really couldn't help but follow her out. And down. To wherever she might lead him, whether there was a telephone at that destination or not. He just hoped that when they got there—wherever they were going—it wouldn't be quite so hot.

Then again, he was beginning to suspect that Butternut, Alabama, was a place that he needed to explore more fully, in all its . . . states. And what better guide to have than Miss Mamie Calhoun? And really, he thought further, when all was said and done, there were one or two things to be said for heat.

Under the right circumstances.

And these circumstances, he couldn't help but note, were feeling righter all the time.

Boy, what lousy circumstances, Mamie thought as she watched Preston Atherton IV gaze gloomily at his dinner plate. First, when he made the phone call he'd had to make, he found out that Sam Butternut had taken off for parts unknown until the end of the week, on account of he'd gone on one of his infamous fishing jaunts. Then Mamie'd had to explain to him that Sam's infamous fishing jaunts were famous for lasting a heckuva lot longer than "until the end of the week." Then Preston had gone upstairs to his room to work and had fallen asleep, face-first, on his itty-bitty little computer.

And even though the waffle-weave design from the keyboard had faded from his cheek a long time ago—and hadn't been what Mamie was laughing at in the first place, honest—his catnap had left him feeling surprisingly frustrated and foul-tempered. She herself usually felt pretty dang good after a nap during the hotter parts of the summer. But not Preston. Noooo. All he'd been able to do was grumble about how much he'd veered from his schedule by catching a few z's. And although Mamie had tried to lighten his mood some by reminding him how much catching up he could do now that Sam had disappeared indefinitely, she'd had to admit that he hadn't been much cheered by the realization.

Now, on top of all that, he hadn't enjoyed his dinner at all. Oh, he'd tried very politely to fake it, had done his best to assure Mamie that each and every item on his plate was one of his most favorite dishes in the whole wide world. But she'd suspected right away that he'd never even had chicken 'n' dumplins in his entire life. Because not only had he not eaten a bite of it, using the lame excuse that the heat had ruined his appetite—like she was supposed to believe something as dumb as heat could make a man like him lose *any*thing—he'd actually said he was worried about his cholesterol.

His cholesterol, she thought again, shaking her head in

disbelief. Like who cared about that if it meant giving up chicken 'n' dumplins? The man must be a total moron. Or else a Northerner. And there were those in Butternut who'd consider those two things totally interchangeable.

Fortunately for Preston, Mamie wasn't one of them. She was quite confident that there were some Northerners who weren't morons. Leastways, she was willing to suspend her judgment on that score until she actually met some Northerners. Well, more than one, anyway. She just figured that Preston's problem was that he needed a little time to adapt to his new surroundings. 'Course, with Sam gone fishin', it was looking like Preston was going to have plenty of time for adapting.

And just when had she started thinking about him as "Preston" instead of "Mr. Atherton," anyway? That was kind of odd. And dangerous to boot.

Thankfully, her thoughts were scattered then, because Preston . . . Mr. Atherton . . . that cute guy from New York . . . pushed his plate forward and stood up. She supposed she should feel gratified that he'd at least finished his iced tea, but honestly. At this rate, he'd fade to nothin' but skin 'n' bones before the week was through.

Mamie was forced to rethink that assumption once Preston was standing, though, because she realized it would take a lot more than a week's starvation to diminish that man. There was just way too much of him. And every last inch of it was quite delicious-lookin'.

Oh, dear. Now where had *that* thought come from? Well, actually, she knew perfectly well where that thought had come from, and it *wasn't* her head. No, that thought had come from a different body part entirely, and it wasn't one that should be doing any thinking. It was one that was made for a whole 'nother activity, an activity in which Mamie hadn't participated for quite some time. Which, now that she gave it more consideration, went a long way toward explaining why that body part was thinking the things it was.

Or something like that.

She pushed a fistful of curls off her forehead and moved

out from behind the registration desk, where she'd been watching Preston Atherton IV not eat his dinner. "All done?" she asked as she strode toward him.

She'd changed her clothes earlier that afternoon, hoping to make herself look a little more like the Bide-a-Wee's owner, as opposed to the hotel gardener, and not because she just wanted to look nice for Preston Atherton IV. Really. She hadn't. That had been the furthest thing from her mind when she'd put on this dress that just so happened to be the one that showed off her eyes better than anything else in her wardrobe. Truly, it had. No foolin'.

Now she wiped her damp palms against the lightweight green-and-yellow-print sundress that had been all she could tolerate having against her body in this heat. Well, she conceded, she supposed she could tolerate *some*thing else against her body in this heat, if she had to, but only if she was naked at the time, and only if that *some*thing just happened to be some*one*, namely Pres—

Stop it, she ordered herself with such vehemence that she came to a halt midway between the registration desk and the object of her desires. Um, or rather, the object of her affections. No, wait, uh, her attention. Yeah. That was it. The object of her attention. She squeezed her eyes shut tight for a moment and had a quick chat with that body part that ought not to be thinking. Then she opened her eyes again and found Preston standing barely a foot away from her, and she totally forgot what she had just said to that body part, or whether or not it had agreed with her anyway.

"Dinner was delicious," he told her with a smile that was clearly forced. "I appreciate your going to all the trouble you did."

His dark hair was damp with perspiration just from sitting down at the table, and she had to curl her fingers into her palms to keep herself from reaching up and gently pushing the wayward locks back from his forehead. When he'd realized he wouldn't be eating with Sam, he had changed out of his businessman clothes and into a loose-fitting, short-sleeved white shirt of some breezy, gauzy fabric and baggy khaki trousers. Now, much to her dismay,

Mamie found him to be infinitely more approachable than he had been before.

She really had to work hard not to approach him.

"You barely touched it," she replied, telling herself she did *not* sound accusatory or hurt when she said it. Just because she'd made that particular dinner special for him, because it was the best thing she knew how to make, that didn't mean he had to enjoy it, now, did it?

He glanced over his shoulder, toward the table he had just vacated, then back at Mamie, shrugging. "It's the heat," he told her. "I just don't have much of an appetite."

She nodded her understanding, but she didn't really believe him. "I'm sorry Sam took off without telling you," she said.

"It's not your fault. There's no reason you should apologize."

This time Mamie was the one to shrug. "I kinda feel like I'm a representative of Butternut, since this is your first visit here and all. Sam's taking off to go fishin', when he had an appointment with you? Well, even if it's not at all surprising, it was very rude of him to do it. So, on his behalf, I apologize."

Preston smiled. "Well, then, I accept your gracious apology. And I'll just hope that Mr. Butternut comes back soon."

Mamie nodded. She hoped so too. Because the sooner Sam came back, then the sooner he could get down to business with Preston Atherton IV. And the sooner the two men got down to business, then the sooner that business would be concluded. And the sooner that business was concluded, then the sooner Preston would go back to New York City. And the sooner Preston went back to New York City, well . . .

Then the sooner Mamie could go back to feeling the way she had felt this morning, before she'd made his acquaintance. Namely, ordinary, average, and normal. And, of course, hot. Then again, she was starting to realize that it wasn't just the heat wave wrapping Butternut that was making her feel so hot. No, even if it were January right now, she'd still be suffering from the heat. Because she'd no doubt have memories of Preston cluttering up her brain for some time to come. And there wasn't anything cool about those.

"Well, I'll just go clean up," she said, taking a few hesitant steps past him.

"Can I help?" he asked, surprising her.

He seemed surprised by the offer himself, she noted when she spun around to face him. Because the look on his face suggested he'd never intended to say what he had.

Reluctantly, she shook her head. "Nah, that's okay. You're a guest here, and even though I know you Northerners think we have funny ways down here, I assure you that we do know how to be hospitable. There's no way I'd make you do your own dishes." She smiled. "Not unless I catch you trying to skip out without paying your bill."

"There's little chance of that happening," he assured her with another one of those toe-curling smiles of his. "After all, I do still have to meet up with someone, someone very important, at that, before the week is through."

There was a mischievous little twinkle glittering in his dark eyes when he said it, Mamie noticed, and a funny little warmth spiraled through her. Because somehow she knew he wasn't just talking about Sam Butternut when he said what he did. And somehow she knew that the "someone very important" had almost nothing to do with Preston's business.

Humming lightly under her breath, for no reason she could rightly name, Mamie went off to clear the table and clean up. And as she went, much to her surprise, from behind herself, she heard Preston Atherton IV humming too.

four

Just because the sun went down in Butternut, that didn't mean there would be much relief from the heat of the day. But as far as Mamie was concerned, the evenings held other, less tangible, benefits that made the heavy air a bit more bearable. Things like the melodic trilling of late-feeding birds, the chip-chip-chipping of the cicadas, and indolent, balmy breezes that at least offered the illusion of falling temperatures. The sky darkened to black velvet, and the stars . . . oh, the stars. They lay scattered across the night sky as if someone had spilled a fistful of diamonds there. And they seemed to go on . . . they seemed to go on forever.

Mamie sighed with much contentment as she flopped into the white wicker swing that hung at one end of the Bide-a-Wee's big wraparound porch. With the tips of her toes, she pushed herself into motion, smiling at the familiar creak and jangle of swing and chain that chorused as one with each lazy motion.

Back . . . forth . . . back . . . forth . . .

Creak. Jangle. Creak. Jangle.

Now *this*, she thought, was livin'. Nothing came close to a casual country night, even in summertime, when the heat was so, well, hot. Because after a day of hard work and physical labor, there was nothing that brought more satisfaction than taking a break and focusing on what was truly important.

Doin' nothin'. It was life's greatest reward.

She closed her eyes and hummed to herself the same tuneless song that had accompanied her throughout the after-dinner cleanup. And she inhaled deeply the aromas of honeysuckle and juniper—and, of course, her roses—along with the lingering scent of chicken 'n' dumplins.

She couldn't help smiling when she recalled again the horror-stricken expression on Preston's face when she had announced the entire dinner menu that evening. Northerners sure did have funny ways about them. She couldn't think of a single person in Butternut who wouldn't *jump* at the chance to have fried corn and creamed onions in the *very same meal*. But Preston Atherton IV had been too worried about his cholesterol.

Cholesterol, she muttered distastefully to herself yet again when she remembered. Shoot. Like that was really a problem. Everybody knew it was your lifestyle that would kill you faster than anything else. High stress levels were far more deadly than high cholesterol levels. And Preston's lifestyle seemed like it was one that was loaded with stress. If he didn't learn to relax and stop worrying so much about sticking to his dang schedule—and useless things like cholesterol—he was going to drop dead of a heart attack.

Back . . . forth . . . back . . . forth . . .

Creak. Jangle. Creak. Jangle.

Thinking about him must have conjured him up, because Mamie heard the squeak and slap of the screen door just as her thoughts were fading. Slowly she opened her eyes and saw him striding across the porch toward her, but where earlier that day he had walked with such brisk purpose and unmistakable intent, his steps now were a bit more leisurely and unfocused.

All in all, he looked a *little* less uncomfortable than he had earlier. Then again, that wasn't saying much. Earlier, he'd been rigid enough to snap clean in two.

"Hey," Mamie greeted him, still toeing the swing lazily.

Back . . . forth . . . back . . . forth . . .

Creak. Jangle. Creak. Jangle.

"Hello," he replied. He came to a halt when a good four feet still separated them, shoving his hands into his trouser pockets and leaning against one of the porch supports. "I was rechecking Atherton Industries' upcoming annual report when I heard the swing through my window upstairs," he added, nodding his head in that direction.

"I hope it wasn't too distracting," she told him. Not that she did anything to slow her swinging, of course. A little distraction might be a good thing for Mr. Preston Atherton IV. He seemed to have so few of them in his life.

"No, no," he hastened to assure her. "Not at all. In fact, it was rather . . . soothing."

Well, now, that was good to hear. Maybe there was hope for him yet. Mamie nodded her agreement. "There've been a few nights when it's gotten so unbearably hot," she told him, "that I've come down here and slept on the swing." She smiled. " 'Course, it's not all that unbearable right now."

He chuckled. "Speak for yourself. I've never felt anything like this before. I mean, it gets hot in New York, but not like this."

"It's the humidity," she told him. "I know that sounds like a cliché and an easy way out, but it's true. The humidity makes the air real heavy, and harder to breathe. That's what makes it so miserable."

"If you say so."

"It's true. You should come back down here in the fall or spring. It's real nice then. Even when the temperatures get up there."

He eyed her curiously, and only then did Mamie realize she'd just pretty much extended him an invitation to come back down and see her sometime. Hastily, she added, "Once we get the Danny Jim Robinson Festival all organized and official-like, Butternut's gonna be a real tourist attraction. You mark my words."

Preston nodded, then sighed. "Yes, well, I wish you luck with that. Me, I don't think I'll be able to manage another trip down here. Unless, of course, something comes up with Butternut Industries that would require my presence."

Of course, Mamie thought. He'd never do anything unless it was for business reasons.

"Well, then," she said, "you better make sure you see the best of Butternut while you're here this time."

He smiled. "Well, you know, Miss Mamie, I think I have been."

Funny, she thought, but the way he looked at her just then—all soft and dreamy-like—made her feel as though maybe he thought he was seeing the best of Butternut, right here, right now, right on the front porch of the Bide-a-Wee Bed and Breakfast. She swallowed hard and kept swinging and told herself she was surely imagining things. But the easy back-and-forth motion and the reassuring creak-jangle of the swing suddenly seemed more frantic than it had before. As did the pounding of her heart and the rush of blood through her veins.

With no small effort, Mamie focused on slowing both the swing and her pulse rate, succeeding fairly well in the first endeavor but failing miserably with the second. Goodness. What was it about the man that made her feel so odd? So tingly and uncertain and fuzzy-headed and dizzy and . . . and . . . and . . .

Hot.

Because suddenly it wasn't the heavy, humid summertime air that was making her own personal temperature rise. No, it was Preston Atherton IV, a man she'd just met. A man whose life ran counter to everything she knew and loved and held dear. A man who had absolutely no interest in anything other than running his business and keeping to his schedule. A man who would be in Butternut for a few days.

It was a familiar enough feeling, though, this tingly, dizzy stuff. Mamie might not have traveled far beyond the outskirts of Butternut, but she'd been around the block a time or two. She was a healthy, red-blooded twenty-seven-year-old woman, after all, and not some blushing virgin.

Well, not too much of a blushing virgin. Not a virgin anyway. Not really.

Oh, all right, so she wasn't *that* well versed in what went on between a man and a woman. She wasn't completely ignorant. This wasn't the first time Butternut had been caught in the grips of a massive heat wave, after all. Mamie had had a boyfriend or two along the way who'd . . . you know . . . helped her through those long, hot summers. So to speak. But one had left to find work in Birmingham a few years back, and she'd happily tossed rice over the other one last winter, when he'd married Daphne Sue Montrose.

This particular hot summer, well . . .

Men were in short supply. Local men, anyway. This outof-towner, however . . .

Now you just stop right there, Miss Mamie, she ordered herself. No way was she going to start something like that with a man who was only going to be in town for another day or two. Eventually the heat wave would pass. But anything she might get going with Preston Atherton IV would have lingering effects that would go on far beyond the summer. Mamie Calhoun didn't give her heart—or any other body part, for that matter—lightly. And she was more than certain that her heart wouldn't travel well. If Preston took it back to New York City with him, she'd probably never see it again. And, focused as he was on business and all, he probably wouldn't take very good care of it, either.

So as intriguing as she found the long, lusty look he was currently throwing her way, she forced herself to glance in another direction. "You want some iced tea?" she asked him. "Or some lemonade?"

Preston smiled when he heard Mamie's offer. He really did like the way she talked. "Iced tea" became "ahsed tay" and "lemonade" sounded more like "limmin-aaayde." Of course, her charming speech patterns weren't the only thing he liked about her. Far from it. In fact, he couldn't think of anything he *didn't* like about Mamie Calhoun. Which was odd, seeing as how she had nothing in common with anyone he considered a friend. Then again, he mused further, he didn't have that many friends—close friends, at any rate. Or even one . . . close friend, he suddenly realized.

Odd, that. He'd never given it much thought before, but now he recognized the truth in the revelation. Certainly he had scores of acquaintances, and he never lacked for invitations to parties and such. And he generally enjoyed himself at social gatherings and never felt excluded. Well, not really. No more than anyone else would. If he sometimes felt a bit, oh . . . bored and disinterested at such functions, that was only because he went to so very many of them, and after a while they all ran together. It wasn't because he was dissatisfied with that way of life.

Was it?

No, of course not.

Still, it was rather odd, he thought again.

Even odder was the fact that he hadn't experienced any of those feelings of boredom or distraction since making Miss Mamie's acquaintance. On the contrary, he felt more comfortable with her—and more captivated by her—than he did many people in New York that he had known all of his adult life.

How did she manage that? He wondered. What was it about her that simply invited a warm, familiar, enchanted response? Even having spent only an afternoon and evening in her presence, he felt as if he'd known her for years. And even though he knew little about her beyond her name and occupation, somehow those details didn't seem at all important.

He liked her. It was that simple. He had liked her from the beginning. Even when she'd accused him of being . . . irregular. And liking her, he supposed, was all that really mattered.

He pushed himself away from the porch railing against which he had been leaning and took a few more steps toward the gently swaying, softly creaking, musically jangling swing. He wanted to sit down beside her, but hesitated without being issued an invitation. So he simply crossed to the other side of the porch and leaned his back against the side of the house. He hooked one ankle over the other, then folded his arms across his chest.

And he wondered why he suddenly felt so awkward.

"So," he ventured, nudging the strange feeling aside for now. He smiled, hoping the gesture didn't look as nervous as it felt. "What do you Butternuttians do in Butternut after the sun goes down?"

For a moment she didn't answer his question, only turned to squint at him as if the yellow-tinted porch light had just gone a tad dim. Then, "Do?" she echoed, clearly puzzled by the question. "What do we *do*?"

He nodded, braving an indulgent smile. "Yes, do. What do you do? Go dancing? To the movies? To the theater? Any of those things ring a bell?"

She arched her eyebrows as she gave some thought to the question. "Yeah, we do all those things here, just . . . not during the week. Those are more for the weekend. Special occasions, like."

This time Preston was the one to arch his eyebrows. "Going to the movies is a special occasion?"

She nodded. "Well, yeah."

"All right," he conceded, masking his surprise as best he could. "Then what do you do in the evenings to pass the time during the week?"

This time she smiled. "We don't really *do* anything. We sit out on the porch and enjoy the quiet evenin'. Or we go out back and visit with the neighbors over the fence. Or we watch a little TV or read or listen to the stereo. Or we just . . ."

She pushed the swing into motion again. Back and forth, Preston noted. Creak. Jangle.

"We just swing," she concluded. "I s'pose if someone's feeling especially adventurous or restless, they take a walk, but me . . ." She shrugged philosophically. "I like swingin'."

Funny, Preston thought. But suddenly the simple prospect of sitting on a porch swing with Miss Mamie Calhoun sounded like a lot more fun than taking in a Broadway premiere and having drinks at Elaine's afterward.

Unable to help himself, he dipped his head toward the vehicle in question. "Mind if I join you, then?" he asked.

For a minute she seemed almost panicked by his question. Not that she moved a muscle, but her eyes did widen in what appeared to be alarm. As quickly as she had reacted, though, she recovered her composure. She didn't answer his question, however.

"I promise I'll let you keep driving," he threw in for good measure. He lifted his chin toward the swing. "You seem to know what you're doing."

Finally, finally, she smiled. And despite the darkness surrounding him, somehow it seemed to Preston as if the sun had just come out.

"I've been doing it most of my life," she told him. "Ever since my legs were long enough to reach the porch." And then, after only a brief hesitation, she moved over to one side of the swing and patted the flowered cushion beside her. "C'mon over," she invited. "I'll teach you a thing or two about drivin' swings."

He smiled again at the way she said the word "swings," turning it into "swangs." Still, she didn't need to ask him twice. Hiding his enthusiasm as best he could—and telling himself not to think about why the simple act of sitting on a porch swing could make him so enthusiastic in the first place—he took a seat beside her. He made himself scoot to the opposite end and leave a nonthreatening foot of space between them, but even at that, Mamie seemed closer than she had ever been to him before. And at that realization, what had been enthusiasm suddenly rocketed right to ardor.

Truly. Ardor. Preston couldn't remember the last time he had felt ardor—or even eagerness—for anything. Well, anything other than his work, naturally, and *that* ardor was nothing like *this* ardor. He made a quick mental note to himself, to schedule some time for ardor when he got back to New York. Because it felt good, this ardor. And it had come about simply because Mamie Calhoun had invited him to swing with her.

How very, *very* odd.

And how very, *very* intriguing.

He said nothing as she set the swing in motion again, only stared forward at the length of the porch and the dark yard beyond. The night was scented with floral fragrances that he scarcely recognized—except for the roses, of course. And the sounds . . .

Preston was so used to living high above the city that he could barely describe any sound other than jets flying overhead, or the hum of the air conditioner, or the occasional siren howling from the street below. Here, however, was an orchestra unlike any he had ever heard before—birds and bugs and wind and swing. Somehow they all combined into a symphony of surprising sophistication. And, strangely enough, he realized, he could enjoy a nightly performance for free.

"Yes," he said softly, "I can see where *doing* something at night here might be a tad unnecessary."

He turned to look at Mamie, only to find that she, in turn, was inspecting him. And rather intently, at that. Her amazing green eyes were fixed on him in a way that made his heart trip a time or two in his chest before leaping to an alarming pace. His fingers convulsed on the cool metal chain that held the swing, but he could manage no other physical motion. Her gaze entranced him, enthralled him, made time stand utterly still.

Back . . . forth . . . back . . . forth . . .

Creak. Jangle. Creak. Jangle.

The slow, steady pace of the swing coupled with the easy, regular rhythm of sound was hypnotic. All Preston could do was sit there and gaze at her and feel himself slipping away to a place he'd never visited before. Then again, as pastimes went, gazing at Mamie Calhoun and visiting a new place with her wasn't such a bad one at that.

A single russet curl danced in the breeze at her temple, and without even thinking about what he was doing, Preston lifted a hand to brush it back. Immediately, he realized he shouldn't have done it. Not because of anything Mamie said or did in response, but because of what happened to *him* as a response.

The moment he brushed his finger over the silky curl, a thrill of something hot and urgent ran through him from fingertip to chest, as if he'd just touched a live wire. Instinctively, he jerked his hand back, but not as far as one would retreat—should retreat—when one feared for one's safety. And only for a second, at that, because without even realizing it, he moved his hand forward once more, to tuck the errant tress behind her ear. Even that small motion wasn't enough, however, and he trailed the pad of his thumb over her warm cheek on the journey back.

Mamie's lips parted softly at his unexpected—for both of them, clearly—gesture, but she said nothing. Nor did she move at all. For one bright flash of time, the two of them remained joined by fingertip and soft cheek, linked, as far as Preston was concerned, by some soul-deep wanting that he couldn't for the life of him understand.

And then, as quickly as it had happened, the moment dissolved, dissipated, disappeared. And he was back sitting on a porch swing amid a chorus of crickets, beside a lovely young woman who seemed much too good to be true.

"I . . . I'm sorry," he stammered, dropping his hand back to his side. But that strange frisson of electricity still shuddered faintly around his heart. "I was afraid—" He halted himself, biting back a surge of panic that erupted from only God knew where. Frankly, he was afraid of too many things to voice them, he realized. Too many things even to think about. "I was afraid . . . I was afraid your hair would get in your eyes. I guess I shouldn't have—"

"No, it's all right," she interjected.

But as if she feared he might try to "help" her out again, she hastily brought her own hand up to shove her hair—all of it—back from her forehead and temples. Quickly, she freed the questionable ponytail caught at the crown of her head, stuffed the escaped tresses back into it, then replaced the rubber band that held the lot together. Immediately, though, a few dozen curls escaped again. But neither she nor Preston moved to contain them.

"The, uh . . . the humidity," she said again, as if that explained everything.

Preston, however, was more inclined to think it was the heat. Because he could conjure no other reason but heatstroke for why his sanity and good sense had abandoned him the way they had. Here he was, sitting on a porch swing in Butternut, Alabama, with a woman he had just met, and he was feeling things he'd never felt before in his life. Good things. Things that had been missing before. Things he had never imagined he *could* feel. Things that made him want to stay right here, on this porch swing in Butternut, Alabama, so that he could more fully explore each and every one of them.

Explore them and something else, too, he realized. Or, rather, some*one* else. Because suddenly, thousands of miles from New York City—the most exciting place on the planet, as far as Preston was concerned—he'd met someone more interesting, more exciting, than anyone he'd ever known.

Miss Mamie Calhoun, he thought then, was going to take some investigating before he headed back home. Fortunately for Preston, Samuel Butternut looked to be even more elusive than before, and that bought him a little extra time. Funny how, only hours ago, the prospect of spending even one extra minute in Butternut had generated such feelings of doom and gloom and defeat inside him. Now he was feeling rather delighted by the prospect.

Gee, he thought, evidently that old adage was true. You really did learn something new about yourself every day. And naturally, right on the heels of that revelation came another. Preston realized he couldn't wait to find out what new discovery he would make about himself—and Miss Mamie—tomorrow.

five

Preston awoke to his first full day in Butternut only to become immediately disoriented. And that was because he immediately experienced some of the most bizarre sensations he'd ever experienced in his life, even more bizarre than the ones he'd experienced on the porch swing the night before.

And those had been plenty bizarre.

Normally, he awakened in his Fifth Avenue penthouse at precisely 6:30 A.M., to the fragrant aroma of Blue Mountain coffee (whose brewing process had been programmed to begin at precisely 6:18 A.M.), to the soft strains of Mozart (whose overture had been programmed to begin at precisely 6:28 A.M.), to the feel of crisp cotton percale sheets (he preferred his nights cool, therefore programmed his climate control to a nighttime setting of seventy-two degrees Fahrenheit, which cut off at exactly 6:15 A.M.), and to the sight of a bedroom furnished in spare, geometric Bauhaus design.

This morning, however . . .

This morning, the aroma of coffee was mingling with the mixed, and decidedly pleasant, aromas of bacon and pancakes—he could feel his arteries hardening already. Instead of Mozart, the music that greeted him through his open window—at least, he was fairly certain it was music—was filled with twangs and trills and "y'alls" and what sounded suspiciously like hound dogs. There were no cool cotton sheets tangling with his limbs, because he had kicked them all to the foot of the bed during the night. This would be a result of the fact, he realized quickly, that the morning temperature of his room was—just a hasty estimate, to be sure—about four hundred degrees. And the decorative mood of the room surrounding him was not so much Bauhaus as it was . . . Our House. Very homey. Very folksy. Very nice, actually.

Preston closed his eyes and lay back on the mattress for a moment, letting the change of venue sink in gradually. In addition to the twangy music, he heard birds singing outside. How interesting. Although he knew that birds existed in New York City, he lived much higher up than most of them did. And with his bedroom windows pretty much fused shut, he wouldn't have heard them singing anyway. And even if he'd heard them singing, he wouldn't have heard them singing, because he would have had his mind on something else—business.

However, now that he did hear the birds singing, he realized it was a rather nice sound. How . . . interesting.

And dallying with the aromas rising from the kitchen downstairs, Preston noted another wafting in through the open window, the scent of . . . roses. Heavens, he was actually stopping to smell the roses. Or, at the very least, lying in bed to smell the roses. Truly, this was an extraordinary experience all around.

With one hand he rubbed away the last remnants of sleep from his eyes, and with the other hand he felt blindly about the nightstand until he located the Breitling wristwatch he had dropped there so carelessly the night before. It hadn't even occurred to him to worry that someone might break in and steal the expensive timepiece. He'd left his window open as well, in deference to the heat, and he hadn't once felt concern for the safety of his person or belongings.

Call him unrealistic, but he simply could not imagine that any self-respecting criminal would ply his trade in a place called Butternut.

With a sigh of what felt like . . . contentment?—oh,

surely not—Preston dangled his watch in front of his face and tried to focus on where its hands lay. The time, he finally discerned, was—good heavens, could that be correct?—ten-thirty.

Ten-thirty?

He shot straight up in bed and inspected the watch again, to make sure it was running properly. True enough, the second hand spun languidly around the numbers at its usual rate. Still not believing the evidence, however, he darted his gaze to the antique clock on the dresser opposite his bed. Ten-seventeen, that one read. Well, of course, it wouldn't be precise, would it? Not if it belonged to Mamie Calhoun. And it would naturally be running slow. Still, it was looking very much like Preston had—he swallowed hard before admitting it—slept late.

Slept late, he echoed to himself. It was unthinkable. Inconceivable. He hadn't slept this late since . . . since . . . well, he'd *never* slept this late before. It wasn't in his nature to sleep late. Preston never, ever, deviated from the schedule that was his life. Yet upon waking on his first full day in Butternut, he had done just that.

It's the heat, he tried to tell himself. Surely that was the only explanation. In this heat, the body just naturally shut down. It was a survival mechanism. Yes, that was it. This sort of thing would have happened to anybody. And his subconscious, which never betrayed him, had known that Samuel Butternut had left town, so there was no reason to rise for an early meeting. His subconscious had therefore allowed Preston to catch a few extra hours of sleep.

Of course. That explained things perfectly. It was all due to his subconscious.

Still, it wasn't in his nature to miss so much of the day, and even though he didn't have any scheduled appointments, he had no desire to remain idle. An idle mind without a specific, well-tailored agenda, in Preston's opinion, was a lost mind. And he didn't want to lose his mind. Especially in Butternut. Who knew where it might possibly turn up?

Rising from bed, he hastened to complete his morning

toilette—which now included peeking out the door like some self-conscious college coed, in an effort to be certain that no one was looking when he hied himself down to the bathroom to shower and shave. Quickly, he did both, then—again with the self-conscious peeking out the door—he hurried back to his room. After dressing in suitably casual attire of lightweight gray trousers and lightweight cotton—though tastefully patterned—shirt, Preston looked . . .

Well, he looked like a limp rag, he thought as he inspected himself in the mirror. Honestly. The temperature must be hovering just below the spontaneous combustion level on the thermometer today.

Although what he needed at the moment, more than anything in the world, was a cup of piping-hot coffee, the prospect of drinking anything that wasn't frozen held little appeal. And as delicious as the bacon and pancakes had smelled earlier, what Preston was really craving at the moment was, he realized with some dismay, a big bowl of sleet.

He cleared the stairs and followed the lingering aroma of fried pork to what became an expansive kitchen that, like the rest of the house, was furnished in Antebellum Quaint. Lacy curtains billowed in the hot breeze that skimmed through the open window, brushing against white cabinets with glass doors that offered a view of the crockery dishes stacked neatly inside. Rush-bottomed, ladder-back chairs stood sentry around a butcher-block table, the hardwood floor beneath covered by a massive braided rug. Although cluttered with pots and bowls and other kitchen essentials, the room was clean. Not to mention empty.

Too empty. And too clean, really, Preston thought. Breakfast, clearly, was over for the day. And Mamie, it appeared, was gone. A screen door opposite him rattled against the breeze, and Preston strode toward it, peering out into the backyard. The first thing he noted was the source of the roses that he had stopped—or, rather, lay down—to smell earlier. It was, after all, a bit hard to miss them. They were, quite simply, everywhere.

They sprouted from fat bushes along a tall, whitewashed

fence at the back, spilled from beds along a cobbled walkway that bisected the yard, climbed trellises around the porch. They were pink, they were yellow, they were red, they were white. Some were splashed with orange and purple, others were a mix of tints to which he couldn't quite do justice, should he try to identify them.

And the smell . . .

Involuntarily, he inhaled deeply, filling his nose and lungs with the ripe, sweet scent of the bounty, then grew dizzy and intoxicated, so unwilling was he to let the breath leave him. Finally, of course, he did exhale. And immediately after, he gasped for more.

Never in his life had Preston seen such a rich collection of warm color. And something inside him that had been taut and rigid for longer than he could say suddenly softened and eased and broke free.

A quick, brief movement from the back of the yard caught his attention then, and he turned toward it to find Mamie. Or, at least, a part of Mamie. The back part, to be precise, sticking out from between two of the most extraordinarily colored of the rosebushes at the very edge of the yard. Her rounded rump was covered—barely—by lovingly faded cutoffs, and her feet—naturally—were bare.

He watched as she pushed herself out from the roses, then marveled at the fact that, somehow, she didn't seem to quite separate from them. With her wild russet curls and cheeks flushed from the heat, and the pale-yellow sleeveless blouse clinging to her torso, she seemed almost to be one of the blossoms that bloomed so flagrantly about her.

No, that wasn't quite right, Preston thought, taking a few involuntary steps toward her. Mamie was infinitely more beautiful than a mere, pedestrian rose. She was . . .

That thought—and his breath—got stuck then, because she lifted her fingers to her forehead to push back a handful of damp curls. When she did, she arched her back into a stretch that was, very, *very* erotic. It was made more so by the way her plump breasts strained against their brief cotton confines, and any hunger for food that Preston might have been suffering was immediately replaced by a ravenous need for something else entirely.

He halted midstride at the realization and found himself standing midway between Mamie and the house, totally paralyzed and unable to take a step further in any direction. Good heavens, he thought. He wanted Mamie. No, more precisely, he *wanted* Mamie, he corrected himself. He desired her. He craved her. He hungered for her.

Her. Even dismissing the reminder that he'd met her less than twenty-four hours ago—which was no small dismissal, granted—the utter voraciousness of his appetite for her very nearly overwhelmed him. To put it in basic terms, Preston didn't feel things—anything—with the depth or keenness of this . . . this . . . this *thing* that he felt for Mamie. Whatever it was winding through him at such an alarming rate, it was unlike anything he'd ever had inside him before. And he felt it for her. A virtual stranger. A virtual stranger with whom he had absolutely nothing in common.

Immediately, though, he knew that wasn't quite correct. Although he had only met Mamie yesterday, he *knew* her better than he knew most people. He wasn't sure why that was—probably because she gave so much of herself right off the bat—but it was true nonetheless. Certainly the two of them had shared only a few perfunctory conversations since his arrival at the inn, but when he thought back to the night before, to that brief moment when he'd touched her silky hair and her soft cheek . . .

He still wasn't sure exactly what had happened, but at that moment the two of them had joined on some indistinct, intangible level. And on that level, they knew each other. They *knew* each other. He could think of no other way to describe the sensation.

But even knowing her as he did, Preston couldn't quite fathom the attraction. She just was not the kind of woman he normally found himself wanting. Not that he had really wanted that many women in his life, he recalled, but he was by no means inexperienced. Still, even his most passionate encounter—and passionate it had been, too—now seemed tepid and clumsy in light of what shuddered through him simply watching Mamie Calhoun stretch her limbs against a background of roses. Yet she had nothing, absolutely nothing—save that indistinct, intangible something that he couldn't even identify—in common with him.

His instincts clamored for him to turn around, to run away, to escape this place, this moment, this revelation, before he did or said something he would regret later. But Mamie chose that moment to glance up from her botanical labors, and when she did, Preston knew—he *knew*—that she experienced exactly the same strange sensation and revelation he had experienced himself only a moment ago.

She *wanted* him. Desired him. Craved him. Hungered for him. Just as he did her. And she didn't understand it any more than he did.

With the recognition that her condition mirrored his own, Preston's paralysis evaporated. And although he seemed to have no control over what he was doing, he strode forward, slowly covering the distance left between them.

"Good morning," he greeted her, struggling to keep hidden the strange miasma of emotions rumbling through him, even though he suspected she knew as well as he did what was going on.

In response, she glanced briefly up at the sun. "It's almost 'Good afternoon,' " she pointed out.

"True enough," he acknowledged. "I don't normally sleep to such a late hour," he added. "I'm frankly amazed that I did here. It's the heat, I'm sure."

She smiled at him, and he knew she didn't agree with his assessment at all. "If you say so," she told him.

"I missed breakfast, I assume."

She nodded. "But you're right on time for lunch. There's still some chicken 'n' dumplins left over from last night, if you're interested."

Preston was. *Too* interested. Even having enjoyed only a few bites before the heat had ruined his appetite, the meal she'd fixed last night had given his taste buds a cataclysmic orgasm—even if it had shaved at least six months off of his life span, thanks to the arteriosclerosis factor. Still, it was almost worth dying young if it meant eating from such a smorgasbord every day.

"Actually, I think a salad would be just fine," he replied reluctantly.

She pushed herself up from the ground, and, chivalrously—at least, he told himself he was only being chivalrous, even if, deep down, he suspected his motives were far more self-serving—Preston extended a hand to help her up. She hesitated only a moment before folding her fingers against his, then he tugged her gently to a standing position. As gentle as the tug was, however, something—he had no idea what, honestly—made him pull just a tad too hard. Just enough to cause Mamie to—accidentally, of course—stumble forward a bit. When she did, he caught her capably—naturally—but she still ended up leaning against him, her hands splayed against his chest to steady herself.

It was, Preston decided, a very nice position to be in. And, not quite able to help himself, he covered one of her hands with his.

She glanced up at his action, her clear green gaze locking with his. He noted a faint sheen of perspiration dewing her upper lip, and, with the thumb of his free hand, he deftly, gently . . . slowly . . . wiped it away. His hand lingered at her mouth, however, and somehow he found himself grazing her lower lip as well—that full, ripe, luscious lower lip—with the pads of his index and middle fingers.

Soft. She was so soft . . .

Her lips parted slightly and her eyes fluttered closed at his gesture, and color bloomed in both her cheeks. The rich narcotic scent of the roses intoxicated him, and Preston began to lower his head toward hers. Close . . . Closer . . . And yet closer still . . . He was so, so close . . .

Suddenly he felt the hands that were spread open on his chest tense, and before he realized what was happening, Mamie pushed. But she didn't push him away so much as she pushed herself away from him. And somehow, that went a long way toward reassuring Preston that what he'd done hadn't overstepped the bounds of propriety. Better yet, it reassured him that what he'd done might very well

happen again, and that next time it might end a little differently.

"I, uh . . . I think I have some tomatoes that are ready for
picking," she said as she disentangled herself from his mea-
ger embrace. "They're looking to be pretty yummy this
year, too," she added quickly. "They love the heat and the
humidity, you know. So when we do have these unbearable
heat waves, at least we get some good tomatoes out of it.
That's something, I suppose."

Mamie knew she was beginning to babble, but honestly,
what else was she supposed to do? She'd just nearly kissed
a man she scarcely knew.

Of course, it didn't feel like she scarcely knew Preston.
On the contrary, the hours spent with him felt more like
years. From the moment she'd laid eyes on him the day
before, she'd felt as if she were welcoming home an old
friend instead of making a new acquaintance. She had no
idea why that might be, but there it was, all the same. Preston Atherton IV, for all his strange ways and odd customs,
felt like a piece of Butternut, as far as Mamie was concerned.

Still, that didn't mean she ought to go around kissing the
fella. Even if she was the proprietress of the Bide-a-Wee
Bed and Breakfast, kissing the clientele sorta put profes-
sional hospitality into a whole 'nother light.

"I think I have some cucumbers ready to come out, too,"
she tossed over her shoulder as she made her way toward
the small vegetable garden on the other side of the yard.

Belatedly she realized that cucumbers probably weren't
the best thing to be discussing at the moment, all things
considered. Not when she'd just felt Preston's, um . . . cucumber . . . pressing against her thigh as she'd fallen against
him. And quite the blue ribbon winner it was, too, she
thought before she could stop herself.

She halted near the garden and hoped the blush she felt
firing her face hadn't traveled anywhere else on her person—well, nowhere that Preston might see, at any rate,
seeing as how there was little she could do about the heat
. . . *down there.*

"A cucumber would be great," he said, coming to a stop beside her.

Yes, it would, Mamie thought involuntarily, squeezing her eyes shut tight as the idea became far too graphic for her comfort. "Okay," she muttered. She scanned the garden quickly until a plump, ripe cucumber caught her eye. Oh, no. She was going to have to reach down there and pick that up while Preston was watching her. Hold it in her hand. Carry it into the house. Then take a knife and—

"Here's a good one," she said hastily, bending down to scoop up a less, um . . . well-endowed . . . version of the vegetable.

"Oh, no," he countered, stooping beside her. "That one's much too small." He pointed to the plump, ripe one that had so reminded her of their embrace. "That one would be *much* more . . . appropriate."

The way he lingered over that last word made her brave a glance in his direction. She found him smiling at her in a way that told her his own thoughts were pretty much following hers. Quickly, she dropped her gaze back to the garden, toward the tomatoes. But those, too, suddenly seemed so sensual, so erotic, that she just couldn't quite bring herself to go over and pick one.

Once more Preston seemed to know exactly what she was thinking, because he said, "I see two luscious-looking tomatoes over there. Why don't I just go and help myself?"

Mamie closed her eyes and just rolled with the sexual wave of pleasure that washed over her. What else was she supposed to do? If handling suggestive vegetables was as close as she was going to come to pleasures of the flesh this summer, then by God, she would enjoy it as much as she could.

"Yes," she finally managed to say. "Why don't you? Help yourself, I mean. To the tomatoes, I mean."

But Preston had already done just that. When she opened her eyes, she saw him standing beside one particularly fruitful vine, fingering two round, rosy tomatoes as if they were the most erotic handful he'd ever had the pleasure to grope. Her mouth went dry as she watched him gently squeeze first one and then the other, rolling his fingertip over their dark centers near the stem before plucking them delicately from the vine.

Damp heat flooded her, and she closed her eyes again to wait it out. She really was going to have to get a grip on herself, she thought. Otherwise she was going to wind up letting Preston get a grip on her that would be much farther reaching and infinitely more troubling.

"These look good," he said as he returned to her side, gently palming one of the fruits in each hand. "Plump. Full. Tasty," he added, not even trying to hide the sexual innuendo in the comments. Then, as if he hadn't already said far too much, he added slyly, "I think I'd like to . . . have . . . these."

It was too much for Mamie to tolerate. Her fingers convulsed on the cucumber she still held in her hands as she thrust it toward Preston. "I just remembered that I have to run into town," she lied. "I hope you don't mind fixing your own lunch. I know that's terribly rude, to make you do that, but I . . . I . . . I . . ." She took a giant step backward. "I really do have to . . . run."

And then, making good on her promise, Mamie spun around and bolted for the back door.

SIX

Preston eyed the two tomatoes sitting side by side on the kitchen counter, then took another bite of his peanut-butter-and-jelly sandwich. The big cucumber likewise taunted him from nearby, and he shifted his weight uncomfortably from one foot to the other, hoping to alleviate some of the tension tightening his own cucum—

Oh, for heaven's sake, he thought. When was the last time he'd indulged in something as adolescent as turning vegetables into sexual double entendres? Actually, thinking back, he couldn't recall *ever* indulging in anything that adolescent, even when he'd *been* an adolescent. Which was probably why it had been so much fun doing it with Mamie. Well, that, and the fact that she was just so damned cute when she blushed.

He grinned when he recalled the look on her face as he'd told her he wanted to *have* her tomatoes. Priceless. It had been absolutely priceless. And if she looked that scandalized at the mere suggestion of him tasting her tomatoes, he wondered how she'd look when he actually did open his mouth to savor her full, plump, naked—

He inhaled deeply and forced his gaze away from the full, plump, naked tomatoes that sat on the counter teasing him. And he wondered where Mamie had hied herself off to in such a rush. He supposed he had no one but himself to blame for her hasty departure. Evidently, he'd pushed her too far with the tomato comment. Still, it would have been nice if she'd hung around a bit longer and played juvenile games with him for the rest of the afternoon. It had been a long time since Preston had had this much fun.

Come to think of it, he couldn't recall ever having this much fun. And how odd. He hadn't even scheduled it in.

And speaking of schedules . . .

Good God, he thought, he'd completely abandoned his. Of course, with Samuel Butternut having gone AWOL the way he had, there wasn't much of a schedule to maintain. But that didn't mean Preston should simply throw his schedule away. On the contrary. He simply needed to adjust it so that it included his newfound priorities.

Instinctively he glanced down at his watch. 1:33. All right. He could work from there. Starting at 1:35, he would have lascivious thoughts about Mamie Calhoun. Then, at precisely 2:00 he would fantasize about her. Nothing too graphic—he'd save that for the evening hours, where it would be more appropriate, not to mention more productive—but a quarter hour . . . no, make it thirty minutes . . . of good fantasizing wouldn't be out of place.

At 2:30, he thought, he could pencil in a snack. All that fantasizing and lascivious thinking would doubtless require refueling—he was, after all, only having a peanut-butter-and-jelly sandwich for lunch, seeing as how he hadn't had it in him to chop up the vegetables; it would have been inhuman. Then, after his snack, at 2:50, Mamie ought to be back from running her dubious errand. So 3:00, he decided, was the precise time that he would strike up a suggestive conversation. That, naturally, could go on for hours, so he'd best leave the remainder of the afternoon free. Dinner at 5:30—with Mamie this time, of course. He would disregard her protests this evening and help her with the cleanup afterward, which should bring them to roughly 7:45.

The perfect time to retire to the porch swing, he thought. Two hours more of conversation—some suggestive, some not—along with a bit of seemingly innocent, but very electrifying, touching, and then the sun would be well down. And then, at exactly 9:45 . . .

Well. That would be the precise time that he leaned forward and kissed her, he decided. Yes, 9:45 would be a very good time for that, indeed. And then, if he was very, very lucky—and Preston prided himself on being a very, very lucky man—then maybe, just maybe, he could carry Mamie up the stairs to his room, then up more stairs to his bed, and they could schedule in a night full of passion.

And who said schedules had to be dull? he thought. Why, this one was promising to be rather exhausting.

Glancing down at his watch, he realized it was time for him to have his lascivious thoughts, so he closed his eyes and did just that. He did, after all, have a schedule to maintain. He only hoped Mamie was as good at keeping time— or, rather, making time—as he was.

Unfortunately, he was forced to realize late in the afternoon that Mamie Calhoun seemed to have no concept of time— or, worse, schedules—whatsoever. Because she didn't return from her errands at the hour that Preston had assigned to the task. Nor did she return the hour after that. Finally, fearing that he might never see her again, he took it upon himself to go looking for her. This, however, much to his pique—and he really did dislike getting piqued—required him to go out and explore . . .

Butternut.

Fortunately there wasn't that much of the town to explore. He ought to be able to cover all of Main Street in, oh . . . he glanced as his watch and did some mental tallying. About a nanosecond ought to do it, he decided. Even if it took as much as half an hour—something he considered laughably impossible, seeing as how the whole of Butternut couldn't possibly take more than fifteen minutes— he could still squeeze in dinner with Mamie at the allocated 5:30 on the dot. Since there would be no time to cook anything themselves, however, they'd have to make do with Fern and Moody's home cookin' at the café across the street.

Oddly, though, he realized as he pushed the screen door open and stepped out onto the front porch, home cookin' was sounding considerably less dissatisfying than it had at this time yesterday.

Even with the sun hanging low over the trees and the porch steeped in shade, stepping out the front door of the Bide-a-Wee felt very much like walking into a sauna. Despite his short sleeves and the lightweight fabric of his clothing, Preston was immediately overcome by the heat and dampness. But the heat and dampness, strangely enough, didn't bother him quite as much as it had a mere twenty-four hours ago. Because he knew something now that he hadn't known then, and he was learning that there was something of a trade-off to it all.

True, the heat was unbearable at times, but what resulted from that heat turned out to be some rather pleasurable consequences.

Like brevity of clothing, for example, he thought, recalling Mamie's snug cutoffs and even snugger tops. And like wild, unruly auburn curls that begged for a man's touch. And misty lips that lured fingers to intimate touches. And iced tea sweeter and more savory than the most full-bodied wine. And raging rosebushes riotous with color and rampant with intoxicating scents. And nights so still, so quiet, so peaceful, that nobody wanted to do anything except sit on a porch swing and enjoy the company of another human being.

Yes, he decided. There was a lot to be said for hot summers. Come to think of it, there was a lot to be said for Butternut, too. Suddenly he found himself hoping that Samuel Butternut's fishing trip lasted considerably longer than 'til the end of the week. Because strangely enough—and it was *quite* strange—Preston realized he was in absolutely no hurry to get back to New York.

He strode to the end of the walkway that curled along the front yard, then drove his gaze up one side of Main Street and down the other. Amazing, he thought. Not a soul in sight. Were this Broadway, at this hour, thousands of people would be spilling into the streets, heat wave or no.

Taxis would be honking, trucks would be rumbling past. All manner of movement and sound and sensation would combine to create Preston's world. Yet here in Butternut, Alabama, the world had come to a halt.

Oh, no, wait. Not quite a halt, he noted. Because there, at a white frame house toward the end of the street, a brown-speckled dog ambled out from beneath a porch and into a shady spot at the edge of his yard. Preston smiled when he realized he'd just witnessed rush hour in Butternut.

He glanced up and down the Main Street again, vexed. Surely it couldn't be difficult to find Mamie among the handful of buildings lining both sides of the avenue. He was certain she couldn't have strayed far from the inn, simply because there *wasn't* a far from the inn. It was only a matter of deciding which of the local establishments she'd chosen for her escape—or rather, her errand, he reminded himself. As if he believed *that*.

Ultimately he found her at the first place he checked, namely Fern and Moody's directly across from the Bide-a-Wee. She was sitting alone at a table in the very back of the restaurant, perusing a menu that sported a pen-and-ink rendition of what appeared to be a pig wearing naught but a chef's hat and a large grin. In his hand, the millinery-bearing porker held a sign that read, if Preston wasn't mistaken, COME 'N' GET IT!

Well, all right, then. He would.

"That must have been some errand you had to run," he said as he folded himself into the chair opposite Mamie's, taking some small satisfaction in the way she nearly leapt out of her skin when he did. Her eyes, when she met his gaze, went wide with panic, then immediately softened with the smile that curled her lips.

Good, he thought. He didn't mind scaring her a little bit—after all, why should he be the only one? But he wanted that fear to be far outshadowed by the prospect, however iffy it might still be, of pleasure. "You've been gone for hours," he added knowingly. "No wonder I found you sitting in a restaurant . . . of sorts. You must have worked up a substantial appetite."

"I, uh . . ." she began articulately. To that, she added a very eloquent, "Um, that is . . ." And then she followed that up with a resounding, "Ah, actually, I mean, um, well, see . . ."

Preston held up a hand to stop the elegant flow of words. "You don't have to explain," he told her.

She arched her eyebrows in surprise. "I don't?"

He shook his head. "No, you don't. Believe it or not, I know *exactly* why you did what you did."

That seemed to worry her a bit, he noted. "But—"

"And besides," he interjected before she could regain her equilibrium—he didn't want her to have hers back until he had his back, too, and he didn't see that happening anytime soon. He glanced down at his watch before hastily continuing, "According to my schedule, if we have our dinner now, then we'll still have plenty of time for the really important things that I have slotted for later."

"The really important things?" she echoed. "Slotted for later?"

He nodded, hoping that the fact that she could only mimic what he was saying himself meant that she was really, really nervous. It would help enormously if she was as uncertain about what the evening ahead held as he was. Why that would be helpful, Preston couldn't very well say, but there it was all the same.

"Really important things," he assured her, noting reluctantly that now *he* was the one doing the mimicking, and wasn't that just *too* interesting? "For example, I can't wait to show you what I have planned for nine forty-five."

seven

At 9:42 that evening, Marnie found herself sitting exactly where she had been the night before, in her porch swing, with Preston Atherton IV sitting beside her. But this time he was sitting a lot closer than he had been the night before, had even draped one arm along the back of the swing behind her. And this time the rhythmic back-and-forth motion and the musical creak-jangle accompaniment weren't nearly as comforting as they had been the night before. And this time there was an awkwardness between them that hadn't been there the night before. Because this time she and Preston were barely speaking a word to each other.

Oh, their dinner conversation had gone along just fine— they'd chattered like magpies all through that. Not about anything in particular, but about everything under the sun. She'd heard things about Preston she hadn't begun to suspect. For instance, she'd had no idea that he had been voted "Prettiest Eyes" in his high school senior class superlatives. She wasn't exactly surprised by the revelation, but it had been unexpected.

She'd also learned quite a bit about his childhood, snippets of essential information such as that his dog was named Buddy, that Twister had been his favorite game, that he'd unscrewed his Oreos *before* dipping them in his milk, that he'd listened to his transistor radio and read by flashlight long after his parents went to bed, and that he'd never quite gotten the hang of the clarinet.

Mamie, in turn, had revealed all her vital statistics, too. She'd told Preston all about her cat, Mick, that she'd been an absolute whiz at Clue, that she'd preferred her Oreos intact while dipping, that Butternut always got lousy radio reception after dark, so she'd had no musical accompaniment herself while *she* read by flashlight after her aunt Gert went to bed, and that she herself had never been very good on the piano. And, of course, there was the fact that she herself had been voted by her senior class "Most Likely to Succeed." But then, there had only been fourteen people in her senior class, and all of them had been voted something.

All things considered, it had turned out that she and Preston had quite a few things in common, after all. Funny how stuff worked out sometimes.

And funny that their conversation had stalled the way it had the minute they sat down on the swing. 'Course, that might have been on account of how Preston was sitting so close, she conceded. Or it might have been on account of how he'd asked her not to turn on the porch light, because he wanted to watch the lightning bugs in the dark. Or it might have been on account of how the night sky was so littered with stars and a fat, full moon just right for lovers. Or it might have been on account of how she found herself feeling about him just now.

Because here she sat, all alone in the dark with a man who she realized she couldn't keep telling herself she didn't know. Even having met him such a short time ago, she realized she knew Preston Atherton IV pretty dang well. And knowing him only made her want him all that much more. And wanting him, she knew, was an impossible thing. Because, as much as they had in common, there was no way a man like him could ever be happy in a place like Butternut. And, as much as they had in common, there was no way a woman like her could ever be happy in a place like New York.

Oh, sure, she wouldn't mind visiting a time or two. It would be very exciting. But she couldn't imagine sharing a town with millions and millions and *millions* of people. New York, she was sure, was noisy and fast and tall and bright, and probably it went on for miles and miles until forever. She'd grown up in Butternut, which, granted, did go on for miles and miles, but those miles were filled with cows and corn and horses and hay, not millions of people. It was neither noisy nor fast here. And it certainly wasn't tall or bright. It was slow and peaceful and languid and cozy. And Mamie just couldn't handle living her life any other way.

"What are you thinking about?"

The question stirred her from her reverie the same way a cannon shot might have. As a result, she snapped her head around so fast she almost lost it. And when she did, she heard Preston chuckle low, saw the soft smile that curved his mouth and warmed his eyes, and felt the dance of his fingertips as they skimmed along her bare upper arm.

Oh, boy, she thought. This was gettin' interestin'.

She remembered a couple of other hot summer nights sitting on this very porch swing with handsome men she knew very well and cared for very much. And she remembered how, and where, those couple of hot summer nights had ended up—namely, the bedroom. Now her heart hammered rapid-fire against her rib cage, because back then, what she'd felt for those men when she'd ended up doing what she had with them . . . Well, back then, she'd fancied herself in love. But what she'd felt back then . . .

What she'd felt back then was *nothing* compared to what had erupted inside her for Preston. And all he'd done so far tonight was touch her a few times. And not even in any of the important places, either.

Not yet, anyway.

"Nothin'," she lied in response to his question. "I wasn't thinkin' about anything."

He chuckled again, and the low, lusty sound wrapped itself around her like a comforting blanket. Dang. Just what she needed. Something else to make her feel hot.

The fingers brushing over her upper arm skimmed higher, to the opening of her sleeve. Slowly, he traced the outline of the yellow fabric, firing off little detonations along the way, tiny explosions that seemed to reverberate deep in her midsection. Mamie swallowed hard, but she couldn't quite bring herself to look at his face. Instead, in the pale blue patch of moonlight, she watched the way his blunt-tipped fingers moved along the sun-darkened skin of her shoulder.

"You sure didn't look like you were thinkin' about nothin'," he told her, dropping the *g* on two of the words to imitate her drawl.

She wanted to smile, but was just too nervous. "Then what did I look like I was thinkin' about?" she asked him. Finally, finally, she found the courage to brave a glance at his face. And she was just in time to see his smile fall some.

"Actually," he said softly, "you looked kind of troubled about something. What's wrong?"

Instead of answering, Mamie pushed her toe against the porch and set the swing into easy motion again. Back . . . forth . . . back . . . forth . . . Creak. Jangle. Creak. Jangle. And, pretending the answer didn't matter at all, she asked him, "What's New York City really like?"

He sighed heavily in response, and somehow she got the impression that he didn't much want to talk about his hometown. In spite of that, he replied, "It's big. Busy. Alive. There's so much energy there, so much . . . so much life. So many people, of all different kinds. Performing all kinds of jobs and roles. There are a million sounds, a million sights, a million things to do at any given moment. It's hard to describe unless you've been there. Or else," he added, sounding a bit hesitant. "Or else . . . go there."

She smiled sadly. "No chance of that."

He smiled not at all. "Why not?"

She shrugged. "I dunno. I'm not much of a city person, I guess. I don't think I'd be comfortable in a place that big, with that many people around."

"You might like it more than you think."

She gave the concept some consideration before finally shaking her head. "No. I'm happy here. This is the kind of life I want. The kind I need."

And why was she telling him that? she wondered. It wasn't like that was something he wanted to know.

She glanced back up at his face again, not out of any curiosity over his reaction, but because he had begun to strum his fingers lightly up and down her upper arm again. But this time, when he reached the edge of her sleeveless blouse, for just the briefest, tiniest of moments, he ducked his fingers inside, beneath the fabric. At the sight of those darting fingers, and at the quick rush of heat over her skin, Mamie's breath caught in her throat. Then she inhaled deeply and silently willed her heart rate to slow down. She'd almost succeeded when Preston said something that made her pulse leap right back up into triple digits.

"You could come back to New York with me . . . for a visit, I mean."

His voice was very low when he said it, and his gaze was fixed not on her face but on the fingers that were playing about the opening to her sleeve. Mamie told herself to say something—anything—in response, if for no other reason than to be polite. But before she could utter a word, he hastily continued, still avoiding her gaze.

"I mean, you yourself said you don't have any bookings here at the Bide-a-Wee. You could come up for a week or so. I'd be happy to show you the sights. It would be fun. And exciting." Now, finally, he did glance up from her shoulder to meet her gaze. "For both of us, I'd wager."

Mamie swallowed hard. "I . . . Where would I stay?" she asked. "I can't afford a hotel up there. They probably cost a hundred dollars a night."

He smiled. "More like two hundred. At least."

She gaped at him. "Two hundred dollars a night? Just for a hotel room?"

"Well, they do have the facilities right there in the room," he told her. "You don't have to go down to the end of the hall."

She smiled back. "I've heard that such places existed, but I didn't know it was true," she said playfully. "Imagine. A bathroom right there in your hotel room. Modern conveniences. What will they think of next?"

He held her gaze a moment more in silence, then told her, "You wouldn't have to stay in a hotel, Mamie."

She wasn't sure where she found the strength to do it, but somehow she managed to put voice to the word, "No?"

He shook his head and dropped his gaze back down to her shoulder. Once again, he started up with the slow . . . maddeningly slow . . . oh, she wasn't sure she could stand it, it was so slow . . . to-and-fro movement of his fingers over her bare flesh.

"No," he replied. "You could stay with . . . with me."

Mamie inhaled another slow, deep breath and released it as evenly as she could manage—which, ultimately, wasn't very even at all. "I . . . I could, huh?" she stammered.

He nodded. "If you want to."

Oh, she wanted to, she thought. She wanted to real bad. The offer was so tempting. But it would be the height of foolishness to agree to such a proposal. No, not a proposal, she corrected herself. Not even close. What Preston had just made was a proposition, plain and simple. And propositions rarely turned out the way they were supposed to.

"Thank you," she said softly. "But I can't."

The fingers skittering along her arm faltered for a moment, hesitated, then began to move in that maddeningly slow way again. And to make matters worse—or, rather, better . . . maybe—the arm he'd stretched along the back of the swing dropped some and landed, not too surprisingly, across Mamie's shoulders.

"Why not?" he asked.

" 'Cause . . .'cause I belong here . . . here in Butternut. That's why," she told him.

He looked up then, fixing his dark gaze intently on her face, something that made her glance away, to some vague point behind him. She found herself staring at a big daddy longlegs, caught in a slice of moonlight, who had affixed himself to the wall of the house.

And, as if from a great, far distance away, she heard Preston say, "It wouldn't have to be forever, Mamie."

She nodded slowly. "I know, Preston. That's the problem. It wouldn't be forever."

"Oh, Mamie . . ."

Something in his voice, something husky and uncertain and needful, made her turn her attention back to his face. And when she did, her breath caught in her throat, because for just the merest of moments, she saw something in his eyes she dared not hope was true. And then, just as her amazement turned to astonishment, he dipped his head toward hers. For a second, just a tiny, infinitesimal second, he hesitated, as if he weren't quite sure what to do. So, impulsively, Mamie helped him, tipping her own head up to his, meeting him—almost—halfway.

His mouth covered hers in a slow, easy kiss, exploratory and tentative, as if he wanted to take his time figuring things out. Mamie, of course, was content to let him do it. Because she realized, not much to her surprise, that she wanted to take her time, too.

The fingers on her arm grazed up over her sleeve, along her shoulder, and past her collar, to caress the delicate indentation at the base of her throat. The skin-to-skin contact caused a whir of electricity to spiral through her torso, puddling in her belly before spreading lower still. Not sure when she had decided to do it, she found that her own fingers had gone exploring too, had curled around Preston's warm neck and threaded into his dark hair.

It felt so good to touch him, even so gingerly. It had been so long since she'd held a man this way, so long since she'd *wanted* to hold a man this way. So long since any man had come close to making her feel like . . . like . . . like a woman. So long.

So *long*.

She skimmed her thumb lightly over his rough jaw as she lifted her other hand to tuck it inside the collar of his shirt. The skin she encountered beneath was warm and damp and alive, seeming to shiver and shimmy everywhere she touched him. And the more she touched him, the closer their bodies came together, until Preston had roped one arm around her waist and pulled her tight against him.

And then things really got interesting.

The lips that grazed hers so softly seemed to lose focus

for a minute, because she felt them skimming insistently along her cheek, her jaw, her temple, her forehead, before moving down to her throat. Instinctively, she drove her fingers more insistently into his hair, pulling him closer still. Then she tilted her head to the side, to facilitate his exploration, sighing her contentment . . . and something else, too—she wasn't quite sure what. When she did, she inhaled a great breath of him and immediately grew intoxicated by the heavy, heady, masculine scent that filled her nose and lungs.

Dizzy from the sensation, she dropped her hand to the top button of his shirt and, without even thinking about what she was doing, freed it from its binding. The next button quickly followed, then another and another, until she could shove her hand beneath the fabric and find more of him to investigate. Impatiently, she opened her hand over the center of his chest and felt his heart pounding wildly beneath her palm. She felt the bunch and dance of solid muscle beneath her fingertips, felt the dark hair tangle around her fingers, as if trying to trap them there forever.

And it was with no small surprise, or dismay, that Mamie realized she wanted to be there forever. Holding Preston. Forever. Kissing Preston. Forever. Doing . . . other things . . . with Preston, too.

Forever.

Before she had the chance to ponder that revelation beyond its superficial meaning, he returned his mouth to hers and kissed her again. But whereas before he had brushed his lips over hers with a gentle and tender rhythm, now he was more insistent. More passionate. More demanding. More . . . more *everything*.

And Mamie, very willingly, gave him all he asked for, and commanded even more for herself in return.

She opened her mouth under his, and he instantly took advantage by thrusting his tongue inside to taste her. As he deepened the kiss, she felt his fingers working feverishly at the buttons on her blouse, quickly unfastening them one by one by one. When he'd freed them all, he began tugging her shirttails free of her shorts. That done, he cupped his hand over the lacy confines of her brassiere, palming her breast expertly before raking the pad of his thumb purposefully across the nipple.

Mamie gasped at the blatant, oh-so-erotic, liberty, but instead of urging him to halt, she arched her body forward, more completely into his grasp. Preston uttered a low, predatory growl and moved his hand higher, pushing the strap of her bra down over her arm until her breast spilled free of its confinement. Then he covered it with his hand again, more possessively this time, filling his palm with her, weighing the plump flesh as he stroked and caressed it.

It was almost more than Mamie could bear. She threw her head backward, ready to give him everything he demanded, everything he wanted, everything she needed to give him in return. Then she remembered they were sitting on her front porch, and although they'd never bothered to turn on the light overhead, they were still on public view to anyone willing to look hard enough to find them.

At the realization, she leapt up blindly from the swing and, without explaining her actions, fled toward the front door. The screen slapped against the jamb behind her as she raced toward the stairway, then echoed the sound again when Preston followed her through. He caught up with her at the foot of the steps, curled his fingers around her bare upper arm, and pulled her back toward him. Then he dipped his head to hers and captured her mouth again, in a *very* commanding kiss. And then Mamie was in his arms once again, right where she'd been before, right where she wanted to be forever.

Except that this time they were much, much closer to her bed. And this time there was almost no chance that they'd be caught by anyone passing by outside. So this time she couldn't think of a single reason why they should stop.

Preston seemed to understand that, too, because he pushed her shirt completely off her shoulders then and hastily unfastened her brassiere, tossing it too to the floor. Then he shrugged out of his own shirt and pulled her close, pressing their damp, heated bodies intimately together. The sensation of rough hair grazing her tender breasts made Mamie cry out in frustration, desire, need. She splayed her hands over his naked back, reveling in the power and strength and heat she found there.

As she explored every solid ridge of muscle, every firm line of sinew, Preston mimicked her motions, running his hands over every last inch of her bare back. Again and again he kissed her, carrying her higher and higher each time. And lower and lower his hands wandered, until he cupped them over the taut curves of her denim-clad derriere and pushed forward, rubbing himself languidly, wantonly, against her when he did. The sensation that shot through her on that intimate contact was . . .

Oh.

Electric. Erotic. Explosive. Mamie felt as if someone had launched a bottle rocket much too close to her person and it had penetrated her to the very deepest part of her soul. When he pushed her toward himself again, the delicious friction of his body ignited her from thigh to breast. Gripping his naked shoulders with insistent fingers, she lifted herself on tiptoe to meet him.

This time Preston was the one to cry out his need, his frustration, his anguish, in a low, guttural voice that she scarcely recognized as his. His hands on her bottom clenched tight, his fingers digging low, to where her brief cutoffs ended and her legs began. He curved one hand under her thigh and jerked upward, opening her to himself, wrapping that leg halfway around his waist. And then he slammed his body into hers again, and Mamie nearly came apart at the seams.

Only then did she realize how far the two of them had carried what had started off as an innocent kiss. And then she realized that their kiss had been anything but innocent. It had been generated by a need too great for either of them to ignore, by a passion that neither of them understood, and, at least for her, by a love that she had never known with anyone else.

Because she understood then that the reason she reacted so intensely, so immediately, to Preston was because somehow, even over such a short passage of time, she had fallen in love with him. And if she allowed what they were doing to continue . . . If she allowed her heart to rule her and made love to him now, the way she wanted so very much to do . . . If she discovered with him that ultimate joy that came with total physical intimacy . . . If Mamie did all that, she'd never, ever, be able to let him go.

And he would go. Of that, she was certain. And when he did, he would take a part of her with him. A part that would stay with him forever. A part she would never recover for herself.

Of course, he'd leave something of himself behind in Butternut, too, she thought vaguely. But it would be little more than a memory. A memory made of moonlight and passion and the lingering scent of roses. It wouldn't be Preston. He'd be long gone.

When that final, desperate thought finally lodged in her mind, Mamie shoved herself away from him, out of his embrace. Before he could stop her, she bent to scoop up her shirt and brassiere, then turned and ran up the stairs as fast as she could go. His surprise at her action bought her a few precious seconds, because although he quickly followed her, Mamie made it to her room and slammed the door shut behind herself. Immediately, she turned the key in the lock, then, in near complete darkness, she leaned back against the door, panting for breath and fighting for coherent thought.

She wasn't surprised by the *boom* of Preston's fist pounding once against the door, but she flinched at hearing it anyway. That single action was all that came, however, because what followed was a silence broken only by her own rapid respiration. After a long moment she heard his hand slide away, followed by a softer sound, one she could only think was his forehead resting against the heavy oak door.

And then, "Mamie, what's wrong?" he asked softly. His voice held no rancor, no disappointment, no frustration. Only genuine solicitude and honest puzzlement. "Why did you pull away? Why did you lock the door? Talk to me."

She closed her eyes and drew in a few more deep, steadying breaths before answering. Finally she said, in a voice just as soft as his, "I can't do this, Preston. I just . . ." She inhaled slowly again, then expelled a rough, ragged breath. "I just . . . I-I can't."

He, too, hesitated before saying anything more. But after a moment, he tried again. "Look, Mamie, I know what just happened . . . I know it seemed to come out of nowhere, but I think it was inevitable. The minute we met, there was just . . . something there. I don't know what it was, but you felt it too. I know you did."

"Yes," she agreed sadly. "I felt it too."

She heard him sigh, then, his voice a bit heartier than it had been, he continued. "I know you and I haven't known each other long, and I know we have absolutely nothing in common. But this thing between us, Mamie. We need to figure it out."

She bit back a strangled, defeated sound. Did he really think that? she wondered. Could he have possibly missed what was so obvious to her?

"Nothing in common?" she echoed. "Preston . . . we have *everything* in common. Don't you see that? Everything that's important, anyway. And I . . . we . . ." She swallowed hard and sighed deeply again. "Knowing that you're so . . . so . . . so *perfect* for me, so *right*," she said, "and then having you leave . . . I just can't do it, that's all. I couldn't stand it. Knowing you're out there in the world, but that I'll never see you again . . . I can't do it."

There was a long pause from the other side of the door, then, so quietly that she almost didn't hear, he asked, "You think we have everything in common? You think I'm . . . perfect for you? That I'm . . . that I'm . . . right?"

She nodded, then realizing he couldn't possibly see the gesture, she replied, "Yes. I do."

Another lengthy silence, then, "I see," he said softly.

She wondered if he really did. Wondered if he understood what was happening—what had already happened—as well as she did. And she wondered, too, if he felt as hopeless and helpless as she did.

Because it sure was clear to Mamie. She loved Preston.

And she couldn't have him. Even though the two of them complemented each other perfectly, they could never be together. As alike as the two of them were in all the ways that counted, their worlds would never mesh. He was a businessman with expensive tastes, used to big-city living. She was perfectly content with her empty bed-and-breakfast and her yard full of roses.

Well, not quite *perfectly* content, she conceded reluctantly. But there was little she could do about that now.

She heard another sound coming through the door then and turned her head to listen. But when she finally recognized what it was, she closed her eyes tight against the tears that threatened. Because she realized that the sound she was hearing beyond her bedroom door was the soft scuff of Preston's footsteps . . . as he slowly, methodically, walked away.

eight

As fortune—or rather, *mis*fortune, as Preston was more inclined to consider it now—would have it, Samuel Butternut returned from his fishing trip the very next morning. That was likely due, he thought, to the fact that it was raining like a . . . like a . . . What was that delightful phrase Mamie had once used? Oh, yes. Raining like a . . . big dog . . . in Butternut.

He stood in the dining room of the Bide-a-Wee Bed and Breakfast, the bag of goobers on a nearby table, having once again donned his business armor of suit and tie in anticipation of Samuel Butternut's arrival at the appointed 2:00 P.M. But seeing as how that was still a good thirty minutes away, Preston only gazed through the screen door at the curtain of rain pelting the great outdoors, his mind on something other than business. Not surprisingly, his thoughts were lingering on Mamie Calhoun.

And he hadn't even scheduled any thoughts of her to linger that morning. No, he'd rather thought he would wait and schedule that for after he got home. Because he knew lingering thoughts of Mamie were going to be inescapable upon his return to New York. He'd no doubt be blocking out a good portion of each day just so he'd have time enough to manage them.

For this morning he'd scheduled, in mental indelible ink,

his efforts to not think about her at all. Because once his business with Samuel Butternut was concluded—at approximately 4:30, by Preston's estimated agenda—he would go upstairs to pack his bag and leave the Bide-a-Wee, and Mamie, once and for all. He was booked on a flight from Birmingham to New York at 9:48 that night.

Naturally, that made him think about what he'd been doing at 9:48 *last* night, which in turn—since those memories included Mamie—brought back those lingering thoughts of her. And that, once again, just threw him way off schedule.

Oh, the hell with it, he thought, allowing himself to think all he wanted to about Mamie Calhoun. About how she had felt all warm and soft and willing when he'd held her half-naked in his arms the night before. About the wild, raucous heat she had generated inside him, just by the simple act of touching him. About how close the two of them had come to coupling in the most basic, intimate way a man and a woman could. About how she had fled from him before that could happen. And about what she had said to him a few minutes later through the barrier of her locked bedroom door.

Preston . . . we have everything *in common.*

Knowing that you're so . . . so . . . so perfect *for me, so* right *. . . I can't do it.*

She couldn't do it, he echoed morosely to himself again. She couldn't make love with him last night because he was perfect for her. Because he was right. Because they had everything in common.

Because she loved him?

Somehow, that was the question that had been circling through his brain over and over again since he'd retreated to his own room last night. Was that what she'd been trying to tell him, without having to tell him? That she loved him? Could it be possible?

He told himself he should just forget about it. All of it. But there was no way that was going to happen, he knew. No matter how much he tried to schedule in forgetting Mamie Calhoun, there was no way he would *ever* forget Mamie Calhoun. Because she was, if nothing else—and certainly, she was *plenty* else . . . He sighed again. Unforgettable. That's what she was.

His life was never going to be the same.

Certainly he could go back to New York as planned—as scheduled—and return to his penthouse with all its modern conveniences that were programmed to act and react according to his instructions and his agenda. He could return to air-conditioning and facilities that *weren't* located in a cramped room at the end of the hall. He could return to a bed that didn't require climbing a flight of stairs to get into it. He could return to being groomed by his father to take over a company he'd never really been sure he wanted in the first place.

Oh, joy. Oh, bliss. Oh, rapture.

Funny, but as joyful, blissful, and rapturous as he'd once thought his future—not to mention his present—to be, he realized that he'd never really known what any of those things were. He could say that, because he *did* know what they were now. Now that he'd met Miss Mamie Calhoun. Now that he'd held her in his arms and joined his mouth to hers and clung to her in ways that he had never before known were possible. Now that he'd fallen in love with the kind of woman who turned his world—himself—completely upside down.

Love, he echoed to himself. Was that truly what it was he felt for her? After such a short time? It must be, he decided, because what he felt for Mamie was utterly different from anything he'd ever experienced for anyone else. Infatuation, he knew well. Desire, he knew very, *very* well. But neither of those came close to describing the feelings he had for Mamie.

Feelings of hope and promise and contentment and happiness. Feelings of connection and admiration and possibility and serenity. Feelings of respect and communion and mirth and life.

What else could inspire all those things in him, but love?

And now that he had recognized his response to her, what was he going to do about it? She had already made it clear that she wouldn't be happy in New York, and even without attempting it, Preston was inclined to agree with her. Mamie didn't belong there—that was clear. Then again, was he all that happy in New York himself? Because he was beginning to suspect that maybe he didn't belong there either, and that perhaps he belonged . . .

Somewhere else.

He recalled the way Mamie had looked, surrounded by her roses, as if she were a part of the lush landscape behind her. He remembered how she had looked sitting on the porch swing that night, serenading him with the musical creak-jangle of wicker and chain. He thought back on the way she had sat at a scarred Formica table in Fern and Moody's, studying a paper menu that invited, "Come 'n' get it!" No, he couldn't imagine her anywhere but here. And he couldn't imagine himself anywhere without her. So the question now was . . .

Could he imagine himself here with her?

"Preston?"

He jerked around at the sound of his name uttered in that lyrical, lilting voice, and found Mamie standing at the foot of the stairs. Instead of her usual uniform of cutoffs and brief shirt, she had donned a dress the pale-yellow color of butter. As always, she was barefoot, and that made him smile.

She had avoided him since sunup, even with the relentless rainfall. She hadn't gone anywhere, but she'd somehow managed to be wherever he *wasn't* in the inn. Every time he'd entered a room, it was to hear her footsteps retreating, and he'd been left with nothing but his memories and the lingering fragrance of roses. Finally, he'd just given up exchanging a word with her until it was time for him to leave. Now, however, that was looking unlikely.

Both the giving up of exchanging of words . . . *and* the leaving, he realized. Astonishingly enough, however, the thought of not leaving, of not returning to New York anytime in the near future, of staying here in Butternut, Alabama, with Mamie for a while . . . or forever . . . Well, the thought just didn't alarm Preston as much as he might have thought it would, once upon a time. On the contrary, the thought actually made him feel rather. . . . good. Rather peaceful. Rather right.

"Sam just called," she told him. "He said he was going to be a little late getting here, but he promised he'd make it by two-thirty. Just between you and me, though, I wouldn't expect to see him before suppertime. He was wrapping some new flies when he called."

Preston nodded, only mildly surprised to realize that he was bothered not at all by the way Samuel's non-appearance would throw off his schedule. Because, really. What good was keeping a schedule when it was filled with things you didn't want to do anyway?

"That's all right," he said. And, just like that, he felt as if a huge weight tumbled right off his shoulders. Wow. That felt . . . wonderful.

Mamie arched her eyebrows in obvious surprise. "It is? I mean, it'll mess up your schedule, won't it?"

He smiled and shrugged. "Ever since coming to Butternut, I've been rearranging my schedule," he said mildly.

She wrinkled her nose in apology. "I'm sorry about that. It's just sorta the way things are down here."

"I know it is. And I'm not sorry at all about it. Because now seems like a rather good time to rearrange my schedule again. Only *this* time, I intend to make sure I stick to my agenda."

Her confusion was compounded by his statement, but she said nothing in reply.

Preston couldn't help but chuckle, mostly because he just felt so damned good. "Mamie," he said, "we need to talk."

This time her brows arrowed downward in obvious concern. "I thought we said everything we needed to say last night."

He shook his head. "No, we didn't say nearly enough last night. We didn't even cover the highlights. Well, except for maybe one," he hastily amended.

Her lips parted fractionally, as if she needed a little help breathing. "And which highlight was that?" she asked, her voice sounding distant and shallow.

He shoved his hands in his trouser pockets and began to stride toward her, slowly, leisurely, taking his time so he didn't spook her the way he had last night. Finally, he halted, when only a few inches separated them. And even though he wanted to reach out to her and pull her into his arms, he decided not to push his luck. Not yet.

And he told her, "The one about me being perfect, being right, for you."

Her gaze wavered from his not at all, but she swallowed with some difficulty. "And what, uh . . . what were the highlights we missed?" she asked.

A wayward russet curl dangled near her cheek, and Preston, unable to help himself, reached up to loop it around his index finger. He found some reassurance in the fact that she let him do it, but not enough to venture any further advance.

He fixed his gaze on the silky tress wound about his finger as he told her, "Well, one of those highlights we missed was about how you're so perfect, so right, for me, too."

She inhaled a quick breath, and he switched his gaze to her eyes, noting how her pupils expanded to nearly eclipse the pale green of her irises. She offered no other response beyond that hasty gasp, however, so he had no way of knowing exactly what she was thinking.

"You're right, Mamie," he said. "We do have everything that's important in common. The way we are together . . ." He sighed softly. "I'd wager there are people out there who've been together for decades who couldn't possibly know each other the way you and I do."

"Oh, Preston . . ." Her voice broke on his name, and she didn't continue, but her eyes filled with moisture that somehow made them seem even larger, even deeper, than they already were.

"And I'd also wager there are people out there who've been together for decades who couldn't possibly . . ."

"What?" she asked almost soundlessly when he left the observation unfinished.

He hesitated, thinking maybe it was still a bit too soon

to put words to the feelings that were planting themselves so resolutely in his heart. "Well," he began slowly, "let's just say that I'd wager that there are people out there who've been together for decades who couldn't possibly . . . feel for each other the way you and I do."

She bit her lip, and two fat tears spilled down her cheeks. But all she did was repeat, "Oh, Preston . . ." leaving the declaration incomplete once again.

His heart hammered hard in his rib cage as he looked down into her eyes and saw her emotions as clear as day, emotions that mirrored his own. She loved him. Even if she was no more ready than he to admit it aloud yet, the two of them were most definitely of one mind on that matter. And suddenly, nothing seemed impossible.

He completed the final step that brought his body flush against hers, then framed her face with both hands and thumbed away her tears. The gesture was fruitless, because two more took their place, but instead of sobbing, Mamie laughed—a rich, happy, triumphant laugh that warmed Preston to his very heart and soul.

Great. They'd finally gotten rain and a break in the heat, and now he was going to start feeling warm all over again. Funny, what he'd begun to think of as his short, hot summer in Butternut was looking to last a good bit longer and be a good bit hotter.

"I'm not going back to New York tonight," he said suddenly, but not so impulsively. Deep down, he realized the decision had been made long before now. "I'm staying here, Mamie. With you. We have a lot to talk about. A lot of things we need to do together." He smiled. "And true to Butternut tradition, I don't want to rush any of them."

She laughed again, but this time she was clearly uncertain. "But what about Sam? What about Butternut Industries? Aren't you s'pose to have some kind of merger? Didn't you once tell me you were s'pose to take over for your father someday?"

"That's fifteen years off, at least," he said, knowing it was true. "Probably more. My father is the kind of man who will work until he just can't work anymore. He has plenty of time to groom someone else to take over, someone who's far more interested in the position than I am."

"But the merger . . ."

"Oh, I'll take care of all that," he assured her. "I won't shirk my responsibilities there." He pulled her closer, pressing his forehead lightly to hers. "But I won't shirk them here, either. Once the merger is complete . . ." He shrugged, totally unconcerned. "I think I deserve a vacation. It's been years since I've taken one. And what better place to have one than Butternut, Alabama, birthplace of Danny Jim Robinson, soon to be tourist attraction? I kind of like it here," he added. "In fact, I like it so much, I might just look for work here."

Mamie gaped at him. "You're a businessman, Preston," she finally pointed out. "What're you gonna do here in Butternut?"

He smiled. "Go into business."

"What kind of business?"

He draped his arms over her shoulders and pulled her closer still. "Well, I hear the planning commission here has great things in store for Butternut."

She nodded, smiling, then wrapped her own arms around his waist. "That's true enough," she said with a smile.

"And, being a businessman, I happen to be very good at planning," he said. "I have *lots* of ideas."

"I did sorta notice that about you early on," she told him, a merry twinkle dancing in her eyes. "But I haven't noticed any of your ideas being particularly businesslike. If you know what I mean."

He grinned suggestively. "That's because you've only been witness to the ideas I have about you. And those have been anything *but* businesslike."

"I did sorta notice that, too."

"Well, then, Miss Mamie," he said, "I suggest we consider a merger, you and I."

He could tell she found that proposal *very* interesting. But all she said was, "Oh?"

He nodded. "Yes, and it's a very unbusinesslike merger, too."

Rather hopefully, she asked, "And just when do you plan on scheduling this merger?"

He tilted his wrist toward himself and idly noted the time, then hastily unfastened his watch and tossed the expensive timepiece over his shoulder. "Oh, I don't know," he said. "Maybe today. Maybe tomorrow. Maybe today *and* tomorrow. For now, I'd like to just see how things develop."

Mamie nodded, smiling brightly. "Sounds like a good plan to me."

Preston smiled back. It did sound like a good plan. He hastily completed his agenda for the next, oh . . . sixty or seventy years. Yes, this time, he thought, it was definitely a schedule he could keep.

Pride and Prejudice

Emily Carmichael

one

The Hyatt Regency in downtown Chicago was not some cheap roadside inn that would admit just anyone. Normally the patrons were required at least to have opposable thumbs and walk upright. The standards had been relaxed a bit for the coming few days, however, and on this evening a number of four-legged guests paraded through the lobby, most leaving damp pawprints on the polished marble floor and trails of muddy water droplets across the plush carpeting. At least, the management hoped the droplets on the carpeting were water. The International Kennel Club of Chicago, which was the host of the annual canine extravaganza in the adjoining McCormick Place Convention Hall, had assured the Hyatt that well-mannered show dogs would never mistake expensive carpeting for grass or potted plants for trees.

Certainly the dog that pranced through the entrance just before eleven that night wouldn't make such a rude mistake. She was much, much too civilized for that. Moreover, in spite of the messy February slush that covered the streets and sidewalks, her tiny paws left not a smudge on the floor—which is more than could be said for her mistress, whose designer aerobic training shoes left waffled footprints as she crossed to the check-in counter.

"Josephine Blake," she told the desk clerk, shaking the

water from her stylish leather jacket. "I have a reservation."

The clerk smiled with Hyatt hospitality. "Damp out tonight, is it?"

"A bit more than damp. Wind, snow, sleet—take your choice." Self-consciously, she finger-combed short, curly hair that had been tangled by the wind. Her shoulders were too tired to do anything but slump, and she could feel her mascara running. Even the waterproof "twenty-four-hour" stuff gave up after an eighteen-hour day and a two-block walk through snow and sleet.

"Here you are, Ms. Blake. Sixty-seven twenty Highland Drive, Chicago? Staying until Monday?"

"Right. We're here for the dog show. The manager said it wouldn't be a problem to have Priss stay with me in the room."

"No, indeed. We're honored to have such a celebrity in residence." The clerk stretched over the counter to admire the little black-and-white papillon, whose butterfly-wing ears came alert at the attention. "Of course I recognize you, Miss Priss. My daughter's a big fan. Before you leave, you'll have to give me your autograph to take to her."

Josie was the creator of the nationally syndicated cartoon strip *Miss Priss*, but her little papillon was the star and the inspiration of the strip. Priss's cartoon alter ego was as familiar to most people as Dagwood or Snoopy. The diminutive celebrity soaked up all the fawning she could get.

"Priss will be glad to give your daughter a pawtograph. In fact, if your daughter comes in some evening, she could probably get a Priss kiss right on the nose. Priss is big on that."

"That'd be terrific. She'd be thrilled. Me, too."

Josie obligingly scooped up the dog and held her face to face with the clerk, a sensible-looking thirty-something lady who blushed with pleasure when Priss's tiny tongue snaked out and delicately kissed her powdered nose. Tired as she was, Josie laughed. She always got a kick out of seeing a six-pound dog reduce an adult human being to a fit of childish twitters. That happened a lot when Priss was around.

"Oh, she's such a doll!"

"Can you take the key, Priss?"

The clerk held out a key card for Priss to take in her tiny jaws. "Look at that!" she chortled as the dog dropped the card in Josie's hand. "She's better behaved than my daughter."

"The room is . . . ?"

"Oh, sorry! Five-oh-eight. Fifth floor. Elevators are through the lobby on the left. Would you like help with your luggage?"

"Thanks, but I have my own cart."

As Josie wheeled her luggage to the fifth floor, Priss rode grandly on top of the pile—two suitcases, a case containing her drawing board and art supplies, a tack box, a folded grooming table, and a plastic bin containing dog food, dog dishes, dog toys, and special liver treats.

"You're lucky you're not bigger," Josie grumbled to the dog. "I'd make you pull it. What a day! All I want right now is a hot bath and a cozy bed."

The key card snicked neatly into the slot and the door clicked open. Josie flicked the light switch as Priss jumped down from the luggage pile and bounced into the room. "Don't go looking for crumbs under the bed, you little hairy Hoover. You'll get dust up your nose and—"

She stopped short when something black, white, and shaggy rose from the bed.

"What on earth . . . ?"

Josie's gasp was echoed by Priss's shriek of alarm, a sound that might have come from an abused squeaky toy. The shaggy beast was a border collie, and it was not alone. A man appeared from the tangle of sheets and blankets. Propped on one elbow, displaying an alarming expanse of nakedness, he squinted against the light and growled a bleary "What izzit?"

Priss launched herself into Josie's arms, where she voiced her indignation with furious yapping.

"Omigod!" Josie felt her face flame. "I'm so sorry! This must be the wrong room."

"What?" the man grumbled. "Stop that goddamned noise!"

Surprisingly, Priss shut up. The man glared at them both.

"I am so sorry!" Josie repeated. "So sorry!" She backed toward the still open door and stumbled over the cart carrying her massive pile of luggage. The luggage toppled, and she and Priss toppled with it, landing on the floor with an "oof!" from Josie and an indignant yap from Priss.

"Good lord!" the man said in disgust. He tore off the bedcovers and started to come to her aid.

"God, no!" Josie clapped a hand over her eyes. "Don't get up."

As if just then realizing his state of undress, he mumbled a surly, "Sorry." Seconds later came the all clear. "You can uncover your eyes now."

Josie cautiously peeked through her fingers. He'd pulled on a pair of exercise shorts that covered the essentials but not much more. From head to toe he was rock-solid and lean, with muscles in all the right places and a height made even more imposing by her perspective from the floor. Her face flamed again as she lowered her hand from her eyes. "I don't know how this happened," she babbled. "I thought the card only worked in the right door, you know, and I thought the room number was right. I guess I was more tired than I thought, and my eyes must have played a trick, you know, because I surely wouldn't have just barged in on a man in bed, especially a naked . . . oh, shit!" Josie frequently babbled when she was nervous, and she hated it. She was twenty-eight years old, successful, and in a tax bracket that forced her to employ two accountants. She shouldn't lose her cool just because she was sprawled on the floor of a hotel room at the feet of an all but naked and entirely teed-off man who had an intimidating stare that rivaled that of his equally teed-off border collie.

"You okay?" the man asked.

"Just dandy."

He offered a hand up. Gingerly, she took it. His hand was broad and hard. Sinew and muscle corded the arm that pulled her to her feet. This guy was no office jock, or if he was, he was a lumberjack in his off hours.

Priss yapped for attention, but promptly fell silent when the man's gaze shifted to her.

"She okay?"

Josie scooped up the little dog and tucked her safely under an arm. "She's fine. If she weren't, she'd be doing her Camille act. She doesn't have a stoic bone in her body." For a moment, Josie couldn't bring herself to look away from the man, no matter that staring was terribly rude. She felt like an idiot. She *was* an idiot, standing there ogling the guy while he waited for her to get the heck out and leave him in peace.

A worried whine from the border collie brought Josie out of her momentary trance. She tore her eyes away with a sheepish look. "Let me just pick up my luggage and get out of your hair. Like I said—" Her eyes brushed past the number on the open door, then jumped back to it. "Five-oh-eight. This is the right room! You're in my room!"

"I beg your pardon," he returned in an exasperated tone. "This is my room. I checked in at five, ordered room service, talked to the desk clerk a couple of times—this is definitely *my* room."

"Well, it's my room as well," she snapped. The coveted hot bath and cozy bed were going up in the smoke of hotel incompetence, and Josie wanted someone to yell at. "Where's the phone?"

He gestured to the bedside table.

"If you don't mind," she said curtly.

"Be my guest."

She set Priss on the bed, where the papillon struck a queenly pose and eyed the border collie, who sat alertly at his master's side. The border collie, for his part, afforded the tiny dog only a passing glance as he regarded the whole situation with judicial gravity.

Josie tapped impatient fingers on the table while she waited for the desk to answer. Finally, "Hello, this is Josephine Blake. You double-booked my room—five-oh-eight. There's someone already in here. I want to . . . no! Wait! Damn!" She cast a halfway apologetic look at the man, who looked almost as impatient and tired as she felt. "Hold," she explained.

He nodded, yawned, and stretched. Oh, how he stretched. Josie wished he would put on some clothes. Or maybe she didn't.

"Hello! Yes, Mr . . . Well, yes. No, I didn't stumble into the wrong room. How would my key card have worked in the wrong room? Your reservations people . . . But can't you . . . ? What? All right. Yes. Give us a minute."

The fellow had propped his very tight butt against the low dresser and leaned back, his arms folded across his chest. George of the Jungle, Josie thought. She was going insane, and she really, really needed some sleep.

"The manager wants to see us."

"He does, does he?"

"Yes, he does."

He looked longingly at his bed, then sighed. "I guess I'd better put some clothes on, then." He opened a drawer where T-shirts and jeans were arranged in two precisely aligned stacks, then another drawer that contained rolled pairs of socks—all in a row, marching in military precision beside neatly folded undershorts.

Josie diverted her eyes from the undershorts.

"I'm Scott McBride, by the way. And the border collie is Iowa."

"Josephine Blake."

"So I heard."

Scott McBride and his clothes disappeared into the bathroom, leaving Josie to wait with the two dogs. Priss made eyes at Iowa, who ignored her and stared directly at Josie as if to warn her she was in the room merely on tolerance. She sank wearily to the bed, collapsing onto her back and stifling the urge to laugh. It was the great gift of her life that she was able to see the humor of just about any situation—one of the reasons she was able to make a living writing a comic strip. She didn't see anything here that she could translate into cartoon whimsy for *Miss Priss,* but the lingering image of her sprawled like an idiot on the floor, hiding her eyes from a naked man, did strike her funny bone.

The sound of water running in the sink reminded her of the bath she was missing, and her laughter became a groan. Both Priss and Iowa regarded her with curiously cocked heads.

"You wouldn't understand," she told the dogs.

Scott McBride and Iowa. Josie had actually heard of them. Anyone who had ever opened a dog magazine had probably heard of them. Scott was a hotshot trainer of herding and obedience dogs. Iowa had won so many herding trials that when he walked into an arena, the sheep stood up and saluted. Everything from *Dog World Magazine* to Animal Planet cable television featured material either by Scott or about him. Josie had never paid much attention. She and Priss were into conformation competition—the beauty contest side of dog shows. They had little interest in anything that required actual training. That was too much like work.

Josie laughed again, thinking that herding trials and such might hold more interest now that she'd seen Scott McBride naked.

"What's so funny?"

Josie looked up to see the man himself, looking down at her with clear gray eyes. A crisp T-shirt tucked into slim-cut jeans. He turned to the closet and slipped a denim shirt off a hanger.

"I think I'm glued to the mattress," she sighed.

He simply lifted a brow at her, inspiring her to make the effort to get up. If this guy had a sense of humor, it didn't show.

"Will the dogs be all right while we're gone?" she asked.

"Iowa won't touch your little dog."

She took offense at his tone—as if her beautiful little papillon was beneath the border collie's notice. "Well, Priss certainly won't provoke him. She's a very private sort. She likes her space."

The situation did not improve in the manager's office. Once the facts were established, the night manager—a Mr.

Grimes—was all apology. Unfortunately, the hotel was completely booked. Mr. Grimes himself made calls to other establishments in the area. Rooms were available, but none that allowed four-legged as well as two-legged guests. This was downtown Chicago, after all, one hotel reminded them with a sniff.

So only seven hours before she and Priss had to walk into the show ring, pressed, dressed, combed, fluffed, and bright-eyed, Josie sat in the Hyatt lobby with her chin cradled disconsolately in her hands.

"You do have a place to go, right?" Scott asked.

"Oh, sure. I can sleep in the car. Or find some motel in suburbia twenty miles down the road."

"Didn't you tell Mr. Grimes you were from Chicago?"

"Did I?" Josie asked glumly. "Was that when I was threatening the guy with my Mob connections?"

That elicited a brief smile from Scott. Of course *he* could smile. He had her hotel room, with the cozy bed, and the nice hot bath. The double booking wasn't his fault, she acknowledged. But she was in no mood to be rational.

"Can't you just go back to your place and commute to the show? I realize that staying at the Hyatt is more convenient, but—"

"My stupid condo is being completely torn apart and then slowly reassembled for the next stupid month. So, no, I can't go back to my place. I was going to spend the weekend here, then Priss and I were going to visit my sister in Minneapolis. I suppose I could commute from there," she said sarcastically. "It's only a seven-hour drive."

"Oh," was his only comment.

"Damn. Which one of my friends can I call at—what is it?—half past midnight?"

He frowned, chewed his lip, stared at his hands, screwed his mouth to the side of his face, and then sighed. This was not a man, Josie guessed, that took anything lightly—even other people's problems.

"Don't worry about it," she advised. "I'm a big girl. I can always go back to my condo and sleep in plaster dust."

He cleared his throat. "Well, hell. We're both adults.

There shouldn't be any reason why we couldn't both stay in the room. It's a big room, after all. There's even a couple of empty drawers in the dresser."

She crinkled her brow. "Are you inviting me to be your roommate?"

"I wouldn't put it that way. That makes it sound as if . . . well . . . you know."

Josie was tempted to smile as a warm flush colored his face. "I seem to remember there being only one bed."

"I . . . uh . . . I can sleep in the easy chair. And tomorrow I'll have them bring in a rollaway bed. We could get one tonight, I suppose, but who knows how long it would take them to bring it. I need to get some sleep." He yawned mightily, but slid her a sideways, questioning look. "But maybe you have a husband who wouldn't like it if you shared a hotel room with a man, even if the arrangement was perfectly innocent."

She shook her head. "No husband. Not even an ex. What about you? Is there some wife or girlfriend who's going to leap to conclusions?"

"If I had a wife or a girlfriend, she'd be sensible enough not to take offense at a perfectly harmless situation."

Obviously he didn't have a wife or girlfriend, or he would know better. Where men and women were concerned, there was no such thing as a perfectly harmless situation.

Scott rose and shoved his hands into his pockets. "Well . . . uh, Josephine."

"Josie," she corrected.

"Josie." He seemed to contemplate the name for a moment. "It's getting late. We should go up."

Josie didn't remember accepting his offer, but what choice did she have? She wasn't even sure the bathroom in her condo was useable, and sleeping in plaster dust held little appeal. Moreover, declining would make her look like a prude, or worse, give the impression that she was an unsophisticated, uptight ninny who didn't know how to be cool about something like this. That couldn't be farther from the truth. She was cool. Very cool. Downright cold as the February snow that whirled just outside the door—where she didn't want to go.

"You're right," she conceded. "We should go up."

The dogs waited exactly where they'd been left, Iowa sitting at the foot of the bed and Priss curled on the pillow. The border collie greeted Scott with a respectful wave of the tail. Priss gave Josie a little whine of complaint, but she didn't bother to leave her pillow.

"That's a load of luggage," Scott commented as Josie hauled her bags from the cart to the bed. The wheeled dolly was designed to carry dog crates and grooming paraphernalia into dog show sites, but it served just as well as a personal baggage carrier.

"I'm going to be away from home for a month," she reminded him. "Besides, half this stuff is Priss's."

He spared a glance for the tiny dog perched on her throne. "Yeah. She looks as if she needs a lot of sweaters and hair curlers and nail files and stuff."

Josie took offense. She could be easygoing about people poking fun at her, but she didn't sit still for someone insulting Priss. "Priss is a very smart, sturdy little dog. I do not paint her nails or fou-fou her hair. She's quite beautiful just the way she is." She darted a significant glance at Iowa. "A dog who performs in public—in any arena—should look its best. A little time spent brushing and bathing never hurt any dog, even a border collie."

Scott seemed amused at her barb. "Us working guys don't bathe but twice a year, do we, Iowa?" With a sparkle in his eye, he deliberately scratched his ribs.

Josie rolled her eyes. The man did have a sense of humor, but it was warped. "I wouldn't want to keep you working guys from getting your beauty sleep. Feel free . . ." She gestured toward the easy chair. "I'll just unpack and take a bath, if you don't mind." She slanted him a superior smile. "Come on, Priss, dear. We fou-fou females do bathe, you know."

Priss joined Josie in the bathroom, leaving the boys to themselves. As Josie sank into a tub of steaming water, she closed her eyes in bliss. Priss regarded her morosely from where she had pancaked herself on the cool tile floor. "Be polite to them," Josie instructed in a low voice. "They could have left us to fend for ourselves."

Priss just sighed.

Josie turned the hot-water spigot with her toe to draw more water. She breathed in the steam and sank up to her neck, reflecting on the interesting twist of fortune that had put her in a hotel room with Scott McBride, of all people. Scott McBride had some of the best working border collies in the country. He was also notorious for his opinion, expressed in numerous articles and training seminars, that a dog should earn its place at the dinner table. He had no time for the purely beautiful, amusing companions whose sole purpose in life was to get hair on the sofa and harass the family cat.

Then here come I, thought Josie with a smile, *with a six-pound papillon princess who believes the human race is on earth to serve her and only her.* Josie certainly didn't care that Priss's only useful function was to amuse her mistress. After all, Josie's only function in the world was to amuse the readers of her comic strip, and she didn't consider herself to be superfluous. Nor did she feel obligated to justify her existence with an outmoded work ethic.

But work ethic glowed about Scott McBride as strongly as the Force glowed about Obi-wan Kenobi. The poor guy was a trudger—she could tell already. A hunk, but a trudger nevertheless.

When they slipped out of the steamy bathroom, only the light by the door was lit. Josie peeked around the corner to find a Scott wrapped in a blanket and passed out on the easy chair—all for the best, because her nightwear, a T-shirt decorated with the motto "Papillon Power," fell only just past her lace panties. She hadn't packed with the idea of sharing her room with a man, and while her garb would never appear in a Victoria's Secret catalog, she wasn't comfortable with the prospect of flashing her lace-clad buns at a total stranger. Turning off the light, she tiptoed to the bed as unobtrusively as possible.

All stealth ended when she stumbled over her luggage cart. "Ow! Dammit!"

A grunt came from the figure in the chair, and a dark, broad-shouldered shadow rose and reached for the lamp.

"Don't turn the light on! I'm fine! Go back to sleep."

"What time do you want to get up? I have the alarm set for six-thirty."

Normally Josie didn't acknowledge that the world existed at six-thirty in the morning—only at dog shows, which insisted upon starting at a thoroughly uncivilized time of day. "Six-thirty is fine."

"Well, good night, then."

"Good night."

She sank into the already rumpled bed. The sheets had a decidedly masculine scent. Not unpleasant. Some sort of fresh-smelling soap. A hint of shaving lotion.

A slight thump signaled Priss's arrival. The dog claimed part of Josie's pillow and settled in with a long-suffering sigh. Josie waited for sleep to descend, but relaxation was nearly impossible as she lay there listening to Scott shift and move about in his chair. Guilt crept over her. She had tossed the poor man out of his bed, after all—not very polite after he'd offered to share his room.

It sounded as if he was doing battle with his blanket. A battle royal, or perhaps the still night, or perhaps her guilt, magnified the sound.

"This is ridiculous!" she finally said out loud. "I can't throw you out of your own bed."

"I'm fine."

"Well, I'm not. I can't sleep if I'm feeling guilty about you sleeping in that stupid chair. This is a huge bed. There's no reason why you can't sleep on one side of it and me on the other."

His protest was halfhearted, and soon he joined her in bed. They weren't really sleeping together, Josie told herself, just sharing a piece of furniture, no different than sitting on the same sofa together. She did hope, however, that he had at least left on his BVDs when he'd stripped down.

Sleeping with Scott was no easier than sleeping with

guilt, Josie found. She lay very still as he tossed about in search of a comfortable position, then, when he grew still, she squeezed her eyes shut and tried not to picture that broad, bare chest rising and falling, rising and falling in time to his quiet, even breathing. The image made her want to squirm. His body heat reached across the space between them, like a warm hand, to remind her she wasn't alone.

Get a grip! Josie warned herself. She was certainly not interested in Scott McBride. Not a smidgen. She could listen to him breathe and picture him naked beneath the bed-covers all night without one iota of anything but idle curiosity. There was not a thing about him that moved her.

He did have nice eyes, though. And his smile, when it made a rare appearance, wasn't one of those smiles that just scratched the surface. It seemed to go right through him. It was, Josie had to admit, a very nice smile.

Thinking about that smile, she finally fell asleep.

Priss perched on Josie's pillow, six pounds of papillon indignation. She was not accustomed to sharing a room, much less a bed, with anyone but her Josie. The Scott person was alarmingly big, and the border collie was working class from the tip of his ears to the last toenail on his clunky foot. Boring and completely beneath her notice.

Priss, after all, was an aristocrat. Since the sixteenth century, papillons had sat on the laps of lords, ladies, kings, and queens. They counted Marie Antoinette and Madame de Pompadour among their admirers, and aristocratic ladies wouldn't dream of having their portraits painted without one of their favorite little dogs at hand. Priss's heritage was inscribed in every fiber of her being, and she would no more consort with the common classes than she would pick a fight with a mastiff.

Not that her Josie was a reigning queen, or even a blue-blood, for that matter. But bluebloods were in short supply these days, so the former companions of the upper crust had to lower their standards somewhat if they wanted bed and board. Josie had her good points, however. She was an artist, and artists, even though they weren't much use to anyone but themselves, were generally considered the elite of the human race. If society didn't think so, at least the artists did. Better yet, Josie had the good sense to center her art on the acme of God's creation—namely, Priss herself. Priss's wit and wisdom, interpreted by the cartoon art of Josie Blake, appeared daily in newspapers all over the country in the guise of a comic strip. Priss was the inspiration, and Josie took care of the legwork, drawing the cartoons, writing the dialogue, and dealing with sundry annoyances such as editors, agents, deadlines, and merchandising rights.

Priss was satisfied with the situation. Life was quite wonderful, and if her Josie would play the cards right, Priss's piquant little face would soon grace everything from T-shirts to coffee mugs. One might think that such crass commercialism was below an aristocrat of Priss's stamp, but in America, notoriety was the next thing to royalty. Royalty, Priss figured, was right up her alley.

So why was she sharing her digs with this dog from the lower orders? She supposed necessity made for strange bedfellows, but a border collie, of all things! Border collies were snobs, convinced that they alone had any claim to intelligence and talent. Big bossy brownnosers is what Priss considered them to be. Work, work, work, work. That was all they thought about. No imagination. No creativity. No independence. They trotted through life with the sanctimonious attitude that if something needed doing, they were the ones to do it, if something needed fixing, they were the ones to fix it, and if someone needed to be told what to do, they were the ones to do the telling. Nothing irritated Priss quite so much as a know-it-all. And that's what the other dog was—a know-it-all and a snob, lying at the foot of the bed and pretending to have not a bit of interest in her.

Priss gave him a distant sniff. She knew his game. Of course he was interested in her. How could he *not* be interested in her? She was adorable. Everyone said so. Much more adorable than he was, though he was handsome, in a rough-cut, male sort of way. And he did wear the supremely confident air of a dog with a job, a dog who knew his exact place in the scheme of the universe and was well satisfied with it.

Priss sniffed in disdain, got up, turned her back to the other dog, and curled into the bend of Josie's knees. Much to her alarm, Iowa got up also, indulged in a leisurely stretch, and before she could squeak in protest, leapt onto the bed on feet that were swift and silent as a cat's. Josie stirred but didn't wake as Priss crowded close to her for protection.

But the bigger dog merely settled onto his own little piece of the king-size mattress and watched both Priss and Josie. Annoying in the extreme. Priss glared, but Iowa simply laid his big head—almost as big as she was—on the mattress next to her. After a suitable interval of indignation, Priss accepted the situation. He was a handsome rogue, and obviously under her spell. She decided to be magnanimous and let him stay.

two

Scott woke long before the alarm went off. His body was tuned to five o'clock, the time he rose each morning to run two miles before feeding the dogs and livestock and beginning the round of tasks that defined each day. No matter that the night before had been a late one, not to mention an interesting one, his body wanted to start moving at five.

He had intended to run this morning to loosen up both himself and Iowa, but under the circumstances, he doubted that was a good idea. His bed partner still emitted soft, feminine snores, such tiny sounds that Scott couldn't decide if they came from the woman or her ridiculous overgrown mouse of a dog. They were all very cute, he couldn't deny—the petite snores, the woman, and even her silly dog. But he knew very little about this Josephine Blake other than the fact that she smelled good, looked better, and could wield a very sharp tongue. He wasn't about to leave her alone in his room.

He tried to go back to sleep, shifting to search for the warm comfort of Iowa to make the strange bed feel more familiar. But Iowa wasn't curled at his feet. Iowa, Scott discovered in the dim red light of the clock radio, was on the other side of the bed, tucked into the bend of Josie's knees and sandwiching the poor papillon between his bulk and the woman's body. The light was just sufficient for

Scott to discern the uncertain look the border collie darted his way. Okay? the look asked. Am I doing right? Is this where I should be?

More to the point, Scott mused was either of them where he should be? What was he, the always-in-control Scott McBride, doing in bed with a ditzy woman he didn't even know? Not that they were actually "in bed," in the most interesting sense of "in bed." He liked women who were sensible, practical, and down-to-earth, and jazzy Miss Josephine with her polished nails, stylish hair, and irreverent, cutting humor did not attract him at all. Not one little bit. Despite that flawless skin—no doubt a trick of artful makeup. Despite the sexy way her generous mouth curled upward at the corners. Despite the interesting way she packed all those curves into such a petite package. Despite the soft woman-scent of her sleeping just a foot away, with her T-shirt stretched across full breasts and the bedcovers kicked away from one shapely bare leg.

With a groan Scott turned over and yanked the covers over his head. He was not in the mood to deal with morning fantasies.

The alarm buzzed a long time later, or what seemed a long time to Scott as he lay sleepless, too aware of the woman next to him. The buzz was a raucous, unpleasant noise, but he couldn't shut it off without reaching across his bedmate, his soft, warm bedmate with her flimsy shirt and tempting curves. So the alarm continued to buzz until a feminine, manicured hand groped from beneath the covers and tried to smash it flat. It was one determined alarm, because it kept buzzing. Finally, Josie groaned and threw back the covers. She squinted at the clock radio, fumbled for a moment, then managed to hit the off switch.

"Good morning," Scott said brightly.

She twisted around, looked at him in blank amazement, then reached for a blanket to shield herself. Her hand encountered Iowa instead.

Josie's shriek inspired the same from Priss. They sounded like two mice on the rampage until the woman gathered her wits and clamped Priss's tiny yap with a finger and thumb. "Sorry. I'm not used to waking up in such a crowded bed. Not that I haven't . . . I mean . . ." Her very blue eyes locked onto his face, and she clamped her lower lip in her teeth. "Never mind. Why is your dog looking at me like that?"

"I guess he thinks you're part of his flock."

"Sheesh!" she grumbled, then collapsed back onto her pillow and covered her face with her hands. For a moment, Scott could have sworn he heard a snore.

"Josie?"

"Huh?"

"Didn't you say you had an early ring time?"

"Uh." She sighed, then peeked from between her fingers. "Turn around till I get into the bathroom. I'm not decent."

His imagination going into high gear, Scott did as she requested. He heard the rustling of covers, the thump of feet hitting the carpet, a soft curse along with the din of something—a shin, perhaps—crashing into the stupid scaled-down freight car she used to haul about her entire household. When the shower turned on, he opened his eyes. Amazed, he looked at the mess she'd managed to make during the two minutes she'd been awake. A suitcase lay open on the foot of the bed, looking as though it had burped up the colorful array of clothing that spilled over the bed and onto the floor. A pair of panty hose clung precariously to the corner of the bed with one toe trailing onto the floor. Silk mingled with jeans. T-shirts hobnobbed with lace and frills. And all were in disarray.

"Good lord!"

Iowa whined softly, echoing Scott's sentiment. Apparently Josephine Blake was not a morning person.

Scott dressed while his roommate was in the shower. By his standards, he was downright spiffy in khaki trousers and a nondescript pullover sweater. His sneakers were clean— at least they were cleaner than his jogging shoes—and his socks matched. This was the limit of Scott's sartorial elegance. He didn't own a suit, and he refused to live any kind of a life that required a suit. Before the shower quit running, he had made his bed, fed Iowa—while Priss watched with great interest—shaved, swiped at his hair with a comb, made coffee in the little coffeemaker by the sink, and fetched in the breakfast he'd ordered from room service the night before.

The bathroom door opened to exhale a great billow of steam. Josie came out in a loose T-shirt and designer jeans that appeared to have been steamed onto her. Scrubbed and flushed, her face was little-girl fresh. Her hair was wet and curly, framing her face in a dark, gleaming halo.

For a moment Scott stared, entranced, his mouth slanting into an appreciative smile. So much for his speculation that her looks owed something to artful makeup. He wondered why she bothered with makeup at all.

She looked back a challenge, as if daring him to be as cheerful as he'd been earlier.

"There's plenty of breakfast for both of us," Scott offered.

She looked at the scrambled eggs, bacon, pancakes, and coffee he'd set out on the table. "How nice." She smiled weakly and looked as if she might gag. "Maybe a banana and coffee. What I would give for a Starbucks French Roast."

She made do with the Maxwell House provided by the hotel.

"You sure you don't want more breakfast than just a banana?" Scott asked. "There's lots of food here."

"No, thank you." She eyed the stack of pancakes he was topping with maple syrup. "You always eat like this so early in the morning?"

"It's late."

"Are you kidding? The sun isn't even up. The only time I see this hour of the day is when I'm at a dog show."

"You miss the best part of the day."

Josie rolled her eyes. "Where are you competing today?"

"Obedience and agility." He glanced at Priss, who sat on the bed as close as she could possibly get to the table, her eyes fixed wistfully on the bacon. "I've seen some papillons do quite well in performance events like obedience and agility."

"Not that one." She smiled fondly at the little dog. "She does quite well at sleeping and eating."

"I take it she's only in conformation, then?"

"Oh, here we go. Why do you performance people always use that tone when talking about conformation?"

"It's a beauty contest. Dogs should prove they can do what they're bred to do."

"Papillons were bred to be beautiful."

"Besides. It's political. The judge looks as much at the handler as the dog."

"Like your reputation doesn't do you any good when you walk into the obedience ring or herding arena. The great herding guru Scott McBride?"

"Great herding guru?" Scott repeated with a grin. "I like that." He was absurdly pleased that she knew who he was.

"I'm not sure I would like to be known as a sheep guru. Baaaa!" She grimaced comically.

"It's a living." He gestured at her with a piece of crisp bacon. "How do you make yours?"

"I'm a cartoonist."

He chortled. "A cartoonist?"

"*Miss Priss.* We're in six hundred papers nationwide, daily and Sunday."

Scott winced at her sharp tone. "Oh, yeah. I've seen it a time or two."

"Don't you read the newspaper?"

"Sure. The important parts."

"No *Peanuts? Beetle Bailey? Dick Tracy? Brenda Starr?*"

"Why would I?"

"Because they're more fun than the latest political scandals, wars, drive-by shootings, and Third World coups. Don't you ever relax?"

"Sure."

"When?"

"Well . . ." Scott was certain he occasionally did things just for the fun of it; he just couldn't bring a specific instance to mind off the top of his head.

"Aha!" she crowed. "So serious. I'll bet even showing

dogs is serious with you. You go into the ring to get more students, more dogs to train. Not for the sheer joy of you and your hotshot dog kicking the competition's butt."

Scott couldn't deny it, but he resented her superior tone. "What's wrong with having a good work ethic and taking life seriously?"

She waved a hand in airy dismissal. "Dull. Dull, dull, dull. I have a work ethic, but I have fun. Life's meant to be enjoyed, not endured."

"Maybe I enjoy work."

"Um."

She bent over to pick up clothing that had fallen out of her overstuffed suitcase. Presented with a view of a very attractive jeans-clad tush, Scott wondered if Josie would appreciate what he was enjoying just at that moment. Sometimes the simple things in life were also the best.

"I have to get out of here," she told him. "Lots of stuff to haul over to the show."

Scott was perversely reluctant to have her disappear. Pretty Josie Blake, with her sybaritic attitude, was rather like the strange flavor of some bizarre foreign dish—like the hot salsa that had nearly blistered his tongue in Texas. It had a bite, but it was almost impossible to leave the stuff alone.

"I could help you. Iowa and I have to get down there as well."

In the middle of rearranging her ridiculous dog paraphernalia on her ridiculous cart, she stopped and offered him a spontaneous, infectious, light-scattering, sense-shattering smile. "Thanks" was all she said.

Scott couldn't help but smile back.

Chicago's International Kennel Club Dog Show was a "benched" show, which meant that each dog occupied an assigned spot in a designated row of slightly raised wooden platforms. There the dog had to be displayed all day, except when in the ring to be judged. The papillon spaces were understandably small, like the dogs themselves. Josie had to do a bit of juggling to get her cartful of equipment into her assigned area.

"Is this a dog show or a beauty salon?" Scott asked as he plugged in a doggie hair dryer that was bigger than Priss herself.

"Don't start," Josie warned him. Nevertheless, she was grateful for his help. She would still be struggling down the hotel hallway if it hadn't been for him.

Iowa had his nose plastered against the wire grating of Priss's little kennel. Priss looked down her nose at him, but she barked indignantly when Scott called the border collie away.

"She's got him bedeviled," Josie noted.

"He's a sucker for the ladies."

Josie gave the border collie an assessing look. "He's quite a handsome fellow, really. You should show him in conformation."

"Ruin a good working dog by turning him into a beauty queen? Not likely. I'd just as soon put pink bows on his ears and polish his toenails."

She snorted. "There speaks the voice of prejudice. You're a snob, Scott McBride."

Scott just smiled. "You're welcome, I'm sure."

Maybe she was being a wee bit touchy, Josie reflected. "Sorry. Did I mention that morning isn't my best time of day? I'm better behaved in the afternoon."

"Nah. You're right. To each his own."

They stood for a moment, awkward, silent, amid the confusion and noise of the show—the conversation, barking, laughter, and blaring loudspeakers muted to a dull background. Josie noticed for the first time how changeable his eyes were. This morning they had looked clear, pure gray. Now they appeared to be soft and green. They were very nice eyes. Quiet, deep, crinkling sometimes with a smile only hinted at by his mouth. She wondered how often Scott McBride smiled and people didn't even notice, not unless they looked closely and knew him very well. She couldn't boast the honor of knowing him well, of course. Wouldn't ever.

"Well . . ." He stuffed his hands in his pockets. "Gotta go."

"Yeah. Good luck in whatever."

"You too."

He started to leave, then turned back. "Maybe you'd like to catch a bite tonight. We can brag about our respective victories."

Surprised, she fumbled for an answer. The invite sounded a lot like a date. She didn't want to give the wrong impression. They were sleeping in the same room, and the situation could get awkward if he thought dinner might lead to a cozy bedroom scene—even if the hotel had promised them a rollaway bed tonight. Then again, kicking back with Scott might be fun. His straightforwardness was surprisingly refreshing in a world where most practiced the art of conversational pussyfooting.

"Well . . . sure. See you later, I guess."

He gave her a high-voltage grin, then headed off, Iowa trotting in a perfect heel position at his side. Priss called after them with a single yap. Iowa looked back without breaking stride, then disappeared with Scott into the crowd of exhibitors and spectators who were beginning to crowd the hall.

Josie bit her lower lip and sighed.

Priss yapped again.

"Oh, all right!" Josie took her out of the kennel and set her on the grooming table, where the tiny dog whined impatiently. "If you're thinking of seduction, little miss, just think again. He's not your type at all."

A laugh came from the bench next door. "You talking to Priss or yourself, Josie?" A round, rosy face appeared over the plywood partition, complete with blond ponytail and Cheshire-cat grin.

Josie laughed. "Hi, Sharon. What are you doing sneaking around in there?"

"Just getting your competition settled comfortably in her kennel. Who's the hunk? And are there any more where you got him?"

"Your husband wouldn't approve."

"I can window-shop, can't I? Nice tush. Superior pecs. I'll bet his abs are awesome."

"Didn't notice," Josie fibbed. As she remembered it, his abs were indeed awesome, and his other parts weren't bad either. But she wasn't going to tell Sharon that. "I think that's a very superficial way to judge a man."

Sharon simply laughed and invited herself over to sit on the bench next to Priss's kennel, where she held her face up to Priss for a friendly dog kiss. "I'm sure he's got other stuff I could judge much less superficially, given half a chance. Who is he?"

Josie started combing through Priss's coat. "He's Scott McBride."

"And . . . ?"

"And what?"

"You say that name as if it's someone I should recognize."

"Border collies. Herding champions. Obedience champions. Last year's top agility competitor."

"Oh, I don't follow that performance stuff. I'd gladly follow him, though, wherever he led. He's USDA Prime cut."

Josie rolled her eyes.

"Hey! How many real men do you see around dog shows? Where'd you meet him?"

"I'm sharing a room with him, believe it or not."

Sharon gave a whoop that started a frenzy of barking up and down the row. "Oh, you sly bitch! I saw you two weeks ago at the show in Milwaukee, and you didn't say a thing!"

"I only met him last night."

Another whoop. "You slut!" Sharon said with a delighted laugh.

Josie felt her face grow warm. She really shouldn't have put it so baldly, without explanation. But Sharon always teased her about being a straight-arrow prude. Of course, compared to Sharon, Madonna was a straight-arrow prude. Josie broke in to Sharon's laughter. "It's not like that." Good thing she hadn't mentioned sharing a bed.

"Did you hear that, Megan?" Sharon called across the

aisle to a gray-haired lady with a papillon under each arm. "Little Josie's shacking up with a border collie guy."

"We're not shacking up," Josie denied. "The Hyatt double-booked the room. I had nowhere else to go, so he suggested we could share."

"How convenient!" Sharon chortled.

"He's not my type. All work and no play. Takes life way too seriously."

"Josie, Josie, Josie!" Teresa Gilbert chimed in from three benches down. "A guy who looks like that one can take anything he wants, seriously or not."

"That was Scott McBride in the flesh?" Megan asked. "I saw his picture in *Dog Fancy*. Looks like a classic to me."

"Maybe Josie finally has a winner," added Mary Jo Richards. Her papillon, a little male who had once won Best of Breed at Westminster, barked his agreement. "She can't pick a winner in dogs, so maybe she can do a better job with men."

By now advice and opinions were being lobbed in by the entire row. Josie had to laugh. It was rather unbelievable that any red-blooded woman could share a bed with a man like Scott and not at least be tempted. Not that *she* was tempted. Nope. No way. She liked to get the most from life, but a one-night stand, or even a one-week stand, just plain wasn't smart.

"Take it easy on that poor dog's coat," Sharon advised. "Taking first place over Priss won't be half as much fun if she's bald."

"You'd better groom your own dog, lady. Not that the judge is going to look your way once he's laid eyes on Priss."

The talk turned to dogs and gossip—always an important part of any dog show.

Sharon and her little pap didn't win that day, but neither did Josie and Priss. Priss placed third, and Best of Breed went to the dog who'd won Best of Show at Westminster a couple of weeks before. Josie had spent much of her time in the ring scanning the spectators for Scott rather than paying attention to her dog, which just proved, she reflected later, that she'd let the banter at the bench turn her head. A pack of prancing papillons was much too frivolous to interest Scott McBride, and why on earth would he want to see Josie Blake strut around the ring?

"Priss looked nice," Sharon told her on the way back to the benches.

"Thanks. So did Molly." She chucked Priss's competition beneath her tiny chin.

"Want to shop till we drop?" Sharon asked.

"You got it."

The rest of the day was a time to relax, spend money on dog stuff, eat junk food, and watch other breeds being judged. Josie peeked in on the agility competition, where a crowd of screaming maniacs—or so it seemed—cheered on an Airedale terrier who dived through tunnels and scampered over teeter-totters, jumps, and other imaginative obstacles. A border collie waited at the gate, ready to compete next. But it wasn't Iowa, and the handler wasn't Scott. Not that she'd wandered over there to see Scott, Josie told herself. Scott was the farthest thing from her mind.

Back at the bench, Josie did her stint at public relations, both for papillons in general and for her comic strip in particular. She had decorated her benching area with a collage of *Miss Priss*. A little publicity never hurt anyone, and there were still people out there who needed to be convinced that a chuckle or two was worthwhile. Like Scott "I only read the serious stuff" McBride. Priss sat on her grooming table, soaking up attention, basking in the limelight. Once she was recognized as *the* Miss Priss, the crowd around their bench increased. With the help of Josie and her little inkpad, she gave out "pawtographs" on personalized Miss Priss trading cards. She allowed one sticky-fingered little boy to feed her cotton candy—until Josie called a halt. Another kid almost lost his hot dog when he waved it too close to her face.

When the crowd thinned out, the papillon people opened their coolers and set out a potluck lunch of three-bean salad, cold cuts, and brownies. While they ate, they critiqued the day's judging, indulged the dogs with a cold cut or two, and generally relaxed. Usually Josie enjoyed this part of a dog show, when the competition was over for the day and people became friends rather than competitors. Today, however, the conversation, jokes, and gossip held only the surface of her attention. She had the strangest urge to look in on the obedience competition. Just curiosity, she told herself. So what if she'd never before shown an iota of interest in such things? Perhaps her horizons were expanding. An obedience trial could be exciting—she'd heard. She wouldn't know, as she'd never really watched one.

You're a pinhead, Josie scolded herself. *Fixating on a man you've known less than twenty-four hours. Incipient insanity. Just plain silliness. Get a grip, girl.*

She would not make a fool of herself by ogling the obedience rings, Josie vowed. She would stay right where she was, right where she belonged, and at dinner she would not act like a dim-witted ninny. With any luck, an evening spent with Mr. Work-a-day McBride would be boring enough to cure her of this silliness once and for all.

When Scott got back to the hotel room, Josie was already there, or so he gathered from the steam billowing from beneath the bathroom door and the song from the musical *Ragtime* warbling accompaniment to the shower. Priss was enthroned on Josie's pillow. Scott simply shook his head and picked a path through the strewn-about feminine clothes.

He had already changed to clean jeans and a sweater when the bathroom door opened and Josie danced out, still singing, wrapped in a voluminous towel and drying her hair. Before she got too far into the room he called out a warning: "Man on the floor!"

"Yikes!" She danced back into the dressing room. "Sorry. I didn't know you were back."

"Ready to eat?"

"Will be in a minute."

A minute turned into thirty while she dragged her suitcase into the dressing room and did whatever women do between taking a shower and stepping out the door. She emerged looking casual but quite together in cotton slacks and a soft angora crewneck sweater. Tiny diamonds twinkled in her earlobes, and a small matching solitaire hung just below her collar. Scott suspected that Josie Blake was put together whether she was going to Burger King or the Ritz. She was a designer jeans sort of woman, and he was an overalls sort of man.

"I thought we could just go to the dinning room off the lobby."

She hesitated an instant, then smiled. "Sure. Why not?"

Of all the restaurants in Chicago, the Hyatt dining room was probably the last place his roommate would have chosen to eat. But Scott wasn't a man with a sophisticated palate, and he had no intention of pretending. He wasn't out to impress Josie Blake. He really wasn't. And if he repeated the denial often enough, he might convince himself.

"So how did your day ago?" Josie asked cheerfully as they were shown to a booth in the dining room.

"Okay. Iowa won his agility class today with a perfect score. The obedience competition didn't go so well. Second place with a score of 198."

She tsked sympathetically. "The slacker lost two whole points. You must be furious."

Scott gave her a crooked smile. "You're being facetious."

"Poor Iowa. If you hold him up to those kind of standards all the time, he probably has an ulcer. Did you hang him up by the ears and pound him with a rug beater?"

"Not yet," he said with a smile. "I might hang myself up by the ears, though. I let myself get a bit distracted." He wasn't about to tell her he'd let his eyes stray to ringside, thinking she might have come to watch. As if she didn't have better things to do.

"Oh, well." She shrugged. "You lost. Did you have fun anyway?"

"Fun?" He didn't know what to answer.

She clucked like a mother hen. "You need help. You definitely do."

"Don't we all. How did your day go?"

"We lost miserably," she admitted with a grin. "Obviously, the papillon judge didn't know what the heck he was doing, or he would have put Priss first. No matter. Priss held court for her fans, and—"

"She has fans?"

"Of course she has fans. Unlike some dreary souls I could mention, many people do enjoy reading the comics."

A guy had to watch what he said around this woman, Scott decided. But it was refreshing, in a way, to meet a lady who didn't mind butting heads.

"Did you have fun losing?" he asked. Turnabout was fair play, after all.

"We had a great time. I love dog shows. They're so utterly, completely, totally silly in so many ways. How can one help but have fun?"

"Uh . . ." It was difficult to think of an answer to that.

"For instance, do you see that fellow sitting with the two older ladies at the corner table?"

"What about him?"

"He's quite well off. Last year bought a forty-thousand-dollar van for his dogs. Wants them to be comfortable on the way to shows. He has chihuahuas, by the way. Do you know how many chihuahuas you can fit into a forty-thousand-dollar van?"

"With or without the tacos?"

She laughed. He liked the way her eyes lit up when she laughed.

"Here . . ." She grabbed a napkin and dug in her handbag for a pencil. Within minutes she'd drawn a van crowned with a TV antenna, chugging along sprouting chihuahuas from every window. It was ridiculous, but he had to chuckle.

"Oh, I can be wicked," she told him with a smile.

By the time their dinner came, she'd told him stories about more than one dog show acquaintance. Amusing stories. Not malicious, or gossipy. Often affectionate. Always illustrated by a quick, stylized cartoon. And he found himself telling her tales from his own life that certainly hadn't seemed amusing at the time, but perhaps he hadn't been looking for the humor. Josephine Blake always did, apparently.

She lived in a different world than he did, looked at the same picture and saw different things, valued a different set of rules. And yet Scott McBride couldn't remember ever having quite such a good time.

Iowa lay in the geographic center of the bed, intensely aware that Priss, perched upon Josie's pillow, had been eyeing him steadily since their people left. He didn't acknowledge her attention. She was scarcely a dog—with those huge ears and that feathery, silky hair. Neither was she a rodent that he could chase or a sheep that he could intimidate. What she was, Iowa perceived, was a nuisance.

He didn't much like being away from his farm. His sheep were constantly on his mind. His assistants, Streak, Moe, and Laddie, were sheep-sitting, but they were a bit sloppy as far as Iowa was concerned. He itched to be in the home pasture, to have the scent of wool in his nose and the thunder of cloven hooves in his ears. Work was bred into every fiber of his being. Work, work, work. Work, sheep, work, sheep, work, sheep. Even in a plush hotel room, on a soft bed, the need made him twitch with dissatisfaction.

Except when that little ball of silky fur with the big ears stared at him just that way. What did she think she was doing? If she was bored, then she could pick up her mistress's clothes that spilled from the suitcase onto the bed and thence onto the floor. Such casual disorder was a disgrace. At Josie's farm, the sheep were probably scattered all over the place, just like her clothes. Chaos and confusion. She obviously needed a good border collie to run her life. Certainly this useless puff of a dog couldn't keep things in order.

Priss gave a single annoyed yap—a childish ploy to get Iowa's attention. The border collie raised his head and rumbled a soft growl. One didn't bark in hotel rooms. Such behavior was unacceptable. But the little delinquent wasn't impressed. She sprang up from her pillow, feathery tail wagging, eyes full of delighted mischief, and bowed in an invitation to play. When he ignored her, she bounced around the bed in wild abandon, scattering even more clothing in sad disarray.

What to do? What to do? The little pipsqueak needed a good setdown, and if she'd been bigger, Iowa wouldn't have hesitated to give her a piece of his mind. But he couldn't run the risk of harming her. That was strictly against the code. She was, temporarily at least, in Scott's care, which meant she had to be guarded and kept in order. But she was so tiny.

Tiny and berserk. Tiny and . . . well, rather cute, really. She was a celebrity of sorts, and perhaps celebrities didn't follow the same rules as ordinary dogs.

Priss sprang to the floor, bounced a few times, then leapt back onto the bed only inches from Iowa. Alarmed, he backed away, right over the edge and onto the floor. Mortally embarrassed, he gave Priss a hard stare. Border collies were famous for their intimidating stares. The "border collie eye," it was called, and Iowa was very proud of his.

Priss seemed unconcerned. She yapped again and leapt off the bed, practically at Iowa's feet. Unafraid, she butted him with her tiny head, scampered away, then regarded him with bright eyes. Her outsize ears moved back and forth like a semaphore signal. The message was plain.

She was cute, Iowa admitted. Useless, but cute. What harm would it do to play her game for a while? He could show her who was boss. Teach her proper respect, and tire her out so she wouldn't bug him.

He gathered himself with great dignity, then pounced. With a delighted squeak, Priss took off. The race was on, and a bit of fun it was, Iowa had to admit. Leap here, pounce there, roll together on the floor, careful not to hurt the little squeaker. Fun, fun, fun. A strange new concept. But Iowa could get to like it.

three

All dogs were required to be in the benching areas by ten-thirty each morning of the show, and not much before that hour on Sunday the papillon people started to drift in. Papillon judging time on Sunday was two-thirty in the afternoon, so most handlers, including Josie, had taken the opportunity to sleep in. Josie was not by nature a morning person. She could work or play late into the night, but dragging herself out of bed had always been a challenge. This morning had been no exception, especially since she and Scott had adjourned to the lounge after dinner and had stayed there almost until closing. When they'd returned to the hotel room, a rollaway bed had appeared at the foot of the bed they'd shared the night before. Scott had insisted on taking the rollaway, and Josie had spent half the night wondering when he would give up his tossing and turning to join her on the king-size mattress. The other half of the night she'd lain awake wondering if that was what she wanted him to do—and why.

Sharon was in a folding chair reading a dog magazine when Josie arrived. As Josie deposited Priss in her kennel and stuffed her bag of grooming equipment under the bench, Sharon greeted her with a glint of mischief in her eye. "You look bright and chipper this morning."

"Do I?"

"Absolutely. Roses in your cheeks. Getting along with the sheep man?"

"We get along all right."

"Wooo-hooo!" Sharon wasn't buying the casual act. "More than roses in the cheeks. I do believe you're blushing, Miss Blake."

"Of course I'm not."

"Yes, you are. Tell me."

"There's nothing to tell."

"That's not what your face says."

"Well, my face is lying. Have you seen my dog dryer?"

"I pushed it under the bench when I left last night. You were in such a hurry to get out of here that you left it out for any Tom, Dick, or Harriet to swipe." She lifted a knowing brow. "Anxious to get back to your roomie?"

"Sharon, you're impossible. I've known the man less than two days."

"Just trying to liven up the show a bit."

"I'd think it was plenty lively if Priss won today. That would finish her championship, you know."

"Too bad she has to get past my Molly first."

They launched into the familiar ritual of competitive banter. No dog show would be complete without it. Josie was glad the diversion had worked. If she'd told Sharon that she'd had a date with Scott the night before, she wouldn't hear the end of the teasing in a year of dog shows. Not that their dinner had been a "date." They were scarcely even friends, and certainly not potential lovers. Certainly not.

Josie lifted Priss to the grooming table and started to comb out the silky black-and-white fur that feathered so fetchingly on her distinctive butterfly-wing ears and proud little tail. The papillon had gotten amazingly mussed and tangled in an evening of doing nothing but lying on a pillow. As Josie worked, her mind drifted around to Scott McBride. The man was a lot more fun than one might expect, seeing that he was so straight-arrow, bucolic, and hard-wired for work. He was very attractive, she had to admit. And kind, especially when it came to animals. He did truly adore Iowa, had prattled on about the border collie at every opportunity, and his expectation of perfection seem to grow naturally from a deep respect for both the dog and himself. The men of Josie's set—young, smart, ambitious professionals who worked hard and played harder—seemed to respect little besides money and ambition. They were polished, politically correct, and always focused on themselves—their needs, their goals, their lifestyles, their futures. Scott McBride was focused as well, but his focus seemed rooted in something more solid—a foundation that involved more than wants and needs.

Josie didn't quite understand it, and certainly she wouldn't have time to explore it. The next morning they would go their separate ways. More than likely she would never see him again.

"Josie, do you have some grooming spray I could borrow?" Megan asked from across the aisle. "My bottle leaked all over my tack box. What a mess!"

"Sure thing." Josie smiled and tossed her a spray bottle. "Take this. I have another."

Strange what an expansive mood she was in this morning.

Priss patiently endured the comb picking at her fur. All this dog show stuff was very old hat. She could do it with her eyes shut. This morning, she was tempted to do just that. A pleasant sort of weariness had her in its grip, and not the sort that came from boredom, or too many liver treats, or too many hours greeting fans and giving kisses to strangers. This weariness came from such a bout of romping as she had never before known.

Teasing Iowa had been second nature. Priss was a superior dog, after all, and Iowa had a holier-than-thou uppity gravity that simply begged to be toppled. Besides which, Priss had been bored. In her dither over the Scott person, Josie had forgotten to give Priss her squeaky mouse when she left the room. Priss could while away hours with that squeaky mouse. But Josie had thoughtlessly left it in the suitcase, out of her reach, along with her ball, her stuffed hedgehog, and the soft, fuzzy snake she like to drag around. Iowa had been her last resort.

Who knew the stuffed-shirt border collie could be such a lark? What fun it would be to have a friend like Iowa. But Iowa would disappear when the dog show was over, unless Priss could do something about it.

A few minutes later, with the combing finished and her fans not yet thick in the aisles, Priss got an idea. For a tiny dog with a tiny brain, Priss had a wonderfully creative mind. Josie had stepped across the aisle to help someone trim dog feet. She trusted Priss to stay put on the grooming table. Hanging on the partition between benches was Josie's jacket, and sitting beneath Priss's grooming table was a bag jumbled full with brushes, combs, spray bottles, grooming powder, and half a dozen different kinds of scissors.

Priss considered both the jacket and the grooming bag, then cautiously eyed Josie, whose back was turned. Iowa was a nice friend, for a border collie. Priss didn't want him to go away. The Scott person was okay too, even though he was only human. If Josie was smart, she wouldn't want him to go away either.

But truthfully, sometimes Josie was dumb as a rock. She was lucky to have Priss around to help.

Priss tiptoed to the very edge of the grooming table, where she could just manage to stick her head in the pocket of Josie's jacket. She emerged with the hotel key card in her mouth, which she promptly dropped into the grooming bag. It disappeared between a bottle of Coat Shine and a tub of Bright White Coat Powder.

Satisfied, Priss dropped her jaw in silent doggie laughter. She'd like to see that smug border collie match this caper for being creative!

Priss's commando raid on Josie's room key might not have accomplished a thing if Josie hadn't broken a nail while putting the hose on her dog dryer. Josie hated imperfect nails. She spent good money every week on a fancy French manicure, and appearing in public with a jagged, broken nail was like walking down the street in mismatched socks.

Her nail file, however, was in the hotel room.

"I'm sure I put the stupid key card in my pocket this morning," she said, rummaging through her jacket pocket.

Priss yawned.

"I couldn't have been stupid enough to leave it in the room!" She dug into the depths of her handbag, looked in her jeans pocket, searched beneath the bench, and even peered into the grooming bag. Nothing.

"I don't have a file with me," Megan sympathized. "Can't you just chew it down to make it look better?"

Josie gave her a look, then went on searching for the key.

"I've got a whole manicure case in the hotel room," Josie said. "I can't believe I left that key in the room. Sometimes I think my brain cells wake up at least three hours after I do."

"I'll bet your roommate has a key," Sharon suggested from the next bench over. "Do you know where he is?"

Josie dropped into a folding chair with a sigh. Of course she knew where Scott was. She had resisted the urge to stroll over to the obedience area all morning, telling herself that she was asking for trouble and being rather obvious about it at that. She looked at Priss, who looked back with bored unconcern. "Come on, Priss. Want to go for a little walk?" When Sharon laughed wickedly, Josie gave her a flip smile. "Hey! I can't go into the show ring with a broken nail, can I?"

She found Scott and Iowa in the obedience ring labeled Utility Class. Josie didn't know much about obedience competition, other than that it had always looked like too much work. She did know, however, that utility was the very top level of competition, filled with impossible-looking feats for both dog and handler. Scott and Iowa were in the ring with a clipboard-bearing judge and two other teams, one of which was an attractive blond woman with a golden retriever who nearly matched her in hair color.

"That's a neat trick," Josie commented, taking a vacant seat at ringside beside an avidly watching woman with a poodle on her lap. She wondered if she could somehow work that hair color bit into a *Miss Priss* episode. "Who do you suppose dyes to match—the handler or the dog?"

"Ssssssssht!" the woman beside her cautioned. "The judge is giving out awards. These three are the only teams that passed in utility today."

"Oh." From the woman's tone, Josie guessed the fate of the world hung in the balance. She resigned herself to reverential silence and settled Priss on her lap. In the ring, Scott and the woman endured patiently as the judge explained the rules of the competition just completed—as if everyone watching didn't know already. Well, Josie admitted to herself, she didn't know. But then, she didn't care. Except, of course, she hoped that Scott had won. He did look like a winner standing in that ring—calm where she would have been all twittery and nervous, confident and solid and down-to-earth as solid oak.

Beside her, poodle woman broke the silence with a furtive whisper. "That's Scott McBride in the ring, you know."

"Indeed!" Josie whispered back, as if Scott McBride were truly someone special. "Who's the woman?"

"Sandy Travis. Her dog was top obedience golden retriever in the country last year. She and Scott were a very hot item up until six months ago. She'd dearly love to beat him."

"Wouldn't we all?" Josie was quite good at sounding knowledgeable when she actually knew very little. In her father's opinion, that talent was the only thing that had gotten her through college.

The poodle woman loosened up a bit. "I'm sure she'd settle for him as a consolation prize, though."

Wouldn't we all? Josie repeated silently, surprising herself a bit. "Still an item, are they?"

"Heavens, no! She's taken up with a rottweiler person, of all things!"

"Such a disgrace!" Josie smiled and took her cue from the woman's tone.

"I'm sure she'd be willing to take Scott back, though."

It made sense—Mr. Sobersides and Miss Steely-eyed Supercompetitor. To Josie's eye, the pair of them looked perfectly matched, each glowing with a competitive determination that was very serious indeed. Josie felt a bit out of place. She tried to think of anything in her life that she took so seriously. Certainly not a dog show. And certainly not her profession; she was a cartoonist, after all.

Applause greeted the long-awaited announcement of the scores. Scott and Iowa won by a margin of half a point. Blondie, who was awarded second place, appeared to be less than pleased, though she congratulated Scott with as false a smile as Josie had ever seen. The third-place team, a little Welsh corgi and a middle-aged man, simply looked grateful to have survived.

She had to remember Blondie's cutting smile, Josie reflected. It was the perfect expression to put on Dilly Cat, who was Priss's constant nemesis in the comics. Not that Sandy Travis was a nemesis of any kind. Josie certainly didn't care if the blond bimbo had carried on a dozen affairs with Scott McBride. The slut.

Josie had to smile at her own transparency.

In the midst of fellow competitors shaking his hand and clapping him on the back, Scott was calm and relaxed, his hand naturally falling to Iowa's head to scratch the dog between the ears. He said something that made even Sandy Travis smile. No gloating, no snubbing the lesser beings around him. Josie smiled. Scott McBride was a genuine guy, and she almost regretted that after today, the most she would see of him would be his picture in *Dog Fancy* magazine.

"Josie!" He brightened when he spotted her. "What are you doing here?"

She got up as he stepped out of the ring to greet her, dumping Priss onto the floor. "I came to watch," she admitted. The room key and the all-important broken nail were forgotten.

Priss yapped, audibly demonstrating that she was not an obedience dog.

"She says congratulations," Josie interpreted.

"Thanks, Priss. But Iowa's the one who gets the congratulations. He was really on today."

"She was talking to Iowa, not you."

He laughed. "Naturally. Did you see us work?"

"We didn't get here in time."

"Sandy gave me a run for the money. I got lucky there."

Lucky to be rid of Sandy? Or lucky to win the prize? Josie grinned at her own wickedness.

"Of course, if Priss had been entered, both you and the blond duo would have gone down in defeat."

Scott chuckled and regarded the papillon, who was cozying up to Iowa, bouncing around the border collie's legs and nudging him under the chin. "Priss might surprise you. I've seen those little wind up toy dogs do very well at obedience trials."

By now, Iowa was bouncing as well. He crouched into a play bow, then sprang into the air, all four paws off the ground, landing in front of Priss, then on top of her, leaving just enough room for her to spring out from beneath him.

Scott regarded the two playmates in amazement. "Iowa, what the heck are you doing?"

At his master's tone, the border collie instantly folded into a perfect sit at Scott's side, gazing at the man with adoring, somewhat embarrassed eyes.

"Oh, let the poor dog have some fun!" Josie said.

"He's still got work to do. The herding trial is this afternoon. He's got to keep his mind on his business."

Josie bent down to scratch Iowa's nose. "Simon Legree here never gives you a break, does he, sweetie? Tell him all work and no play makes Iowa a very dull boy." *And Scott as well, if he isn't careful.* "What time is the sheep thing? I'll come cheer for you."

Scott looked pleased. "We'll be in about three-thirty."

"Good." She picked up Priss and challenged him with a smug smile. "That'll give you time to show up at two-thirty and cheer for Priss. Ring five."

"Uh . . ."

"Come see how the rest of us live. I promise the fou-fou powder won't rub off on you."

He looked embarrassed.

• • •

Scott was a bit embarrassed, but he did show up in time to see Priss and Josie triumph over the competition to earn Priss's show championship. He felt like a stranger in a strange land among the conformation show rings. In ring five, papillons pranced about in a circle, not so much trotting as bouncing on their little toothpick legs, tails and butterfly ears erect. In ring six, Pomeranians paraded about like so many dust bunnies with legs. Across the aisle in ring four, Irish setters strutted in their brilliantly red silky coats, looking supremely smug despite the fact that none of these so-called sporting dogs had ever flushed a bird or heard a gun fired.

Groomed to a perfection that matched their dogs, the handlers strutted their stuff in an intricate, much-rehearsed dance—up and back and around the ring, stopping just so, giving the judge superior, knowing looks implying that all the other dogs in the ring were trash.

Scott made the effort not to laugh at the gravity lent to the whole ridiculous farce. The place was redolent with grooming powder and coat spritzes. Fur was trimmed just so, whiskers snipped, toenails manicured. Not since the last Miss America pageant had so much useless pulchritude been on display. But at least the human beauty queens paid some homage to talent, whereas the canine version got by on looks alone.

To a man like Scott, who had always judged everything—human, mechanical, or animal—on suitability for a specific purpose, the whole thing seemed an awful waste of time.

Only one of these fou-fou creatures held his interest, and that was Priss. The papillon was rather appealing all on her own, Scott had to admit, but her attraction rested more with who was on the other end of her leash. Miss Josephine Blake was as cute as her dog, talented (in a frivolous sort of way) and smart, and she had a way of making a sensible guy forget what he was doing and where he was going. She could also be prickly as a porcupine and could get her tail up just about as quickly as the skunk who sometimes lived under his barn. Josie was far more attractive than either of those creatures, however.

She saw him when he took a seat at ringside, gave him a delighted little wave that drew curious looks from her companions in the ring, and nearly missed a signal from the judge that he wanted to see Priss trot around the ring. Josie obviously took the contest a bit less seriously than some of the other competitors, but that was no surprise to Scott. Josie was probably the least serious person he'd ever met. She saw humor, irony, and incongruity everywhere she looked, yet seemed to regard everything and everyone with a tolerance and even affection that saved her from cynicism.

Priss strutted her stuff with attitude that belied her tiny stature. The judge apparently approved, because he pointed her out as the winner. Josie gave a whoop of joy, and a number of spectators applauded. Josie's uninhibited display of joy, hugging the second-place winner and doing a little victory dance outside the ring, was a breath of fresh air in the prevailing stuffiness. He got up to congratulate her when she tore herself away from the crowd and came toward him. Bouncing almost as joyfully as her little dog, she laughed and hugged him impulsively. Hair that smelled like lilacs brushed his cheek in a silky caress, and the sudden, unexpected press of her body against his threatened to shoot his blood pressure through the roof.

Awkwardly, he thumped her back. "Congratulations. Nice win."

"Priss is a champion! This was the very last win she needed!"

"Super."

Jose pulled away, artlessly unaware that she'd just about set him on fire. "Wasn't she terrific?"

"Stupendous."

Scott couldn't take his eyes off her as she accepted the congratulations from her friends. She glowed. She grinned like a kid with a piece of candy. She was one of those people who turn joy into an infectious contagion, spreading it in every direction. How could anyone look at her and not smile? How could any man be near and not want to kiss her?

The last thought jumped into his mind unexpectedly. As a distraction, he picked up Priss, held the smug little celebrity level with his face, and congratulated her personally. "Not bad, Miss America. But what else do you do?"

Unfazed, Priss stretched out and gave him a dainty kiss on the end of his nose.

"That's what else she does," Josie told him with a laugh. "Aren't you impressed?"

Scott just grinned and handed the tiny dog to her mistress. He'd gotten a kiss after all, but it was from the wrong girl.

"I'm headed out to get lunch," Josie said. "Want to come?"

"Can't. Iowa and I are on sheep in about fifteen minutes."

"That's right! We'll grab a burger and come to watch. Tell Iowa to knock 'em dead."

"I think knocking the sheep dead wouldn't really please the judge."

She chuckled at his attempt at humor, then tucked Priss beneath one arm and headed toward the benches, looking over her shoulder to give him a victorious thumbs-up, whether for Priss or Iowa he wasn't sure. Josie Blake was a whirlwind, capable of creating chaos in a man's mind and making mush of his better instincts. Overexposure to such a woman could no doubt be damaging to his mental health.

Josie missed the herding trial, diverted first by sharing a cheeseburger with the proud new champion, then by a flood of Priss fans in the benching area who sought pawtographs from the star of the comic pages. By the time she made it to the big indoor arena, the sheep were evident only by their smell and the spectators were filing slowly out of the bleachers. The area around the sheep pens was clogged with border collies, Australian shepherds, a cattle dog or two, and one short-legged little Welsh corgi. Handlers wore boots, jeans, flannel or denim shirts, ball caps or battered cowboy hats. In the chic yellow suit and silk blouse that she'd worn into the show ring, Josie felt like Little Miss Muffet at a jamboree stomp. Certainly she drew some curious looks as she pushed through the press of dogs and handlers toward Scott, who seemed to be the center of the pack.

"I missed it!" she told him. "How did you do?"

"Him and his dog whipped all our butts," a big fellow with another border collie declared.

"Really? That's wonderful!" She colored as a dozen sets of eyes came to rest on her, staring in a way that reminded her that if Scott had won, then these people had lost. "I mean . . . uh . . ."

A tall woman gave Scott a good-natured poke. "Not like we're not used to it. All McBride has to do is show up with Iowa and he whips our butts."

Almost everyone joined in the laughter, and Scott looked as if he might shuffle his feet and say "Aw, shucks!" at any moment. Josie felt a surge of purely unwarranted pride. Scott McBride wasn't hers. He was a mere acquaintance. But all the same, he surely was something standing there looking like Captain America and Farmer John rolled into one.

When Scott introduced her around, a fellow by the name of Moe told her, "We're going to make Scott buy us a celebration dinner. Come along, why don't you?"

She dithered until Scott smiled at her. "Of course Josie is coming. She's got something to celebrate as well. She finished her championship today."

"Not surprised," said an older gent with a twinkle in his eye. "She looks like a champion to me, boy."

"My dog's championship," Josie added with a wry smile.

"What do you have?" the tall woman asked.

"A papillon."

A few eyebrows raised, and there was a soft snicker from somewhere, but most were polite.

As it turned out, only seven of them went to dinner— four men and three women, counting Josie, who hardly felt that she rated full membership in the group. All except Josie were herding enthusiasts and border collie worshipers.

Two of the group were from out of state and were eager to try true Chicago-style pizza, so they all crowded into a cab and went to Giordano's, where they secured a large corner table, three large pizzas, and several bottles of good Italian wine. It didn't take long for the party to grow a bit rowdy. Scott was the quietest one at the table, Josie noted. Of course, he was buying, so he might have regarded the flowing wine and thick, sloppy pizza as mixed blessings.

"Did you see my O'Henry work today?" asked Eugene Kraft, whose florid face almost matched his red hair. "Lordy! If it hadn't been for that one stubborn ewe, we would have had a great run. That was a crank sheep if I've ever seen one."

"Scott's Iowa didn't have any trouble with that crank sheep," one of the women reminded Eugene with a grin.

"Hell!" Moe commented. "That Iowa wouldn't have trouble with the devil himself."

"That true, McBride?" another asked.

Scott gave them a crooked smile. "Iowa's a good dog. A good worker."

"And here you left him in the hotel room while you go out for pizza!" Josie said. "Iowa and Priss should be chowing down on pepperoni and cheese. After all, they did the work today."

Apparently no one saw the humor in the image, because she got a barrage of blank looks. At least Scott had a twinkle in his eye.

"Who's Priss?" a woman asked.

"Josie's papillon," Scott told her. "Cute as a bug."

"Oh."

The discussion turned back to herding, sheep, and border collies. As the wine flowed, the border collie stories got bigger, rather like fish stories exchanged among fishermen. To hear these people talk, border collies invented the wheel and then the cart, the carriage, and the sports car to go with it. Long before the pizza was exhausted, Josie lost her patience. She was the first to fawn over a dog. Priss was an excellent example of that. But abject worship at the altar of an entire breed was taking things a bit too far.

"Listen to you people," she finally said. "You talk as if border collies invented fire, wrote the Magna Carta, and walked on the moon! Border collies aren't the only dogs with talent."

Again with the blank looks.

"Besides, you give no credit to yourselves. I'll bet any dog could learn to herd if the trainer is good enough. Even my Priss."

One of the women laughed, and slowly all but Scott and Eugene with the flaming red hair joined in. Scott was being polite, Josie was sure. After all, he could end up sleeping with Priss tonight. It wouldn't do to be laughing at her behind her back.

But Eugene had a wicked look in his eye. His face had gotten redder with each glass of wine. "This sounds like an opportunity," he boomed above the laughter. "Everyone's been piling it on about how great ol' Iowa is, and what a good trainer ol' Scott is. I say let 'im prove it."

"If you ask me," a more sober voice said. "Iowa proved it today."

"Yeah, yeah, but that's Iowa. Like Josie says, a real trainer should be able to get some results from any dog. Right?" He looked to Josie for confirmation.

"Well . . ."

"Sure! That's what you said. Now, Scott here enjoys a certain reputation as a trainer, but he's always worked with border collies. I'd like to see what he could do with a more unlikely sort of dog."

"Like what?" one of the women asked. "A Belgian sheepdog? A corgi?"

Eugene grinned wickedly. "Scott, m' friend, I'll bet you five hundred bucks you can't train the dog of my choice to . . . let's make it easy . . . all the dog has to do is pass a herding instinct test. Easy as pizza pie. All it has to do is show the tiniest bit of interest in sheep. Five hundred easy dollars."

Scott looked uninterested.

"What dog?" Moe asked.

"Josie's little papillon."

"What?" Josie squeaked.

Scott looked up. "Train Priss?"

"You got it," Eugene said smugly. "Five hundred smackers."

"This is ridiculous!" Josie declared.

"Weren't you the one who said any dog could be trained to herd sheep?" Moe asked with a chuckle. Everyone had started to grin by now.

"Well, yes, but . . ."

"I could do it," Scott said. "Sure."

"Oh, no! Not Priss."

"I could do it by the Wisconsin Sheepmen's trial. Two weeks away."

"You are all insane," Josie declared. "You've got sheep pellets for brains."

"Come on, Josie," Scott challenged. "You said you can't go back to your place for a while. Just come up to my farm instead of going to Minnesota. I've got an extra room. Priss would have a good time."

"I've got to work," she said lamely.

"If you can draw your cartoons in Minnesota, you can draw them in Wisconsin."

"Priss might get hurt. Those sheep are really big."

"I wouldn't let Priss get hurt."

"Come on, Josie!" the table chorused. "You're the one who started it. Put your money where your mouth is!"

"What if you lose your five hundred dollars?" she asked Scott.

He smiled at her. Funny how a smile could change a face from merely attractive to devastating. That smile blew through every Stop sign in her brain and crashed right through to her heart. Josie knew Priss wasn't the only one in trouble.

four

Put your money where your mouth is. How many people, Josie wondered, had gotten sucked into trouble with that particular challenge? As the northern Illinois suburbs flew by, she thought of all the reasons why she should be headed to her sister's place instead of to a sheep farm—or did they call it a ranch?—in Wisconsin. Farm, ranch, what difference did it make? It had sheep, and it was in the middle of nowhere.

Josephine Blake did not belong on a farm. Priss did not belong on a farm. They were creatures of asphalt and concrete, thriving on traffic noise, sirens, and big-city boorishness. Josie expected a security guard at every door, a Starbucks on every corner, and a bagel bakery in every block. Her idea of a walk in the country was a stroll in Grant Park, and Priss refused to walk on grass that wasn't mowed and trimmed.

Why hadn't Josie thought of those things when she'd sat like a stupid mope at the pizza parlor? How had she let herself get roped into this ridiculous proposition? Somehow the thought of spending another few days with Scott had infiltrated her brain and turned it to mush.

No matter, Josie told herself. This little trip should cure her of any illusions she harbored about Scott McBride. Ten days on a farm, hobnobbing with chickens and sheep, should convince her once and for all that she and the stalwart farm boy were oil and water, mismatched as any two people could be. Scott might have a droll smile and kind eyes. He might have amusing flashes of humor and an old-fashioned sense of chivalry that made a girl feel safe, even in his bed. He might be solid, rooted, and quietly sure of himself. But he was totally not Josie's type. Totally.

Sitting on the passenger seat, fastened into her little doggie seat belt, Priss yawned audibly. Josie reached over and scratched her head. "You'd better get some rest while you can. Scott isn't going to put up with any lollygagging. He's a taskmaster if I've ever seen one."

As they rolled northwest, strip malls and car sales lots gave way to small-town quaint. Drydock harbors and marinas clustered around picturesque lakes, and houses with docks in their back yards sported huge screened-in porches overlooking the water. Living in such a place might be acceptable if one just had to live in the countryside. But Josie already missed the city. She wanted the theater district and tall buildings and edgy excitement. And right then she wanted a French Roast from Starbucks.

An hour and a half and a world away from Chicago, she crossed into Wisconsin with its little farm burgs and spreading, winter-brown farm fields. The farmhouses and barns could have been imported from the nineteenth century. Rural charm lay so thick upon the land that Josie almost choked. At every curve of the highway she expected to see a horse-drawn plow and Ma and Pa Hayseed posing with a pitchfork.

Nestled among all this peace and quiet was the McBride homestead. A two-story white farmhouse set well back from the highway, shaded by oaks that might have been there a hundred years and more. A big weather-beaten barn stood off to the side among a bewildering array of fenced pens, and a scattering of other small buildings completed the frontierlike setting. One of those buildings looked suspiciously like an outhouse. Josie sincerely hoped it wasn't.

With a sinking heart she turned into the drive—dirt,

gravel, and mud. Not even paved. She and Priss truly had reached the end of the earth.

Scott watched out the kitchen window as the Lincoln Navigator SUV pulled into the driveway. Josie had a strange notion of first thing in the morning. She'd taken Monday to get her things together and promised to be at the farm first thing Tuesday morning. He could understand her need to get things together, for at the time she'd said it, on Sunday night, her "things"—including clothes, books, drawing board, dog toys, and her tractor-trailer size luggage cart—had been scattered over a good part of their hotel room. He supposed that since the time was a whole hour before noon, this could still, strictly speaking, be classified as morning. But it was hardly the same thing as "first thing."

Iowa put paws on the windowsill, whined, then gave a single bark in greeting to the new arrivals. Scott gave the dog a wry smile. "Do you think we've bitten off more than we can chew?"

Iowa's look seemed to suggest that Scott should find an easier way to get a few days with a good-looking woman. Scott laughed. "Come on, you. We'd better say hi to our newest students."

Josie looked like a Lord & Taylor model in wool slacks, a silk knit top, and a spiffy leather jacket. She surveyed the farm with a carefully neutral expression but relaxed into a genuine smile when Scott came down the porch steps.

"Hi, there!" he greeted her. "You're here."

"We're here."

"You're a brave woman."

She chuckled in that way she had, a subtle bubble of amusement that communicated somehow that everything in life was subject to laughter. "I am brave. Actually"—she glanced around with a smile—"I'm beginning to think I'm, uh, what do you call that phobia of open spaces?"

"Agoraphobia."

"Right. Not quite that. Agriphobia, maybe. Fear of farm fields and unpaved surfaces. What is this beneath my feet?"

"Dirt?"

With a twinkle in her eye, she kicked at a clod with the toe of her stylish leather ankle boot. "The planet is really made of this stuff?"

"As far as I know."

She shuddered theatrically.

The guest room upstairs was scarcely big enough to hold Josie's luggage. Scott had to wonder just how many clothes a woman needed for a few days mucking about a farm, but his heart warmed to her when she admired his grandmother's quilt on the bed. "Gran was the best one at needlework that I've ever seen," he told her. "I don't think that lady bought a single piece of clothing or linen in her entire life."

"Incredible," Josie agreed. "Is she still alive?"

"No. She died at eighty-six. Up to the day of her death she still sheared her own sheep and mowed her own lawn."

"Unbelievable."

Scott couldn't decide if what he heard in her tone was admiration or outright consternation.

Before taking his guest on a tour of the farm, he dug through his sister's chest of drawers for more suitable clothing. They survived the awkward moment that resulted when he held up Tricia's baggy sweater and thrust it against Josie for size. "You're just not very big," he said, inserting foot into mouth.

She raised one reproving brow, but the twinkle in her eye softened the rebuke.

"I mean . . . uh . . . Tricia's a broad-shouldered sort. Uh, big-boned, you know."

"I know what you mean," she assured him in a dangerous voice. He thought better of shoving the foot any farther down his throat. "Are you sure your sister won't mind me borrowing her clothes?" Josie asked in a more forgiving tone. "I have jeans and a sweatshirt somewhere here."

Scott could imagine what those designer jeans cost, and whatever sweatshirt adorned Josie Blake was bound to be made for fashion rather than for slogging about a farm. "She won't mind. She just leaves the stuff here for when she comes to visit. She helps with the shearing in spring."

"Is she great with a needle, too?"

"Not bad. Gran taught her."

"Make homemade bread. Put up jams and veggies? And maybe rewire the house while she's at it?"

"She doesn't do electrical work. She's a hell of a plumber, though."

Josie smiled faintly. "Of course."

To hear Josie talk during their tour of the farm, Scott might have thought she'd never seen a chicken up close or met a horse firsthand. Carrying Priss under one arm, cautiously picking her path through the half-frozen mud of the yard, she regarded everything with the curiosity of a space traveler visiting a strange planet. Even dressed in Tricia's worn, baggy jeans, huge sweatshirt, and dilapidated but serviceable parka, she exuded big-city style.

"Why didn't you warn me the rear end of a horse is not a good place to stand?" she demanded at one point.

"I thought everyone knew that."

"We don't have many horses in downtown Chicago."

"What about the horses that pull the carriages along Michigan Avenue?"

"They have the decency to carry bags beneath their tails."

Scott chuckled. "Well, aren't you glad now that you're wearing Tricia's rubber barn boots?"

She emitted a snort of disgust.

She liked the ducks, though, laughing at their noisy greeting and quacking back at them in a fair imitation. And Tricia's milk cow, hand-raised from a calf, got a cautious pat from her mittened hand. The fake outhouse—a prank by Scott's brother—drew a disbelieving groan when she saw it.

"Don't panic," he told her with a grin. "We're not that old-fashioned. We got indoor plumbing just last year." At her momentary look of horror, Scott had to hoot. "You actually believed me?"

She blushed—an attractive habit of hers. "Of course not! Not for a millisecond." At his continued laughter, she lifted her chin a notch. "It's very rude, you know, to laugh at a person's ignorance."

"Sorry." A few more chuckles escaped him, though, in spite of her scowl.

She huffed along at his side for a moment, but it would take more than a bit of joshing to dampen Josie's irrepressible spirit. When they looked into the barn, she immediately exclaimed in delight. "This is really picturesque, Scott. If you cleaned up all that straw and stuff, this would be really quaint."

"It's a barn, Josie. It's supposed to have straw and stuff."

"Oh."

"Does that dog of yours ever walk on her own feet?" he asked as they headed toward the sheep pens.

She glanced down at Priss, whom she had stuffed inside her jacket. "She doesn't like to get her feet dirty."

He rolled his eyes. "All dogs like to get their feet dirty."

"Not this one."

They sheep bleated greetings and trotted toward the fence.

"How sweet," Josie commented. "They're happy to see you."

"They think I'm here to feed them."

Both Josie and Priss sneezed as the odor of sheep dung and dirty wool reached them on the cutting February breeze.

"Put Priss down beside the fence. Let's see if she's interested in them."

Josie set the dog down as if she were handling fragile porcelain. They both watched for a spark of canine instinct to light her eyes, even a faint reflection of the possessive ardor that riveted Iowa's gaze as he stood eyeing his charges. Priss was equally riveted, but by Iowa, not the sheep.

"Look at the sheepies, Priss," Josie urged. "Aren't they cute?"

Scott butted his forehead against a fence post and laughed helplessly. How did the woman do it? he wondered. She was ridiculous and endearing at the same time. He couldn't remember ever laughing so much in one afternoon, both at her and with her.

"What are you laughing at now?" she demanded.

"Your dog," he lied, chuckling.

"Don't laugh at her. You'll hurt her feelings."

"Poor little princess."

Josie laughed at his mock sympathy. She couldn't stay testy for long. "Why is she so fascinated by Iowa?"

"Because he's a hardworking guy. All the ladies like a fellow who makes a good living."

"Oh, go on!" Josie swiped at him playfully.

They laughed at one thing or another all the rest of the way around the farm. She made fun of the rooster who cock-a-doodle-dooed even though it was half past noon ("Can't you reset him, sort of like an alarm clock?") and the peacocks that wandered at large ("What is this place? A zoo?")

"Actually," Scott informed her, "there's a fair market for their molted feathers."

She snickered. "Of course we wouldn't want to keep around anything that's just nice to look at."

Scott was rather proud of the farmhouse, which had stood since 1898. It was a model of orderliness; he'd made sure of that before Josie arrived. Even though she'd shown a marked lack of concern for neatness, he didn't want her to think he was the typical slovenly bachelor with pizza between the cushions of the sofa and dirty socks draped over every chair.

She surveyed the spartan, pristine rooms like an artist looking at a bare canvas. "A little color would make this place absolutely darling. Have you ever thought of putting down some area rugs? Maybe Oriental style. Your eye could still appreciate the beautiful hardwood floor at the same time your feet would revel in the cushy softness of rich wool. Rugs would add a lot of warmth . . ." She glanced at his carefully neutral expression and suppressed a smile. "Surely you, of all people, appreciate the many advantages of wool. It can do more than keep sheep warm, you know."

"I suppose the place is a bit plain. My sister keeps telling me so."

"Your sister is a wise woman. But it's a lovely house, Scott. As I drove up here I was thinking it was just like driving back through time. I guessed nineteenth century."

And not in a complimentary way, Scott guessed. Josie Blake was a thoroughly modern woman if he'd ever met one.

"So . . . When does Priss start?"

He smiled wickedly. "You mean when do you and Priss start?"

"Me?"

"You're a team, right?"

"I'm not a sheepherder. I'm a cartoonist."

"I promise I'll defend you from the vicious sheep. Of course"—he pulled a solemn face—"that's supposed to be Priss's job."

She threw a sofa cushion at him.

As he had four students scheduled for that afternoon, Scott gave Josie a temporary reprieve. She was quite willing to walk down to the big arena, with Priss stuffed warmly inside her jacket, to watch as his shepherd wannabes worked their dogs. Between yelling at his students—and occasionally praising them—he tried to explain the fine points of working sheep. She listened attentively, a lively interest lighting her eyes.

"You know, I could do a whole series for *Miss Priss* using this." She gave him an innocent smile that thinly disguised a streak of wickedness. "You don't mind being the guest star of a cartoon, do you?"

It was going to be a long, hard two weeks, Scott feared. But damned if Josie Blake didn't make life more interesting.

A loud metallic clatter woke Josie from a deep sleep—a noise akin to Godzilla throwing a tantrum with the kitchen skillets. Her heart jumped when Priss bounded onto her chest, stiff-legged, and howled.

"Up and at 'em! Rise and shine!" came Scott's call from downstairs.

Josie groaned and pulled a pillow over her head. The

room was dark as the middle of the night. That was because it was the middle of the night.

"Come eat breakfast before I throw it away!"

"Throw it away," she mumbled into the pillow. "Like I care." The man was inhuman. Anyone who got up, much less ate, at this hour was inhuman.

For a moment she thought he'd given up, then the sounds of boots on the stairs warned of unpleasantness to come. A knock sounded on the door.

"Josie?"

"Go 'way!"

"Time to get up."

"Not for me it isn't."

"I'll do to you what Gran used to do to me. She'd throw back the covers and smack a load of snow on my bare . . . uh . . . my bare self."

"You wouldn't dare."

When he laughed, Josie reflected that "wouldn't dare" might have had the unfortunate ring of a challenge. She had a sudden vision of Scott plucking back the bedclothes, lifting her T-shirt, and rubbing snow on naked skin. The image flashed through her mind with a fire capable of turning a whole snowman to slush.

"I'm getting up!" she yelled.

"You've got five minutes before a snow bath." He laughed again, and the boots tromped down the stairs.

"Sadist," she mumbled, dragging herself out of bed. When bare feet hit the cold floorboards, she cursed. Only the threat of snowballs up her shirt kept her from diving back into the sack. She longed for the thick, soft, warm carpet that covered her bedroom floor, the cheerful patter of talk on her favorite radio station, the morning sun streaming through a window that overlooked Lake Michigan and the park along the shore.

Priss yawned and curled into a silky ball on the pillow that Josie had recently vacated. Josie gave her an annoyed poke. "Rise and shine, lazybones. You could get a snowball, too."

As she stumbled into the kitchen and collapsed at the

table, Scott greeted her with disgusting cheer. "How do you like your eggs?"

"Sometime after eight in the morning."

"Hell! That would be lunch."

She glared. "What time is it?"

"Late. Five-thirty."

She groaned. "You don't want to sleep away the best part of the day, Josie," he insisted. "I've already milked the cow, collected eggs, and fed all the livestock."

"And plowed the north forty, no doubt."

"Not this time of year."

"Lord save us!"

"But I did jog a couple of miles with Iowa. Do you like duck eggs?"

She gave him a look, then dropped her head onto the table. "Coffee!" she begged. "Just give me coffee!"

"Not a morning person, hm?" He put a huge platter of scrambled eggs and crisp bacon on the table and another plate piled high with buttered toast. Josie thought she might throw up, but then salvation came in the form of a huge mug of strong black coffee. Not Starbucks French Roast, but at this point, anything hot and caffeinated would do. Next to her full cup Scott put an old-fashioned coffee percolator.

The first few sips of the brew made her feel almost human. Human enough, at least, to appreciate the sight of Scott sitting across the table from her. How could anyone look that good at such an hour? It wasn't natural, but it was almost incentive enough to crawl out of bed—or to stay in bed, a wicked imp whispered in her ear, if the guy was in the bed with her. What would it be like, the imp continued, to wake up each morning to a tousled Scott McBride, those gray-green eyes warm and sleepy, his jaw shadowed with masculine stubble, the body warm and supple from sleep, but still hard and demanding with all that country vigor flowing through his veins.

Josie nearly choked on her coffee.

"Too hot for you?" Scott asked.

Early mornings, Josie decided, were definitely dangerous.

Priss didn't mind the farm. Everywhere her nose pointed, there were interesting smells that went with interesting creatures. Fat, quacky ducks. Busy chickens. A sleepy-looking cow. The horses were alarming when they snorted or stomped their big feet, but looking out from her warm cocoon inside Josie's jacket, she felt safe and secure. The border collies were snobby, but one expected that from border collies. Iowa was still willing to play when they were in the big farmhouse. When they were outside, however, he was always bossing the other dogs or the ducks or chickens or horses . . . or sheep. Big, ugly, stinky, stupid sheep. The sheep were the only things spoiling this little vacation.

Priss hadn't cared much for the sheep when she saw them from outside the big arena. Looking at them from inside the arena, she cared even less. They were worse up close. Far worse. Especially since Josie insisted she stand on her own four feet. Her paws were getting muddy, and those stinky pellets lying all over the ground weren't raisins, that was for certain. The smell made her sneeze.

"Look at the lambs, Priss," Josie urged. "Aren't they cute?"

Priss pressed up against Josie's legs.

"They're just babies, sweetie. Go take a good sniff. They won't hurt you."

Priss knew the stupid creatures were baby sheep, but as far as she was concerned, they weren't a bit cute. They had sharp little hooves and were likely to bounce this way and that for no reason at all. They definitely weren't cute.

"Let's try something else," the Scott person suggested. He took hold of Priss with his big hands so she couldn't follow as Josie walked around the huddle of sheep. No amount of whining and pitiful looks would make him pick her up and take her to safety. Priss decided he was not a nice man after all. She was sorry she'd encouraged Josie to seek him out.

"The dog's instinct is to bring the sheep in your direction," he told Josie. "For now just encourage her to chase them a bit. She'll learn that they'll move away from her, and once she gets it, she'll think it's fun."

Scott let Priss go. She immediately backed up and sat on his boot. Firm as concrete, she was determined that she would not budge. The boot lifted gently, dumping her onto the ground. Mud squished between her toes. Life had suddenly gotten very difficult.

"Come, Priss!" Josie called. "Get the sheep!"

What a ridiculous notion.

"Sheep, sheep, sheep!"

The sheep, Priss decided, could go stuff themselves.

Josie knew that look on Priss's little face. It was going to take a miracle to budge the tiny dog from where she stood—unless someone opened the gate to the arena. In that case, she'd be gone in a little black-and-white streak.

"Scott, this is hopeless."

"Never hopeless," he said. "Some ladies just take a while to adjust to new ideas, new surroundings."

Strange, Josie mused, that he was looking at her, not Priss, when he made that pronouncement.

Unexpectedly, Iowa moved. He'd been lying still as a statue in one corner of the arena, staring alternately at the lambs and at the unmoving papillon. Slowly he got up and walked sedately toward the lambs, who bleated and moved away. Then he looked meaningfully at Priss.

Expression still recalcitrant, Priss picked up her little feet and walked daintily toward him. Iowa moved again. The lambs moved again. Priss moved again.

"Good girl, Priss."

The papillon gave Josie a disgusted look, but she continued to follow Iowa as he pushed the sheep in Josie's direction.

"What do I do?" Josie squeaked.

Scott crossed to her side, took her by the shoulders, and pulled her backward. The lambs were moving faster now, heading straight for her. Suddenly she shared Priss's opinion of the thundering herd. They weren't cute at all.

"Always be on the opposite side of the sheep from your dog," Scott told her.

"What the hell does that mean?"

His firm hands guided her, turning her to walk one way, then another as the sheep changed direction, causing the dogs to change direction as well. Iowa was fully engaged now, crouching low to the ground, glaring at the lambs when they dared to set foot where he didn't want them to. Priss was watching the border collie, not the sheep.

"Try it on your own." Scott abandoned her. His steadying hands left, taking with them their warmth and security.

Suddenly she felt awkward. Bleating lambs rushed at her, surrounded her, pressed against her legs, and toppled her into the mud. Both Iowa and Priss regarded her with mild surprise.

"Oops!" Scott commented with a laugh.

Josie wanted to throttle him.

"Try again."

"I suppose *you* never did that," Josie snapped as Scott plucked her out of the muck.

"Nope."

The man was infuriating. Here she stood, caked in filth from the butt down, conquered by a pack of puny lambs, sniggered at by a couple of uppity dogs, with a backside bruised black and blue. If Scott McBride was even halfway human, he'd sympathize. All she saw in his eyes was a gleam of amusement. The man's sense of humor was twisted.

Then she saw herself through his eyes, and she couldn't help but laugh. "You know, don't you, that if you win this bet, you owe me at least a filet mignon at the best, most expensive restaurant in Chicago?"

Scott just smiled, battling the warmth her laughter sent to his heart. He'd seen frustrated students cuss, yell, sulk, even weep. But Josie stood there, slimed and sore, and laughed. Then threatened him with a posh restaurant. She could transform any experience into a good time—probably even that posh restaurant.

"Are Priss and I the most inept pair you've ever seen?"

"I've seen worse," he lied.

Normally he had little patience with livestock dimwits, and this pair could earn the dimwit championship hands, and paws, down. But Josie was special. He was just beginning to realize how special. He was, Scott admitted, crazy to feel this way, crazy to have jumped at the chance to lure her to the farm, and crazy to think something might come of it. No matter, he wanted to keep her here for the brief time she'd promised him. He wanted her to like it here, to like the farm, the sheep, the dogs, and most important of all, to like him. Her warmth and brightness gleamed like the sudden appearance of the sun in a dull gray world.

Scott had never thought of his life as dull or gray before he met Josephine Blake, but she gave him a new perspective. She was the wrong woman for a serious-minded farm boy, and he was the wrong man for a ditzy, latte-drinking city girl. But tell that to his heart, with her standing there surrounded by bleating lambs, covered in half-frozen mud, and smiling a smile that brought heart into her eyes. Every one of her smiles brought heart into her eyes. That was Josie.

It was hard to keep from wanting her. He didn't even want to think about loving her. The whole thing was too impossible.

"Well, what are you standing there for?" he said gruffly. "Get the sheep moving. Get Priss's attention."

She was willing to try again, bless her. Scott motioned Iowa to lie down. By now Priss should have gotten the basic idea.

Josie patted a lamb on its woolly head and cooed, "Come on, sheepies. Let's go for a walk." Scott tried hard not to laugh.

She moved off. The lambs milled in confusion. Priss gave them a look of disdain and moved to be near Iowa. Scott shook his head in frustration.

"Iowa, go," he commanded. The border collie was up in a flash and picked up the lambs before they descended into total chaos. Priss followed. But now Josie was in the wrong place. She blocked Iowa's path.

"No! Not there." Scott strode over to show her how to position herself. Just as he touched her shoulder, Iowa inexplicably dashed between them, knocking Josie off balance. She teetered. Scott caught her, and there she was in his arms, her cheeks flushed, her lips parted in surprise. So he kissed her. It seemed the logical, sensible thing to do.

Her mouth was warm, giving, just like Josie herself. After an instant of surprise, she melted against him in delicious acquiescence, and everything in the world disappeared but her soft mouth, her warm, supple body, and the sudden sweet communion between them.

Iowa stood watching Scott and Josie, his tongue lolling in satisfaction. Scott was happy. He could feel it. Josie was happy too. All they had needed was someone to step in at the right time. If a job needed doing, there was no one like a border collie to get it done.

He glanced at that silly Priss, just to be sure she was regarding him with the proper awe. She was. It was only right. He'd shown the little puff piece a thing or two about creativity.

five

What was a kiss? Nothing. A kiss was just a stupid kiss. Isn't that what the classic song said? A kiss was just a . . . a nothing. Meaningless. Little more than a handshake.

Yet Scott's kiss had seemed so much more. It had been a drug in her veins, a bolt of lightning that singed her from the top of her head to the tips of her toes. She'd melted down more completely than a nuclear reactor going haywire. And that was exactly what she was, Josie decided: haywire. Cross-wired, with a serious screw loose and more than one bolt short of a full complement. After Scott's kiss she'd been as flustered as an old maid with twisted knickers. Scott had been red-faced and tongue-tied as well. They'd acted like a couple of kids, avoiding eyes, hemming and hawing, groping for anything to talk about except what had just happened. It hadn't gotten any better in the days since. One would think two adults wouldn't get butterflies in their brains from one simple, meaningless, spontaneous, unintended kiss. But they did. Both of them did.

This shouldn't be happening, Josie told herself. She and Scott were wrong for each other. Scott's best friends were his border collies, and next came the sheep. Scott's idea of a good time was kicking back with a beer and a good book on sheep diseases.

Yet didn't Josie have a best friend who walked on four

legs? Didn't she occasionally—just occasionally, mind you—enjoy a quiet time of putting her feet up, drinking a cup of hot tea, and losing herself in a book?

In the days since the Kiss, like an endlessly repeated recording, the same thoughts kept running through Josie's head. She'd come to think of it as a capital K kiss. There were kisses in a woman's life, and then there were Kisses. Scott McBride's kiss had definitely been a capital K kind of kiss. Even now, six days later, standing in the cold wind outside the duck pen, Josie still felt the flush of its heat and the jolt of its impact. The memory of it was powerful enough to distract her from the goings-on in the pen, where Scott and a flock of ducks were trying to convince Priss of the virtue of running toward the ducks instead of away from them. The contest only skimmed Josie's mind, where the Kiss and its puzzlement flowed endlessly, like a warm current through a cold river.

Beside Josie, Iowa whined. His head poked through the open weave of the fencing and moved from side to side as he followed the action—most of which, unfortunately, came from the ducks. Very little came from Priss.

"Okay, okay," Josie said to the border collie. "We all know that you would make those quackers do exactly what they're supposed to do. Can't you have a little talk with Priss on one of your dates? Give her a hint or two?"

Iowa and Priss's "dates" had become a little private joke for Josie and Scott, ever since Josie's third night at the farmhouse when Priss had deserted her in the middle of the night to curl up with Iowa on the parlor sofa. Wondering what the little papillon princess was up to, Josie had caught the two furry friends sound asleep on the well-worn cushions, Iowa curled protectively around his Priss. Her stumbling about the house in the wee hours had awakened Scott, and they'd shared a chuckle standing in the cold, moonlit parlor. Scott had thrown a down jacket over his bare chest before coming downstairs. Unthinkingly, he'd offered to take Josie into its warmth, and equally unthinkingly she'd snuggled inside the parka, absorbing the heat of his flesh. They'd been half asleep and stupid, but the effect had been

almost as electric as the Kiss. At least, Josie thought grate-
fully, he'd been decently covered in sweatpants, unlike the
first time she'd seen him. Only the chest was naked. That
was enough. When they parted to go back to their separate
beds in their separate bedrooms, they'd been hemming and
hawing again.

The next morning Josie had unpacked her drawing board
and pencil, determined to put her time to better use than
dwelling upon silly, adolescent thoughts. Since she had
proved even more awkward around livestock than Priss,
Josie no longer went into the arena. She was a bit indignant
at Scott's obvious amusement. Surely she wasn't the first
person to get knocked over by a flock of lambs. And any
sensible person would take refuge by climbing the fence
when cornered by a flock of annoyed ducks. Scott had been
no help at all, standing there laughing like a jackass.

After the drawing board came out, Josie felt more at
home. Her pencil happily recorded the moment when Priss,
slimy feet and all, had sprung into Scott's arms to avoid
one particular duck who thought a nine-inch-tall piece of
fluff had no business telling a duck what to do. Josie should
have warned Scott that papillons have springs in their legs,
but the sight of him covered with mud and goop from a
dripping Priss was worth the dirty look he shot her.

Josie also captured the poignant moment when Priss had
touched noses with the farm's aged pony. The two of them,
both shrimps of their species, seemed to have a meeting of
souls in the aisle of the barn. As far as Iowa and Priss went,
Josie's tablets were full of their posturing and playfulness,
along with philosophical and tart little comments that she
imagined the two of them exchanging. Scott complained
that his border collie was being turned into a goof-off by
Priss's constant enticements to play.

"Next he'll be wanting to prance around a ring like some
primped show dog."

"Horror of horrors!" Josie exclaimed. "What a disgrace
if he should earn his championship!"

Scott shot her a disgusted look, but Josie just laughed
and repeated the maxim about all work and no play making

Jack a dull boy. What it did to Jack it could do to Iowa or Scott. "Do you want to be a dull man with a dull dog?" she'd taunted.

"Am I dull?" he'd asked, unnervingly serious as his eyes met hers.

"No," she'd answered simply.

He wasn't dull at all, in spite of his workaday habits. When she had decided that, Josie didn't know. It was sometime before the Kiss, or the Kiss would never have happened.

Not dull at all, Josie thought once again as she watched Scott in the pen with Priss. It was almost endearing the way he patiently tried to get the little dog to understand what she should do. Most dogs had some instinct to work. Even non-herding breeds had an instinctive predatory need to chase, and that could often be refined into actual herding. But not Priss. She wasn't a predator; she was a princess. Her only use for ducks and sheep was for feathers and fleece to stuff her dog bed.

She made a quick sketch of Priss lording it over an anxious sheep who was knitting its own wool into a Priss-size sweater. In her concentration, she missed Scott coming to the fence with a mud-spattered Priss tucked beneath his arm. He grimaced at the cartoon and just shook his head.

"Priss couldn't inspire a sheep to stick its head in a feed trough, much less knit a sweater."

Josie merely smiled. "She does much better at telling people what to do."

"Huh?"

"Who gave who a pitiful look and got a ride out of the nasty ol' duck pen?"

Scott glanced at Priss, who looked up at him soulfully from her comfortable perch under his arm. Somewhat redfaced, he thrust Priss into Josie's arms. "She's cold" was his justification. "And tired. Besides, I've got a student coming."

Eagerly grabbing the excuse, he waved to the driver of a truck coming up the driveway. In the passenger seat rode a tan-and-white Australian shepherd. In the driver's seat was a woman with a bouncy ponytail and a big smile.

"That's Bev Thornton," Scott told Josie. "Really nice working Aussie."

Really nice-looking Aussie owner, Josie noted as Bev stepped out of the truck. Tall and slender, she was the kind of woman who made K mart jeans, an oversize sweater, and a mountain parka look like a designer outfit. Her curly ponytail anchored a perky ball cap, and her makeup-free skin and eyes glowed with natural, energetic health.

Any other place, any other time, Josie would have admired Bev Thornton's style. But the comfortable hug the woman gave Scott and the unmistakable rapport Josie sensed between them put the kabosh on any inclination she had toward sisterly bonhomie. No woman had the right to look that good without makeup.

Josie chewed on a bit of jealousy. First the golden-haired obedience-trial bombshell with her matching golden retriever, and now Miss Hayseed America with her Australian shepherd. The man attracted women like honey attracted flies. Who did he think he was? Mel Gibson?

Josie warned herself to behave. Scott was a hunk, he was personable, and best of all, he was unattached. The combination made him a woman magnet. One stupid, meaningless kiss and Josie had grown claws like daggers.

When the cozy pair ambled over to the duck pen, Scott introduced them. "Bev, this is Josie Blake. You've probably read the cartoon strip she writes—Miss Priss. It's in all the papers."

"No kidding," Bev commented blandly. "I don't read the comics much."

Bad enough she was a natural beauty, a down-home country sort who was right up Scott McBride's alley, but she didn't read the comics. What was wrong with these people?

"But I'm sure it's great," she added, tossing Josie a crumb. "What a cute little dog. A papillon?"

Priss, the indiscriminate little traitor, wagged her tail furiously.

"She just earned her championship at the Chicago International," Josie boasted.

"I'm impressed," Bev lied. "Are you here to work sheep?"

"As a matter of fact, she is. She's going to earn her herding instinct certificate in the trial next weekend." On a freezing day in hell, probably, but this woman didn't need to know that.

"How cute. That'll be a first, won't it? For a little lap dog?"

Scott seemed oblivious to the tensions underlying the words of the exchange. "Dakota ready to work?" He scratched the Aussie's head.

"What is it with all these dogs named after states?" Josie asked as they walked toward the big sheep arena. "Is it the cool thing? Maybe I'll name my next papillon Rhode Island. For being so small, you know?"

Scott laughed. Bev gave her a pale smile. Josie gave herself a point on her side of the scoreboard.

For the next half hour Josie stood at the arena fence, Priss tucked warmly inside her jacket, and watched Bev and her dog work a flock of ten of the most difficult of Scott's sheep, including Icky Ewe, the contrary ewe that Scott brought into the arena only for his most advanced students. Bev and Dakota did everything right, at least to Josie's eyes. Every once in a while Scott would call out a suggestion about some fine point in the performance, but anyone else watching would have seen only the perfect coordination between the dog and its mistress. Unlike Josie, Bev didn't get her feet tangled up in the sheep and sprawl in the mud. Unlike Josie, she always knew exactly where she was going, where the sheep should be, where her dog should be. She controlled Dakota's every move with a mere word or gesture.

Unlike Priss, Dakota actually paid attention to the sheep. He paid attention to his mistress as well, standing still, dropping to the ground, moving forward left, right on Bev's signal or softly spoken command. It was a ballet, a pas de deux between sheep and dog, with Bev the choreographer.

"You have to give them credit," Josie mumbled to Priss.

Scott ambled over to the fence and gave her a grin. "Nice working dog, eh?"

"I suppose, but they don't hold a candle to Priss and me."

Scott laughed, but he didn't look away from his annoyingly perfect student.

Bev stayed for lunch. In fact, she prepared lunch. Her intimate acquaintance with the kitchen indicated she'd done this more than once. When Josie tried to help, Bev shooed her politely out of the way like a conscientious hostess dealing with an overeager guest. Except Bev was a guest too. She just didn't behave like one. She behaved as if she belonged in Scott's house, in Scott's kitchen.

"She's cute," Bev observed about Priss once the six of them had settled down to lunch—-Scott, Josie, and Bev at the kitchen table, Iowa, Dakota, and Priss stationed hopefully on the floor. "It must be nice to have room in your life for something with so little practicality."

Josie just smiled, gritting her teeth and telling herself not to stoop to the level she wanted to stoop to. As a cartoonist, she had a unique resource to deal with people who annoyed her. She contemplated just how she could introduce a caricature of Bev Thornton into *Miss Priss* and take revenge by proxy.

Scott saved her from her own unholy thoughts by offering unexpected support, scooping up Priss and allowing one of her enthusiastic kisses. "She is very cute," he agreed with Bev. "And I'm beginning to appreciate that seemingly impractical creatures can have real value in a person's life." The smile he sent across the table was for Josie alone, and it made her heart skip a beat.

Bev looked from Scott to Josie, lifted a curious brow, and was silent.

Over the next few days, Priss demonstrated that she liked ducks as little as she'd liked sheep. A few feints in the right direction showed that she did have a glimmering of what to do and how to do it; she just didn't believe that such undignified work with dirty, smelly ducks was her proper place. Scott was patient, but also stubborn—almost as stubborn as Priss, and their training sessions provided endless material for Josie's sketch pad. The question of who was training whom was yet unanswered.

Josie was reluctant to admit it, but after just a few days, the farm was growing on her. There was no Starbucks for miles, but a latte made with milk fresh from the cow, cream and all, went a long way toward calming that particular craving. The effluvia wafting from the arena and barn would never be Josie's choice of air fresheners, but one did get used to it. If she was honest, Josie had to admit it was no worse than the hydrocarbon belching of the traffic along Lakeshore Drive.

Scott grew on her as well. Heaven knew he was an unlikely soulmate. The man ate eggs every morning, for pity's sake! And he had to be one of the few people in America who had never watched even one episode of *Seinfeld*. But his smile made up for a lot. The sight of him carefully picking frozen dirt clods from between Priss's little toes made up for even more. And the Kiss stayed in Josie's mind like a warm glow in a dark night.

Bev Thornton came twice more for lessons, once bringing homemade jam. The woman definitely had eyes for Scott—and who could blame her, Josie admitted. Scott's feelings on the matter were a mystery. Men could be oblivious, and also obtuse. Josie tried to tell herself she didn't care. But she did care.

On the Thursday before the big herding test, Mother Nature walloped Wisconsin with ten inches of snow. After a dinner that she had cooked—just to prove she could be domestic if she wanted to—Josie stood at the kitchen window looking out at the pristine blanket of white and the softly drifting flakes.

"I'm going for a walk," she announced on impulse.

Scott sat on the sofa, where Priss perched on his lap and Iowa lay beside him, chin on his knee. "You have snow boots?"

"No. But stalwart farmer that you are, I'm sure you have something you can lend me."

Scott went with her, as Josie had known he would. Iowa, also, and Priss tucked inside not Josie's jacket but Scott's.

"If you fall in those floppy boots," he pointed out, "you'll squish her."

"Okay, tough guy." Josie refrained from mentioning that Priss's stubborn refusal to be anything other than a pampered little princess didn't seem to keep Scott from enjoying her.

The fields and trees were beautiful in their white finery. Even more beautiful, Josie had to admit, than Michigan Avenue dressed up with snow. Profound quiet made the night seem almost primal, and the flakes that whirled about them seemed a curtain that isolated them from the rest of the world, creating a private little capsule with room for only the two of them—no future, no past, no expectations.

"Stopping by Woods on a Snowy Evening." Josie recalled the Robert Frost poem with a smile. "I didn't realize the world could be so quiet. Walks like this must be one of the reasons you like it up here."

"Actually, I don't think I've ever done this before."

"Really? Why is that?"

He shrugged. "I guess because there was no reason to take the time."

"Then why did you come out tonight?"

"I figured you'd probably get lost, then we'd have to call out the Saint Bernard with the brandy barrel to find you."

"Oh, twiddle! I'm not that incompetent!"

They walked a moment in silence as she reflected on the sad case of anyone living with all this beauty and not bothering to take pleasure from it. "Don't you ever do anything just for the enjoyment of it, Scott?" she finally asked.

"Well . . ."

"Something that has no use, no reason other than kicking back and having fun?"

"Once in a while I indulge myself," he said with a wry smile.

"No kidding! Mr. Serious cuts loose now and then?"

"It's been known to happen."

"What? What do you do to have fun? Clean the barn? Shear the sheep?"

"Much better than that."

"Wax the hardwood floors in the house? Build a new henhouse?"

"Something so useless and crazy no sane man would dare."

"You have me breathless with curiosity? What?"

"Take a bet that I can teach a poofball little toy dog how to boss sheep." He glanced down at Priss, whose head and fringed butterfly ears peeked out from the shelter of his jacket. "Isn't that right, Princess?"

Josie laughed and poked him. "Stop making fun of my poor dog! Taking that stupid bet was your idea. If you lose your shirt, it's not her fault."

"She resembles her mother in a lot of ways."

"Oh! Now you're making fun of me!" She poked him again.

"Princess," he accused with a grin.

"Trudger!"

"Trudger?"

"Someone who trudges through life rather than lives it."

"Trudger! Oh, my God! What a fate! Can I be saved?"

"No. You're doomed."

By now they were both laughing. Iowa gamboled around them like a puppy wanting to play.

"You've turned my dog into a ditzhead," Scott reproached her with a suppressed smile. "Look at him. Today he was so busy playing with Priss outside the arena that he was ignoring his job."

Josie feigned horror. "String him up from the nearest tree! He spent two minutes not obsessing on sheep!"

"I think he's crossed the line into hopeless." Scott put Priss on the snow-covered ground, and Iowa instantly bowed in play. Priss yapped and bounded. The snow was up to her chin, but that didn't get in her way. She tunneled first one way, then another, snow flying in all directions. Iowa carefully avoided knocking her down as he crouched, bounced, and rolled in the snow.

"Dogs really do know how to enjoy themselves," Josie commented.

"You think that looks like fun?" Scott asked, a gleam in his eye.

"Of course. Look at them. They're—" A snowball smacked her on the chest.

"Yes, Princess?" gloated the snowball thrower.

"I don't believe you did that!"

He snickered, just before getting a snowball to the side of the head. "Hey!"

An all-out snowball war followed. Even the dogs got creamed, until poor Priss dove beneath Iowa for cover. No one emerged the clear winner. Both Josie and Scott firmly declared victory.

Something about the crisp cold and the soft, muffled feel of the night made Josie slightly giddy. Or maybe it was that last big snowball in the face. She remembered winter games from her Michigan childhood and was suddenly struck with the urge to make a snow angel.

"What are you doing?" Scott asked with a laugh as she launched herself backward into the soft snow.

"Making a snow angel." She flapped her arms and legs in the time-honored tradition. "Come on! Haven't you ever made a snow angel?"

"Why would I want to swim around in the snow and get ice down my butt?"

"Because it's fun!" She scrambled to her feet and admired her angel. "Come on, Scott! Defy trudgery. Hold out your arms." She helped him assume the position. "Then choose a spot with thick, cushy snow, and"—with a hand on his chest, she pushed him backward—"keep your arms spread," she advised as he unsuccessfully flailed to save his balance. When he plopped into the snow, she giggled.

"Yeow!" he complained. "Snow down the britches."

She laughed harder when Iowa and Priss both pounced on him, wanted to join in the play.

"This is great! I wish I had a video camera!"

"Damn but this is cold! At least get the stupid dogs off me!"

Still laughing, Josie reached down for Iowa and found herself caught in a steely grip. Scott grinned up at her wickedly.

"Oh, no."

"Gotcha."

Somehow she landed in the snow with him on top. They both were laughing, then gradually, they weren't. Josie couldn't feel the cold. She was suddenly hot, so hot the snow around her should have melted to a steaming river. So hot she could see her own fire reflected in Scott's eyes.

"What would you do," she asked in a breathless voice, "if you happened to fall for a totally useless woman? One who couldn't milk a cow, or stitch a quilt, or plumb a bathroom?"

His mouth curled at one corner, and Josie would have given a lot to know what he was thinking. But the question flew out of her mind when he kissed her. In fact, everything flew but the feel, the scent, and the warmth of him. There they were, just Scott and Josie, the night, and the snow. The rest of the world went away. And away . . . and away . . . and still away . . .

On the walk home, they were both wrapped in their own thoughts, but at the front porch Scott took Josie's arm and pulled her gently toward him.

"Josie, I think we should talk."

She laughed uncertainly. "We just spent the whole evening talking."

"You know what I mean."

Indeed she did. They might have kissed until their lips froze together if Iowa hadn't brought them back to reality with a cold swipe of his tongue. In fact, they might have done much more than kiss, snow and cold be damned.

Josie let herself be caught by his eyes. "This is a strange time," she told him cautiously. "Kind of like an interval away from the real world, away from real life, even." She touched his cheek. "We need to talk, but let's be smart and have that talk after we've had some time to think. After the trial this weekend. After I've gone back to my real life and you've got your homeplace to yourself again. We might discover this has no more meaning than a dream."

Gently he kissed her. Friendship—where there had been passion. Understanding—where there had been urgency. "We'll talk."

She smiled up at him, then went inside to her lonely room, her lonely bed, to think of him doing the same right across the hallway.

The herding trial—Priss's ultimate test—was Sunday, but long before the judges and exhibitors had assembled early Sunday morning, Josie was a bundle of nerves. After today's trial, she would give Scott that talk he wanted—and more besides, perhaps. It might be the beginning of the rest of her life.

Since that night in the snow, Scott hadn't pressed her, but she felt the weight of question in his every look. The snow had melted, for the most part, but the emotion that swelled between them had only grown. This feeling she had, this merging of friendship and desire, admiration and passion, eagerness and caution, was different from anything she'd ever felt. She was looking over the edge of a chasm, and that was scary. The chasm just might be love. Not a crush. Not a casual flirtation with someone from her own world. Scott wasn't from her world, and casual was the last thing she felt about the man. From the first time they'd met, he'd put her heart on a teeter-totter.

Sunday morning dawned on a transformed farm. The yard in front of the barn was crowded with parked trucks and cars, as was the field across the road. Tables for the trial reports and score sheets sat where Scott's border collies usually lined up to watch the action in the arena. There were people everywhere, eating doughnuts and drinking coffee from disposable cups, talking dogs, sheep, and verbally reliving triumphs and embarrassments from past trials. At their side they had border collies or Australian shepherds. Here and there was a collie dog—one even named Lassie, and one or two short-legged Welsh corgis.

Josie hadn't realized how much she'd come to value the

peace and quiet of the farm until it was invaded by an army of people and dogs. Imagine her, longing for peace and quiet!

The herding instinct test was the first event of the day, conducted with sheep for the large breeds, ducks for the little dogs. Of the dogs that were presented for the test, more than half passed, showing the required interest and ability in moving livestock. Priss, unfortunately, was not one of these. Scott took the ribs coming his way with remarkable good nature, even joking about the papillon's face-off with a duck, little more than a duckling, really, that sent her scurrying behind Scott to peek out from between his legs. Josie wondered how she'd ever believed the man had no sense of humor.

Scott didn't get ribbed very long about Priss, though, for later in the day, Iowa scored the highest marks of the trial, and another of Scott's border collies, a young female by the name of Streak, wasn't far behind. As trucks and cars began to pull out of the driveway and the winter sun rested on the western horizon, Josie hunted for Scott to give him her congratulations—and her apologies. She couldn't help but think that she had gotten him into that stupid bet with her big careless mouth, and she felt awful about him losing five hundred dollars.

She found him in a group around the tailgate of the truck that held two big coffee urns. Bev Thornton was with them. Her Aussie had done very well in its class, and Bev was all smiles and bonhomie. The group broke up even as Josie approached, leaving Scott and Bev sitting alone on the tailgate. Josie came up to the truck just as Bev planted a very thorough kiss on Scott's mouth, showing the same enthusiasm for him that her Aussie had shown for the sheep. Josie stopped in her tracks as Bev whispered a throaty congratulations to Scott and kissed him again. When the bold hussy caught sight of Josie, she broke off the kiss and waved a cheery greeting. Scott turned and saw her, his face a fiery red.

"Congratulations" was all Josie said before turning to walk back to the house.

• • •

Scott knew he was up to his elbows in sheep poop. He'd tried to chase after Josie in her retreat to the house, but he was grabbed not once but three times by people demanding his attention to some problem or another in cleaning up after the trial. At least the delay gave him time to compose a heartfelt speech. She would understand when he told her that he'd known Bev since they were in fourth grade together, that there was nothing between them but a somewhat flirty friendship, with all of the flirtiness on Bev's part. He'd held Bev's hand through two divorces and a number of dog crises, but that was it.

Josie was the one he wanted. He had known her only a couple of weeks, but already he was sure. She brought a brightness to his life, joy to his heart. She made him look forward to getting up in the morning, made him want to expand his horizons, explore new things, be more than he was. They were different, but that could be their strength, he had decided. The important things were what they shared—love of dogs, love of life, love of each other. He could convince her of that, given a chance. Given a few more days, a few more weeks. He couldn't let her stomp off in a huff, thinking he'd been playing with her emotions and playing with Bev at the same time. He cursed Bev's delight in stirring up trouble. The woman was incorrigible, and she'd been teasing Scott about Josie since the first time she'd seen them together.

When Scott finally got to the house, Josie was gone. The guest room looked bare without her things scattered around. The messiness that had first annoyed him had somehow given the room a homey, lived-in look. Priss's toys—the ridiculous pink mouse, the squeaky frog, the little stuffed hedgehog she loved to flaunt in Iowa's face—all were gone.

"Damned stubborn impulsive woman!"

Scott stomped downstairs. On the kitchen table he found a note that he'd missed when he first blew through calling Josie's name. In her bold, artistic hand it read, "So sorry about the bet. I got you into it, so I'll pay you back. Thanks for everything. It's been great, but I hate long good-byes.

P.S.: Read the comics. It'll do you good. P.P.S.: Kiss Iowa for me and Priss."

"Damned stubborn woman!" he repeated. Where would she go? Home, of course. Her condo might be finished by now. How long would it take her to get there? Scott looked at his watch.

Iowa whined, worried about the scowl on Scott's face. Scott gave the dog a long, speculative look. "What would you be willing to do, old friend, to get back your little buddy Priss?"

At the mention of Priss's name, Iowa's tail wagged.

"It'll take something big to convince Josie this could work," he warned the dog. "Something that will tell her we're willing to compromise if she is. What do you think?"

The dog's tail thumped the linoleum floor.

"Right," Scott said with a smile. "I agree."

Two hours later he picked up the phone, stiffened his spine, and pumped himself up on hope. When Josie answered the phone, he spoke in a grave, businesslike tone.

"Josephine Blake?"

"Yes," she said cautiously.

"This is Scott McBride," he said, as if they hadn't shared the last two weeks on the road to romance. "I understand you're a pretty competent dog show handler in conformation. In fact, I hear you just recently showed a persnickety little papillon to her show championship."

"Scott, what the hell . . . ?"

"I have a proposition for you."

Silence. But at least she didn't hang up. Finally, "What kind of a proposition, Mr. McBride?"

"I've got this border collie. Name of Iowa."

"Yes?" Her voice was warmer now.

"Big scruffy opinionated male. But if someone took him in hand, he might turn out to be a fairly civilized creature."

"You're talking about the dog?"

"Who else?"

"Who else, indeed?" The familiar laughter brightened her voice.

"Iowa has a couple of problems. He's a bit lovesick, and

maybe a little bored with the rut of his life. He thinks you're the only one to help him. The only one."

"Do tell."

"Yeah. That's right. The upshot of it is, Iowa has decided he'd like to be a beauty queen . . ."

epilogue

A cold February wind whistled along the lake shore in Chicago, but in the fifth-floor hallway of the Hyatt, where Josie Blake wheeled her luggage cart toward her room, all was warm and cozy. Atop the pile of suitcases and dog paraphernalia, Miss Priss rode in grand style. At the next day's Chicago International Dog Extravaganza, she was entered in her first obedience competition.

"What a day!" Josie grumbled. "All I want right now is a nice warm bath and a cozy bed."

It had been a long day indeed. That morning Josie and Priss had been in New York City, putting "pawtographs" on copies of her new cartoon collection, *Perfectly Priss.* Their plane had arrived at O'Hare two hours ago after being delayed by fog and sleet, and in less than eight hours, Priss would step into the ring to prove she had brains as well as beauty.

The key card snicked neatly into the slot and the door clicked open. Josie flicked the light switch as Priss jumped down from the luggage pile and bounced into the room. "Don't go looking for stuff under the bed, you little hairy Hoover."

A border collie launched himself from the bed with a jubilant bark, and Priss shrieked with joy. At the same time, a man rose from the tangle of sheets and blankets. "What izzit?" he mumbled just before being buried by the cavorting dogs.

Josie shut the door behind her. "Oops!" she chortled. "Must be the wrong room."

But it was too late. The man had disentangled himself from the dogs and climbed out of bed to take her in his arms.

"You don't have any clothes on, sir!"

"You have too many clothes on, ma'am."

She laughed. "Hello, Mr. McBride."

"Hello, yourself, Mrs. McBride."

"Did you know we've been married three months this very day?"

"I knew that."

"And do you regret having a border collie who's a beauty queen and a wife who sleeps until nine?"

"Not unless that wife regrets living in the back of beyond and having a husband who smells like sheep."

She took a long, sensuous sniff of his bare skin, then slowly smiled. "You don't smell like sheep."

"And you're not going to sleep until nine. Mostly because I have plans for your not sleeping at all." He grinned. "After all, I haven't seen you in four whole days."

"Four whole days!"

"You know you can't stay away from me. Never could."

"Who couldn't stay away from whom?"

"Princess."

"Trudger."

"City slicker."

"Hayseed."

She laughed as he carried her to the bed, tossing a shoe into one corner of the room and throwing her jacket into another. Her habits hadn't changed much. Neither had his. But they were working it out. She had moved to the farm and was learning to milk a cow. Scott was learning to live with the new Oriental rugs, the microwave, and the expresso maker on the kitchen counter, not to mention the huge entertainment center in the living room. What's more, a new Starbucks was going up just ten miles from the farm. Scott would learn to live with that as well.

Iowa and Priss watched, by now used to the horseplay, the occasional spats, the teasing, and the long, blissful silences. Humans, they agreed, were nice pets to have around. But don't try understanding them.

The Princess and the Adventurer

Elda Minger

To Eric Edson,
who taught me the value of opposites
And so much more.
I'm forever in your debt.

one

He saw her the minute she entered the Mexican cantina.

Matthew Kinkaid passed a hand over the stubble on his chin as he stared at the woman. Nope, you couldn't miss her. She stood out like a debutante at a monster truck rally. If her perfectly pressed khaki pants and crisp, long-sleeved white blouse hadn't given her away, then the jaunty little Indiana Jones hat perched on her head and tied firmly beneath her chin, would have.

Matt sighed. Tried to look away, but couldn't. Wished he could simply remain at his out-of-the-way table and concentrate on his Corona. Impossible. The boys in this place would eat a woman like this one alive within minutes. She didn't stand a chance, even if she did remind him of a rather prim schoolteacher looking over a bunch of grubby children. He loved old movies, and for a moment flashed on the image of Deborah Kerr in *The King and I*.

Matt continued to study the woman as she approached the bar, her stride graceful yet at the same time purposeful and determined. Even as he started to rise out of his chair, he wondered how she'd ever found a place like this, on the edge of the Mexican jungle. And she didn't seem at all like most of the women he had to work with. When finances ran low on his various treasure expeditions, he had to tolerate the trophy wives of businessmen who were determined to experience the jungle on their terms. Essentially, he was reduced to being a jungle guide to the brattiest people on the planet. Those women, those wives, were a major pain in the butt.

But this woman seemed . . . different.

Then again, maybe not. But she was sure different from the usual female that turned up in a cantina like this one. As Matt began to walk toward her, a rather clichéd line made his lips twitch upward in a smile.

What's a nice girl like you doing in a place like this?

By the time he'd made it to the bar, trouble had already started.

She spoke fluent Spanish and had an excellent accent, but the bartender already seemed annoyed with her, as were several rather heavyset men who were approaching.

Damn. He wasn't looking for a fight. Not now.

As Matt came up behind the woman, he took a glance over her shoulder at the photo she held in her hand. The four-by-six color snapshot showed this woman and a man with ruddy red hair, a couple of days' growth on his chin. They were hugging each other, clearly happy and smiling like mad for the camera. He wondered who the guy was, and was amazed to find that he was actually curious.

The bartender, Luis, had an amused smile on his weathered face as he dried a glass with a rather grimy white dish towel. He'd seen it all before, and Matt knew he was just waiting for everything to go down. Matt had scoped out his surroundings long before he reached the bar, and he knew exactly who else was approaching. He'd formulated a plan just as quickly.

"She's with me," he announced to the room in general, then grabbed the woman's arm, swung her around, took her in his arms, and hugged her.

She stiffened for an instant, long enough for him to whisper in her ear, "You'd better go along with this if you want to get out of here alive."

He realized she probably had no idea what kind of place she'd stumbled into. This bar, this cantina and its customers, perched on the edge of a thick and primitive jungle, paid absolutely no attention to any societal rules or structures. A woman was totally on her own here. And a certain kind of woman was fair game.

"What?" Her voice sounded soft and breathy and tickled his ear. She smelled like rosewater and mint, as opposed to mud and sweat.

He lowered his voice even further, hugged her tighter.

"Lady, I don't know what possessed you to come here, but there are several men approaching the bar right now, and I don't think they have your best interests in mind."

"And you do?"

"Let's put it this way—I'd like to see you make it back to the States in one piece."

"How gallant of you." But she relaxed a little, even though that spine stayed rigid. That was what had reminded him of a schoolteacher—she had perfect posture.

He stepped back, confident that she was going to go along with his plan—which at this point, he was making up on the spot—until he could find a way to get her out of this godforsaken place.

Nodding at the several beefy men who were approaching them, he said in Spanish, "Ah, it's a good day when a man's sister comes to visit him." Sister, these men could understand. A brother standing up for his sister or his mother was a very Latin concept. No one would disrespect a sister.

To a man, they hesitated.

Matt smiled, then draped a possessive arm around her shoulders. And realized he still didn't even know her name.

"Why is she here?" one of the men demanded, no doubt smelling a ruse.

Matt decided to go all out. He hadn't been in Mexico for the last seven years without picking up the local color and culture.

"Our mother. Our poor mother has been ill. Isn't that right?" He glanced down at the woman by his side and realized in a heartbeat that she knew exactly what he was about.

Smart. Logical. He liked that in a woman.

A long silence, pregnant with meaning, then one of the shorter men piped up. "What's wrong with her?"

"Her heart," the woman said, surprising Matt. "She's had heart trouble for many years, and despairs of my shiftless brother ever returning home. So I came here to get him."

Rumblings and mutterings rose from the group, as several of the men thought this over. A mother with heart trouble. A sister who would brave the jungle to bring her wayward brother back into the fold.

Finally, one of the men in back spoke up. "It's been a long time since we've seen a woman who looked like you in these parts."

Uh-oh. Matt gave them an easy smile, at the same time maneuvering his body so the woman stood partially behind him.

"And longer still, once I get—Maria home, where she belongs."

Maria. The trump card. That name had immense power in these regions. Mother Mary, and all she stood for. Most of these men had gone to mass at least once in their lives, and several wore small gold crosses around their necks. Symbols had meaning for them. He held his breath, hoping that this final ploy would work.

"Hmmm." The man in the front of the small crowd, a tall, heavily muscled individual who looked like he should be a World Wrestling Federation star, considered this. Sweat gleamed on his bulging forearms. His shiny black hair fell to his shoulders; his dark eyes expressed both distrust and disdain. Matt was absolutely positive that his worn denim vest concealed either a knife or a gun. He stared at the man, who was clearly the leader of this group. Several long seconds passed, and he felt his heartbeat speed up.

A medley of grunts and mutterings followed. Then, in response to a very subtle signal from the man in front, the crowd slowly, reluctantly, dispersed.

"Allow me to escort you to my table, Princess," Matt muttered, taking her arm in a firm grip. Not wanting anything else to go wrong, he practically dragged her along the worn wooden floorboards.

"Princess? Why did you call me that?" She stumbled, then started walking rapidly after him.

"Because you're about as out of place here as a princess in a pigsty, that's why."

She said nothing as he guided her to his table, but once they sat down, she put her backpack aside and leaned forward.

"Thank you for what you did back there. I—I didn't see that coming."

That surprised him. He'd expected more of an argument. "How would you know, unless you frequent these sorts of establishments on a regular basis?"

"I don't."

He narrowed his eyes as he studied her.

"No kidding. My next question—what the hell is a woman like you doing in a place like this?"

She handed him the photo.

He studied it for a moment. She and the mystery man looked so happy in the snapshot. She was wearing a pink sundress, and the man was dressed in jeans and a slate-blue polo shirt. What looked like a birthday party was going on behind them, balloons and a cake, presents, even a banner on the wall.

"Who is this guy?"

"My brother."

Oh, no. He could see it coming a mile away.

"He's missing." He said the two words in a totally flat voice, then glanced away from her. The last thing he wanted was to get involved in something like this.

She didn't say anything, and when he finally looked up, he saw tears shimmering in her eyes, those incredible gray eyes, as she fought her feelings. And he had the sudden feeling that this wasn't a woman who cried all that often.

Hell. He was a sucker for female tears, but she didn't need to know that.

"Come on, Princess, don't tell me you've decided to find him yourself."

She took a pristine white handkerchief with an embroidered monogram out of her pants pocket and dabbed at her eyes. "Isabelle." She blew her nose, then wiped it delicately. "Isabelle Burke."

He was amazed to see that this woman could even blow her nose in an elegant manner.

"Isabelle." He considered this for a moment, then held out his hand. "Matt."

She hesitated, tucking the folded handkerchief back in her pocket, then took his hand, her grip surprisingly strong. "Matthew. I've always loved that name."

No one had called him Matthew since his mother had died.

"Matt," he said quietly.

"Matt," she said, then took the picture out of his other hand.

"Have you seen him?" she said as she extracted a small leather-bound book out of her dark green backpack, carefully placed the picture inside its pages, and then stuffed the book back inside the backpack.

"No. But that doesn't mean anything." Curiosity got the better of him. "Where was the last place he was seen?"

"Very close to here. He was looking for—" She stopped. Hesitated. Glanced around, then leaned in close. "Can I trust you?"

He almost laughed. In a place like this, with a total stranger, he found it odd that she should ask such a question.

Intrigued, he said, "Why would you even ask me a question like that?"

"Well, I think I can. It's very logical, if you think about it."

He'd always been a great believer in gut feelings, but this woman intrigued him.

"Go on."

"You saw me enter the bar, and noticed trouble brewing. And you came to my rescue, with no thought for your own personal safety." She leaned back and started to take off her hat. "That alone tells me you're an honorable man."

He couldn't take his eyes off her as that hat came off. It revealed straight pale-blond hair done up in some sort of ridiculously sophisticated yet simple twist, flawless porcelain skin, and cheekbones that would have done both Deborah Kerr and Grace Kelly justice. She was a looker, all right.

Her picture hadn't done her justice.

Trying not to stare, he said, "You can trust me."

She leaned forward. Lowered her voice.

"He found the jaguar. The City of the Sun."

Now she had his complete and total attention. Matt leaned forward, every muscle in his body tensed.

"What?"

"He found it." She sat back. Smiled. "I was so incredibly proud of him when he told me." Her expression changed. "But that was the last I heard from Tom."

"How did he—"

"He's very smart," she said, and Matt found himself almost hypnotized by those cool gray eyes.

"Tom's been coming down here, first for summers and then for entire years, for more than a decade. Though his degree is in archaeology, he's always had a fascination for treasure legends."

"But he found it! That means it really exists!" Matt realized he was whispering, and he looked around to make sure no one had overheard. In a place like this, talk about money and treasure could get a man killed.

"By accident. Tom wrote to me right after his discovery, telling me that he was planning to go back into the jungle and, with the natives' permission, see if he could borrow the statue of the jaguar for his museum."

"His museum." This story was getting wilder by the minute. Whatever had happened to the good old days of treasure hunting, when all a man desired was to melt down a jaguar statue, take the gold—and the emeralds and diamonds it was supposedly encrusted with—and head for the hills?

The Caribbean, more specifically. Any island would do. That was his dream—the one big score that would enable him to retire from this rat race, lie back in a hammock beneath a shady palm tree, and do absolutely nothing for the rest of his life.

"He runs a museum in San Francisco. Tom's dream was to make the jaguar accessible to as many people as possible. He wanted the world to understand its beauty, and the beauty of the people who created it."

"But not the money."

"Oh, no. If Tom has just enough money to finance his various expeditions, he's happy."

"Hmmm." Matt considered this. A noble explorer. Well, Tom was certainly a better man than he was.

Her next question caught him off guard.

"Will you help me?"

"With what?" He stalled, not wanting to get involved.

"Finding Tom."

Matt considered this. Long and painful experience had taught him it wasn't wise to jump into anyone else's business. That is, unless there was something in it for him.

It was just a basic law of survival. And his own personal—and cynical—code.

"Will you help me find him?" she said.

"What's in it for me?"

She leaned forward. "I can pay you."

"How much?"

She named a sum that made him smile.

"I'd need at least three times that much."

He didn't miss the anxious expression in her eyes.

"All right, Matt. I can meet that price."

For some reason, he felt like a worm. Couldn't meet her eyes. What was it with this woman, with her shining blond hair and high cheekbones, her perfectly pressed pants, her cool white shirt, and her wild story about this brother of hers? How could she possibly be making him feel guilty? He'd thought he'd given up on guilt a long time ago.

"Forget it."

He didn't miss the quick sheen of tears in her eyes, but he had to admit she controlled herself admirably.

"No, Isabelle, not forget the rescue. Forget that second

price." He couldn't believe the words that were coming out of his mouth. "I'll take the first offer."

Slowly, she smiled, and he watched, fascinated, as her entire face changed. This woman was beautiful, and the thought made Matt glance around the dark cantina again. You never knew who could be watching.

"Put your hat back on, Princess," he growled. "The less this crowd sees of your face, the better."

She did as he told her, and Matt decided that things couldn't be that bad if she was this tractable.

He sighed. Either they'd find the remains of this brother of hers or he'd locate the man in the flesh. And then—

Matt smiled. Suddenly his island dream, his early and total retirement, seemed so much closer to reality. Because there had to be more treasure in the City of the Sun than that jaguar statue, didn't there? Perhaps another statue, or a dagger with a jewel-encrusted hilt. Hell, he'd settle for plain gold, and lots of it.

And he was just the man to find it.

He walked her back to the room she said she'd rented. For some reason he didn't want this woman to get into any more trouble. They could've met up in the morning and started their quest, but he wanted to make sure she was safely tucked in for the night. A light rain had begun to fall, turning the jungle into a steam bath. Their boots stuck in the mud, making small sucking noises as the two of them made their way toward her lodgings.

This small gathering of shacks on the edge of the jungle was home to only a few people. Word would've gotten around that the American adventurer had a sister—and a stunner at that—visiting him. But they would have to be on the move shortly, because his story wouldn't hold up for long. A man wanting to fulfill his baser desires eventually wouldn't care whose sister she was.

"How did you get here?" he said, taking her backpack and hoisting it on his back. She'd refused his help with it at first, but he could see she was tiring. And he realized that it had probably taken a lot of courage for her to enter that bar in the first place. A grudging sort of admiration for that action surprised him.

"My brother had a friend, a local guide. I hired a private helicopter to fly me into the jungle, and he brought me here."

He wondered at that, at how many people would go to this much trouble to find a missing sibling.

"What does the rest of your family think about this wild-goose chase?"

He didn't miss the determined tilt of her chin. "Our parents died in a skiing accident when we were little. My grandfather raised us, but he passed away almost two years ago. Tom is all the family I have."

Matt considered this. That explained the closeness he'd sensed between them in that photo. He had no family, hadn't thought about anyone but himself for years. His focus had been on finding treasure, and lots of it. The entire rationale for heading out and settling on his Caribbean island was so that he'd never have to deal with people again.

He found himself feeling a grudging kind of admiration for this woman. Clearly unequipped for the kind of adventure she was embarking on, she had only determination— and courage—going for her.

And him.

"All right," he said as they started up a flight of rickety wooden steps that ran along the back of the ramshackle building on the far end of the town. "I'll pick you up at sunrise and we'll start our search."

She glanced behind her, and he could tell she was nervous as they started up the stairs.

"You don't have to come all this way—"

"I just want to make sure everything's all right."

They stopped at the threshold of her door. It had been broken off its hinges, and the inside of the room looked like a tropical storm had hit it, the contents flung haphazardly all over the place. Matt stood behind Isabelle, and he saw the sudden stiffening of her shoulders, the way her slender hand grasped the door frame in order to steady herself.

He eased past her and went inside.

Someone had gone to an awful lot of trouble here. Someone had turned the mattress over, pulled out the dresser drawers and dumped them, even torn out part of the wall.

Someone was looking for something.

He turned toward Isabelle, still standing in the doorway. Still in shock. Matt set the backpack down and crossed his arms in front of his chest.

"Okay, Princess, suppose you tell me what's really going on?"

"A map!" Matt ran his hands through his hair in an agitated gesture. "Oh, terrific! Who else knows about this map your brother told you about?"

"No one. Except—"

Matt leaned back in his chair. "Think hard, Princess. Think real hard. Because I don't like getting involved with treasure hunters when the parties involved choose not to let me in on all the details."

They'd relocated to the outskirts of town, to the run-down house he called home on a temporary basis. But it was clean, and both bugs and snakes kept their distance. It was dry during the rainy season, offered shade from the hot sun and warmth from the night air, so as houses went, this one did the job.

They'd swiftly packed up what was left of Isabelle's things, salvaging what they could, and now they sat at the kitchen table, "kitchen" being a relative term, as the entire house was the size of a small bedroom.

"No one except who?" he said, prompting her.

"Whom," she said softly.

"Whatever. Spill it."

"Except Frederico," she said. "Tom's guide. But he wouldn't—"

"I don't *care* if he wouldn't, there are plenty of guys in this area who would take tremendous delight in getting that information out of him any way possible, if you get my drift."

"Oh." He watched, fascinated, as her porcelain skin

turned even paler. "Oh, no." Her expression imploring, she turned toward him, her hands twisting together in agitation. "Then I've put him in terrible danger!"

"I've sent a couple of guys I trust to check things out—they should be back by morning, before we leave."

Darkness had fallen, and along with it came the sounds of a jungle at night. Leaves blowing in the wind, those of the rubber tree over his small shack of a house tapping against the tin roof. Strange rustling sounds coming from the jungle floor. Insects clicking. Matt was well used to them, but he noticed the way Isabelle reacted to the tiniest noise.

"Take it easy. I've got a few booby traps around the house. No one can get to me without my knowing it."

"How can you live this way?"

He wondered how much he could tell her, then decided he owed her a modicum of honesty. "I'm sacrificing everything in the present for a great future."

"What does that mean?"

"I'm in this for the big score."

Comprehension dawned in those intelligent gray eyes. "Money?"

"What else makes the world go 'round?"

She considered this. "Don't you get lonely?"

"Are you offering?"

That beautiful skin flushed a deep pink. "I didn't—I mean—"

He felt like a heel. "Hey, forget I said that. Look, you need to find your brother, and I need some treasure. Sounds like a fair trade to me."

"You sound so cynical, Mister Kinkaid."

He couldn't believe he'd told her his last name. In the circles he ran in one name was sufficient, but she had a certain little way of worming information out of him. He'd have to be cautious in the future. After all, she was his business partner, nothing more.

"Cynical is my middle name."

She studied him for a long moment, with what Matt

would call her "governess look." Damn if she didn't remind him of Deborah Kerr.

"I don't think you're all that cynical, Mister Kinkaid. For if you were, you would have left me to my own devices in that bar."

"English, please," he said, and he couldn't help the way his lips began to twitch into a smile. She had the strangest way of making a point!

"You wouldn't have helped me if you were as terrible a man as you think you are."

"Ah, I just wanted a few more beers. If there'd been a big brouhaha over you, I wouldn't have been able to drink in peace."

She considered this, and he had the damnedest feeling she was studying him.

Finally she said, "You'd be a lot more attractive if you shaved."

"You offering again?"

This time she laughed. He ran a hand over the stubble on his jaw.

"Hey, it keeps the bugs at bay." He glanced around the small room. "You take that hammock over there, I'll sleep by the door."

"But that floor—"

"Don't worry, Princess. I've slept on a lot worse." He gave her what he hoped was a glowering look. "Now, get some sleep. I'm going to need you bright-eyed and bushy-tailed in the morning."

"Mister Kinkaid, you're not sleeping."

She sure had that governess thing down. Thank God she didn't have a British accent, or all bets would be off.

"And neither are you."

"I'm too . . . excited."

That surprised him.

"Excited?"

"Yes. I've never done anything like this before."

"What is it you've done before?"

"What do you mean?"

"Do you have a job, or just Daddy's trust fund?"

She didn't seem insulted by his remark. "My parents left us a certain amount of money, and Grandfather gave each of us our inheritance when we reached twenty-one. I bought myself a small house in San Francisco and invested the rest."

She kept turning sharper and sharper on him. He found that he liked it. She was the sort of woman who kept a man on his toes.

"What do you do for laughs, Princess? Do you work?"

"I take pictures."

"You're a photographer?"

"Yes."

"You've had pictures published? Like in magazines?"

"Yes. I even brought my camera. It was in my backpack, thank goodness."

Thank goodness. The last time he'd heard that expression, it had come out of his mother's mouth. He smiled in the darkness.

"What do you know about the City of the Sun?" she said quietly

He liked the sound of her voice in the darkness.

"Not much, except that I hope we find mountains of gold there."

"Do you want to know anything about it? It might help us with our search."

He decided to humor her. "Sure."

"Tom found it because some Indians in the jungle told him about a cave and a stream that ran nearby. He's so good with languages, he was able to find out how things had come into being."

In spite of himself, Matt found that he was interested. "Go on."

"My brother also knows a lot about natural healing. When one of the older men, a shaman for the tribe, was dying, Tom gave him something that helped ease the pain. Before the man died, he told Tom about the City of the Sun."

"How to get there and everything?"

"Yes. But he also told Tom how it all happened. And he told him not to worry about finding it, because there were no ghosts or spirits guarding the treasure."

"Really." He didn't believe in that stuff.

"Laugh all you want, Mister Kinkaid. To these people, the spirit life is very real."

That damn governess thing. He almost felt ashamed of himself—but not quite.

"Go on."

"The Indians mined this particular source of ore for a long time, amassing quite a fortune in gold—"

"Now we're getting to the good part!"

"—but eventually, when the Spaniards found them, back sometime in the sixteenth century, they forced the Indians to give it all to them."

"Then why isn't it in some Spanish museum? Or with some rich European family?"

"Because of the Royal Fifth."

"Royal Fifth?"

"One fifth of all the treasure—and there was a considerable amount—was set aside for the king of Spain. The soldiers put that amount aside, in a particular area, and sealed it off. Then they tried to take all the rest themselves. But they met with tragedy."

Matt stirred in his makeshift bed on the hard wooden floor. "Wait a minute—this isn't going to be one of those deals where you get to take the jaguar for your museum, but we can't touch the rest of it, is it? I mean, this stuff isn't cursed, is it?"

"How much would you need?"

"A lot."

"Define a lot."

"Enough so I wouldn't have to work for the rest of my life, and then some."

"I'm sure I could talk to the tribal chief and come to some sort of agreement. After all, you're risking your life to bring me to my brother."

"And the treasure," he reminded her.

"Of course."

"Go on," he said, lying back down and trying to get comfortable. He rarely had company in his small house, and until now, that one small hammock had suited him just fine.

"My brother had heard of this City of the Sun, also called the City of Gold—"

"Oh, I like the sound of that."

"—and when the shaman told him it was true, his only real interest was to find the jaguar, clean it up, and put it on display so that all the world could see it."

"What a guy." But in a bizarre kind of way, Matt meant it.

"He wrote me a letter and told me about the jaguar, about gold earrings and bracelets, piles of gold coins, even a gold chalice."

"He saw all this?"

"Yes. But he didn't want to exploit the Indians, so he made an agreement with the chief to take the jaguar for two years, then bring it back."

"This guy was going to bring it *back* to the Indians?"

"Well, yes. It belongs to them. They worship the jaguar as an animal of great strength and power. Their statue means a lot to them."

"Hmmm." Matt considered this. "But you're sure they won't mind if I take enough gold to finance my final expedition?"

"And what expedition is that?"

Briefly, with as much economy as possible, he told her about his dream to find a quiet island in the Caribbean, kick back, and enjoy life for the rest of his days.

"It sounds lonely to me."

"Trust me, Princess, it'll be just fine. You just send me a brochure from that museum of yours and let me know how the exhibit goes."

"I will." He could feel her hesitation in the dark. "There's only one thing that troubles me."

"What's that?"

"The shaman told my brother that there were several people who had approached the treasure and had a horrifying experience. They almost went mad from it."

"Not me. I know how to deal with large amounts of gold."

"Be serious, Mister Kinkaid. I think we have to use the utmost caution, much as my brother did."

He decided to humor her. "All right, Princess. Whatever you want."

His eyelids felt heavy, he was just about drifting off to sleep when she said, "I'm glad you agree with me. And that's the reason that I've decided to trust you enough to show you the map."

two

Anger, Isabelle decided, didn't really suit her host.

Matt was angry, all right, He'd rolled up off the floor, lit a candle, and now stood over the hammock, staring at her. She got out of it with as much grace and economy as possible, thankful for the expertise she'd acquired from the hammock she'd put up in her own backyard. She remembered longingly the summer afternoons she'd lazed away in it with a terrific historical romance and a glass of icy lemonade.

That was about as much of an adventurer as she usually was.

"You have a *map*." His voice once again had that peculiar flat tone.

"Well . . . yes."

"And you didn't think this was a valuable piece of information? Something you should tell me about as soon as possible?"

"But I did."

"No, Princess, you said that your brother had *told* you about a map. There's a difference."

She refused to let him intimidate her, even though her heart thundered in her chest and her mouth was suddenly dry. She was alone at the edge of the jungle, in a small house with a man she'd met only a few hours ago. A man she hardly knew.

But a man who'd been enough of a gentleman, beneath his rather boorish exterior, to rescue her from a band of ruffians. And she had to remember that this was also the man who was going to help her find her brother.

"Mister Kinkaid, surely you can appreciate the fact that I might have mixed up my words, or not thought them out as carefully as I should have. I'm tired, I wish I could have a hot bath but I know I can't, I've traveled a long way . . . and I want to do everything I can to assure you that I didn't mean to deceive you."

Isabelle watched, fascinated, as his expression slowly calmed. His chiseled features were cast in sharp relief by the soft glow of the single candle. She saw his lips begin to twitch.

"How come, for such a little thing, you have to use such big words?"

She straightened her back the tiniest bit, tried to draw herself up taller, but she was no match for his six feet and something.

"What should I have said?"

"How about, 'I'm tired and I might have screwed up'?"

She considered this. "All right. I screwed up."

Those lips twitched again. Actually, he was a rather amazing specimen of a man, tall and fit, his body a mass of hard muscles. His forearms alone were incredible. Unruly dark-brown hair fell below his shirt collar. He clearly hadn't felt the need to get a haircut in many months. The stubble on his jaw didn't do anything to camouflage the strength of his bone structure. She loved action adventure movies, and he reminded her of a young Harrison Ford.

Actually, this Kinkaid was quite handsome. Even when he was angry and those dark-blue eyes flashed with suppressed emotion. Even when he stood glaring at her, his body taut with frustration.

She tried a different tactic.

"You have to understand, I'm new at all this. This treasure hunting, and surviving in the middle of a jungle."

He smiled, and she forced herself not to stare at him. Lord, he was good-looking.

"The middle of the jungle." He paced to the small kitchen table and set the candle down on top of it, then ran his hand through his hair. "The middle of the jungle." He shot a look her way, his expression one of complete frustration. "Princess, if you think this is the middle of the jungle, you're in for a rude awakening once we walk into the real thing."

"I can keep up with you."

"What, you're about to tell me you do your half hour on the Stairmaster three times a week? That won't cut it out here."

She folded her arms in front of her chest. "What exactly do you have in mind?"

"Give me the map, and the picture of your brother. I can move faster and get more done without you."

She stared at him for a long moment. "No."

"This isn't some kind of pleasure trip, Princess. Things could get very messy, and, pardon me for saying so, you don't strike me as the messy type."

"I screwed up once. It won't happen again."

He glowered at her, and she made an attempt to glower right back.

There was a part of him that could barely keep from laughing at the expression on her face, that scowling, elegant face. But a part of him remained dead serious. She was smaller and weaker than he was, and he found himself not wanting to expose her to any danger. He wanted to protect her, and the feeling made him absolutely disgusted with himself. It wasn't often he felt this way—toward *anyone*—because feelings of this sort could be a sign of real weakness in the kind of life he lived.

"I'm going with you, Mister Kinkaid," she said quietly. "And you can't stop me."

He remained silent, studying her. Considering.

"What would you do, anyway?" she said. "You're too much of a gentleman to leave me here to a worse fate than any I could find in the jungle with you."

He absolutely hated the way she could see right through him. But she didn't need to know that.

"I wouldn't be too sure of that," he replied, then tried to look fierce but clearly failed. Damn, it was frustrating when she wasn't even scared of him!

The silence grew between them until Isabelle finally said, "I have to find Tom."

He hated it when she played on his emotions. What little of them he still admitted to having.

"Hey, it's a bitch that your brother's missing. I can appreciate that, but—"

"Don't you want your gold, Mister Kinkaid?"

"What I want," he said through gritted teeth, "is for you to stop calling me Mister Kinkaid. Matt will do just fine."

"But you look like a Matthew."

Couldn't this woman make any sense? He ran his hands through his hair again, then decided to take another approach.

"Where's the map?"

She advanced toward him until they were face to face, as though she was looking up and he was looking down at her. Those eyes—she had the most incredible gray eyes.

"Not until you agree to take me with you."

He sighed. Tractable? How had he ever thought she was tractable? If he didn't take her along, have her where he could keep an eye on her, who knew what kind of havoc her good intentions could wreak?

"Fine."

"Promise me," she said.

"You have my word," he ground out between clenched teeth.

She hesitated, and he said, "Don't push your luck."

"I believe you," she said, approaching her backpack and kneeling before it. "Because I sense that, underneath all that grime, that facial stubble, and that wild hair, there's a gentleman waiting to come out."

"Oh, no. Don't make this into one of those romantic stories, those fairy tales—"

"They're not just stories. Don't you believe in love, Mister Kinkaid?"

Did he believe in love? All he wanted was to see the frigging treasure map, and here she was, delivering some sort of discourse on love.

"Get the map," he said shortly.

"Well," she said, digging through her backpack, her back toward him, "you must have strong feelings on the subject, or you wouldn't be reacting so forcefully."

Matt counted to ten, thinking the entire time that this woman couldn't even carry a normal, plain backpack. No, this one had strange mesh pockets on the side and enough inner pockets to confuse anyone. Definitely an amateur traveler's—no, a *tourist's*—bag.

He took a deep breath. "Maybe I'm a tad grumpy, Princess, because neither of us is going to sleep a wink tonight and we have—at the very *least*—a twenty-mile hike tomorrow."

"Hmmm. Twenty miles." She considered this as she pulled a packet out of her backpack.

"At least." He'd never walked twenty miles in a week, let alone a day. If there was an easier way of doing something, he was the expert at finding it. But he wanted to scare her.

"And I suppose the next thing you'll be telling me is that there are hideous grizzly bears in the jungle."

"No. Just snakes and spiders and all sorts of creepy, crawly things. Ants. Fire ants. Huge termites. Oh, and don't let me forget the leeches—"

"Spare yourself, Mister Kinkaid. I'm coming with you." She approached the table, slid a document out of an envelope, and spread it on the scarred surface of the table.

"The City of the Sun," she said softly. "The City of Gold."

His breath almost caught in his throat as he stared down at the carefully crafted map. Excitement built inside him as he recognized some of the landmarks.

"That town . . . and those ruins . . . I know where they are." He looked up at her. "Is it drawn to scale?"

She nodded. "Tom's meticulous about such things."

"Then it's about a two-week journey from here."

"Two hundred and eighty miles away?"

Lord, she was quick. He hadn't even realized he was talking out loud, more to himself than to her. Matt pretended to study the map closely, regretting his twenty-mile deception earlier. More like three hundred miles away, through dense jungle . . . but if they could find a pilot . . . depending on how close he could drop them . . . and how they would arrange a pickup afterwards . . .

"You're sure you can get us there?"

He nodded his head, entranced with the map. He'd never held an actual treasure map in his hands before. Things were definitely looking up.

"The deeper we can fly into the jungle, the less time we have to waste walking. But I don't want anyone getting too close to that city, so it'll still mean at least a couple of days on foot." He glanced at her. "A couple of very *rough* days."

His words went right over her head.

"I want to talk to the tribal chief when I get there. I have to see if he has any idea where Tom went."

He sighed. She wasn't going to give an inch. Well, she had a point. If it weren't for her and her missing brother, he wouldn't even know where to begin looking for the City of the Sun.

"You got it, Princess," he replied, his gaze still on the map. "As long as I get my gold."

She placed the map in a fanny pack she had around her waist, then went back to the hammock and actually fell asleep. Matt sat by the door for a while, then made himself a cup of strong coffee.

An actual treasure map. And an actual treasure. Things were getting better and better. His dream of island living actually seemed within reach.

The soft tapping at the door brought him out of his thoughts instantly.

"Who is it?" he whispered.

"Miguel," came the reply, and as Matt recognized the

voice, he opened the door and let his friend and contact inside.

Isabelle came awake the moment he opened the door and, rubbing her eyes, swung herself out of the hammock and came to the table. Matt offered her a cup of coffee, then poured one for Miguel.

Miguel spoke softly and rapidly in Spanish, and Matt was suddenly glad he wasn't going to have to stop and translate everything for his partner. At least she was bilingual. Hell, she could probably outsmart him in two languages.

"He escaped!" Isabelle said in response to Miguel's soft-spoken words. "Frederico escaped."

"Yeah, but we don't know how much these people—whoever they are—got out of him." Matt glanced around his small house. "We're leaving now."

"What do you mean?" Isabelle said. "It's not even sunrise."

"My gut feeling tells me that if we don't leave ASAP, we're going to have some unwelcome company. What do you think, Miguel?"

The little man took one last sip of his black coffee and set his cup down. "I'm going to go hide at my sister's until this whole thing is over."

"Give it a couple of weeks," Matt said, patting his shoulder. "Come on, Princess, let's hit the road. The story is, we're heading back home to dear old Mom."

She didn't know how he did it, but he found them a pilot within the hour. They went back to the cantina and sat at an out-of-the-way table, with their backs to the grimy wooden walls until the person Matt was searching for came in the door.

"Remember," he whispered to her as he stood up. "We're taking the money you would have paid me and offering it to Ed if he'll get us to the nearest airport. But once we get there, I know a buddy I can trust who'll fly us in close to the City of the Sun. I know it sounds like we're taking the long way around, but we'll get there much sooner."

"You're right," she said, taking his arm, uneasy at the

way some of the men in the cantina were looking at her. "And we'd better get out of town."

By midafternoon, they reached a tiny airport in a town she'd never heard of. Ed had had a little trouble getting his run-down helicopter to work, and she'd waited patiently while both he and Matt worked on the machine.

Matt must have seen the worry in her eyes when the helicopter finally fired up, because he whispered, "I'm not going up in anything I think might come right back down. That should reassure you, Princess."

She simply followed him.

Now she stood on the tarmac, watching as he joked and laughed with yet another man, this one a short, barrel-chested individual named Roderick.

Isabelle stared off into the lush green beginnings of jungle undergrowth, the plants encroaching on this small slice of civilization. Then she turned her attention to the pale blue sky, the sun a blazing ball of brilliance overhead. Both the temperature and the humidity were overwhelming, and she pulled at the front of her blouse where it stuck to her skin. Though she would've given anything for a bath, there was no time. They had to get to the interior, to the lost city, as quickly as possible.

She glanced over as Matt came sauntering toward her, a confident smile on his face.

"All set, Princess. Rod says he'll fly us in for free, in exchange for an hour alone with you in one of the back offices."

She glared at him. Narrowed her eyes. "Very funny."

"Hey, what fun is it if I can't even tease you?" He lowered his voice as she fell in step by his side and they headed toward the white helicopter. "What gave me away?"

"It's only logical."

"How so?"

"You know I would never do something like that. So you wouldn't have even suggested it. And you want to get to the City of the Sun as much as I do."

"What would you say," he said, "if I told you that in the

beginning of my most delicate negotiations, Rod tried to get me to agree to that original deal?"

She glanced up at him as they both approached the helicopter. This one looked a lot better than the first one they'd traveled in.

"I'd say you were a most intelligent man to have turned him down."

She continued walking away from him, feeling his eyes on her every step of the way.

Nothing could have prepared her for the view of the jungle from a helicopter. So many shades of green, such a huge horizon, such an expanse of sheer wildness. Isabelle glanced over at Matt, who seemed to be enjoying himself as he talked with Roderick. Though the man had most certainly suggested the sordid little arrangement Matt had described, Isabelle couldn't fault him as a pilot. Roderick knew what he was doing.

Matt had taken a furtive look at the treasure map before they took off, making a few necessary notes on a small piece of paper that he now kept in front of him. After a slightly longer time than she'd expected, he signaled to her that they were very close to the spot where they were to disembark.

"I'll take you in as low as I can," Roderick said over the noise of the propellers.

"Fine," Matt said. Isabelle nodded and gave him a tentative smile.

They were almost there. Very shortly she would find out what had happened to her brother, and that couldn't happen soon enough for her.

"Shouldn't we be going this way?" Isabelle asked, indicating the opposite direction.

"Nope." He was in a good mood, and felt supremely confident. "I had him overshoot the site. That way, if he decides to help out those other guys, they'll be going in the wrong direction."

"Unless they have a copy of the map."

Matt stopped dead in his tracks. "Now you're telling me that there might be copies?"

"No. Frederico never saw it. I only told him I was here to find Tom."

"Then why even bring it up?" His good mood was disappearing as fast as morning mist.

"I can't be responsible for anyone else Tom might have told."

"Any ideas?"

"No. He was closest to me, and there were a lot of things he trusted me with that he told no one else."

"Well, let's hope this was one of them," Matt threw over his shoulder as he strode ahead. "Any more of your little revelations and you're going to kill me."

She said nothing, merely followed in his wake.

He glanced back over his shoulder. "I'm teasing, Princess."

She looked up at his face, then continued walking. Something was clearly bothering her.

Matt felt vaguely uncomfortable, though he had absolutely no idea what he'd done wrong. Something, obviously, if she wasn't speaking to him. He cleared his throat.

"We have at least a day's travel ahead of us. Maybe two, depending on the terrain. Don't you think things are going to be a little uncomfortable if you refuse to talk to me?"

She held up a hand in a "Back off" kind of gesture.

"You really are mad, aren't you?"

"I didn't think it was funny."

"What?"

"Roderick."

Comprehension dawned. "I would never have agreed to it! I told you, I was teasing!"

"There's always a little bit of truth behind any joke, don't you think?"

This woman could ask the damnedest questions. "No. I think sometimes a joke is just a joke."

She said nothing. They continued walking, the jungle a thick canopy of green above them, the sounds of birds screaming in the hot, humid air.

"Princess, come on—"

"Don't call me that."

"Oh, excuse me, Your Royal Highness."

"Thank you." She could frost a window in the middle of the jungle with that tone.

They walked in silence for a good half hour, and Matt wondered how she did it. A few times he looked back at her, quickly. She never saw him, as her entire attention was on where she was putting her feet, step after careful step. He had to admit that she was doing an excellent job of keeping up with him.

Drenched in sweat, her hair in a makeshift braid down her back, that hat perched on her head, she looked entirely out of her element. But those long, sleek legs encased in khaki pants kept pace with him.

Another swift glance provided a distinctly enjoyable view from a masculine standpoint, as her crisp white blouse had wilted and was plastered to her body with sweat. Her face seemed paler, and he took pity on her.

"Let's take a quick break."

She stopped, then unzipped one of the side pockets on her elaborate backpack and brought out what looked like a wrapped candy bar.

"What have you got there?"

"One of those Power Bars. You know, protein bars. This one's chocolate banana with antioxidants."

Aha, she was speaking to him again. He had no idea what an antioxidant was, and he didn't care. At least she was talking.

"Here's some water, Princess."

They drank in silence, and he could hear her breathing, slightly heavier than normal. He'd have to watch it, be sure he didn't overtire her, because he suddenly had the feeling that she was going on nerves alone.

"Tell me something funny about Tom," he said, wanting to lighten her mood. Maybe if she thought about her brother, it would give her a little more strength.

To his absolute horror, her gray eyes filled, and she looked away.

"I'm sorry," she whispered.

He didn't say anything, just stood very still, with no idea what to do next. He'd rather have come across a group of headhunters than have to deal with a crying woman.

She swallowed, then said, "I'm sorry I was—the way I was earlier. I'm just so worried about Tom."

It all made sense. The poor kid had to be worried sick about her big brother, her only family left in the entire world.

"Hey, it's okay. Anyway, don't you think you'd know if Tom were dead?"

She stared at him.

"You know. Instinct."

She pleated the wrapper of her protein bar with her fingers, then stuffed it back inside her backpack and zipped the side pocket. "I don't know. I don't usually rely on instinct."

"What do you go on, Princess?" Even though the nickname bugged her, it suited her.

"Logic."

He'd never met a woman like this one. A cool customer one minute, crying and vulnerable the next. But he realized that no tears had actually fallen.

This Isabelle Burke showed a lot more control of her emotions than most women.

He had to do something.

"Well, for what it's worth, I don't think he's dead." He had to give her some sense of hope, or she'd never make it through the jungle, even a one- or two-day journey.

"You don't?"

He just about despised himself for the hope he saw shining in those gray eyes, but he couldn't think of any alternative. The middle of the jungle was not the best place for an individual to give up all hope and have a complete emotional breakdown.

"I don't." He decided to embellish his opinion, hoping like mad that Tom actually was holed up somewhere. "We would have heard something back at the village."

"Of course!" Her expression changed, her eyes sparkled,

her cheeks flushed with color. Matt simply stared. She hadn't looked this animated since he'd first met her at the cantina. And he found himself hoping Tom was still alive.

She handed him the canteen, then wiped her palms on her khaki pants.

"Let's keep going, I want to get to the City of the Sun as soon as we can."

They walked for the remainder of the first day and set up camp as soon as darkness began to fall. Which was hard to gauge, because many of the places they walked through were pretty shaded, what with the towering canopy of the jungle.

He had some idea of how tired Isabelle was when she didn't even object to sharing a tent with him. Matt almost took pity on her as she collapsed on her sleeping bag without saying a word and within half a minute was breathing deeply.

She was going on heart alone. There was nothing about this woman that made him believe she was even vaguely prepared for a journey like this, yet she'd been determined to come with him. It humbled Matt, because he also knew that her reasons had absolutely nothing to do with treasure and everything to do with her brother.

Privately, he wondered if Tom was still alive.

Matt ate a solitary dinner, tired enough that he didn't heat anything up but just ate food out of his pack. *Some dinner, all right.* Dried beef and a ripe banana, and a few pieces of a chocolate bar. And water, of course, to make up for all his perspiring. The jungle, even shaded, was a hot and humid place. A lush, green oven.

He studied Isabelle as she slept and wondered how she would feel in the morning. Probably stiff as hell, what with all the walking they'd done. He wondered if she would even make it through the second day. He really should have insisted on leaving her at a seaside resort hotel while he went after this brother of hers. She'd look a hell of a lot more at home on a beach, relaxing by the ocean in a bikini, than here in the jungle, bathed in sweat. She was an elegant woman, and her world had certainly never included anything like this.

Or anyone like him.

He lay down on his sleeping bag and stretched. He had already taken off his boots, after being sure the tent was thoroughly zipped up. You had to be careful about all the things creeping and crawling on the jungle floor. He stretched gingerly, flexing the muscles in his legs, then relaxing them. He hadn't walked this far in a long time, and he had a feeling he might be a little stiff in the morning.

The minute he closed his eyes, he slept.

The first thing she noticed when she woke the following morning was that her legs felt as if they were on fire. The second thing she noticed was that she was sprawled on top of Matt Kinkaid. Directly on top of him. Their bodies pressed together as close as was humanly possible. And she wasn't so much of an innocent that she wasn't immediately aware of the effect she was having on him.

If the physical proximity of their bodies hadn't given his sensual feelings away, that grin on his stubbled face would've done the job.

Horrified, she tried to move away, but every muscle in her legs and lower back protested, on fire, rigid with pain.

"Ow-ow-ow!" she said as she rolled off him, the jungle floor barely cushioned by the tent floor and her sleeping bag. Jarring her body activated that pain all over again.

"A little stiff?" Matt asked.

She would have died rather than tell him, so she cautiously tried to sit up.

"Oh, no more than I expected." At this moment, she would've killed for a Jacuzzi. Even thinking about the warm, bubbling water seemed to bring on more pain.

"Are you going to be able to keep up with me today?" He didn't seem to be gloating, so she chanced a look at him. He seemed genuinely concerned, but she couldn't risk telling him the truth and not continuing with him or, worse, losing a day or two while her body got accustomed to the rigors of the journey.

"I—I think I can." It wasn't exactly a lie. Not exactly.

"What time do you want to head out?"

She closed her eyes for a moment, summoned up her will.

"Give me just fifteen minutes."

He felt sorry for her. But damned if he didn't admire her for trying, as he watched her slowly cleanse her face with a wet cloth moistened with water from one of their canteens. And as he watched her tortured movements as she slowly brushed out and rebraided her blond hair, he had to admire her courage. If there was an entry for "stiff upper lip" in the dictionary, well, they should put Isabelle's picture right beside it.

He'd already formulated a plan by the time she was ready. She walked up to him, her pack on her back, and he could tell that each movement, each step, was sheer torture.

"You can't walk," he stated flatly.

"Mister Kinkaid," she began, and he decided to hear her out.

"Go on."

"I'm afraid you were right. I didn't think, I didn't take into consideration that this might be a little too rough for me—"

"But I did." He liked the fact that he could be her hero, even if only in this small way.

She looked up at him, clearly puzzled.

"We're less than one day away from where we need to be by nightfall. I calculated things so we were dropped fairly close to the tribe. We can leave most of our supplies here, and come back for them later."

"But I still don't think I can—"

"I'll carry you."

She flushed a bright pink, and he wasn't sure if it was because of the physical intimacy of the act, or if she felt helpless, or angry at herself, or both. All he knew was that he'd certainly enjoyed their physical proximity this morning. With another woman, it might have led to something. With Isabelle, he'd had an urge to protect her. Again.

"I can't ask you to carry me."

"Sure you can. How are your arms? Can you still carry that pack?"

She nodded.

"We'll just take out some of your stuff and put in some of mine, especially food and first aid items. How about it?"

She nodded her head, and he could see the stress lines at her mouth start to soften.

"That would be—that would be fine."

He liked carrying her.

Isabelle still had her backpack on while he carried her piggyback style, his arms supporting her bent legs. He'd felt like a cad, hearing her breathy little whimpers of pain as she maneuvered her legs into the necessary position, but he knew it would take a lot less out of her than actual walking would.

He liked the feeling of her arms around his neck, the closeness. Her softness. And he *really* liked the feeling of her breasts pressed up against his back.

Oh, a man could dream, all right. He had about as much chance with a woman like Isabelle as a pig did with a poodle. There was no place in his life for a woman like her. And no place in his dream, either. For he had a feeling that Isabelle would always be engaged with the world, doing something for someone, while his goal in life was to get as far away from civilization and its problems as possible.

But for now, he could enjoy her. When she wasn't driving him crazy.

"Look at that!" she whispered, as a particularly brilliant butterfly of cobalt blue and bright yellow flashed past them. "Oh, how gorgeous!"

Golden butterflies had never really interested him before. Gold itself had been his goal. He didn't want to be one of those guys who pretended to be interested in stuff as a way of getting a woman into bed. It wouldn't work with Isabelle, anyway; she would see right through him. With any other woman there would have been thoughts other than travel on his mind as they walked deeper and deeper into the jungle and became more and more isolated, just the two of them. With this woman, he found, he just wanted to look after her. Protect her.

Be a better man.

He blinked, then shook his head slightly. Sweat dripped into one of his eyes, stinging.

What could he have been thinking?

"Wait a minute," he heard Isabelle say. "I want to get my binoculars out."

"Binoculars? I would've left those back with the other stuff."

"Not these." He heard the smile in her voice. "They're quite compact, and fit nicely in one of the side pockets."

He remembered those damn mesh pockets, and stood still while she managed to reach behind with one hand and grab the binoculars. Somehow he couldn't find it in his heart to be mean enough to prevent this woman from viewing a butterfly.

"Want to take a look?" she whispered after a minute.

"Sure."

She handed him a pair of binoculars slightly smaller than a pack of cigarettes. They weighed practically nothing, and his hand dwarfed them. But he put them up to his eyes and got a stunningly close look at the brilliantly colored butterfly.

"Isn't it just glorious?"

Again, he had that quick image of Deborah Kerr, this time out on a field trip with a recalcitrant charge.

"Lovely."

She didn't seem to notice the sarcasm, simply plucked the binoculars out of his hand and took another look.

"Where do you get these toys?"

"What do you mean?" she said.

"That backpack of yours. And those field glasses."

"Oh." He had his head turned just enough that he could see her lower the glasses. "A friend of mine works in a travel store near the museum, and she lets me use her discount."

"Hmmm." He considered this. "Any other little gadgets I should know about?"

She smiled. "Only on a need-to-know basis, I think."

He almost laughed out loud. Then, remembering the gold they would find at the end of this journey, he said, "Let's get going."

"I couldn't agree more," she said, and from the twisting around behind him, he assumed she was putting the teeny binoculars back in that pack.

"How are the legs?"

He could almost feel her embarrassment and modesty as she replied, "Still a little stiff, but much better for not walking. Thank you, Mister Kinkaid. I don't know what I would have done without you, I really don't."

Deborah Kerr, thanking the savages. He muttered something under his breath and started walking, determined to keep his mind on gold, more gold, and gold alone.

They didn't take another break for quite some time after the butterfly. Matt concentrated on putting one foot in front of the other, staying on course. They'd made good time this morning, stopping briefly for lunch, then continuing onward. But he'd determined that they had no more time for silly sight-seeing, no matter how wonderful the colors and textures were, or what she wanted to see.

According to his calculations, they should be meeting up with this mysterious Indian tribe any minute.

"Matthew," she whispered.

He wondered why she hadn't called him Mister Kinkaid. Then seconds after that, he sensed they weren't alone.

Shadowy figures flitted through the trees. He caught a glimpse of face paint, of bright, curious eyes. Deciding that prudence and caution were the best course, Matt gently eased Isabelle off his back and kept her behind him. Then he glanced behind them and suddenly realized they were surrounded, shadow people on all sides of them.

So much for that plan. There didn't seem to be any way he could shield Isabelle, and he wasn't entirely sure that these people were part of the tribe he was aiming to find.

"Any ideas, Princess?" he said, his voice low. "Because right about now would be as good a time as any to put them into practice."

three

Matt tried to shield Isabelle from the painted warriors as they came closer, clearly curious yet still looking fierce. But she had other ideas, popping out from behind him and placing herself in plain sight.

"Stay close to me, Prin—" He stopped abruptly as one of the first tribesmen looked up at Isabelle, then set down his spear and knelt in front of her. He lowered his head until it almost touched the jungle floor.

Amazed, he watched the dozen or so others do exactly the same thing.

"I don't know what the hell you just did," he muttered, "but your timing couldn't have been better."

She looked up at him, and he was amazed to see her eyes sparkling and her cheeks flushed a bright pink. Isabelle may have been feeling many things, but fear wasn't one of them.

"How do I tell them to get back up?" she whispered. "This is awful!"

"No," he said, touching her arm. "Trust me. This is not bad. And it's a hell of a lot better than getting killed."

"There's really no need to use language like that," she said softly. "My father always told me that men resort to swearing when their vocabularies aren't very extensive."

"English, please," he whispered, actually afraid that he

might laugh. He'd been in some pretty strange situations in his life, but this was shaping up to be one of the strangest.

"What I meant is—"

"It's okay, Princess. I get your drift. I'll watch my mouth while you're around." He gestured toward the tribesmen, their foreheads still low, their spears still on the ground beside them. "What should we do about these guys?"

"Do you think they speak Spanish?"

He gave her what he hoped was a reassuring smile. "Let's give it a try." He cleared his throat, then said—in Spanish—"Please stand up!"

Nothing.

Again, in Spanish—"There's no reason to bow."

He looked at Isabelle and shrugged his shoulders.

She cleared her throat and tried Spanish once again. "Now, I'd like you all to come to your feet—"

Instantly, gracefully, the group collectively came to its feet, but kept a respectful distance.

"What did I do?" she whispered in English, for Matt's ears alone.

"Beats me. But keep doing it."

She glanced around. "Would you please—" She hesitated, and he saw her lips twitch. Isabelle actually thought this was funny!

"Would you please—take me to your leader?"

He made a snorting sound in a feeble attempt not to laugh.

"This is quite wonderful," she whispered to him. "I've always wanted to say that!"

If he hadn't seen it, Matt would've never believed it. The painted tribesmen actually *carried* Isabelle back to the village.

He, of course, got to walk behind—with the blasted backpack. Muttering to himself all the way.

"What did she do to them?" he said to himself as he tripped over a root on the jungle floor and almost lost his balance. "I spoke Spanish. She spoke Spanish." He thought furiously as he raced to keep up with the villagers, who had placed Isabelle on some sort of crude chair, almost like a primitive rickshaw. Now four or five of the tribesmen were carrying her as if it were a total honor.

They couldn't seem to do enough for her.

He just didn't get it.

"It has to be that governess thing," he muttered, while keeping a careful eye on his feet and the jungle floor. "It's attitude. She has exactly the right attitude, that Deborah Kerr, Grace Kelly type of thing. With a little bit of Hepburn thrown in."

But that still didn't feel right. Instinct told him something else was going on, something he still hadn't put his finger on. Puzzled, he looked up ahead, as Isabelle's rickshaw almost disappeared into the jungle's gloom.

Matt decided that now wasn't the time to think about this. He would just concentrate on keeping up with these guys. Clad in skimpy loincloths, every single one of them had a sleek, runner's body, tight with muscle and not a spare ounce of flesh. Clearly, junk food had yet to invade this part of the world. And twenty miles a day would be no problem for these people. Matt was sure they'd never even heard of a Stairmaster.

Their village was a masterpiece of artful concealment.

One minute you saw jungle, the next you could barely make out various huts and stone circles. Matt had dealt with tribes before in the course of his wanderings, but none had struck him as being this . . . magical. There was really no other word for it. They'd arrived at dusk, which added to the effect.

The men set Isabelle down in a small clearing, and women and children seemed to simply appear out of the dense jungle growth to stare at her. Again, that kneeling and bowing, that total subservience. Again, she gently asked them to get to their feet. And of course she met their "fearless leader."

The chief was younger than Matt would have expected, until he remembered that Isabelle had told him that their shaman and tribal leader had recently passed on. This chief was in his early twenties, a bronzed god, with high cheekbones and dark, glittering eyes. He would've looked at home as an exotic runway model. Standing briefly clad in the middle of the jungle, he radiated presence. Even Matt had to admit he was a magnificent specimen of a man.

And, thankfully, he knew a lot more Spanish than the rest of his tribe did.

"Tom taught me," he said, as they sat together just outside his hut. He'd brought them water to drink and fruit to eat, but Matt was still uneasy. Perhaps it was the way the tribal chief's darkly inquisitive eyes kept coming back to Isabelle. She'd taken her hat off, and the chief couldn't seem to tear his gaze away from her pale blond hair.

Tom had apparently taught the natives a lot more than Spanish. According to the tribal chief, whose name sounded something like Kenta, Isabelle's brother had come into the tribe's life at a time when they were struggling. He'd shared everything he had with them, the most precious being his knowledge of herbs that even their medicine man hadn't known about.

"He saved my father from so much pain," Kenta said.

"I was sorry to hear about him," Isabelle replied.

"It was time for him to transform."

Matt had to hand it to these people. To them, death certainly didn't seem like the traumatic event it was in the civilized world. There seemed to be an acceptance, a peace about the whole process.

He knew Isabelle had to be anxious about her brother, so he asked, "Do you know where Tom is?"

The tribal chief nodded his head. "He was seen by one of our men. I asked him to go after your brother and bring him back safely to us." He glanced at Isabelle, and Matt could tell the man was fascinated all over again. If they didn't watch it, she'd end up being the queen of this entire group. And that thought made him decidedly uneasy.

"Don't worry," the chief said. "He'll bring Tom back to you."

Isabelle could barely blink back her tears, she seemed so

relieved. As she leaned forward to thank the chief, Matt noticed the small gold sun on a chain around her neck. He also noticed the way the chief kept glancing at the medallion.

That's it. That sun had some sort of significance.

He asked her about it as soon as they were alone in the guest hut.

"Did Tom give you that?" He indicated the medallion around her neck.

"Yes. It was part of the treasure that the shaman said he could take with him. It was given to him as a gift, and he sent it to me and told me to wear it always. The shaman told him it contained powerful magic. Protection."

"That's what did it, Princess. That's what had them bowing in front of you." He massaged his leg, still sore from the unbelievably challenging trek to the village. "And that's what got you a ride."

"I asked them why they didn't carry you," she said.

He sighed. "This should be good."

"They said that it was right and proper that my consort should walk."

"You're kidding!" Consort? He was her *consort*?

"I tried to change their minds, but they seemed remarkably insistent."

Consort. He still couldn't get over that word.

Matt started to massage his other leg, knowing that if he didn't do something to loosen the muscles, he was going to wake up stiff as a board the next day.

"So," he said, watching Isabelle as she searched inside that incredibly complicated backpack for a washcloth, "what's our plan of action?"

"I think," she said, pouring some water from one of their canteens onto the soft cloth, then wiping her face with it, "that we should enjoy ourselves tonight. Kenta told me that the entire tribe is preparing a feast in our honor."

In your honor, he thought. *The consort will probably have to either sit at your feet or grovel down at the end of the table.* If there even was a table.

It wasn't a comforting thought.

"Just make sure I get something to eat."

She started to laugh as she took her hair out of its braid and ran a brush through it.

"I mean it. If they tell you that your consort has to eat entrails or something, I'm out of here."

She had to set down her brush, she was laughing so hard.

"I'm dead serious, Princess. You're not the one who had to keep up with those Marathon Men today."

"I'm sorry," she said, wiping her eyes and picking up her brush. Her other hand reached out and touched his knee in a conciliatory gesture. "I'll make sure you get plenty to eat tonight."

"Lizard wasn't exactly what I had in mind," Matt whispered to Isabelle in English as he eyed the chunks of meat still sizzling on their skewers. Their plates were sturdy green leaves. There was also some sort of grain piled high, next to a starchy, bananalike vegetable that looked like plantain, along with some green vegetables in some sort of sauce and a baked yam.

But the lizard was clearly the main course, and the delicacy. A delicacy reserved for honored guests—and their consorts.

"I'm sure they wouldn't give us anything they thought was harmful," Isabelle said, and he could tell she was attempting to reassure him. "From what the chief tells me, this is considered a delicacy in these parts."

Matt eyed the chunks of meat, wishing he were groveling somewhere, waiting for a few scraps to be thrown at his feet. It wasn't that he was a fussy eater, but—lizard?

"I don't think we should hurt their feelings," she muttered to him, while smiling at the entire tribe. Everyone had turned out for the evening's festivities. And everyone seemed to be watching them.

"Then why don't you go first, oh Sun Goddess," Matt muttered.

She surprised him.

"All right."

He watched as she took a bite of the strange meat, chewed it, then swallowed. And he had to hand it to her, because she gave them all a beautiful, brilliant smile, then rubbed her stomach in circular motions with her free hand, a gesture of complete satisfaction.

Excited murmurs rose from the crowd.

"Don't overdo it," Matt cautioned her. "Or we'll be eating Godzilla on a stick for breakfast, lunch, and dinner."

"It's not that bad, you big baby. It tastes a lot like chicken. And there's some kind of spice or rub they've used, it almost tastes like oregano."

"Not the Colonel's eleven herbs and spices, I'll bet."

"Will you stop fussing? They did a study on that chicken and found out those eleven herbs and spices were mostly salt, and that's bad for your blood pressure—"

"Bad it might be, but I'd trade this lizard kabob for a three-piece meal, extra crispy, in a New York minute."

She dug her elbow into his side unobtrusively so no one would notice.

"Maybe we could ask them to deep-fry a few chunks for you," she said. "Would you just take a bite, Matt? They're watching. And please remember that they went to a lot of trouble for us."

He eyed the kabob. Actually, if he hadn't known better, he would have sworn it was chicken. Mustering up his nerve, Matt took a bite and chewed it. The taste filled his mouth, and he was genuinely surprised. Not tough or grainy, as he'd expected. The wild meat practically melted in his mouth, it was that tender. And it did indeed taste an awful lot like chicken.

Isabelle nodded and smiled, and those murmurs started up again.

"Good enough for you?" he muttered.

"I expect you to finish that entire kabob."

There it was, that governess thing again. And that posture. Come to think of it, she could be a queen. It wasn't that much of a stretch.

He enjoyed the rest of the meal, recognizing the plantain and figuring that the green vegetable must be a relative to peppery-tasting watercress. The chief had also broken out some kind of private label, a homemade brew that tasted like a very spicy rum and packed quite a kick.

"Go easy on that stuff, Princess," he cautioned Isabelle. "I don't want to see you dancing on the tables at midnight."

"We're sitting on the jungle floor."

"It's a figure of speech, Sun Goddess. You know, just a lowly consort's way of reaching for a laugh."

"Oh, Matt, are you still upset about all that?"

He rubbed his left knee. It still ached. At thirty-six, he was getting too old for these Iron Man marathons. Or maybe he just wasn't in the greatest shape. Not like Kenta, Lord of the Jungle, over there. Bare-chested and superbly muscled, with black hair that flowed to his shoulders, he looked like he belonged on the cover of a romance novel. And Matt suspected that Isabelle was the sort of woman who loved romance novels.

While he, with his sweat-stained clothing and ragged hair, his stubbled chin and bad knee, could have been Central Casting's definition of a bum. Make that a bum who was also a consort.

"You have to admit, being a consort isn't exactly a flattering job description. I liked it better when I was your guide."

She put her hand on his knee, and a different type of tension invaded his muscles.

"You're still my guide, Matt." She glanced up as another plate was set in front of them, this time with something on it that looked like dried meat. Their server bowed low, then spoke rapidly in Spanish.

"Great," Matt muttered. "Lizard jerky. In case we get hungry tonight."

"I think it was very thoughtful of them." She smiled up at the native, then rubbed her stomach again.

"He's taking you *where*?"

"Hot springs. Kenta says there's one not too far away. Can you imagine it? I'll finally be able to take a bath!"

"And where will fearless leader be?"

"Oh, Matt, I'm sure he'll give me some privacy."

"*Some* being the operative word. For all you know, Princess, accepting his invitation to the hot springs could be the equivalent of going to the No-Tell Motel."

"Your imagination is disgustingly vivid."

He heard the sound of chewing in the dark.

"You aren't actually eating that stuff, are you?"

"It's quite tasty. And I was nervous at dinner, so I didn't eat as much as I would've liked."

He snorted. "That's true. I hadn't considered that being a goddess is such hard work. Nothing at all like a consort—"

"I can't believe you're still mad about that."

"How about this, Princess? How about I get to wear that necklace tomorrow?"

"I don't think we should confuse them."

"Hah! I knew you'd have an excuse."

"No, it's not an excuse, it's the logical approach to take. But perhaps I have something in my backpack that you could wear—"

"A consort in drag. Terrific."

"No, I meant around your neck."

"At this point, I'm considering a noose."

"Matt! It can't possibly be that bad."

He couldn't put a finger on why he was behaving so badly. Well, yes, he could. He didn't like the idea of the tribal chief taking Isabelle to an isolated spot, this hot springs, and being alone with her. There was no telling what might happen.

It hit him with sudden certainty that he was jealous. That green-eyed monster had him but good.

"I have a jade horse on a chain—"

"Forget it. These people have never seen a horse—they'd probably decide to eat it. And me."

"They're not that uncivilized." He heard rustling as she searched through her bag again, using a small flashlight as her source of light.

"I have a Kermit the Frog key chain—"

"Fantastic. I can be Wart, Great God of Frogs. Nope,

Princess, I'd probably wind up on the menu for their next feast, on a skewer right next to Godzilla."

"What is this thing you have about being eaten? I can't help you if you're going to be so disagreeable. The last thing I can offer is a golden rose, it's a lovely pendant—"

"Too feminine." He abruptly changed the subject as she clicked off her flashlight and lay back down on her side of the guest hut. "Why don't I come with you to the hot springs?"

Dead silence. Obviously she didn't like the idea.

"Unless, of course," he said slowly and carefully, "you *like* the idea of being alone with the chief."

Another silence, then—

"Matt, are you jealous?"

She had such an advantage over him, being able to see right through him. It was disconcerting that she could see his motives and emotions almost as quickly as he could. And she probably had a better understanding of them, to boot.

"Me? Jealous? Oh, no. I'm just a noble consort, not wanting my Sun Goddess to be left in any danger. And if you're planning on taking off your clothes in front of Bomba the Jungle Boy, you'd better think again. Because we're in the middle of the jungle, and civilization and manners travel only so far."

"The chief would never touch me."

"The chief is a man!"

"And what's that supposed to mean!"

"Exactly how much experience do you have with men, Princess?"

Her stunned silence told him everything. Even in the dark.

"Oh, no," he said.

"Oh, no, what?" she replied.

"Please don't tell me that I also have to worry about virgin sacrifices."

Her silence gave him his answer.

"Some of us aren't as adventurous as you are, Mister Kinkaid."

She'd called him Matt before, earlier at dinner and tonight in this hut. Now they were back to Mister Kinkaid. He knew he was heading toward the doghouse, and that she didn't like to discuss such private matters, but he had to continue.

"How old are you?"

He could almost see her lifting her chin in the darkness.

"Twenty-four." She hesitated. "Almost."

He groaned.

"And you never—nothing ever—"

"I attended an all-girls school. And college was the same."

The extent of her non-experience boggled his mind.

"Yeah, but if you graduated at twenty-two, there's almost two years there where you could've—"

"I was busy taking pictures."

"I see. Just sublimated that sexual drive right into your work."

"*Mister* Kinkaid. I didn't sublimate anything. I have feelings just like any other woman." He heard her take a deep breath. "Perhaps I was just waiting for the right man."

A horrible suspicion flitted into his mind. "Don't tell me the right man is our chief?"

"A woman could do worse than have her first experience with a noble savage."

He sat up and raked his fingers through his hair. "There you go again, Princess. For a woman who claims she's logical, you have the damnedest way of making everything sound like a novel, or a movie, or a—"

"Romantic fantasy. Spare me, Mister Kinkaid. I don't need you to remind me that I live in a world of dreams. But I don't consider them to be dreams. If I want to believe that people are capable of great things, including great and noble emotions, that—is—my—prerogative."

He knew she was really mad at him now, when she didn't even bother to use contractions and emphasized each and every syllable like that. It was too bad she hadn't considered teaching as a career. She could scare the holy hell out of her pupils.

"Listen," he finally said into the tense darkness. "Just consider that I've been around the block a few more times than most guys—"

"I'm sure you have."

He gritted his teeth. How could she, with the simplest inflection, make that one sentence sound nothing like a compliment?

"What I'm trying to say is, you've been raised largely in a world of women, so you might not know how the average man's mind really works."

"And you're prepared to enlighten me."

"Well . . . yes."

"Please don't, Mister Kinkaid. I'd like to finish this trip with at least a few of my illusions not completely shattered."

What a vocabulary. What a woman. Disgusted with the way things were going, Matt turned his back on her. Forget it. She could dance naked in front of the chief for all he cared. She could offer herself up to him, and once he claimed her, he would never allow her to leave this place. She could eat lizard for the rest of her life and have that wildly romantic existence she seemed to want.

It was nothing to him.

He followed her to the hot springs the following morning.

Matt wasn't proud of his actions, but he knew he couldn't live with himself if something really bad happened to Isabelle. Prickly and logical she might be, cool and collected, but she was also a twenty-three-year-old virgin who might not know quite what she was getting into.

To his amazement, the chief simply walked her to the hot springs, chatted with her for a few minutes, and indicated the safest place to enter the water. Then he turned his back and walked away, seeming to melt into the dense jungle.

Oh, and he'd also carried that ridiculous backpack for

her, carefully setting it on a flat, dry rock when they reached their destination.

Matt knew he should leave, as he watched Isabelle take a bar of soap out of one of the mesh side pockets. He stood and stared as she took down her hair and started to brush it out, the pale blond color gleaming in the small shafts of sunlight that made it to the jungle floor.

Leave. Now.

But his body didn't want to follow his brain.

Time to go. She doesn't need your help.

He couldn't seem to walk away. It was as if he were rooted to the spot.

Water flowed over flat rocks, collecting in a deep pool. The surface of that pool shimmered slightly, and he knew the water would be hot and bubbly, perfect for bathing or soaking out the aches in his muscles.

Perfect for making love . . .

He shook his head, dazed, determined to walk away. If Isabelle discovered him watching her, she would accuse him of being a Peeping Tom, and she'd be right. A dirty old man. He was twelve years older than she was, and he felt decades older in life experience. Jaded. That's what he was, and he'd never felt it weigh so heavily on him as it had last night. He was jaded, and it had taken a twenty-three-year-old virgin to point that out to him.

He continued to watch Isabelle as she finished brushing her hair and put the hairbrush back into her pack, then took out a change of clothing.

Hey, the chief walked away. Obviously he thinks she's safe here. Leave her alone.

Then another thought crossed his mind. What if the chief thought she really *was* a goddess and was therefore invulnerable? How could he possibly know what the man really thought she was? What if there was some sort of danger lurking in the jungle that Isabelle was unaware of? What if she suddenly needed his help?

Yeah, like soaping that spot on her back she can't quite reach.

He knew he was in big trouble when she started to unbutton her white shirt. He looked away, ashamed of himself, then glanced back, irresistibly attracted.

The lacy white bra that covered her breasts took his breath away. He'd seen enough black lace lingerie to last him a lifetime. Who would've thought that a pristine white bra would be his downfall?

She took off her boots and socks, then slid the khaki pants down her legs. Matt felt his mouth go dry, his body tighten, and every impulse he possessed forced him to stay rooted to the spot where he stood. He couldn't have moved if his life had depended on it.

Her panties were just as pretty as her bra, white and lacy and incredibly brief. She turned, and he realized it was a rather racy little thong. And he wondered if Isabelle was as cool, logical and contained as she almost always appeared.

Not with that underwear . . .

Then she unhooked her bra, and all bets were off.

Oh, she was a goddess, all right. Her breasts were beautiful, not too big, not too small, just right because they were hers. He couldn't look away as she quickly skimmed off the thong, picked up her bar of soap, and waded into the spring.

He almost felt the hot water as she did, and was close enough that he could hear her sensual gasp of pleasure as it closed around her naked body. Then she ducked beneath the water and surfaced, skimming her hair off her face. The lush jungle greenery and colorful wild orchids made an exquisite backdrop for her bath. Matt felt as if he was watching a live video of any red-blooded male's secret fantasy come to life.

She started to soap her body, her arms, her shoulders, then her breasts . . .

He heard a soft moan, then realized the sound had come from him and bit down on his lip hard to stifle anything further. This was torture of a particularly poignant kind, since Matt knew the two of them would never connect. It would be like mating a grizzly bear with Bambi, for God's sake. But he decided that he would take pure delight, pure pleasure in this moment. And then when he was lying in that hammock in the Caribbean sometime in the near future, a rum-and-fruit-juice concoction in hand, all he'd have to do is close his eyes to remember the sight of a naked Isabelle in a jungle pool surrounded by flowers.

She was a pagan goddess come to life, and he watched as she indulged in her bath. Smiled while she lathered her hair and ducked her head beneath the water. Watched silently as she floated on the pool's surface, her pale gold hair fanned out around her in the water.

And at the same time, he felt old and tired. Used up.

He was ready for that hammock. Hell, the way his knee felt, he might be ready for a walker.

When she walked out of the water, he was reminded of another movie, *Dr. No*. The scene where Ursula Andress came out of the water and up on the beach in that incredible bikini. But Isabelle looked even better, vibrant and alive.

Wanting to make sure nothing happened to her, he waited until she was fully dressed, then remained very still within the jungle foliage as she passed him on her way back to the village.

He followed her until she reached their hut and put her backpack inside, and he saw her leave with her camera in hand. It was another one of those technological marvels she adored, this camera smaller than her palm. But he was absolutely sure she would capture some stunning images.

Visions of Isabelle, clean and pure and glowing, coming out of that jungle pool made him think about the way he looked and felt. Sweaty. Grimy. His stubble, threatening to turn into a full-blown beard, was now at that awful in-between stage that made him look his absolute worst.

Several of the tribesmen had been more than happy to run back and find the supplies they'd left behind yesterday morning, so Matt ducked into the hut he shared with Isabelle and grabbed a change of clothing and the necessary toiletries. Then he headed out toward the pool, whistling.

He could clean up with the best of them. And he couldn't wait to see how a particular goddess reacted to a clean-shaven face and freshly washed hair.

four

She'd never seen him without stubble. As Matt came striding into the village, Isabelle naturally turned her attention toward him and focused on his face through her camera lens.

What she saw astounded her.

He was actually handsome, devastatingly so. Oh, she'd known he was handsome before, but somehow, all cleaned up and freshly shaven, Matt Kinkaid made an impression on her senses all over again.

"You look absolutely wonderful," she said as she fell into step beside him.

"I'm glad I meet with your approval, Princess."

She walked with him to their hut, where he hung up his damp clothing.

"I wish I'd thought of that!" she said.

"What? Washing your clothes?"

"I only brought two sets in my backpack, and I'm already sweating in these."

"Hey, I'll help you wash them if you want." When she blushed, he realized she might not want him handling her unmentionables. Lord, she was modest. "Look, I'll go to the spring with you and look the other way."

"Did Kenta show you where it was?"

He kept his answer deliberately vague, not wanting to

risk her discovering he'd been watching her bathe. "One of the men told me—I can't remember which one."

"Wasn't it fabulous?"

He nodded, then to change the subject, said, "Let's get your clothes."

They actually had a good time. If someone had told him that he, Matt Kinkaid, would get an enormous kick out of washing clothes on a rock in the middle of the jungle with Miss Goody Two-shoes, the princess, he would've told them where to go. But that was before he'd met Isabelle.

There was just something about her . . .

He tried not to stare as she rinsed out her lacy underwear, tried not to remember how terrific she'd looked filling it out. Instead, he concentrated on helping her wash the white shirt. She'd changed into a light blue shirt and another pair of khakis. The hat remained the same, wide-brimmed and practical, shielding her face from the sun. But not much sun reached this part of the jungle through the dense canopy of trees, so she wore it down her back, the leather ties around her neck. He had the feeling she just kind of liked keeping it with her.

Comprehension dawned. "Did Tom give you that hat?"

She smiled up at him as she gave a last twist to her white lace panties, wringing the water out of them. "Yes. Every time he'd go away, he would bring me back lots of presents. He said this hat reminded him of the Indiana Jones movies." She hesitated, then said, "I think he enjoyed spoiling me."

Matt could easily understand why. Isabelle would be fun to spoil.

"What other kinds of things did he bring you?" He noticed that she seemed to have utter confidence that her brother would return, and he found himself glad that she did.

"Straw purses. Foreign money, books, little statues. He brought me a wooden elephant that I have on my desk at home. And a tiger."

"Hmmm." Matt considered this and realized that in all

his travels and adventures he'd never had anyone to bring gifts to.

"Oh, and postcards, lots of postcards. He never had time to write them, so he would just buy them and bring them back to me so I could imagine all the places he'd been. Tom doesn't like to travel with a camera. He doesn't have to, he can make you see anything with his words." She looked up and around the jungle, then sighed, her clear gray eyes shining. "But I never imagined I'd see it myself. Or that it could all be so beautiful."

There she went, astounding him all over again. Most of the women he'd worked for, usually the trophy wives of businessmen who wanted their big jungle adventure, bitched and moaned endlessly about the heat, the lack of amenities and privacy, the bugs, the food—the list of complaints was endless. Matt realized that Isabelle was one of the few women he'd ever met who found the same sort of beauty in a tropical jungle that he did.

And who actually liked lizard meat.

"I know what you mean," he said quietly. "I never get tired of it."

"You're like Tom that way," she said. "It's in your blood."

"What, like malaria?"

She laughed. "No, the desire to travel. Journey to new places, see new things."

"And you never had that desire?"

"I did—in my dreams. In my books. But I was always a little—afraid."

"You, Princess? Afraid? Pardon my skepticism, but you don't strike me as afraid of anything."

"I was afraid when I came down here looking for my brother."

"Nope. Sorry. I don't buy it. *Afraid* would have meant staying in San Francisco and hiring someone else to find your brother for you. Coming thousands of miles to find someone you love is not being afraid. That's called courage."

She considered this. "But there was nothing else I could do. I had to find Tom."

She just didn't get it. She had no idea how many people there were out in the world who would've left Tom to his own devices, brother or not. It was one of the things he really liked about her, the way her fresh, innocent take on the world contrasted with his world-weary one. In a strange kind of way, she was starting to give him back his faith in people. Maybe they weren't so bad after all.

But he was still heading for that island in the Caribbean.

"Well," he said, glancing down at the clothing in their hands. "We should get back to the village and see what they've cooked up for dinner tonight. Perhaps a lovely spider stew."

"Mister Kinkaid!" But there was a hint of laughter in her voice and a soft smile on her lips. Damn, she was beautiful. Just standing there with that blond hair of hers, she lit up her little corner of the world. He could understand how Tom thought she was special.

They had some time before dinner, and Isabelle spent it writing in her journal.

"This is exactly how I pictured it!" she said, finishing the last sentence with a final flourish of her pen and closing the green leather-bound book with a snap.

"How?" He was lying on his bedroll, his hat over his face, snoozing. He would never be as industrious as she was, not if he lived to be a million years old. And he would bet his last dollar that her penmanship was perfect, precise and orderly. She was probably the type who could write straight sentences on unlined paper. The thought made him smile.

"Oh, I always wanted to travel like this, off the beaten path somewhere, and keep a journal about all my adventures and take pictures to help me remember them."

She was different, all right. Other women might spend their vacations emptying out their husbands' bank accounts, but Isabelle liked living in the moment and recording her adventures afterward.

He could almost picture her as a grandmother, her hair up in that same elegant twist. Several of her grandchildren would gather at her feet in her little house in San Francisco, probably one of those gingerbread Victorians. She'd read to them out loud from her journal, keeping them enthralled with tales of her adventures and showing them mounds of glossy pictures. There would be lots of laughter, kisses and hugs. And afterward, homemade cookies and milk, then straight up to bed.

Deborah Kerr would've been proud. Or was it Anna he was thinking of? Anna and the king . . .

What was it with this woman, that she could cause him to start seeing such pictures in his mind? Lovely domestic pictures, with such a rosy glow. He hadn't thought about anything remotely connected to family in years. Yet here he was, thinking of Isabelle with grandchildren, while he would be lying in his hammock somewhere in the Caribbean, listening to the sound of the waves, a drink in his hand . . .

For a moment Matt panicked. For this first time in as long as he could remember, that image didn't stir him quite the way it used to. What was going on? Was this woman making him go all soft in the head? Life in the Caribbean was *exactly* what he wanted, and he was closer to getting that life than he'd been in years.

"I have to get some air," he said abruptly, then sat up and walked out of their hut, needing to put some distance between the two of them.

Twenty minutes later, he was heading back when he ran into the chief, who indicated with gestures that he should come over. And a few minutes after that, Matt didn't know how he was going to break the news to Isabelle.

Impossible. Tom couldn't be dead. But that's what the chief had told him. That's the reality that his tribesman, the best tracker in the entire village, had come back with.

How are you going to tell her . . .

Images of a crazy little museum in the heart of San Francisco flashed through his mind, along with that gingerbread Victorian. Her pictures probably hung on some of the walls, and she'd probably had her brother over for dinner often. She'd said her parents had died in a skiing accident when she and Tom were children, and he had a sudden image of a little girl, her blond hair pulled back tightly in a ponytail, holding on to her brother's hand for dear life. Tom had been more than a brother to Isabelle, of that he was absolutely sure.

He couldn't tell her. He couldn't be the one to break the news.

"Do you want me to tell her?" the chief said quietly.

For a moment he was tempted. Let someone else be the bearer of bad news. But he couldn't take the coward's way out; he wouldn't be able to live with himself. Even though she would probably hate him for telling her, he had to be there to help her, to protect her. He owed her that much.

Matt realized he would've done anything to take this pain for her, to make it his own. She was a courageous woman, but this was the worst sort of news, the worst sort of pain. It was so final, and so unnecessary.

"I'll go."

She'd come out of the tent to meet him, and he saw that apologetic look in her eyes.

"I came to apologize, Mister Kinkaid. I talked your ear off, and you were trying to take a nap, and—" She saw the expression on his face and stopped. And he knew the exact moment when realization flooded through her, and she knew what his expression meant.

Matt could've handled things better if she'd cried, if she'd burst into tears and thrown herself into his arms and pounded her fists on his chest. Instead, she just stared at him, and he realized she was going into shock.

This was so much worse. He reached for her hand, but she pulled back as if his touch burned her. Clasped her hands together, looked up at him, her gray eyes pleading. Her voice sounded tight and constricted, low and intense.

"But they think—they think he's coming home."

He said nothing. Couldn't. He couldn't give this woman

false hope. As much as it killed him to hurt her this way, there was no way to make this better.

"He'll be—he'll be—" She turned around and lowered her head, and he wanted so badly to take her into his arms, to at least put his hands on her shoulders and try to offer her some of his strength. But he didn't, because gut instinct told him she would shatter if he touched her. Her spine was rigid, but her perfect posture was off. Her head was lowered, and Matt was reminded of summers on his grandfather's farm, trying to get an ailing Thoroughbred to stand, because once one of those proud horses went down, there was no hope.

She stood that way for almost a minute, and he remained silent, taking his cue from her, letting her lead the way down this terrible path.

"How did it happen?" That elegant head was still bowed, but her voice had steadied.

"They think—they think he fell down the side of a cliff."

"The body?"

"They haven't found it yet, but the chief's sending out a search party."

She nodded her head, the gesture ever so slight.

"Would you thank the chief for me? We'll get your gold, and then I guess we can be on our way."

He wanted to shake her, yell at her, but he couldn't. He wanted to tell her that she had to feel it sometime, in some way, and that keeping it all inside would kill her.

But he didn't say anything. He simply stared at her back, trying to figure out what to do, when she made the decision for him. Her knees buckled, he grabbed for her, and managed to catch her before she hit the ground.

Swinging her up into his arms, he carried her back to their hut.

All night long, members of the tribe left offerings of friendship, comfort, and affection at the hut's door. And all night long, Matt lay next to Isabelle, not touching her, just offering her his silent company. He was a wise enough man to know there was nothing he could say to make this hurt better.

When she came to, there was a painful moment when he knew from her expression that she hadn't remembered. Then the knowledge flooded her eyes and she closed them. She'd pretended to sleep, pulling a light blanket over her shoulders, but he wasn't fooled.

Now, close to midnight, he still didn't sleep. He couldn't. So he heard her voice when she finally spoke.

"Matthew?"

He didn't have the heart to correct her.

"Hmmm?"

"Would you . . . could you . . . hold my hand?"

Such a small thing to do when he wanted to take all the pain away. He reached for her hand, and it felt cold to his touch. And so delicate.

"Do you want to talk?" He had to ask. She'd been so quiet, it frightened him.

"No."

A short silence, then—"Do you think he—" Her breath caught. Hitched. She cleared her throat. "Do you think he—suffered?"

The truth could be a real bitch. "I hope not."

"I hope it was . . . quick." He could tell by her tone of voice that she'd finally started to cry.

"Ah, Isabelle," he said, pulling her into his arms and resting his chin on top of her head. He'd been with crying women before, but never one who seemed to cry with her entire body. She simply shook with her grief, and he held her and wondered if there had been any way he could've seen this coming that moment a few days ago when she'd walked into that bar.

"Please don't let me go," she whispered against his bare chest, her voice muffled. He'd taken his shirt and boots off, and wore only his pants. She was still fully clothed, except for her belt and boots which he'd removed as she slept—or rather, tried to sleep.

"Never." He held her even tighter. "Never."

He couldn't let himself imagine the life she had ahead

of her. Letting herself into that empty house. Walking down to the museum and telling her brother's coworkers he wouldn't be coming back. Starting her life all over again without the person she loved most in the world.

If he'd had a heart, it would be breaking by now.

It was.

"Don't go back," he found himself saying. He kissed the top of her head. "Stay here with me." Somehow he couldn't bear the image of her letting herself into the empty house and knowing that her brother would never be coming over for dinner again.

She sniffed, then fished in her pants pocket and found her handkerchief, blew her nose. "I can't possibly burden you any more than I already have, Matthew."

Matthew. That was a good sign.

"You're not a burden, Isabelle. You've brought—a lot to my life that was missing." He thought quickly. "And I don't want you going back to San Francisco alone. Not right away, anyway."

"You're very sweet," she said softly. "But I can't ask you for your charity—"

"It's not charity," he said, his voice almost a soft growl. When was this woman going to get it through her head that he saw her as a woman? Matt suddenly found himself frustrated with the divisions between them. He didn't want to be her employee anymore. He wanted . . . he wanted . . .

Acting totally on instinct, he lowered his head, found her mouth in the darkness with his own, and kissed her.

And kissed her. And kissed her again. And put everything that he was feeling and couldn't quite put into words into those kisses.

Something caught fire, and he realized she was kissing him back. And a part of his mind registered the fact that he might be taking unfair advantage, kissing her at a time like this—

But it felt right. He continued kissing her and slowly lowered her to her bedroll, covering her with his body as he did so. He took most of his weight on his forearms, as she felt incredibly fragile below him. Then he rolled to the side and snaked one arm around her shoulders, then slid it lower so he supported her back and pressed her closer to him as he kissed her.

He groaned as he felt her hands slide over his chest, then slowly come up around his neck as she hung on for dear life. He didn't quite know what was happening between them, because he'd never felt anything like this. He'd had plenty of experience in the course of his adventuring, but he'd never been with a woman when it had felt like this, when *he* felt as if he wanted to emotionally pour all that he was feeling into her with each kiss, each touch, each—

He fumbled with the buttons of her blouse, tossed it aside. He found the clasp of her bra and unhooked it, then slid the lacy straps off her shoulders. He slid his hands through her hair, pulling out the few pins that held it in place. It was happening too fast, but that felt right, too.

He had her completely undressed within minutes, her hair loose around her shoulders, her body lying naked beneath him. All the while he continued to kiss her, to devour her. He couldn't seem to get enough of her, her touch, her scent, *her* . . .

For one last moment, sanity surfaced.

"Tell me if you want me to stop," he whispered, his voice rough with suppressed need. "Tell me now, or I'm not going to be able to stop." She was like a drug in his veins, a substance he couldn't get enough of, ever.

"No," she whispered against his mouth. "Please."

It touched him deeply, that she was asking for something she knew nothing about. And he wondered if she would be repulsed by his need, by the sheer, raw physicality of the act. He wanted to make her first experience a good one, but he didn't know if he could because he was caught in this powerful current as deeply as she was.

He swiftly shed his clothes, then rose up above her, settled himself between her thighs. She opened for him as if she'd done this many times before, and the sheer, physical feeling of *rightness* gave him hope that this wouldn't be too bad for her, this first time. And he realized, with a sudden moment of clarity, that they'd been heading for this moment since the first instant he'd seen her in the bar.

He kissed her again, then brought his forehead to hers and whispered, "This has to happen."

She moved beneath him, restless, and he heard her whisper against his ear one single, breathy word.

"Yes."

That one word fired his blood like nothing ever had before, when he realized that though she might be a little afraid of the unknown, of what was about to happen between them, she wanted it to happen as much as he did.

That one "yes" gave him permission.

He parted her thighs wider, then touched her between her legs, making sure she was ready. She jerked at the contact, so taut, so sensitive to his touch. He found her wet and warm and ready for him, and knew he didn't want to delay the inevitable any longer.

He took his weight on his elbows and reached for her head, threading his fingers through her glorious hair. He covered her mouth with his own, kissing her deeply and parting her lips with his tongue.

She moved upward, toward him, moving restlessly beneath him. His body pushed her thighs even farther apart as he found the entrance he sought. He felt her stiffen for just an instant as he first slid inside, and she was so tight around him that he almost stopped. But hesitating would only give her time to become more scared, and he didn't want her to be scared of this, never of this.

With a strong, determined thrust of his hips, he took her.

She cried out, breaking the kiss, her body stiffening in an instinctive reaction to the pain. It was almost as if she was trying to throw him off her, but he stayed close, fully sheathed, covering her, pinning her down. Her breathing came in panting little gasps, and he lowered his forehead to hers and kissed her mouth, her cheek, then the tip of her nose.

"It won't feel bad for long," he whispered. Her heart had to be racing; he could feel the humming tension coming off her body.

"Okay," she said, but he heard the doubt in her voice.

He had absolutely no experience with virgins, had no idea if the first time could be any good at all for them. But if there was one chance in a million, he was going to give it to Isabelle.

He remembered one of the gifts that had arrived outside the hut's door in sympathy that evening, one of the few he'd taken inside. A flask of that homemade liquor, the rum drink—at least he thought it was rum—with the kick to it. Well, it couldn't hurt to give Isabelle a little bit now. It would certainly help her through this, and would ensure that she slept through the night.

"Here," he said, handing her the flask. It had been near his bedroll, and he hadn't even had to move away from her to reach it.

She groped for it in the dark, then raised the flask to her lips. He heard her take a drink, then her soft gasp.

"I spilled some!"

"Where?" He lowered his head and licked up the droplets that had splashed over her neck and her breasts, and as he did so, he felt her most feminine muscles constrict around his heavy arousal.

"Oh!" Her voice had that breathy, surprised quality he loved.

"Drink a little more," he said. "It'll relax you."

"I'm sorry I'm not—doing this right."

He almost laughed out loud, but he knew he couldn't risk hurting her feelings.

"You're doing everything right, Princess."

She lay back down after that second long drink and reached up for him. He lowered himself down on top of her, and slowly eased out of her, then pushed back in.

"Better?" he whispered.

"Hmmm."

He liked the sound of that sigh. He liked it a lot.

He kept their rhythm slow and steady, wanting to build her arousal, wanting to give her everything. And she caught fire again, moving beneath him, crying out, but different cries this time, not cries of pain but cries of pleasure. Her hands dug into his shoulders, the nails biting into his flesh, but he didn't care. She was with him, she was taking pleasure from what he was doing, and that was all that mattered.

He picked up the pace, his strokes stronger now, more insistent, pushing strongly inside her, then pulling back, then pushing in again, giving her his strength, letting her see the depth of his need. She responded, caught up in a sensual fire, her hips moving in tempo with his thrusts, her neck arching, her cries growing louder as they began to take that climb.

Her response aroused him so strongly, it was so pure and free. It amazed him that she should have decided to let him be her first lover, and though it took a bit of the edge off his own pleasure to stay in the moment and gauge her response, he was determined to see her through it all.

He knew she was close when she grabbed at his shoulders, then his arms, then she cried out sharply and he felt those incredible contractions squeezing him, caressing him. Matt breathed deeply to delay his own response and waited until she was finished.

"Oh," she said when she could talk again.

He kissed her, a soft and tender kiss while his mouth curved upward in a smile.

"Oh," he said, then slid more deeply into her, then pulled back out.

"Oh!" she said. Then, "I guess we're not done yet."

He considered that this was her first time and he didn't want her to be too sore. "Only if you want to be."

"But—no, I don't."

He kissed her again. "All right, then. Do you want to rest a little bit?"

"No." He liked the fact that she didn't even hesitate.

He rolled over onto his back, taking her with him so she ended up straddling him. Then, before she could consider this new arrangement, he grasped her hips firmly in his hands and began to establish their rhythm, pushing up as he pulled her toward him. She gasped in response, and he saw the way her head lolled back on her shoulders.

He kept the insistent rhythm going, easing her down against him so he could kiss her, cup her breasts, mouth her taut nipples into hard peaks of pleasure. Her second climax was quicker coming than her first, and while she was still in the throes of it, he rolled her over, buried himself inside her, and thrust strongly as his own release washed over him, shaking him to the core.

Afterward, when he could move again and think coherently, he touched her shoulder, smoothed a piece of hair out of her face.

Fast asleep. He wondered if it was the native liquor or their lovemaking. But in the end, it didn't matter.

Matt tried not to waste a lot of time on guilt, feeling that it was one of the most useless emotions. He rearranged their bedrolls so that the two became one, then covered Isabelle carefully. He settled in behind her, spoon fashion, and slid a possessive arm around her.

Tomorrow would bring its own set of problems. But tonight he'd answered a question that had been burning in his gut since he'd first seen her walk into that cantina. And the answer was yes. She was his, they belonged with each other, and it didn't matter how different they were so long as they had this kind of magic together.

He held her tightly against him, breathed in the sweet scent of her hair. Ever since he'd met her, he'd felt as if she'd challenged him. And he realized that what she challenged him to do was simply to be a better man. To be more than he could be on his own. He knew he didn't have a lot to offer her; she was financially secure, while he lived from job to job looking for that big score. She was a lot more refined that he would ever be. But he loved her with a passion that made up for all that. No one in this world would ever love Isabelle Burke more than he did.

She made a soft little sound of distress in her sleep, and he leaned back as she rearranged herself so that her head rested on his shoulder and she was safely nestled in the crook of his arm. As he looked down at her and kissed the top of her head, Matthew Kinkaid felt a sense of contentment he hadn't felt in a long time. If ever.

• • •

Just before dawn, the tribal chief came to their door. When Matt called out softly and told him he could enter, it gave him a measure of satisfaction for the chief to see Isabelle's naked body in his bed, beneath the blanket. He hadn't been wrong about the man—he caught a quick flash of disappointment in the tribal leader's eyes.

But now the chief knew she was his. Matt had marked her, claimed her, in one of the oldest ways known to mankind.

Quick words were exchanged. The search party was heading out, and Matt told the chief he was staying with Isabelle. The man nodded his assent and left as swiftly and silently as he'd come. Relieved, Matt studied the sleeping form of the woman lying next to him. He would've gone with the search party in a heartbeat, but he knew that if he had, Isabelle would have wanted to come along, and he hadn't wanted that to happen.

He could do her more good here, taking care of her.

She woke up around ten in the morning, and he could tell she was still exhausted.

"Matt?" She looked up at him, and he saw that she didn't seem filled with regret, didn't blame him for what had happened between them. Isabelle was one remarkably self-possessed virgin. Well, not anymore.

"Hey." He touched her cheek with a fingertip. "How're you doing?"

She closed her eyes. "Did they find him yet?"

"No. The search party left at dawn."

She glanced around their hut. "I guess I should get dressed."

"What are you planning on doing?"

She considered this. "I don't know."

"Why don't you rest? Get some sleep?"

"That's all I did last night."

"Well, no," he said, "that's not *all* you did."

She blushed, and he watched, fascinated, as it stained the top curves of her breasts, her neck, and then flooded into her cheeks. She looked down, then pleated a piece of the blanket between slender fingers.

"Thank you . . . thank you for making it so wonderful for me last night."

His eyes stung. It was on the tip of his tongue to tell her he loved her, but he was suddenly afraid. It might not be the best time, considering what had just happened.

"You were wonderful," he said, his voice gruff. "What happened last night—it's never been like that for me before. Ever."

He could give her that, even if he couldn't quite tell her he loved her. And he saw the quick joy shining in her eyes. The blanket slipped, and she was naked from the waist up, and he couldn't believe how much he wanted her. Again. He had a feeling it would always be this way.

"Matthew," she said softly, holding her arms out to him. "I need you."

He went to her, more than willing.

five

"I'm taking the jaguar back," Isabelle said.

Matt knew better than to argue with her.

They'd been in the village for three days since word had come back that Tom was dead. Matt had talked with several of the tribal members who were expert hunters and had heard that they had found several pieces of his clothing and some of his supplies down the side of a sheer drop. Matt wondered if any other men had heard of this City of the Sun, the City of Gold, and of what one man with a blood lust for treasure might do to another.

The ultimate irony in all of this was that Tom hadn't wanted money. His motives had been so much purer.

"When?" he said, studying Isabelle. They were sitting outside their hut, and he was peeling a guava for her.

"Within the next two days."

"I'm coming with you."

"No," she said quietly. "There are things I need to do up in San Francisco. Get the exhibit ready. Pack up his apartment. Organize a service. Make sure the world sees that jaguar." She stared at him, defiant. "It's my way of saying good-bye."

"You're not okay," he said.

"Right now, I feel like I'm never going to be okay."

He ached for her. Setting down the knife and the peeled

fruit, he got to his feet and took her hand. "Walk with me."

"Matthew—"

"Humor me."

They walked out toward the pool and sat on the flat stones, warmed by the sunlight that managed to struggle through the dense canopy of foliage. And though Matt didn't say anything, and Isabelle didn't seem to have any desire to talk, he knew the power that nature had to heal the soul.

She still slept with him at night, making love with emotion that bordered on desperation. He sensed she was trying to feel, to feel anything, because a part of her had locked up tight when she'd found out about Tom.

Matt could understand that she wanted to put Tom's dream into effect immediately. It was as if she wanted to do this particular exhibit in homage to her sibling, because it would represent everything he stood for.

But he worried about her. Matt didn't give a damn about the gold anymore. He didn't even care if she paid him at all. He had enough money in the bank that he wasn't going to starve or want for anything. His needs were simple, and that island in the Caribbean seemed to be fading, drifting farther and farther away.

He knew he would've given all his salary plus a ton of gold to see Tom come striding through the jungle and the look in Isabelle's face when he did. He didn't know why or how this change had come over him; he only knew it had.

"Let's go back," she said abruptly, and he knew her mind was on other things.

They took a longer way back, as he wanted her to get outside their hut and into the fresh air. But he knew that all the fresh air and exercise in the world, the most choice pieces of fruit, and even his constant companionship weren't enough. Isabelle was going on sheer nerves, and instinct told him there would come a time, probably late at night—and soon—when she was going to bottom out.

They were walking along a trail when he saw a particularly vivid butterfly, purple and orange. He'd never seen anything like it, and his first thought was that Isabelle would adore it.

"Take a look," he whispered, and for a moment he saw the pain leave her eyes as she examined the flying insect and took several involuntary steps off the trail toward its brilliance.

And then vanished.

It took him a moment to realize that she'd disappeared.

"Hey!" He turned, looked one way, then the other. Irritation seized him, irritation that covered up his fear. "Princess, this isn't funny."

He heard the sound of coughing.

"Where are you?" he shouted.

"Down here," she called out, then sneezed.

He'd been looking left and right, all around, even up in the leafy canopy. But he hadn't looked *down*.

Keeping an eye on his feet, he walked carefully toward the area where he'd last seen Isabelle. There, before him, was what looked like a hole in the ground.

"Isabelle!"

"Don't come any closer! It'll cave in, and then we'll both be trapped!"

He didn't like the idea of her being buried alive, so he stood very still. "Do you have that little flashlight with you?"

She sneezed again, then said, "Yep! Tom taught me never to go anywhere without it."

"Good. Turn it on."

He didn't hear the soft click, but he did hear her say, "Oh my God."

"Isabelle!" Visions of poisonous snakes filled his head. Deadly scorpions. At this point, even evil spirits or dancing skeletons. "What have you found?"

"I think—I think I can safely say that I've found the Royal Fifth."

The tribe didn't want anything to do with this particular part of the treasure, as they considered it cursed. But they were more than willing to help Isabelle excavate it, carefully dusting off each piece and bringing it to a separate hut where she cataloged it.

This was one of the finds of the century. This was what Tom had been looking for, and it was the ultimate irony that his baby sister should have literally fallen into it. The natives had never strayed off that particular path, because at some time in the past, someone had seen many poisonous snakes in the area.

Matt was glad he hadn't been aware of that. It had seemed like ages passed while he raced to the village with a pounding heart and a throbbing knee and rounded up the necessary men to dig Isabelle out of that sinkhole.

And what a sinkhole it was. Besides all the gold figurines, there were gold coins and bars, more treasure than anyone could imagine.

"You're a rich man, Mister Kinkaid," Isabelle said one evening almost a week after they'd found the stash of treasure. "There's more money in your share than you could spend in a lifetime."

He couldn't imagine a lifetime without her, but he knew she wouldn't listen to him. Not now.

He also sensed he was losing her.

He woke up three days later and instantly realized she was gone.

Glancing around the hut, he saw that everything she owned was missing. He got up and pulled on his pants, about to race outside and start searching for her. Then he noticed the small cream-colored envelope on his pack.

He opened it with amazingly steady hands, considering that his heart was in his throat.

Dear Mr. Kinkaid,

I want you to know that I couldn't have made it through this trip without you. No one could have been kinder or more considerate of my needs.

He thought of how he'd discouraged her from even making this journey. The rude and arrogant behavior he'd displayed at first. And all the times they'd bickered in the jungle, while eating lizard. Even how he'd given her a hard time about being a goddess while he was a mere consort.

No one could have made my first genuine adventure any more exciting. And you were the best part.

His eyes stung, and he blinked rapidly.

I know my behavior may strike you as inexplicable . . .

"Speak English, please," he muttered, his voice hoarse.

. . . but I find that I have to do things this way, for now. I realize that mounting an exhibit in San Francisco may seem a rather strange way to pay tribute to a life that was cut short.

"Not strange at all, Princess," he said softly.

But it's all I can think of to do. I've never been through anything this horrible before, and I didn't want to take it out on you.

She was polite to the end, his Princess. None of those messy emotions for his Isabelle. Deborah Kerr had nothing on her.

"Take it out on me? You couldn't have done that." It comforted him in a strange way, talking to her like this.

I've left you most of the gold coins and bullion, and I want you to take it and pursue your dream of living in the Caribbean. For if there's anything I've realized during this particular journey, it's that life is most certainly too short. So I will think of you, Mister Kinkaid—

"Mister Kinkaid," he muttered. "After all the rolling around we did together, she has the *nerve* to still call me that?"

So I will think of you, Mister Kinkaid, lying in your hammock, raising a glass of fine, aged rum toward the sun, and enjoying the rest of your life. I will remember you with great fondness, especially the brief, intimate time we spent in our hut. A girl couldn't have asked for a better guide in matters of the heart.

Isabelle Burke

" 'The brief, intimate time we spent in our hut'?" He tapped the letter on his outstretched hand. "Oh, no. Not this way. It's not over 'til I say it's over."

He carefully tucked the letter into his backpack, totally

disgusted with himself that he should have slept through Isabelle's departure this morning. What kind of guide and protector did that make him? A laughable one, that's what.

As he left the guest hut, one of the women from the village came up to him and smiled.

"Did your woman enjoy the sleeping potion I prepared for her?"

Pieces of that particular puzzle clicked into place. She'd urged him to drink some of the potent local liquor last night, a little "celebration" of their find. He'd thought there was something strange about that, but he never would have suspected that Isabelle Burke would have stooped so low as to *drug* him!

Glancing around, he realized it was much later in the day than he'd thought. Late afternoon, as opposed to early morning.

He'd lost most of the day, while she'd gotten a spectacular head start. But he was very good at playing catch-up.

He had a long talk with the tribal chief and discovered how she'd escaped.

"We have a charter service that comes in a few times a year," the chief said from his luxurious hut. "I called them on my shortwave radio—"

"Shortwave radio?" Now he thought the tribal leader was making fun of him.

"Sure. This pilot I know, he's a reliable guy, and I told him to see her all the way to her doorstep, along with the treasure. For the kind of money she's paying him, he can afford to do it."

"Shortwave radio," Matt muttered.

"Sure. Hey, this is the twenty-first century! Sometimes we even order in a little pizza, you know what I mean?"

"Pizza?" His stomach growled. "So you people eat lizard when you can afford to fly in pizza?"

One of the young women who had been sitting to the side of the chief started to laugh, and Matt suddenly had the most horrible suspicion.

"It *was* chicken."

The chief smiled. "Free range and organic. Only the best for our guests." His expression changed, grew more serious. "Hey, we have to be careful who we let know what's going on out here. I don't want this corner of the jungle to turn into Mexico City, with crowds and pollution, if you know what I mean."

"I do."

"That's why we all cared for Tom so much. There was nothing that conventional medicine could have done for my father; it was his time to leave us. But Tom's knowledge of herbs stopped his pain. That man managed to bridge our two worlds."

"I wish I'd had a chance to know him."

They were interrupted by shouting and both men raced outside to see several of the tribal guides gesticulating wildly. They were shouting in their own language, and Matt couldn't understand them, but suddenly the chief turned to him with an enormous grin on his face and said, "You may get that chance after all!"

The exhibition was a smashing success.

Isabelle had worked nonstop with a museum team to clean all the figurines and artifacts. She'd also had several of the pictures she'd taken of the jungle and the local flora and fauna blown up to poster size to grace the clean, white walls of the museum. Combining that with innovative lighting and the strategic use of several clusters of large, dramatic plants and fountains, she'd successfully created a tropical ambiance that set off the priceless pieces to absolute, stunning perfection.

The gold gleamed in the soft lighting, and she heard the appreciative gasps that the beauty of the work drew from even the most sophisticated art lover.

The morning she'd left, the tribal chief had told her she could keep those pieces in her brother's museum forever.

"The real City of the Sun has a deeply spiritual significance for my people," he told her. "We've been living in fear for some time, believing that someone might come and try to rob us. It's not the monetary significance, but the damage it could do to the tribe."

"I understand," she said.

"Your brother was family to me." He placed his hand over his heart. "He will always live on in my heart, and in spirit."

"I know." She blinked back tears.

"Those pieces—I give them to you, for him, as a form of tribute to the beauty that was his life."

"Thank you," she said, then hugged him as the pilot signaled they were about to take off. Even though the helicopter made a tremendous noise, she had no fear of Matt's waking up and finding out she was leaving.

Thoughts of Matt now made her particularly emotional, so she concentrated on the exhibit, nodding at one person standing by an elegant waterfall, smiling at another regular over at the far window.

"Tom would've loved this," a voice behind her said.

She recognized the voice and turned, her breath catching in her throat. Matt stood behind her, absolutely stunning in an Armani tuxedo. His hair had been freshly trimmed, his face was closely shaved, and he looked as sophisticated as he had looked rough in the jungle.

"Matt!"

"I have two things for you, Princess. I'm hoping you'll want both of them."

Her heart started to speed up.

"The first one—well, the first one, I know you're going to like." Taking her shoulders in a gentle grip, he turned her so she could see the man who was standing at the entrance of the museum, smiling broadly, taking this all in.

The shock was so acute he actually felt it hit her slender body. She wrenched herself away from him and began to run, and in front of all of San Francisco society attending the opening of this world-shaking art event, she threw herself into the man's arms and burst into tears.

Tom's arms came up around his sister as he held her close, and Matt found he had to clear his throat in order to breathe properly. And he knew that until the day he died, there would be no event in his life that would give him greater pleasure.

Well, maybe one.

He accepted a glass of very good Chardonnay from a passing waiter as he watched brother and sister get reacquainted, and finally Tom steered Isabelle toward him, a smile on his face.

"What can I say?" he said to his sister. "Without this man's best efforts, I would still be trapped on the side of that cliff. He and the chief risked their lives to save me."

He'd fallen off a cliff, but he hadn't died at the bottom. His equipment had gone over the edge, but he'd been trapped on a ledge, with just enough food and water to hold out until Matt and the tribe had found him.

Isabelle wiped her eyes, her mascara smearing, and Matt produced a large white handkerchief from his pocket.

"There you go, Princess," he said softly.

"I can't thank you enough," she managed to get out, still holding her brother's arm tightly, as if she could barely believe he was standing next to her. "I can't tell you what this means to me."

"It's okay," he said.

"What can I do? How can I—"

"Oh, there is one thing." Matt glanced over at Tom. "What do you think? Is now a good time?"

"Now," said Tom, flashing his sister a brilliant smile, "is the most excellent time in the world." He loosened his sister's hold on him, then said, "I think our Mister Kinkaid wants a private word with you, and if I were you, I'd give it to him."

"Okay. But you're going to stay here?"

"I'm not going anywhere, Belle."

He walked over to a crowd of patrons, and in no time was explaining the finer points of one of the figurines, an elegant snake coiled around an image of the sun.

Matt took Isabelle's hand in his and felt her pulse racing.

"Why did you drug me?" he said.

"I knew you'd never let me go."

"You knew right." He brought her hand up to his lips

and kissed the palm. "What can I do to convince you never to do that again?"

"I don't understand what you mean."

He gave her a look, a combination of loving exasperation tinged with just a little bit of worry. She didn't understand the worry until she realized he was getting down on his knees in front of her.

"Matt! Get up this instant!"

His voice held suppressed laughter. "I may have to touch my forehead to the floor like the natives did if you don't agree to marry me."

"Get up! I don't want you to— Marry you?"

"That's the general idea." With a graceful motion, he reached inside his jacket pocket and took out a black velvet ring box. He snapped it open, and she found herself staring at an exquisite three-carat diamond ring.

"Chump change after the City of Gold, I know, but I thought it suited you."

"Oh." She didn't know what to say as he put the ring on her finger. Several people had stopped looking at the exhibit and were beginning to collect in a small crowd around them.

"And no more of this 'Mister Kinkaid' business."

"What about 'Princess'?" she said.

He frowned. "Maybe just at home."

"Matthew?" How she loved saying his name.

"Yes."

She leaned toward him and whispered into his ear, "Yes!"

They didn't spend more than a minute longer at the exhibit, leaving it to Tom, who was in his element and loving every second of it.

As they got out of Isabelle's Mercedes, Matt glanced up at the star-studded sky, then smiled as he saw the house in front of him. A gingerbread Victorian, painted a pastel pink. It suited Isabelle. Then he remembered his vision of her and frowned.

"Matthew? What is it?"

"Do you want children?"

"Of course I do." She hesitated. "Don't you?"

He smiled down at her. "I want to see you with our grandchildren."

Tears misted her eyes as she looked up at him. "I'm going to make you so happy."

They started up the steps.

"Do you still want that island in the Caribbean?" she said.

"Only if you come with me."

"It's a deal," Isabelle replied. "Maybe part of the year here, part of the year there."

"And part of the year in Mexico. We can visit the tribe, as long as you still like eating chicken—"

He laughed out loud when she flushed bright pink.

"He told you. Oh, you must think I'm horrible."

"No, actually I think you're a pretty good practical joker. How did you know?"

"Tom told me in one of his letters. The chief and his tribe have quite a sense of humor."

"No kidding. It almost did me in."

After she unlocked the front door, he swept her up into his arms.

"I know I may be a little premature, but I like the part about carrying the bride across the threshold."

"Why, Mister Kinkaid, I didn't know you were a romantic. I could have sworn you were a much more cynical man."

He kissed her and said, "Not anymore." Then he smiled.

"What are you thinking?"

"Mister and *Missus* Kinkaid," he said. "I like the sound of that, Princess."

She smiled back at him and touched his cheek.

"So do I."